"An enchanting mix of 'romantical dragons' take center stage in a quartet of tales created by writers drawn to the magic and mystery of these mythical creatures. From knights and lords to a modern-day handyman, from exotic Japan to Regency England, these stories soar with imagination, adventure, and magic to delight those who long for a bit of a fairy tale and a lot of romance."

—*Romantic Times*

ENCHANTING PRAISE FOR THE AUTHORS OF *DRAGON LOVERS*

Jo Beverley

"Arguably today's most skillful writer of intelligent historical romance."

—*Publishers Weekly*

Mary Jo Putney

"Putney's writing is clear as crystal and smooth as silk."

—*Booklist*

Karen Harbaugh

"Readers who have been searching for . . . a unique historical paranormal will not want to miss Harbaugh's work."

—*Booklist*

Barbara Samuel

"Barbara Samuel's writing is, quite simply, splendid. . . . Samuel soars with genius in the humanity of her storytelling."

—*BookPage*

Dragon Lovers

JO BEVERLEY

MARY JO PUTNEY

KAREN HARBAUGH

BARBARA SAMUEL

A SIGNET ECLIPSE BOOK

SIGNET ECLIPSE
Published by New American Library, a division of
Penguin Group (USA) Inc., 375 Hudson Street,
New York, New York 10014, USA
Penguin Group (Canada), 90 Eglinton Avenue East, Suite 700, Toronto,
Ontario M4P 2Y3, Canada (a division of Pearson Penguin Canada Inc.)
Penguin Books Ltd., 80 Strand, London WC2R 0RL, England
Penguin Ireland, 25 St. Stephen's Green, Dublin 2,
Ireland (a division of Penguin Books Ltd.)
Penguin Group (Australia), 250 Camberwell Road, Camberwell, Victoria 3124,
Australia (a division of Pearson Australia Group Pty. Ltd.)
Penguin Books India Pvt. Ltd., 11 Community Centre, Panchsheel Park,
New Delhi - 110 017, India
Penguin Group (NZ), 67 Apollo Drive, Rosedale, North Shore 0632,
New Zealand (a division of Pearson New Zealand Ltd.)
Penguin Books (South Africa) (Pty.) Ltd., 24 Sturdee Avenue,
Rosebank, Johannesburg 2196, South Africa

Penguin Books Ltd., Registered Offices:
80 Strand, London WC2R 0RL, England

Published by Signet Eclipse, an imprint of New American Library, a division
of Penguin Group (USA) Inc. Previously published in a Signet Eclipse trade
paperback edition.

First Signet Eclipse Mass Market Printing, October 2008
10 9 8 7 6 5 4 3 2 1

Contents

❧

Dragon
Lovers

The Dragon and the Virgin Princess

BY

JO BEVERLEY

Chapter 1

"**B**eing the Sacrificial Virgin Princess of Saragond *stinks*."

"I'm sure it does, Highness."

"Seven years. Seven interminable years!" Princess Rozlinda leaned forward on the Royal Mage's table. "Not only have I been SVP longer than anyone before, today I *doubled* the previous record. And," she swept on before the mage could speak, "Princess Rosabella's term ended when she was sixteen. How old am I?"

"Nineteen, Highness." But Mistress Arcelsia's aged eyes seemed to say, *Magic cannot solve this.*

Rozlinda whirled away, her skirts brushing knick-knacks, her veil snagging on something. She yanked it free, not caring if the silk ripped. Stupid, stupid thing!

Nineteen and she'd never flirted with a man, never danced with a man, never kissed a man. She hardly ever *spoke* to a man outside her family. She had eight elderly lady attendants whose sole purpose was to make sure the SVP stayed V.

The mage's sanctum lay at the top of the highest tower of the White Castle of Saragond, and through the window, Rozlinda could see all the way to the Shield Mountains. "I feel like a bird in a cage. Look but don't touch. See but never go."

"Now, that's not true, Princess. You can ride out any time you wish."

A moving cage is still a cage. But Rozlinda turned

back, attempting a smile. None of this was Mistress Arcelsia's fault, and a princess should make all around her comfortable. "Perhaps I will later."

When she went riding, her knights escorted her. She'd still have her ladies to protect her from her knights, but they'd be there. Young, virile men in their silver armor and bright, heraldic tunics, so masterful on their prancing white horses.

Much good would it do her. Could anything be more cruel? The SVP Guard should be as wizened as her tutors and her ladies.

"Sit down, Princess. We'll try scrying again. Perhaps you'll see your future."

"As I never see anything," Rozlinda muttered under her breath, "that's not encouraging."

But she gathered her skirts and sat on the stool before the deep golden bowl. In her disgruntled mood, she sat on her trailing veil, dragging her conical headdress to one side. With a hiss, she rearranged herself and pushed the hennin straight so the silken bands beneath her chin weren't choking her.

"I don't see why being SVP means a person has to dress this way."

"Tradition, Princess."

Rozlinda looked at Mistress Arcelsia's white robe and scarlet velvet cloak. "No one wears clothes like yours, either. Doesn't it bother you?"

"Not at all, Princess. They are the outward sign of my position and skill, and very comfortable."

"Mine are merely the outward sign of being the youngest fertile female of the blood, and they're awful."

"Princess, do try to put your mind into a state receptive of magic."

"Fat lot of good it's done so far," Rozlinda mumbled, but only because the mage was drawing water for the scrying bowl and wouldn't hear. They both knew Rozlinda didn't have a scrap of magical ability, but they pretended.

Mages could do magic, or so they said. Rozlinda

rubbed a finger on the rounded edge of the bowl. "Is there some magical way to bring on Izzy's flowers?"

Mistress Arcelsia turned so sharply water sloshed. "No, there isn't, and it wouldn't be right. You know better than to tamper with fate."

"I'd suspect she was concealing the bleeding if she wasn't so desperate to be SVP."

"Princess Izzagonda would never do such a wicked thing. After last time."

Last time, when the ceremony had gone awry.

Mistress Arcelsia poured the water into the bowl. "I'm sure she'll flower before the dragon comes. She's thirteen, after all."

"I'm not afraid of the sacrifice. I'm just tired of the Princess Way. Another year seems unbearable."

"The fates have their reasons."

"The reason," Rozlinda said forcefully, "is that the royal family is having fewer and fewer girls, and no one seems to be doing anything about it."

"There is nothing to be done—"

"Then hasn't it occurred to anyone that we're *doomed?*"

The royal family of Saragond existed solely because their female blood had a mystical power to appease a dragon—the blood of a princess who had flowered but remained a virgin, that was. They married only within their line so that the blood would remain strong.

"Well?" Rozlinda demanded.

Mistress Arcelsia walked behind her. "Clear your mind for magic, Princess. Perhaps you'll receive wisdom." She put her hand on Rozlinda's neck and pushed, so Rozlinda had to look into the depths of the golden bowl. "What do you see?"

Rozlinda sighed and concentrated. She had no magic, but she'd been trained all her life to respect ritual and tradition, and daily magical exercises were part of that. Part of the Princess Way, which was all to do with saving the world when the dragon came. If only it would come today.

"Clear the mind, Princess!"

Rozlinda squinted, trying to see images in the scant play of light on still water. She puffed a breath to stir the surface.

Snakes? Ribbons? A jelly pudding?

"Nothing, Princess?"

Mistress Arcelsia's assumption that as usual there would be nothing snapped Rozlinda's patience. "I see water. A river, I mean, not the bowl. A deep one." Might as well be dramatic. "There's a storm coming. Lightning. A golden fish leaps out."

"A golden fish! An excellent omen."

She suspected that Mistress Arcelsia knew she was lying, but carried on, anyway. "A man catches the fish. In a big, black net."

"Alarming, Princess. What sort of man?"

"A . . ." Rozlinda's imagination faltered. A knight, a prince, a brute? But then she gasped.

She saw a man!

She blinked, but this was no ripple image. It was as if the round bowl had become a window through which she saw a strangely dressed, pale-haired man. He was standing by a river or lake, but in sunlight.

"Describe the man, Princess." Mistress Arcelsia's bored voice seemed from another world, and perhaps it was. Rozlinda was finally having a vision!

"The picture's changed. Now I see a sunlit scene. Countryside. Water. And a different man."

"Tell me more." A sharp tone showed that the mage knew the difference.

Rozlinda strained to catch every detail.

"He's not from around here. Long, pale hair but dark skin. Not like the dark of Cradel. A sort of bronzish gold. His clothes are strange, too. A sleeveless leather jerkin such as a farm worker might wear, but cut tight. And no shirt underneath."

Rozlinda had to swallow. That leather was almost like a second skin and left his brown, muscular arms open to her inspection.

"And?" the mage prompted.

Rozlinda dragged her eyes away from more manly perfection than she'd seen as an adult. She grew hotter. The jerkin went down to his thighs, but his legs were covered by garments as formfitting as her own silk stocking.

"Princess?"

"Green hose, brown boots."

How inadequate. How deceptive. But she felt that if she truly described this man he might be snatched away like a forbidden treat.

It was as if he were drifting toward her, or she toward him. Details became clearer. His arms weren't totally bare. "Metal bands around his arms, upper and lower. They look like gold. Can't be. He's no prince. You can't see this, Mistress?"

"No, it's your vision. Blond hair, you said?"

Rozlinda concentrated again. "Not really blond. More white."

"Old?"

"No, not at all. It's . . . this is a strange word for hair, but it's bone colored."

"I see."

"You do?" Rozlinda tried to sit up, but Mistress Arcelsia pushed her down.

"Tell me more. Tell me everything."

Something urgent in the mage's tone both excited and scared Rozlinda. It had been so long since anything different had happened to her that she didn't know how to react.

"Pale hair. Loose down the back but in thin plaits at the front. Glinting, as if woven with shiny wire."

"Is he alone?"

"Yes. No! He just looked to his side and spoke to someone, but I can't see who. And it would have to be someone in the water. Or in a boat. The water rippled. Perhaps someone's swimming. He's picking up a bag and hanging it from his shoulder. A scruffy bag. Definitely not a wealthy man. A thief, do you think? Is this some warning about thievery? He's walking toward me."

Rozlinda tried to shrink back, but the mage's hand was firm on her neck. This was a vision, she reminded herself. A prognostication or an omen. Important.

"Is there anything else about him that you haven't told me, Princess?

"He walks well." Rozlinda became lost in the easy grace of that walk. Not a trudge, but a smooth swing, as if the whole world was his to walk over and he intended to do it.

As he drew closer, she noted more about his face. It was as handsome as the rest of him, with a square chin, high cheekbones, and chiseled symmetry, but the set of his mouth was grim and his startling pale amber eyes were cold.

And looking straight at her.

"Let me up!"

Mistress Arcelsia's hand clamped her down. "More, Princess. Tell me everything!"

Panting with fright, Rozlinda looked anywhere but at those eyes. "Leather belt. Pouch. Knife. A buckle. It looks to be . . ."

"Be what?"

"Set with dragon-eye stones. It can't be. Only princesses of the blood wear dragon eyes!"

Who was this man? What did this vision mean?

Deep inside, instinct answered: *Nothing good.*

Then the man stopped again and opened his battered bag. He took something from it and fixed it to the front of his jerkin. When his hands moved away, the sun caught it, flaring red.

Rozlinda pushed back with all her strength and at last broke free. She swiveled to look at the mage. "He put on another dragon eye. One as big as my palm!"

"Ah," said Mistress Arcelsia.

"Who is he? What does it mean? Is he . . . is he from *Dorn?*"

Dorn, the mysterious land beyond the Shield. The land from which the dragons swooped out to kill and consume. The land from which all dragon-eye stones came.

"Time will tell." Mistress Arcelsia pulled Rozlinda off the stool and steered her to the door. "You are needed in the apothecary. Your sister is with child again, so mother stone must be prepared."

Rozlinda found herself on the landing outside, her question unanswered, but she didn't go back in. She didn't want an answer. Instead, she wanted reassurance—to be told visions weren't real, that the man wasn't real, that he wasn't from Dorn.

Mistress Arcelsia had seemed frightened. Did her vision portend war?

For seven years, ever since the disaster, Saragond had braced for war, expecting Dorn to exact revenge for the death of the dragon. Gradually, fear had changed to hope, but along with it came the conviction that the next time a dragon arrived everything must be done correctly to the last detail. That conviction, more than rules, had chained Rozlinda to the Princess Way.

Why would it all go wrong now?

For century upon century, every eight years a dragon had come, killed and eaten, then been appeased by the gift of a cupful of blood from the SVP.

Not long afterward, tribute arrived, clear sign that the peace would hold for another eight years—tribute of calming hralla, sweet-smelling versuli, mother stone, and dragon-eye jewels. They were pretty, but their greater value came from their power to prevent pregnancy in princesses of the blood. That was essential if the mother stone ran out between tributes, for without that no blood princess could bear a live child.

Aurora.

With child again. What a fool she was!

Rozlinda set off down the spiraling staircase, her patient ladies falling in behind. Aurora had been told not to get with child again yet—all the women of the blood had—because there was little mother stone left. Which was all Aurora's fault.

It had been Aurora who'd killed the dragon. Or been responsible for it. That act had created the threat of war and, of course, meant no tribute. If her child died in her womb it would be entirely her own fault, but Rozlinda couldn't wish that upon anyone.

She left the tower and hurried down the covered walkway to the apothecary. But then she paused to look at the pictures painted on the stone wall. They were so familiar that she normally hardly noticed them, but today they had new meaning.

The first paintings showed the myths of ancient history; the next, scenes from the War of the Twin Princes. The final scene of Prince Lorien and the remnants of his army fleeing toward the Shield Mountains seemed to roll into the first picture of the Dragon War, showing dragons flocking from those mountains into Saragond. There had been many centuries between the two, however.

All the pictures were faded by time, but the essentials were still clear.

Rozlinda studied the main picture of the Dragon War. The sky was full of dragons, many breathing fire on farms and villages while knights hurled spears and farmers threw stones. More effectively, a group of men operated one of the huge lancing machines that had already killed one dragon. It sprawled on the ground, glittering red, green and gold, impaled.

Those machines had been rebuilt seven years ago, just in case.

The castle walls made up the left foreground of the picture. On them, the king directed defense. Machines mounted on the battlements shot lances at one great circling beast. Its horned head snarled fire at the defenders, a forked tongue clear, and one set of mighty claws held a struggling, screaming man.

What horrible beasts they were.

On the dragon's back, a wild-eyed, howling dragon rider urged it on—a rider with long bone-colored hair who wore a huge red stone in the middle of his chest.

She had definitely just had a vision of a warrior of Dorn.

"Princess, what is it?" asked Lady Petrulla.

Rozlinda looked around, finding her anxious ladies and the sunlit garden beyond them as unreal as if they were the vision.

"You are required at the apothecary, I believe," Lady Petrulla prompted.

"Yes." Rozlinda carried on.

The cluttered, aromatic room welcomed her, but it didn't soothe the jangle of thoughts inside her mind. Had she just received a warning of war? Should she tell someone? There'd been no violence in the man she'd seen, but he had looked foreboding.

Mistress Madder seemed as out of sorts as she. She was muttering, "There's not enough," as she scraped out the ornate pot where the crumbly mother stone was kept.

Rozlinda pulled on plain oversleeves to protect her diaphanous ones. "Aurora is so stupid."

"Only in some ways. She was clever enough to figure out that if Galian of Gar killed the dragon, she'd have to marry him, blood family or not."

"Perhaps he thought of it."

Mistress Madder put the bowl of chips and dust on the worktable. "Who spends the most time studying the rules and traditions of Saragond? The archivists, the king and queen—and the SVP. She did it."

Rozlinda knew the apothecary was right.

By tradition, the mother stone had to be prepared by the SVP, so Rozlinda set to pulverizing it in a pestle. "Do you know if she had a vision?"

"Aurora? If she ever had a vision of more than her own selfish wants, I never heard of it. Concentrate on your work."

Rozlinda looked at the grayish powder. "It's not enough."

"We have to try. If the child dies in her womb, it will be her own fault."

But Rozlinda could tell that Mistress Madder would no more wish that on any woman than she could. She began to add the other ingredients. "No children for me, then, even if Izzy flowers today."

"Not until the next tribute comes. But don't you be in a hurry to pick your husband."

Rozlinda stirred everything together, not saying that she'd made her choice already.

Jerrott of the White Helm, captain of her guard. He of the golden curls and sky blue eyes. The best, the brightest, the boldest, and safely of the blood.

"I'll have plenty of time. Even if Izzy flowered today, I wouldn't risk marriage until next year." She looked at the empty mother stone box. "It could be disastrous."

"There's always dragon eye," the apothecary pointed out.

Rozlinda's hands paused. "Can it be relied on?"

"Absolutely. Three small stones swallowed, and no child can start that month."

Rozlinda stirred again, allowing a little hope. As soon as Izzy flowered, she could marry. Babies could wait. She wanted Jerrott and to cease to be V. But then she grimaced. "I suppose we're short of dragon eyes, too."

"Not that short," Mistress Madder said, with an understanding smile.

Rozlinda poured the potion into a vial, but then, as she stripped off the oversleeves, a new fear shivered in. "What if no more comes? Ever? No more dragon eyes. No more mother stone."

I'll never bear a live child, so I'll not be able to risk conception. I'll have to live as chastely as the SVP all my life.

"Of course it will. As long as everything is done right this time."

"It will be, I promise."

The apothecary looked up. "If you're SVP, yes. But it'll be Princess Izzagonda by then."

"She'll follow the rules, too, I'm sure. We all know the dangers—"

A bell clanged.

It startled Rozlinda, but caused nothing but puzzlement at first. Then the apothecary cried, "The dragon bell!" and Rozlinda's ladies burst in. "Hurry, hurry, Princess. A dragon comes!"

"But it's not due until next year...."

They grabbed her and towed her out. She heard a trumpet blast beyond the wall, and a voice calling. It had to be Jerrott shouting the traditional words. "To horse! To horse! A dragon comes."

Rozlinda laughed, broke free and ran, skirts hiked high. The dragon had come! By evening, Izzy, ready or not, would be SVP. In days there would be mother stone and dragon eyes, and everything would be all right.

Aurora's child would be safe, and she herself would be free to flirt, to kiss, to marry and have children. To cease at long, long last, to be V!

She burst into her chambers just as her mother rushed in through another door, crown atilt, crying, "The bath! The Virgin's bath!"

"Is it really a dragon?" Rozlinda gasped as her clothes were peeled off. The bell still clanged.

"Yes, yes! A clear sighting."

"And just one?"

"Just one."

Rozlinda heard the relief in the queen's voice and knew she, too, had feared war.

"Everything must be done exactly as it should be," the queen said forcefully.

"Of course ..."

"But, Your Majesty," Lady Petrulla whispered, "the princess has no gown."

Everyone froze.

The Virgin must wear white for the sacrifice. All white. No other pure white gown was permitted in Saragond. But there'd seemed no point in preparing the costume for Rozlinda when Izzagonda was expected to take her place.

Chapter 2

"Aurora's," the queen said. "Find it!"

The SVP's gown was ceremonially burned once the tribute arrived. Last time there had been no tribute, and so the ceremony had never taken place.

"It'll never fit," Rozlinda protested. "I'm half the size she was even then."

"Don't exaggerate. And too large is better than too small. To the bath!"

Rozlinda was swept into the next room and into a steaming bath. Many hands scoured her body as others washed her hair, giving her time to think.

This must be what her vision had foretold, though she couldn't understand how one meant the other. Still, it was good. The dragon was early, but it was here. Soon everything would be normal again.

If everything went as it should.

Was it crucial that the SVP gown be new? As the dragons had always come with clockwork regularity, the possibility of a used gown had never occurred before.

Izzy burst in. "It *can't* be a dragon! If she gets a dragon, I'll never get one. Cousin Jesseletta will be ready in time. It's not *fair!*"

"Don't worry, Izzy," Rozlinda said. "If the dragons can come at any time, there may be one for you in a couple of years."

"Zlinda!" the queen protested.

Izzagonda glared. "You summoned it, didn't you? Just to spite me!"

"Why on earth would I do that? And how?"

"You would if you could."

"Of course I would. Years ago. If you were ready, you could have today's thrills with my blessing, and the status of having made the sacrifice."

"Then why can't I? Mother, you heard her. I can take her place! No one need know."

The queen slapped her, the *crack* shocking everyone to stillness.

"Do not even *mention* the possibility of deviating from the tradition, Izzy. Ever. Go to your room and prepare your mind. By tonight you *will* be the SVP, flowering or not, and you will observe every jot of your duties as your sister has always done."

Wailing, Izzy fled.

"Mother . . ." Rozlinda protested.

"She's another Aurora, and I will not have it. Everything must go off perfectly. Everything."

A page girl rushed in. "It's eaten a cow in Prubrook, Majesty!"

She dashed away, and Rozlinda was pulled out of the bath to be dried. She hurried into a silk shift, lace-trimmed drawers, and fine stockings. At least white underwear was common, but this was another deviation. Every stitch she wore should be new, and only the stockings were.

Her mother's tight lips showed she noted it. "Sit!" she commanded, and Rozlinda collapsed onto a chair, her teeth beginning to chatter.

What if this all went wrong?

Two maids brushed Rozlinda's hair, sometimes pulling out knots in their rush, and Rozlinda saw new lines around her mother's mouth. "Don't worry, Mother. I will do everything precisely as it should be."

The queen's face relaxed and she put a hand on Rozlinda's shoulder. "I know you will, dear. You always have. We do understand how hard it has been for you."

Another page girl. "It's eaten two cows in Thretch County!"

Another. "It's taken a pig and her piglets near Cummins. All in one gulp!"

One of Rozlinda's deeper fears surged up. "Once upon a time, the dragons used to eat the princess. What if . . ."

"Ancient history, dear. Probably myth, in fact."

But this dragon had come early. What if Aurora's selfish folly had changed everything?

Perhaps the queen felt her shivers. "Don't be afraid, dear. It's a tiresome business, but there's nothing to it other than a small cut and a little blood. Truly."

Lady Petrulla hurried in, almost invisible beneath a mound of white. "It's ill-omened. It's even stained."

The skirts were edged with dusky green, and a few dark spots must be blood.

"If you can tell me where we may find a pristine white dress, I will be grateful," snapped the queen. "Dress her!"

The mass of perfumed gossamer silk first smothered Rozlinda and then was tugged down so she could breathe. She twisted to look in the mirror. The gown hung off her and puddled on the floor.

"I look like an iced cake that's run!"

"We'll hitch it up with a belt."

In moments, that was done, the bulges of fabric above the waist doing nothing for the appearance.

"Mother!"

"There's a bodice."

The clanging bell was giving Rozlinda a headache.

Another page ran in, eyes wide and bright. "It swept right over the castle! It's enormous!"

Rozlinda's arms were thrust into the stiff, sleeveless garment, which was laced at the back. It was more like a corset, and being slightly built, Rozlinda had never worn one. Thank heavens it was loose.

But the queen said, "Summon the seamstresses. We can make it fit."

"Except in the bust," Rozlinda pointed out, looking down at the jutting, empty mounds. In moments, they were being stuffed with silk veiling.

I look ridiculous, she thought, close to tears. For the most important, most public day of her life, she was going to look ridiculous.

I am the vessel of the blood, she reminded herself. *I am about to make an important sacrifice to save my people from harm and to preserve peace.* Calm settled over her. She'd prepared for this for seven years, so she was glad to have the privilege of doing it. And in hours, she'd be free.

The Keeper of the Jewels presented the tiny crown, no bigger than an apple. Rozlinda hadn't seen it since she'd watched Aurora leave the castle last time. It had looked so pretty, sparkling and trembling on the top of her head, with yards and yards of shimmering veil spilling out of it. Now she wondered.

"How on earth does it stay on?"

"Glue."

"What?"

"Don't fuss. It washes out. Sit."

When Rozlinda obeyed, someone dabbed cold stuff in a circle around the top of her head. "Don't move," the queen commanded, and pressed the crown in place. Rozlinda immediately developed a cramp in her thigh and a desperate need to scratch her nose.

"Mother . . ."

"Just a little longer . . . there. I think it's solid."

Rozlinda shifted, and tiny hairs pulled. "Ow."

"Don't touch it! The veil."

The enormous length of silk was carried over and many hands began to hook it to the crown.

"Ow. You're pulling my hair!"

"Don't be a baby, Zlinda. I hope you're not going to make a fuss when the priest takes your blood."

"Of course not." But that meant she had to grit her teeth and keep quiet as the veil was fiddled onto the crown. At the same time, two seamstresses took in rough seams in the corset.

Another page ran in. "The people are gathering outside the gates, Majesty, calling for the princess to save them."

"No more time, then. Stand up, dear."

Rozlinda did, very carefully, feeling as if the crown might slide off and take most of her hair with it. The bodice still wasn't snug, and the skirt trailed the floor. She must look a mess, and she desperately wanted this to be perfect.

"Did you have a vision before your dragon, Mother?"

"No, dear. To tell the truth, I never really had any sort of vision."

"Nor did I. Before today. I think it was a warning that the dragon was coming."

"Really? A good omen, then, but a shame it didn't come last week. We could have had a new dress made. Are you ready?"

Rozlinda persisted. "Did Aurora have a foretelling? Has any SVP ever had one?"

The room had stilled and everyone was staring at her.

"Not that I know of, dear. You can tell me all about it later. Now, look how well it's turned out." The queen turned Rozlinda to the mirror.

It was like magic.

The white skirts frothed out from beneath the bodice, which gave her the kind of figure she'd only dreamed of. The slight puddling on the floor was rather pretty. Impractical, but pretty.

The twinkling crown, silly though it was, looked delightful, especially as her ladies spread the veil in a shimmering cloud around her. Rozlinda smiled.

"There, see," the queen said, smiling, too.

A page dashed in to announce, "The king and the knights await!"

Rozlinda was almost carried out of her chamber, some attendants managing the veil, others holding up her skirts at either side, her mother crying, "Hurry! Hurry!" and "Careful! Careful!"

When she appeared at the great door, the maddening bell went silent. Instead, she was almost knocked back by the cry of acclaim. "The Virgin! The Virgin!"

It came from all the people below in the castle bailey—her knights, magnificent in their shining armor, dragon lances aloft; the court, gathered in hasty finery to cheer; and all the town worthies who'd been able to cram in.

Her father came to give her his arm down the steps. As he handed her into her white chariot, he said, "Here we go, then, blossom. Off to the dragon's rock, then back for the ball."

Rozlinda tucked in her skirts and veil and took her seat, smiling her thanks at him.

"No smiling, dear," her mother hissed. "Remember, this is a *sacrifice.*"

As her guards took their places around the chariot, Rozlinda made herself look miserable, reminded that once, long, long ago, this sacrifice had been real. The princess had been eaten by the dragon. Had the knights' role then been to prevent an unwilling victim from escaping?

Her father went to take his place in the open carriage behind, along with the Priest of the Blood, who would be carrying the special knife. She wouldn't think about that. Just a little cut, that was all.

Following them would be a train of carriages for other priests and the more feeble gentlemen of high rank. Most of the men would ride, however, and many would be carrying lances as a symbol that they, too, would defend the princess from the dragon if necessary.

Defend, or force?

The chariot rolled through the arched gateway into the crowded town. Marching ahead of her, the Crown Crier began his bellow.

"Oyez, oyez! A dread dragon has come to ravage Saragond. Behold a virgin princess of the blood, who will sacrifice herself to save us all."

The cheer almost deafened her.

"Thanks to you, beautiful princess!" people cried.

"Blessings on the princess!"

"Blessings on the Virgin's blood!"

White flowers settled around her like snowflakes, and Rozlinda wanted to smile and wave. She kept her gaze ahead, however, and her face still. She would be the perfect SVP.

"Oyez, oyez! If any man lay low the dragon and put his foot upon its neck, he will be rewarded by the grateful princess's hand in marriage. Oyez, oyez . . ."

There it was, the ancient remnant Aurora and Galian had used.

Rozlinda noticed the way men in the crowd grinned at her, perhaps imagining for a moment becoming one of the highest in the land if only they were brave and skillful enough.

She'd never thought of this peril.

It was one thing for Aurora to secure the husband she wanted by having Galian kill the dragon. It was quite another to imagine being handed as a prize to just anyone—old or young, wise or foolish, honorable or wicked. When this was over, she was going to get that changed. After Aurora, everyone had to see how dangerous it was.

Over the next hour, as her procession wound through the packed streets of Castletown, then out along the road to Dragon's Rock, the cheering men's faces all looked avaricious. It wasn't even that they desired her; she was simply key to a greedy dream.

Her first glimpse of the rock gave only relief. Soon this would all be over.

As it grew closer, however, foreboding trickled in. The dark rock humped so strangely in the grassy plain, like a slumbering beast that might stir and growl. No one knew how it came to be there. No rock of similar type had been found elsewhere.

No one knew why it so strongly attracted dragons, and why only every eight years. In this case, seven years. Or why an offering of SVP blood here would send the marauding dragon back to Dorn.

When they knew so little, when things were already amiss, how could anyone be sure this ceremony would go as it should?

The chariot drew up where the coiling steps began. The spot was in the shade, but that wasn't why Rozlinda had to fight shivers as she extracted herself, shedding blossoms, and took her father's arm. He looked somber, too, but perhaps he was playing his part—the sorrowful father giving up his beloved daughter for the good of his people.

Rozlinda looked up at the blunted mound. It didn't seem so big until you were close, but now it loomed. The steps cut into it spiraled out of sight then reappeared as they reached the flattened top.

"Right, pet?" her father asked, and she nodded and walked forward, aware of knights, carriages, and mounted gentlemen forming a circle a short distance from the base of the rock. Soon they'd circle it entirely, but they'd be little use if she truly needed protection.

Of course she wouldn't, and Jerrott would be with her. The Captain of the Guard was also Keeper of the Chain, so he was waiting on foot, the delicate silver chain looped around his arm. His visor was up. She thought he smiled slightly in encouragement.

Or anticipation? He had to know how she felt. She smiled slightly back. *Tonight, we will dance.*

The Priest of the Blood led the way up the stairs. Rozlinda followed, telling herself there was nothing truly to fear.

Except breaking her neck.

The stairs were worn with age, and her thin-soled slippers were aptly named. They gave no grip. Thank heavens for railings on both sides, but she didn't have a third or fourth hand to manage her skirts and veil. No wonder Aurora's dress was stained. Silk kept snagging on wood and rock and she had to let go to free it. She felt her father behind her, trying to help, but he couldn't do much. The green rock already coated her hands.

White is the silliest color for this, she fumed. Once

back at the castle, she was going to insist on changes. It really couldn't matter. Dark green would be sensible. A narrow skirt. Gloves and sturdy shoes.

When the spiraling stairs took her to the other side of the rock, a wind made everything worse. It flapped her skirts and whipped her veil around her face.

Her father gripped it from behind. He meant well, but her hair screamed a protest. She carried on up the stairs, tears springing from the pain, from the general, impossible awfulness of this, which was not mentioned at all in the Princess Way.

When she reached the top she stopped in blessed relief, but also because the handrails ended.

Her father nudged her. "Move on, Zlinda."

She didn't want to step out onto the rough, flat top without support. The wind was whipping her veil so hard that she'd already had to put a hand to her crown for some relief. If it got under her skirts, she felt she might fly away.

It had to be done, however, so she picked her way forward over the uneven ground. Her father took her arm and patted her hand. "Not much more now, pet, and Reverend Elawin is waiting."

She nodded, wishing the priest wasn't waiting so close to the edge. One hand on her crown, she let her father guide her, but kept her eyes on the tricky ground. She noted that the large dents in the rocky surface were grooved.

"Are those . . ."

"Marks of dragon teeth, yes, Princess," the priest said, and she looked up to find she'd arrived at the spot. "The dragon took a particularly large bite last time. A good omen."

He fell silent, doubtless remembering that last time had been Aurora's dragon.

Rozlinda stared at a huge, crescent bite. She'd known that the dragon bit off the part of the rock that had virgin blood on it, but . . .

"If Your Highness would kneel?" the priest prompted. He had the blade ready in his hand.

Rozlinda wasn't sure if her sudden quaking was because of the size of a dragon's bite, the wind or the knife. Other men had followed up here—princes of the blood, the royal council and the male elders of Castletown. All watched her, eyes implacable. If she tried to run, they'd stop her.

"It's the wind," she said, trying to excuse her shivers.

"Aye, it's sharp today," her father said, pushing her down into the kneeling position, "but we've not lost a princess yet."

It was a joke, but Rozlinda couldn't wrench her mind from the dark, distant days when the king had brought a daughter to Dragon's Rock to truly sacrifice her to the beast. She glanced at the iron stake to which she'd be chained. Despite every attempt of will, her throat glued itself with dryness and her heart began to panic.

"Highness?"

She looked back at the priest and found he was offering a goblet. The traditional hralla tea. She took it, drank and could breathe again. Blessed hralla. She'd only had sips before when ill, but now she drained the cup.

All cares drifted away, yet her senses expanded. She fancied she could pick out faces down below and almost catch quiet comments made there. She heard music on the wind, perhaps even the song of distant birds. The few flowers still clinging to her gown gave off perfume.

There was another aroma, as well, neither noxious nor sweet. It came from the very rock.

The priest cut the ribbons that cinched in her enormous sleeve and pushed it up to expose her arm, to rub a cream there. To numb it.

Her father held her arm while the priest gripped her wrist. Compelling her, but she didn't mind.

Here came the knife. How beautifully the light played on the long blade. How prettily her blood shone as it swelled and then dripped. Big, glossy drips that the rock drank in, turning black.

Her veil swirled and picked up a touch of blood, as if

licking it. She caught it in her free hand. Mustn't steal any from the dragon.

The dragon she could sense. She looked toward the horizon. Nothing there yet, but she knew where it was just as it knew her, knew her blood. Was drawn to it. She'd wondered sometimes if she really had the blood; how anyone could tell. Now, she was sure.

"There, Highness. A goodly amount."

Rozlinda looked back to see the priest wrapping a bandage around her arm. It quickly showed a line of red. The dark stain on the rock was quite large, but it didn't seem enough to appease a hungry dragon.

Enough to make her light-headed, however.

She staggered slightly as her father helped her up, making jolly, soothing remarks. Around her and below, the crowd roared. She supposed it was a cheer, but it sounded wild. Or perhaps the wildness in the air was a thrumming that she recognized as dragon.

As her father guided her to the stake, Rozlinda's mind continued to explore realms beyond her ordinary senses. How funny, she thought, with a real temptation to giggle, if the dragons were drawn not to her blood but to the enormous amount of hralla in it.

But that made no sense. Hralla came from Dorn. Hralla, dragon eyes, versuli, mother stone. Hralla, dragon eyes, versuli, mother stone. It became a song in her mind. . . .

"The dragon!" The call rose all around like a flock of startled birds.

"That's quick," said her father. "Let's get you chained up, love. Don't want anything to go amiss at this stage."

Jerrott had the long chain already threaded through the loop at the top of the stake, and he and her father wrapped it round and around, lightly binding her arms to her body and her body to the iron.

Not a real chain, she reminded herself. It was as delicate as one she might wear around her neck. Just a symbol. But as a distant shadow took fluid shape, so like a bird but not, Rozlinda strained against her bonds.

"Courage, Princess." It was the merest whisper, but it came from Jerrott. A break with protocol, but so welcome. She met his eyes.

Thank you. Soon.

The lock clicked. Her father and Jerrott retreated. All the men retreated to be as far away from the dragon's bite as possible. But she saw Jerrott pick up his spear. If the dragon tried to eat her, he'd defend her. Even so, as the beat of mighty wings pulsed through the air, ghosts of princesses past, princesses chained here in truth, shrieked warnings.

The horns!

The scales!

The vicious teeth!

Rozlinda clenched her hands. She would not shame herself.

But the beast grew larger and larger. Could a bit of blood be enough? She could see that horned head now, and the crimson-and-gold eyes, fixed hungrily not on the bloodstained rock, but on her! Rozlinda tried to break free then, and found she couldn't. Even such fine chains held tight.

She clutched the iron rod behind her as the beast circled overhead, blotting out the light and beating down stifling, acrid air. Dust swirled to choke her, to sting her eyes. She closed them, screaming in her mind, *Eat and be gone! Go away! Go away!*

She heard the crunch. Felt it in the rod as if the whole rock trembled. Perhaps she heard distant cheers and trumpets of delight, and then the air calmed.

She let go, blinking dust from her eyes. The dragon still circled but up high, as if waiting for something. For more?

Please go.

As if obeying, it beat its wings and soared, but then curved back, flying lower—heading straight for her!

Spears arced up from below, but the knights and men down there were too far away. Jerrott was braced to throw, but waiting.

Throw now, she screamed in her mind. *Throw now!*

The dragon's mouth was a crimson maw, its gray teeth curving blades. Rozlinda fought the chains again, but knew she was about to die.

Then the dragon collapsed across the top of the rock with a thud that shook the earth. Coughing in the storm of dust, Rozlinda stared at wicked talons only feet away, then up at a small mountain of crimson, green and gold scales.

She was saved.

Jerrott had saved her!

She turned to thank him, but he stood, frozen, spear still in hand.

Who, then? Who?

Who, she suddenly realized, would she have to marry?

A man appeared on the fallen dragon's neck. It was the man from her vision—the one with the bone white hair and the pale amber eyes.

His voice rang out in the suddenly silent air. "I claim my princess bride."

Chapter 3

The king silenced the hubbub with a grim roar. Amid settling noise and dust, he asked, "Who are you, sir, and what are you doing?"

The man climbed nimbly up to the peak of the dragon mountain. "What does it matter who I am?" he called out in a strong voice, meaning to be heard by all. "Am I not the savior of the Virgin Princess?"

He spoke in a slightly guttural accent, using complex vowels where simple ones would do.

It must be the remnants of hralla in her that made this seem so unreal, Rozlinda thought. This couldn't truly be happening. Where had he come from, just like that?

Then she knew.

He'd ridden the beast—as a Dornaan warrior would. A pale-haired Dornaan warrior ... but the Dornae didn't *kill* dragons. They revered and adored them. This had to all be a hralla dream.

The man turned on his gold-and-crimson hill, looking like a dream himself. His bare, dark arms were outstretched and glinted with gold as he addressed the Saragondans, but especially the powerful men up here on the summit.

"Does not your sacred tradition say that any man who can lay low the dragon and put his foot upon its neck may claim the sacrificial princess as his bride? I claim that right in recompense for the dragon stolen from us seven years ago, against all rules of harmony and honor between our peoples."

"Sir," called her father, "we apologize most sincerely for that and assure you it will never happen again. But there must be some other recompense."

The Dornaan turned to face Rozlinda. To her, he said, "None."

Jerrott cried out, "May I not challenge this rogue, sire?"

"Be silent."

Her father's tone made Rozlinda quake. This was all real, and she suddenly understood her situation.

The royal family of Saragond existed because the princess blood was essential to peace, harmony and prosperity. Aurora's selfishness had threatened disaster. To refuse this man now could ruin their house.

Nor did she think her father was moved solely by that. He truly believed this ritual was essential. And so, she realized, did she. Despite internal rebellion, she had faithfully followed the Princess Way for seven long years because she believed.

Stillness hovered over rock and plain as everyone waited for her father to speak. In this, his word was law. At last he said, "Captain, give this man the key."

The Dornaan ran down the dragon's leg and strolled toward Rozlinda. She remembered that easy walk. She remembered that enormous dragon eye on his chest. Up close, it seethed in the sun like a bubble of molten rock.

It was real.

He was real.

This was really happening.

Perhaps this was another ritual, Rozlinda thought frantically. A symbolic marriage important to his people?

Or perhaps the dragon needed more blood.

She could do that.

A cup or two more wouldn't kill her.

As he came closer, those cold eyes stole her breath.

I'll give you some fingers and toes, even, she desperately thought.

He extended a hand, and Jerrott stiffly put the key in it. When the Dornaan reached for the padlock, Rozlinda couldn't help but flinch away. Heat beat out from him, as if a fire burned within his dusky skin. Or perhaps the heat came from that dragon eye. She felt that if she were to touch it, it would not be cold like a stone, but hot enough to char her skin.

He turned the key, tossed the lock aside and loosened her chains, unwinding them until they tinkled to the ground. Then he took her hand and led her away—toward the dragon.

She jerked back. "Don't. Please don't feed me to it!" It came out as a pathetic squeak.

"I won't."

Of course not. The dragon was dead.

"Not here, at least," he added, with a touch of grim humor.

Other dragons. Thousands of dragons. In Dorn.

"Come." He tugged and she had to follow, for no one was making a move to help her. It was as she'd thought. In the end, these men would sacrifice her if it suited their own ends.

She stumbled along, one hand holding up her over-long skirts, her veil blowing around her face and trying to smother her. The wind shifted and cleared her face, seeming to clear her mind. She twisted back to look at her father, at Jerrott, at the councilors and lords. "Help me!" she screamed.

Some twitched, but then they looked away.

What could anyone do? Even Jerrott couldn't save her by killing the dragon. The dragon was dead. They could kill the man, but that, she was sure, would mean war. Abruptly hopeless, Rozlinda let him take her to the corpse, as accepting as a dumb animal to the slaughter.

The fallen dragon still gave off heat and a pungent odor of burnt rock and blood, but its fate touched her.

"I can't believe you killed it. You, a man of Dorn."

"You like dragons, Princess?"

"No, but you should."

"I do."

She turned on him. If no man would fight for her, she would fight for herself. "Then why? You can't want to marry me, sir. You must prefer women of your own type."

"You, Princess, are the bride I want."

"Why?"

"Your blood is highly valued in Dorn."

She thrust out her bandaged arm. "If it's blood you want, take more." When he didn't respond, she protested, "You can't drag me off to a foreign land that I know nothing of! I don't speak your language. I know nothing of your customs. How can I make you a good wife?"

He looked down briefly, so briefly that she might have missed it if she hadn't been staring so fixedly at his face.

"I regret any discomfort, Princess, but it must be so. Some of the Dornae speak Saragondan, and you will learn our language as you learn our ways. Seven years ago, the conditions of peace were broken. This is the only means to mend them."

The words reduced her rebellion to dust. *Refuse,* he said, *and there will be war.* Armies of dragons will again stream over the Shield to wreak disaster on Saragond.

Desperately, she looked to her father for help.

He looked older by a decade, but said, "He's right, Zlinda. If he insists on this, by our own laws, there's nothing to be done." He turned from her to the Dornaan. "Sir, do you promise to treat my daughter well?"

"Your Majesty, she will have all honor and respect in my land, as the vessel of the blood and as my wife."

"And who are you in your land, sir? I must know that."

The demand was bluster, but the Dornaan answered. "I am Rouar, Guardian of the Queen, third maj of the second council, Seyer of the Dragon's Womb."

For all that meant, Rozlinda thought. She knew they had a queen, but the queen didn't seem to rule. Instead there were tribes and councils, partly elected and partly appointed, perhaps by inheritance, and everything seemed to be connected to dragons one way or another.

It made no sense to normal people, and his name, with its rolled *r* at the beginning and end, sounded like a multisyllabic roar. At least he obviously held high rank. She couldn't help being glad that she wasn't being snatched up by some vagrant.

She couldn't tell if this Rouar's words meant more to her father than they did to her, but he seemed to have no further resistance to offer.

"Very well, Seyer Rouar. We must agree. We will all return to the White Castle so arrangements can be made—"

"We will be married here. The Priest of the Blood has the spiritual power, and you, Your Majesty, along with your council, have the right of approval."

Now her father flushed red. "Come, come, you must allow my daughter time. Court her a little. Let her gather her bridal chest."

"Alas, I cannot. We must return to Dorn immediately. My wife may return to visit her family later, if she still wishes to."

"If I still wish to! Of course I will. When will this 'later' be?"

"Let us say a half year."

"*A half year?* I'm to be a prisoner until then?"

"No. You are to be a wife. A wife stays with her husband."

"You could accompany me back here."

"I have duties."

"All the time?"

"For the next half year."

Rozlinda wanted to snap that she did, too, but in truth her only duty was to be the Sacrificial Virgin Princess and that was over. Except for marrying the dragon slayer.

And presumably ceasing to be a virgin with him. She

shivered in a deeper way and cast a frantic glance at Jerrott. He was staring grimly at the horizon.

"How can you be so heartless?" she demanded, hat-
ing to be reduced to pleading.

"Princess, I can be as heartless as I must." It was a
flat warning that denied any hope of escape. "Are you a
child to cling to your home so?"

"It is not childish to value family, sir. I pity you if you
do not!"

"Oh, I do, Princess. This is all about family, as you will
learn. Priest, pray thee, do your work."

Pray thee. The first word he'd used that wasn't quite
right. How did he know Saragondan so well when
Saragond and Dorn never interacted beyond this one
ceremony?

A sense of not knowing, of not understanding, swept
through Rozlinda like a cold draft. Uneasy men rustled
all around. Below, silent faces stared up. Had they any
idea what was happening?

The priest stepped forward. "Er . . . do you assent to
use the Saragondan ceremony, sir?"

"Of course."

Reverend Elawin looked around as if hoping someone would intervene, but then raised his practiced, sono-
rous voice. "Then I declare that all present are witness
to the wish of these two, Seyer Rouar of—"

"Just Rouar," the Dornaan interrupted.

The priest gaped, but picked up. "Of these two—
Rouar of Dorn and Rozlinda of Saragond, princess of
the royal house, Sacrificial Virgin of the blood, revered
sacrifice to the dragon . . ."

Rozlinda listened numbly as her attributes rolled
out and the ceremony began. When asked if she willingly and joyfully chose Rouar of Dorn as her husband, she looked from face to face to face. "How can
I say yes?"

"Leave out the joyfully," the Dornaan said. "I assume
the princess is willing to do her duty for her people."

"Do you, Rozlinda, willingly choose Rouar of Dorn as your husband?"

Rozlinda delayed, sure that something, someone, had to intervene. Nothing did. She whispered, "Yes."

When the priest put the same question to the Dornaan, his answer was firm.

Reverend Elawin produced his knife. Rozlinda muttered, "More blood," but she didn't protest as he jabbed the fine point into the pad of her hand and then into the pad of the Dornaan's, nor as her wound was pressed to his.

"Thus you become one," the priest intoned. "May blessings rain upon you, bringing prosperity and fertility in your home and in your land. And," he added hesitantly, "may the blood continue through you."

That phrase was used only at the wedding of a princess of the blood. "Is that what this is about?" Rozlinda asked. "You want princesses of the blood for yourselves?"

"Something like that."

She had to admit that made sense. "Will that mean your dragons won't invade?"

"I cannot say, Rozlinda."

It was the first time he'd said her name, but his doing so didn't help because the word came strangely from his mouth, with a throat-rolled *r* and the *i* stretched almost to an *ee*.

He spoke a foreign language. His people spoke a foreign language. They probably all looked as peculiar as he did, and had strange, even offensive smells and customs. She looked around frantically again, but he hissed something like, *"Zupsisi."*

And the dragon moved.

Rozlinda yelped and backed away, but the man locked her against him as the dragon heaved onto its front, got its legs under it and then rose.

"It's alive!" she protested, yanking against the imprisoning arms. She twisted to face her father and the knights. "He tricked us! That has to invalidate the ceremony."

Her father was slack-jawed, but said, "A wedding is a wedding...."

"It *can't* be."

"There is nothing," the Dornaan's deep, emotionless voice said, "that says the dragon must be dead. Only that the man must lay it low and place his foot upon its neck."

"All the same ..." But then she yelled, "Stop it!"

She was shouting at the dragon, which had circled its long neck to point its huge, red, flaring nostrils right at her face. The point of its long tongue flickered in and out. No one could doubt that deep in its dragon-beast mind it was thinking, *Yum, yum. More princess blood.* It was even drooling a viscous yellow and pink stuff.

The man wasn't controlling her anymore. She was clutching his arms for protection.

"Seesee, behave," he said.

If a dragon could pout, this one did, but it moved its head away, circling it on the long, flexible neck as if inspecting king, knight, priest and councilors. They all flinched back. Then it poked its head off the hill and breathed at the crowd below. Horses reared.

"Seesee!"

The head coiled back to be tucked on the beast's back, perhaps chastened, perhaps sulking. By the blood, the monster behaved like a poorly trained puppy.

"You see, wife, we must go. This is too difficult for her."

The Dornaan said something and then picked Rozlinda up in his arms. The dragon had already lowered its neck, and the Dornaan ran up it to a crest of horn at its shoulders, to place her sideways in a dip behind. She clutched the horn, looking down, stunned, at the equally stunned watchers. The Dornaan slid astride behind her and said, "Go."

The dragon leapt, beating its enormous wings and stirring a stormlike rumble. Rozlinda couldn't believe it could raise its mass, but then it soared like paper on a breeze. Below, Dragon's Rock, father, knights and all she'd ever known shrank smaller and smaller in her horrified vision.

When she saw her home, turrets shining in the sun, pennants bright and lively in a breeze, she burst into tears, sobbing against the velvety warmth of the dragon's bony crest.

Chapter 4

Rozlinda's tears ended as tears must, even when the cause persists. She simply rested there, limp and exhausted. What calm she felt was probably from hralla tea. That must explain why she hadn't thrown a fit earlier, and all in all she was glad of it. It wouldn't have done her any good.

No one could afford to break protocol again. If this was her fate, she would be brave.

She swallowed and straightened—and became aware of being in a man's lap, of his hot hard presence down her left side. She was finally touching a man, in many places, and he was her *husband*. She shied away from that thought, fixing instead on a simpler problem—her runny nose.

"The costume of the Sacrificial Virgin Princess doesn't include a handkerchief."

"The clothing of the Seyer of the Dragon's Womb doesn't include one, either. Use the bandage on your arm."

Teeth gritted at his tone, she did as he suggested, taking in the state of her gown for the first time. When she'd put it on, it had been stained only around the hem. Now green dust covered it, smeared deep in places by her dirty hands. With a grimace, she wiped them as clean as she could on the silk. The dress was ruined beyond hope, anyway.

Yet it was all she possessed. She was leaving home

without money and with only the clothes she wore—ruined, impractical clothing that hadn't fit her well in the first place.

She would not cry again. Presumably, a husband would provide clothing for his wife. And she had done her duty. A harder one than she'd expected, yet still she had done it. For her people and her family. Legends would be woven about Princess Rozlinda of Saragond.

"Mother stone," she said, still looking at her gown for fear of looking anywhere else. "You will send it this time?"

"Of course."

She felt his voice as well as heard it, which was perhaps why his tone seemed softer, even kinder.

"Everything will now be as it should be, Princess. I promise."

She turned her head to look at him, but he was too close and everything about him was too strange. When she looked away, she saw the ground far, far below. And realized it didn't bother her.

"How peculiar not to mind flying."

"A blessing."

"I suppose so. Cold, though."

He put his arms around her, sharing his startling warmth. With that added to the heat of the dragon, she wasn't unbearably cold. What's more, riding a dragon could be seen as a privilege. Had any other Saragondan ever seen their country from this elevation?

She'd almost persuaded herself that she was content with her situation when the dragon tilted in flight. Sitting sideways in silk, Rozlinda began to slide. She clutched the man's arm, hoping his seat was secure. She breathed again, but then the dragon tilted forward, tucked its wings, and dove downward.

Rozlinda shrieked, and kept on shrieking all the way down, blank with terror. She only breathed again when the dragon opened its wings and leveled out. She was still panting when it landed delicately in a field.

She was inhaling to yell her outrage when the Dornaan rose with her still in his arms, put her down, took her hand, and tugged her at a run down shoulder and leg to the ground. The footing was rough, which helped, but she squealed as she went and then crashed against him.

She thumped him with her fists, spitting out pent fury. "You beast. You *monster.* I could have broken my neck."

Then she stared. For the briefest moment, humor had lit his eyes. It disappeared as if a door had been slammed, but at least he wasn't dead to emotions. She was scrabbling for scraps and she knew it, but her unwanted husband's ability to smile, maybe, was a comfort.

But then she grew wary. "Why have we stopped here? So far from Dorn."

"Seesee can't carry us for long periods, especially without eating."

"Eating?" Rozlinda's voice squeaked with fear, because, of course, if this man wanted to feed her to his dragon, it would hardly have been diplomatic to do it in front of her people. How to get her away to this isolated spot? Marry her.

Hot, acrid breath made her whirl. The dragon's tongue was flickering toward her. She edged away, but the dragon stretched its neck and its glistening tongue grew longer and longer. She looked wildly toward the man, but of course he wouldn't help. Even so, she whispered, "Please?"

"Seesee." He went to pound on the dragon's nose, but sounded indulgent. "She's only being friendly," he said to Rozlinda.

"No, she isn't. She wants to *eat* me."

"Don't be silly. Seesee, stop."

The tongue slurped back in.

It wasn't that so much as the word *silly* that calmed Rozlinda's terror to mere fright. Surely he wouldn't call her silly if her fears were true. She inhaled and exhaled, making herself calm.

The Dornaan had taken a forked stick off his belt and

was scratching the beast's eye ridges with it. The dragon seemed almost to purr.

"So your dragon—"

"*Our* dragon—if anyone possesses one, which no one does."

"Ours?"

"Is it not Saragondan law, too, that in marriage all is shared?"

"More or less." Saragondan marital property law was complex, especially for princesses, but if he wanted to share everything, she wasn't going to argue. Talk of such practicalities eased her fears even more. Her heartbeat settled.

She wasn't about to be eaten.

To show she wasn't afraid—much—she walked closer. She ended up near an enormous nostril, assailed by dragon breath, so she turned her head away—to find herself looking into a huge, red-gold shimmering eye. It blinked a dark gray eyelid and then dazzled her again.

"Is that where dragon-eye jewels come from? From their eyes?"

"Their eyes are eyes and decay when they die. Dragon-eye stones are so called because they resemble them."

For some reason that calmed her, too. It appeared she had no escape from this situation, so she needed information. Lots of it.

"There's no pupil. How does she see?"

"Seesee, show your eye."

A gold layer slid upward, revealing red centered with a darker red pupil. Then the golden membrane dropped again.

Rozlinda turned to the Dornaan. "Does she speak Saragondan, then?"

"She doesn't speak at all."

"Very well, does she *understand* Saragondan? And if so, why?"

"She probably only understands my inner voice. My thoughts, if you like. It works better if I speak at the same time, but the language doesn't matter. I use your language out of courtesy to you."

Rozlinda considered this. It helped to concentrate on practical things.

Not on being snatched from her home and family.

Not on being taken to a land of strangers.

Not on being this man's *wife*—with all that implied.

Seesee butted up against her, almost as if in comfort.

Rozlinda flinched away. "Does she understand *my* thoughts?"

"I don't know."

She backed away. "This is intolerable. I can't bear it. *Ow!*" She clutched her crown, turning to find the dragon nibbling at her veil. "Stop it!"

A bit more veil went into the mouth, forcing her to step closer or lose some hair. Then the dragon sucked. Rozlinda staggered hard against its nose, trying to save her scalp. "Do something!" she yelled.

"Tak!"

The dragon spat out the veil. The end was a lump of yellowy slime.

"Ugh, ugh, ugh!" Rozlinda exclaimed, staggering away. "It's *disgusting.*"

A moment later, she was buffeted by dust and wind as the dragon launched into flight.

"You've upset her."

She turned slowly to the man. "*I've* upset *her?* Be she toddler or puppy, she should be trained not to damage things. My veil is ruined, my dress is ruined, and in case you haven't noticed, because you insisted on dragging me away like this, *I—have—no—other—clothes!*"

She was shrieking like a hawker in the marketplace, but she wanted her home, she wanted her mother, she even wanted Mistress Arcelsia and Lady Petrulla. And above all, she wanted a hot bath and some ordinary, clean clothes.

"Is this how you treat a woman, a princess of the blood, even, in Dorn? Is this how you treat a *wife?* Then, sir, I pity all Dornaan women."

He was like a rock buffeted by a breeze. "I truly am sorry, Princess, but it had to be. I cannot amend it, but I do have clothes for you."

Deflated, she watched him shift a pile of stones and pull out the bag she'd seen in her vision. Then he extracted a second one, carried it over to her and took out clothing.

Rozlinda stared, unable to believe the final indignity. "I cannot wear those."

He looked at the bright yellow hose, then back at her. "Why not?"

"They'll show my legs."

"Yes?"

"In Saragond, a lady of any degree of respectability does not show her legs above the calf. Or do they go under a gown?"

He held up the green tunic, which she had to admit was very prettily embroidered with flowers.

"If that reaches mid*thigh,* I'll be surprised."

"You may have mine if you wish."

"Which will reach no lower than my knees." She truly wasn't intending to be difficult, and he appeared to be trying to help, so she said, "Thank you, Sir Rouar, but I'll put up with slime until you can find me something decent."

"That can't be until we reach Dorn, so I recommend the boots at least. Those shoes aren't suitable for walking."

"Walking?"

"Seesee cannot carry us all the time."

She took a deep breath. "You expect me to *walk* to Dorn?"

"Only now and then."

She desperately wanted to hit him. "And then climb the Shield, perhaps?"

"No, she'll carry us over there."

What would happen if she set off to walk back home? Surely no one would expect a princess of the blood to put up with this. That was one reason to change into the low, green boots.

"If they fit, I'll wear them," she conceded.

After a moment, it became clear that he wasn't going to remove her slippers and help her with the boots. Seething, she found a rock and sat to do it herself, trying to calculate how far it was back to the castle.

This rough, uninhabited moorland was nowhere near her home, and the dragon had probably covered a great distance. It had been a long day, and she was weary. . . .

And she couldn't unknot the ribbons. She struggled, making the knot worse and worse as she accepted that she couldn't walk home, anyway.

Even if the Dornaan allowed it, it was too far.

Even if she made it there, her people would send her back.

Even if they didn't, the pattern would remain broken. No tribute would be sent. Aurora's baby would die in her womb. No woman of the blood, including herself, would ever bear a live child. And there would probably be war.

She was simply sitting there, misery a rock in her heart, when he knelt beside her, a sharp knife in his hand. "You would permit me to cut your ribbons?"

She almost felt as if she'd permit him to cut her throat.

"Very well."

He slid his fingers beneath the ribbon, a warm contact she wasn't prepared for, and the knife parted the silk as if it were air.

He pulled off the dirty slipper, then did the same with the other one. He kept hold of that foot, brushed off some dust, and pushed on the boot.

"It's a perfect fit," she said, wriggling her toes.

"The cobbler who makes the royal shoes provided the measurements."

She considered that as he slid on the other boot. It had been obvious that today's events had been carefully planned, but it startled her to learn that the Dornae had been making arrangements within Saragond.

In fact, it frightened her. What else did they get up

to, sneaking around? And if they were able to sneak around, they couldn't all look like him. She was churning with alarm, but with excitement, too. She might be the first Saragondan to explore Dorn. Might she be able to find ways to create harmony between the two peoples? She could keep a journal and one day write a book.

He was still kneeling, looking at her as if he'd like to read her mind.

"Thank you," she said, rising to try the boots, revived by purpose. But then a gust of wind caught her hair, tugging at her crown again. "Now take off my veil."

He rose. "Rozlinda, I don't take orders. A *pray thee* will sweeten it."

"*Pray thee,* then, Sir Rouar, take off my veil."

A brow twitched at her tone, but he bowed, hand to the dragon-eye stone on his chest, and walked to her back. He released the veil from its many hooks, and managed it with little pain. Then he tugged at the crown.

She clutched and yelled, "Don't! It's glued on."

"Whatever for?"

"How else would it stay on?"

He came round to face her. "You have to wear it forever?"

"Of course not. Until the glue can be washed out with hot water. Which, I assume, is not available."

"Not here, no. Again, my apologies."

The words were polite, but he looked as if he thought all Saragondans idiots. He put the veil in her hands and walked away. With no purpose that she could see, he simply moved to stand a few rooms' lengths away from her. Was this some requirement of Dornaan propriety, or blatant rudeness?

Oh, she hated this! If nothing else, she'd always been certain of the correct thing to do and say in every situation. She was expert at reading nuances of behavior, but he was an enigma.

And only look at the veil. It meant nothing to her, but she had so few possessions that its state could break her heart. One end was heavy with dragon goop, most of it was streaked with green dust and there was even the smear of her blood from the ritual that now seemed so long ago.

She couldn't bear to throw it away, but it was too messy to put in the bag. With a shrug, she tied it around her waist like a bulky sash, which reminded her of the bunched-up skirt beneath the bodice, and the breast cups stuffed with silk.

Had it only been this afternoon that she'd dressed? Only hours since she'd approached the Dragon's Rock, expecting giving some blood to be the full extent of her sacrifice? If all had gone as it should, she'd be back home now, enjoying a leisurely bath before the Princess Ball. She gazed sadly in the direction she thought home might be.

Would they still hold the ball? It wouldn't be fair to Izzy not to celebrate her ascendance, and it was part of tradition. Tradition must be upheld. When the mother stone and other tribute arrived, would they build a bonfire even though there was no dress to burn?

That settled one thing. She'd send the regalia back with the tribute. They'd certainly want the crown back. Yes, that way, everything would be just as it should be.

Heartened, she looked to see what else was in her bag. A smaller bag contained soap, cloth, comb, brush, toothbrush and powder. She tried the comb in her hair, but the crown made it painful to comb anywhere.

Three identical garments confused her until she realized that they were tiny pantalettes that would fit snugly and come down only inches on her thigh. She supposed that under the yellow, waist-high hose her full, loose undergarments would bump and bulge all over the place. Another reason not to wear the hose.

She glanced over at the Dornaan, wondering what he wore under his shameless hose. Even active men of Saragond didn't expose their legs above the knee. It was disgusting—but she had to make herself look away.

Face hot, she dug out the remaining contents of her bag. Two . . . shifts? Too short to be shifts. They were a thin underbodice. She looked down at her chest and was confronted again by the two mounds shaped for Aurora's munificence.

She hated these clothes.

She hated the ones he'd brought for her.

And there were no spare stockings.

She checked again, but no. Because she was supposed to wear those obscene hose.

She looked at him again—he as good as naked in his formfitting clothes. Tall, slim hipped and broad shouldered. As graceful in repose as in movement. Her mouth dried and her skin tingled.

He was too dark skinned, she told herself. He wore his hair like a woman's and it was as faded as an old man's.

No, it wasn't. It was almost beautiful.

He wasn't going to get away with ignoring her, whether it was the Dornaan way or not. She hitched the front of her skirt higher into the belt, then marched over to him. "When will we reach Dorn?"

He turned to her. "In three days."

She stared. *"Three days!"*

"Are you sure you don't want to change?"

"Of course I do, but you haven't provided any suitable clothes."

He shrugged. "Then we should be on our way." He returned to the bags.

Rozlinda remembered. Walking. Rolling her eyes, she followed him. "What about the dragon?"

"She'll find us." He picked up both bags and passed one to her.

She looked from it to him. "You expect me to *carry* that?"

"It's not heavy."

To say that princesses did not carry bags would be true, but clearly irrelevant. She was no longer a princess. She was a Dornaan wife, which apparently meant beast of burden.

So. This was the adventure she'd never been allowed

to have and she would embrace it. She took the bag and got the strap over her shoulder. Then suddenly, she laughed.

He looked a question at her.

"I'm trying to imagine what I look like, princess gown billowing, crown sparkling, and booted and bagged like a wandering laborer. Onward, sir, to the Shield, to Dorn, and to my new life!"

Simply to show him, she set off in the lead.

Chapter 5

R ouar of the Dragon's Womb followed his wife along
a rough track, cursing fate. This was the only way,
and he'd never expected it to be easy. But he'd never
dreamed that he would *like* a princess of Saragond.

She was soft, pampered and arrogant, but she was
also brave, high-spirited and resilient. Even Seesee
seemed drawn to her, and it couldn't only be because
of the special blood that pulsed in her veins. The blood
that could save the dragons, and thus his world.

"You'll have to bear with me if I'm slow," she said
without turning her head. "An SVP's life doesn't involve
much walking."

A statement of fact rather than a complaint.

"SVP?" he asked.

"Sacrificial Virgin Princess."

Shockingly accurate. "When Seesee's fed, she'll carry
us to where we can camp for the night."

"Camp?" she asked, dismay escaping, but then
shrugged and marched on with a jaunty step.

By the womb, he wanted, needed, cold distance, but
he should give this remarkable young woman as much
as he could. He moved to walk beside her. "So, what
does an SVP's life involve?"

"Routine. First thing in the morning, correspondence,
which also, of course, includes penmanship and etiquette.
Then history and archives before lunch with my parents,
and discussion of important events. After lunch, magic."

"You can do magic?" He kept his voice calm, but he'd never imagined that problem.

"No. I'm not convinced that anyone truly can, but the study is part of the Princess Way. Then there's dancing, castle management and inspection of my guard."

"The shining knights on their white steeds."

"Don't sneer. If you hadn't had the law on your side, I'm sure they'd have fought you off. After all, Galian killed the last dragon."

Every muscle in his body tensed. That she could speak so lightly of such a terrible deed.

It was as if she sensed something. "I'm sorry. I'm sure that was upsetting."

Upsetting.

A cataclysmic disaster that threatened their whole world . . .

He made himself speak. "It was the cause of your situation."

"I understand that. Someone had to pay for Aurora's willfulness, and it seems to be me."

"Aurora?" He knew who that was, but he wanted the princess's version of the story. He wanted to truly understand.

"My older sister, the last SVP. She wanted to marry Galian of Gar, but Galian doesn't have the blood. We princesses have to marry into the blood to make sure it continues. But what Aurora wants, Aurora gets, so she used the tradition that the man who slays the dragon gets the princess as reward. Which you clearly know."

"Let us say, we learned."

From her wary look, she'd heard the ice in his voice. "It's obvious that Dorn and Saragond don't know enough about each other. I'm hoping that I can learn enough to amend that, to explain each side to the other. To be a bridge, you see. A route to peace. That's a worthy life, don't you think?"

A shocking urge to weep rose up in him. He hid it behind stony indifference that dulled her enthusiasm and made her sigh.

Good. He couldn't bear anything else.

She also stopped talking, which was a blessing. He let her get a little ahead again.

She would be the route to war, not peace. When Saragond learned the truth, it would attack and Dorn would defend. Many would die, people and dragons, but even war was better than annihilation.

Until now he hadn't truly understood why Cheelus had died. He'd studied Saragondan ways, looking for the deep meaning, but now he knew the truth. It had happened because two people had fallen in love, and the man was considered too lowborn for a princess of the blood.

For that a trusting queen had been slaughtered and her guardian had killed himself. For that the whole of Dorn had pulsed for revenge, maddened by grief and by the knowledge that their world must soon die.

The Dornae had been restrained only by this plan, by the hope that Virgin Princess blood could amend all. They'd hoped to wait the full eight years, to preserve tradition as much as possible and not to alert the Saragondans to trouble, but Seesee had indicated that it must be now.

The plan had worked. All that remained was the deed.

Representatives from all the tribes were gathering at the womb, gathering to see Seyer Rouar slit Princess Rozlinda open so that her blood poured out. To watch Seesee consume every drop of blood so that she could miraculously lay eggs again and the dragons would survive.

Rozlinda's brisk step dwindled to a trudge and she felt weepy again, but mostly from exhaustion. It seemed a week rather than hours since she'd risen this morning, and her stomach didn't remember her light lunch. Her feet were comfortable enough in the boots, but her legs ached, her back ached, and her hair pulled, pulled, pulled.

In the end, she had to plead. "When can we stop?"

It was as if he'd forgotten her existence. "My apologies." He looked around and pointed across a scrubby field to some low trees. "There's water over there."

He set off in the lead. Sighing, she scrambled down a rough ditch and up again, clutching her massive skirts in front, then followed him doggedly.

He stopped short of the trees and put down his bag. "Pray thee, Princess, make yourself at ease. I will collect wood for a fire."

He walked away, and she looked around in weary disbelief. What in this rocky landscape could he imagine offered ease? She simply sat in a thistle-free spot. With the merest hint of shelter and a bed, she could go to sleep now, hungry as she was.

He returned with an armful of branches and quickly made a fire. The process was new to her, so it stirred a scrap of interest. He took out a tube and squeezed it. Fire shot out to light the tinder.

"That's clever. How does it work?"

"A combination of rocks."

"You could sell that to us."

"We have no need to."

He sounded as if trade was a disgusting thing. "You must be in need of some things in return."

"Only the blood."

"Then why not include one of those fire things in the tribute to make us even more eager to provide it?"

He looked up. "Tribute?"

"The dragon eyes, the mother stone and the rest."

His expression chilled to ice. "Tribute implies subordination. We send gifts to thank the Virgin, as prescribed in the ancient treaty."

Rozlinda sighed. She'd been trying to make conversation, and he sounded as if he were chewing lemons. The fire was leaping now, but it only made their surroundings more gloomy.

"Do you have food? I'm faint with hunger."

"We'll have a meal soon, but if you please, enjoy

these." He opened his bag and passed her a wooden box. She found cherries and a cake and had to stop herself from gobbling them. She ate three cherries in a rush, and then made herself slow.

"Thank you. These are good." But then she asked, "What?"

He was staring at her, and his expression was no longer indifferent. She didn't know what it was—angry, confused, alarmed?—but he surged to his feet and grabbed a leather bucket.

"We need water," he said, and strode toward the shadowy trees.

He'd left her alone on a rocky plain with night chilling the air and the fire creating shadows all around. She considered following him, but was far too tired.

She dozed where she sat, and started at a *clank*. Her unwanted husband was back and arranging a metal kettle over the fire. For tea, perhaps, but tea wouldn't satisfy her aching stomach. Where was the food?

He suddenly looked to the horizon. "She comes."

Rozlinda couldn't see anything, but then the dragon was circling and settling at a distance. Rozlinda was shocked anew at Seesee's size—and hit by the dusty wind and the smell of burning rocks. Along with another smell.

Fresh blood.

As the dragon waddled closer, she saw its snout was smeared with gore. Rozlinda looked away, but the snout appeared nearby and spat a bloody lump into Rouar's waiting hands.

"Thank you, Seesee. A nice bit of leg."

Bile rose in Rozlinda's throat. "I am not eating that."

"Stop hurting her feelings."

She set her mouth, but a princess should always be grateful for a gift, no matter how inappropriate. She swiveled to face the beast and said, "Thank you, Seesee."

It was almost as if the dragon sighed with disappointment before turning and waddling into the trees. Splintering noises told of trees knocked over, and then a splash said it had reached the water.

Rouar was slicing the bloody meat thinly and threading it onto metal skewers.

"Aren't you going to *wash* it? It's straight from her mouth."

"It'll be delicious. Trust me."

A "ha!" escaped before manners could prevent it. Rozlinda took a big bite of the cake. If she ate it all, it would serve him right. He could have his slimy, disgusting meat all to himself.

"I believe cooks in Saragond rub meat with many strange things," he said.

"*Not* with dragon drool."

"They would if they knew. It tenderizes and adds a delicious flavor. You'll see."

She ate the last piece of cake.

"All meat is disconcerting if you think where it comes from."

"It does *not* come out of a dragon's slimy mouth."

"How else is she to carry it? If she carried it in a claw, it would get dirty when she landed. And besides, if she were startled, she might drop it on the way. I like my dinner."

A smell from the sizzling meat made Rozlinda's stomach rumble. The aroma was slightly sweet, slightly spicy and, yes, delicious. Her mouth started to water. She looked away and hairs pulled.

"I wish I could get this crown off!" she snapped, as if that, too, was his fault. And it was. If things had gone as they should, she'd be crown-free. Bathed. Properly fed. Dancing at her Princess Ball. With Sir Jerrott.

He knelt beside her. "Pray thee, let me try."

He was holding a cup of hot water and a cloth and began to dab at her hair. She looked at the fire, at sizzling meat and smoke; at a whirling insect caught by the light.

She felt a tug and one side of the crown came free. He couldn't avoid pulling some hairs, but she didn't complain. Instead she made herself think of how careful he was being. How gentle. Excellent qualities in a husband.

And the meat did smell wonderful. Perhaps if she didn't think of where it had come from . . . after all, she was going to live in Dorn. They probably drooled their meat all the time.

"How many dragons are there?" she asked.

"Not enough." He was back to sucking lemons.

"Why not?" she persisted.

"It's complicated."

Fine. She needed to know these things, but she was too tired to push. Her fretful mind wouldn't leave the puzzle, however.

Not enough for what?

Not enough to wage war on Saragond?

After all, only one dragon ever came.

What if there was only one—Seesee?

That had to be nonsense. There had been another, the one Galian had killed. Only two? That couldn't be. She remembered in her early days on the Princess Way asking why the dragon came, and why only every eight years. And why it went away.

"Because the sacrifice compels them," the historian had said. "Otherwise dragons would come in flights of hundreds to plunder us, driving us to starvation."

That had satisfied her then, but now it made no sense.

He was easing the rest of the crown free, his other hand steadying her head against the pull.

She shifted, aware of warmth flowing between his hands, and of shivers, stirrings, aches elsewhere.

Her Princess Ball was happening now. Hers as much as Izzy's. She should be dancing, flirting, kissing. She should be receiving a kiss from each of her guards. A delicate kiss, but she'd looked forward to it. Especially Jerrott's.

This man was her husband, key to the exquisite pleasures she'd been promised once she'd done her duty. She swallowed, close to drooling herself. Would he kiss her now?

Then his touch ended. He rose to his feet and her crown tumbled into her lap even as he walked away.

"I need check if Seesee help wants. Attend meat, pray thee."

His Saragondan was awry, as awry as her wits.

She watched him stride away, and then looked at the silly little crown, teardrop jewels trembling in the fire-light, just as she trembled tearfully in every nerve.

Rouar dragged off his boots, then threw himself into the cold water. Seesee raised her snout from drinking and blinked an enormous question at him.

"Drool. Drool on a fertile woman. Nightfall. It's never happened to me like this before."

Queen. Seesee slurped in enough water to shrink the stream. Queen's drool makes women happy.

"Don't you mean *men?*"

Men happy means women happy.

"You're smirking." But the thought of that sort of happiness made him groan. He pushed to his feet, sodden. "She has to be a virgin." In case the princess was checking, he pretended to wash the dragon. He'd swear Seesee chuckled.

How can you find humor in this? It's life and death. Her death.

She's a nice princess.

Had that been *nice* or *tasty?* Dragon speech was often ambiguous.

I like her, he tried. *She's brave.*

I like her, too.

But again, *like* was open to a number of nuances. Rouar leaned against Seesee, for once not finding the dragon comfort he'd known all his life. Could he and the other guardians have misunderstood the dragons? Was this not going to work?

Princess not happy.

Rouar needed to stay far away from the drooled princess, but dragons seemed driven by a need for happiness in all. It had made today difficult for Seesee, and she didn't need more stress. And he should try to ease the princess's last days.

He sloshed out of the stream to his boots. They were dry, but they were the only thing that was. He walked in hose-feet to the fire, stripping off his jerkin. He felt the power of the drool from yards away.

"I turned the skewers," she said. "I don't know if that's right. I've never cooked on an open fire before."

She glanced up at him, then away, and then shot him another wide-eyed glance. At his crotch, then away again.

Parts of him were swelling and his jerkin was no longer covering down there. He dropped his jerkin and grabbed his pack. "I need to change."

He hurried back into the wood, thinking, *I'm Guardian of the Queen, third maj of the second council, seyer of the Dragon's Womb and engaged in a mission to save my world. What am I doing lusting like a raw youth after the one woman in the world I must never touch?*

Seesee stood. Shallow. Lake better.

"There aren't any lakes around here."

It was as close as he'd ever come to snarling at a dragon. He stripped naked, dried himself, and dressed in looser hose and a tunic, pulling his mind into order at the same time. He simply had to keep his distance.

He returned to the fire to find his bride picking glue out of her hair. It was plain brown hair, but thick and shiny. In fact, the firelight dancing on it made it quite beautiful. Like a glossy nut in sunshine. Rippling from her fingers, fluid as it would run over his skin, drowning him . . .

Drool!

He wanted to run back to the stream, but he sat—as far from the tormenting woman as he could while still being able to reach the meat. He struggled to think only of food, but his mouth watered at the thought of the taste of her, of her lips, her mouth, her skin, her sweat.

When he used one of the padded cloths to turn a skewer, his hand trembled so much he almost dropped the meat in the glowing wood.

Queen drool. Dragon drool was an enjoyable stimulus to sex, but queen drool was a whole other thing. Treasured but carefully guarded. He was only twenty-five. Fifteen years ago, when the last dragon had returned to Dorn a queen, he'd been too young to even think about such things.

His mind sharpened. Did the power of the drool mean Seesee was growing eggs already?

No. It had been clear that large amounts of princess blood would be necessary for that. Only a little blood for a ripe young dragon ready to queen, but for an older one who had queened once already, the entire blood of a princess.

Need blood, she'd thought at him. Lots, lots, lots, always with an image of a young woman chained to the rock that was drenched with the blood from her fatal wounds.

Obviously, something had started, however, and the effect would only get worse with darkness. That was when drool had the most power. He felt it growing, creeping over him like fingers on his skin, beneath his skin, like love songs in his mind.

"Is it supposed to singe?" his tormenting princess asked.

Chapter 6

Rouar hastily lifted the skewers off the fire. For courtesy, he should take one to her, but he couldn't risk being that close.

"Like this," he said, picking up a skewer and biting into the meat, not surprised to see her roll her eyes.

She used the other cloth to pick up a skewer, and then gingerly nibbled. Even the sight of her neat, white teeth tightened his balls.

Then she smiled, making him want to groan. "It *is* good. I'm surprised fresh-killed meat is so tender."

"Drool. Tenderizes it."

Among other things. And he was eating it!

"May I have some tea?" she asked.

"Serve yourself."

From her look, the princess had decided the Dornae were hopelessly uncouth, but she poured tea into a cup. "Shall I pour for you?" she asked, making it a clear reproof.

"No, thank you."

She sipped, but then exclaimed, "Hralla. You're trying to drug me!"

"We always drink it at night. It's soothing."

He poured himself some and drank. He certainly needed soothing.

"We only use it for medicine, or for the SVP ritual, of course, because we have so little. Why will you not trade? You seem to have many things we would value."

"We have no need."

He could sense her frustration, so different to his own, but he was incapable of complex thoughts.

"Will I be allowed to send letters to my family?"

He closed his eyes. "Yes, of course." *As long as you are alive.* He had to do better than this. He gathered himself and looked at her. "Family. You have brothers and sisters, I gather."

"Five brothers, two sisters. Izzy is the Virgin Princess now. That should delight her."

"She won't be worried about you?"

She bit off a piece of meat. "Not Izzy. Unless she thinks the same thing will happen to her." She licked sauce off her upper lip, leaving it glistening. "It won't, will it?"

He swallowed his own drool. "No."

"Good." She reached for another skewer of meat.

He'd eaten only half of his first and dared not eat more. "Brothers?"

"Five, as I said."

He'd forgotten.

"One older, four younger." She caught a drip of sauce on her tongue—luscious pink tongue—and relished it. "What do I call you?" she asked, beautiful eyes fixed on him.

"Call me?" He was going to choke, pass out, explode.

"Is it correct for me to call you Rouar?" She frowned. "I don't think I said it right. It feels strange in my mouth."

In my mouth ... He forced himself to bite and chew. "Call me Rou, then."

"Rue?"

He repeated it, but she couldn't get it. "Try Ro. It's closest."

"Ro." She tried to roll the *r* in the back of her throat. A deep, sexy purr. "And I'm Zlinda." She was smiling at him, gilded by firelight. Warm, interested, welcoming ...

He swallowed against a thick throat. "You won't mind me calling you that?"

"We're husband and wife." She ran her tongue down her third skewer of meat, licking the sauce, eyes half closing as she relished it, but still seeming to catch the fire's flame. "What does that mean in Dorn?" she purred. "Being husband and wife."

His mind went blind-blank.

She closed her lips around the end piece of meat and slowly pulled it off. "This is *so* good," she mumbled. When she swallowed, she looked straight at him. "We will share a bed? With all that means? Tonight?"

There was nothing coy in the question. Did drool work on her, too?

"No," he choked out. He needed a reason. "No bed."

She smiled at him. "Do we really need one?"

It was as if an earthquake shook inside of him and a volcano exploded in his head. He was on her side of the fire, licking sauce off her full lips. Her eyes widened, but she licked him back, her tongue like fire.

Distant alarms clamored, but he was deaf and blind except to her. The bravest, brightest, most beautiful woman in the world, pulsing with heat and life. Round, sweet, wet, willing.

He grabbed that marvelous hair, cradling her skull, commanding her lips to him, then plunging his tongue inside to explore her deeper, hotter taste. A clatter told him her skewer had fallen onto stones, but he was lost, lost in the torrid wave of her, her smell, her taste, her essence drowning him.

Their mouths became as one, sweet and spicy with the sauce, hot and deep as the womb itself. They were plastered together, her supple, vibrant body everything a man could ever desire. He fought billows of silk to reach her leg, her silk-covered leg—was ever anything so alluring? Except a silk-covered bottom, so round, so hot, so damp in secret places.

Wife. He tumbled her to the ground, throbbing, struggling one-handed with his clothing—

"Ow! Stop. Stop. Rocks! *Owwwww!*"

One of her flailing fists glanced off his nose. The pain was just enough to bring him out of madness. He heaved away. By the womb, what had he almost done?

She sat up, rubbing her hip, but smiling. "Just rocks. I'm sure we can—"

"No!" he snapped, backing, unable to be anything but rude.

"I'm sorry. But the rocks ... it hurt." Tears glimmered around her eyes.

He wanted nothing more in the universe than to comfort her, to take her into his arms again and drown in her wonders.

To save her.

Temptation slammed into him. If she wasn't a virgin, she would be safe.

But the dragons would die out.

Dorn would die.

"That's why we have to wait," he said desperately. "Until we reach Dorn."

"Oh." A tear escaped to trickle down her cheek. "But won't that take three days?"

Three days. Two more nights. His body pounded with pain, his mind exploded with it. "The river," he said, and staggered off to throw himself into the saving shock of cold water.

Seesee lay coiled in the stream, and he sensed nothing from her. Not alarm, not amusement.

"If I start doing that again, stop me."

But you would enjoy it.

"What's that got to do with it?"

People are funny.

"Coming from a dragon ... Doesn't it matter to you that the dragons survive?"

Yes.

"And don't you need princess blood—to lay eggs?"

Say no, say no.

Yes.

He gave up. Dragons could communicate, but that didn't mean people always understood, even dragoners who lived their lives with them. Among the dragoners they used *dragon sense* to mean "incomprehensible."

Dragons liked their people to be happy, that was clear, but would they put that before their own survival? If so, it couldn't be allowed.

He staggered up, soaking wet again, this time including his boots. As he changed into his last dry clothes, he hoped the ones hanging by the fire would dry overnight, or next time he needed a quick dunking he'd have a problem.

His biggest problem right now was how to survive the night. He had to return to his bride and it would soon be bedtime, womb save him.

Bed. The princess was exhausted. Once she was asleep, he could keep far away.

"Seesee. Bedtime."

He felt her grumble that it was early, exactly like a child, but she waddled out of the woods and wandered the rocky ground until she found a spot to her liking. Then she settled down, neck and tail coiled, wings furled on her back.

Standing no closer to his wife than he must, Rouar said, "Let me show you how to sleep on a dragon, Zlinda."

She gave him a look but rose, an image of dejection, especially when struggling in the absurd skirts. She should get undressed. . . .

By the womb, no.

"I need"—she hesitated—"to go to the river."

"Right, of course." He had to offer. "Do you need me to guide you?"

She shook her head, picked up her bag and walked away, clutching her ridiculous skirts in front, trailing them behind.

Her stained and drooled skirts and the heavily drooled veil tied around her waist like a belt. No wonder she was driving him so completely mad. He wasn't simply affected by bits of queen drool—the princess was covered in it.

He needed to get her out of those clothes.

But how, when he'd not brought any skirts and she considered showing her legs as indecent as a Dornaan would think showing genitals or navel?

Rozlinda picked her way toward the woods, surprised that she could feel even more miserable on this horrible day, but she did. Without that hralla tea she'd probably be howling.

Everything had been so wonderful for a moment and then—*pop!*—it had gone, leaving her empty and feeling hungry even though she'd stuffed herself on that delicious meat. And now she was struggling through trees in gloomy light on her way to piss in the open and wash in a river.

The going wasn't quite as bad as she'd expected, because Seesee had trampled a wide path, so she had only to clutch up her dragging skirts and frequently unhook them from branches and broken saplings. From the Princess Way to the Dragon Path. Perhaps that should be the title of her book, though understanding between Saragond and Dorn seemed less likely by the moment.

I am glad to ease your way, Princess.

Rozlinda froze. Had she imagined that? No, even though her ears definitely hadn't heard anything, she'd heard words. The dragon could talk to her? Did that mean the dragon could hear her thoughts? What if she then told them to Rouar?

Private things.

Remembering what the Dornaan had said about speaking helping, she softly said, "You won't tell him?"

Private things.

Hoping that meant what she thought, Rozlinda plodded to the riverbank. It was only a stream, really, but pretty in starlight, shallow at the edges and chuckling over stones, making sweet music in her hralla'd mind. Perhaps that was it. Perhaps hralla opened her mind to the dragon. She'd be careful about when she drank it, then.

She relieved herself near some bushes, and then settled to washing off as much of the dust from her skin as she could. She unwound the bandage and found the long cut healing well. Perhaps there had been something more than numbing power in the cream Reverend Elawin had used.

The water was cold, but the idea of bathing fully grew in her mind. Why not? She untied the veil, but that was as far as she got. The bodice laced up the back and when she tried to reach the knot, she discovered that the dress's sleeves were surprisingly tight around the shoulders.

She could ask Ro.

Oh, no, not after what had just happened. She could live with the dirt, and the bodice wasn't tight. She could sleep in it. Anyway, she had no nightgown. If she somehow managed to undress, she'd end up sleeping on a dragon, next to her strange husband, in her sleeveless, calf-length shift.

At least she could wash her feet. She rolled off her silk stockings and when she'd washed her feet, she washed the stockings, too. When her feet were dry, she put the boots back on, wondering if the stockings would dry overnight. Perhaps she could spread them on the hot dragon. Anything was possible in this peculiar new world.

When she emerged from the wood, she saw her husband leaning on the dragon, close to Seesee's head, looking dejected. Probably disappointed in his bride. After all, what did she know about men and their ways, never mind Dornaan ones? She wanted to escape, and sleep seemed the best refuge at hand.

She cleared her throat. "I'm ready."

He straightened and offered a hand up onto the dragon. She relished that, clinging a little as she climbed. But then worry trickled in. "Is this safe?"

"Of course. Why?"

Something—a dragon thought?—had reminded Rozlinda that dragons liked SVP blood. She was certainly still V.

"She . . . she doesn't like midnight snacks?"

Something twitched his lips. "You're completely safe here, I promise. And dragon sleeping is cozy. With that and hralla, you'll be off like a baby. Slide down beneath the wing."

Rozlinda considered the situation dubiously, but what choice did she have? She spread the stockings over the dragon's back and then sat down, gathered her skirts, and wriggled under the wing.

He was right. It was surprisingly comfortable. The scales were smooth here, and the dragon was slightly soft and delightfully warm. The big body rose and fell gently with each breath. She'd get used to the smell in time.

"Will you sleep nearby?" she asked, peering up at the black silhouette against the deep blue sky.

"Not yet. Go to sleep."

Rozlinda lay on the warm, breathing dragon, looking up at the densely starred sky, trying to come to terms with her situation, but fighting tears. She believed in duty and even in sacrifice, but why did her path have to be so very hard?

Chapter 7

She woke in daylight, screaming, fighting a choking, stinking monster. By the time she'd realized she was knotted up in her dress, the Dornaan had dragged her from under the dragon's wing. She was panting with panic and her bodice wasn't helping. It had twisted in the night to compress her chest. As soon as she was on the ground, she cried, "Get me *out* of this thing!" When he didn't seem to understand, she added, "The bodice, idiot!"

His brows shot up, but he took out his knife, turned her, and cut her free. She dragged it off and stamped on it. Jumped on it, both feet at once. "I am *never* wearing one of those things again."

"You don't—"

"I know I don't need one. That's the point! I have nothing to confine."

She realized she had her hands clutched to her meager bumps and let go, face dragon-hot. "Now you know the truth."

His eyes flickered between the stuffed cups of the corset-bodice and her. "So I do. It is of no importance, Zlinda."

"So you say."

"So I say. However, I must insist that you change your clothes. You cannot go on like this."

"I cannot wear the ones you brought."

"I could command you."

His tone sent a shiver through her, but she raised her chin. "A princess of the blood is commanded only by the queen."

"But you're not the SVP anymore, are you?"

She shook her head. "That's irrelevant."

"Then explain."

She grimaced and sought the right words. "The women of the blood are above all others. Within the blood, princesses who have made the sacrifice have the eminence, oldest being highest. The princess on the Way is least among us. But no man can command us. It is different in Dorn?"

"We have no princesses in Dorn. A husband may command a wife for her own good. As she may command him to his."

"I don't see how that can possibly work."

"We shall see. Now, your clothes."

"I can manage."

He looked down. When she followed his gaze, she saw that six inches or more of skirt dragged on the ground. When he'd cut the lacing, he'd cut the belt, as well. Remembering how she'd looked in the mirror, she struggled with tears, but she pulled herself together. "May I request"—she tried for courtesy to use his word—"pray thee, that you cut a few inches off?"

"It will ruin it."

"It's already ruined. Besides, the virgin's dress is ritually burned. This one was only available because"—quickly she switched to—"because things were irregular last time."

"How short?"

If dragons gave off heat, this man could give off ice. Rozlinda blinked to clear blurry eyes. "Perhaps six inches?"

He slit quickly through the silk as she rotated. When he'd finished, she looked down at a neat edge circling just above her ankles.

"Thank you. That's much better."

He didn't thaw. Last night might never have happened.

She reached for the strip of dirty silk in his hand, but his hands tightened. "This is part of the death of Cheelus."

"That wasn't my fault!"

Nothing in his icy face changed.

Rozlinda pulled on her boots, picked up her small bag, and took refuge by the stream. This was all so unfair. She couldn't go on. She was aching from yesterday's walking, and the water was icy.

She had a horrible thought. What if this was the way the Dornae lived—wandering homeless through a rocky world with all their possessions in a bag, sleeping on their dragons, washing in streams? Surely Seyer Rouar of the Dragon's Womb, or whatever his titles were, must live in a castle.

Seyer Rouar of the plain clothes and scruffy bag?

"Zlinda?"

She turned and saw her captor in the trees.

"If you want breakfast, you need to come and eat."

If starving would spite him, she might, but she gathered her things and returned to the fire. He had the kettle boiling, slices of bread on plates, and something liquid in a pot. Boiled drool?

Rozlinda looked around. "Where's Seesee?"

"Gone to feed."

Rozlinda stared into the blank sky, stabbed by a new loss. There went her stockings. The delicate silk might have survived a night on the dragon's back, but they wouldn't survive flight. For some absurd reason, that loss seemed tragic.

"Sit and eat."

She sat down and picked up a slice of bread. It was heavy and hard.

He offered her the pot.

"What is it?"

"Honey."

Distrustfully, she tasted it. It was indeed honey, so she spread it thickly and ate, savoring the familiar sweetness. Even this had a strange taste, however. The bees of Dorn must feed off different plants. Strange plants, strange place, strange people ...

He put a steaming cup near her hand.

"Is that hralla?"

"In the morning?"

She wanted to snap that it wasn't her fault if she understood nothing about Dorn and its ways. That if they'd been planning this capture as carefully as it seemed, they should have sent lesson books to prepare her. And known to bring her suitable clothing! But what was the point?

She didn't recognize the taste of the tea, but it was pleasant enough, especially as he'd added honey. She ate, drank and was wiping honey off her fingers with the washcloth when she felt a thrum in the air. She looked to see Seesee swooping down on them, and watched the way the dragon seemed to gather herself in order to land neatly, stirring as little dust as possible.

"She's good at that," she said, trying to be pleasant.

"Dragons try to be considerate."

"So," she said coldly, "do princesses." *Unlike Dornaan men.*

The dragon waddled off to the stream, and the man gathered their cups and plates and followed, presumably to wash them. Rozlinda deliberately did nothing to help. When he returned, he began to pack things away.

"What do you want to do with the strip of cloth?" he asked.

The piece cut from her gown was neatly folded, but it was brown from recent dirt, green from dragon rock, and smeared where Seesee had sucked at it. She should send everything back home, but what would they think of its condition? He'd extinguished the fire, or she might burn it.

Then she "heard" a vague *yum?* and saw the dragon emerging from the woods.

"Perhaps Seesee would like it."

"She's not a puppy to be given a toy."

Rozlinda picked up the silk and walked over to the dragon. "If you would like it, I am most happy to offer it."

For a moment, she thought she'd made a fool of herself, but then the dragon's tongue slid out and snagged it, slurping it into her mouth, where she chewed or sucked with obvious delight.

Rozlinda turned to smirk—and caught affectionate humor in Rouar's eyes again. For the dragon, of course, but it gave her hope. He immediately turned blank. "There's no understanding dragons."

"Or a Dornaan." But Rozlinda returned to help gather their belongings, saying, "Ro, we need to learn each other's ways. Tell me about Dorn. You're organized into tribes, aren't you? By trade?"

He was assembling plates, cups and utensils into a tidy bundle. "More or less."

"And your tribe is?"

"The dragoners, of course."

His tone implied she was stupid to ask, but she would not become irritated. "The clan devoted to caring for the dragons?"

"All people of Dorn care for the dragons."

Patience, patience. Rozlinda stuffed her bodice and belt into her bag, though it could hardly hold them. "So what does that mean—to be a dragoner?"

He grimaced, but she thought it was frustration over having to explain something difficult rather than irritation at her. "We are family with the dragons," he said at last.

"So you are the families that look after the dragons." She wanted to ask, *Isn't that what I said?* but someone had to stay calm in this conversation.

"They look after themselves."

"Then what do you *do?*" So much for calm.

He put his kettle in the leather bucket and the bucket in the bag. "Farm, build, make things, buy, sell. Everything people generally do."

She was ready to bash his head with a rock, but then

something clicked. He'd said, "We are family with the dragons." Did that mean "We are *the* family with the dragons," or "Dragons and dragoners are one family"?

"You mean that the dragons are *part* of the dragoner clan?"

"Isn't that what I said?"

Breath seemed painful. "So the dragon . . . it, she, wasn't . . ." She'd been about to say *an animal* or *a pet*. "She was like a sister, a mother or an aunt?"

It sounded ridiculous, but he said, "More or less."

She looked at the dragon who was contentedly chewing. Already she'd learned that Seesee was more than an animal. *Person* didn't seem the right term, but it was the closest she could come to.

She turned back. "I'm so very sorry. How can I apologize enough for Cheelus's death?"

"You can't. It's done. Forget it."

"Can you?"

"Never."

Hopeless beyond words, Rozlinda ran back down to the stream. Galian and Aurora had done a terrible thing, but they hadn't known. None of them had known. And none of it was her fault!

But she knew now that she was the representative of all that he hated. What was to become of her in his strange, inhospitable land if her husband hated her? If his people hated her.

She tried to find solace from last night, from beautiful passion, but whatever had pulled him to her had battled his loathing, and loathing had won. She hugged her knees and wept.

Rouar halted by the last tree.

He'd come after the princess to apologize, but she was crying, the sort of steady tears that should go with a wail. She, however, sobbed almost silently.

And she still didn't know.

He put an arm around a slender tree, gripping its rough bark.

He couldn't do this.

He must do this.

What did one life matter in such a cause? He'd willingly offer his own—but he wasn't a vessel of the necessary blood. He wished they'd snared her sister. It might be easier to gut that selfish piece. But no. She'd still be an innocent.

At least there was hralla. With enough hralla, by the time he let poor Zlinda's blood drain into the womb, she'd think it the most wonderful thing ever to happen to her.

Could he drink enough before the sacrifice to gain the same bliss? He leaned his head against the bark, fighting tears of his own.

He didn't want Princess Rozlinda to die. He wanted, with ferocity, to step into her reality, where they arrived in Dorn as man and wife; where she set to learning all about her new family and the dragons; where they set up home together, talked together, laughed together, made love and babies together.

And in daylight, that wasn't queen drool speaking.

He choked tears in the back of his throat and bashed his forehead against the tree to try to knock sense into his brain.

"Ro?"

He turned to see her looking at him, lovely eyes concerned. He staggered away, half-blind and panting, to seek the dragon warmth, the smell, the something in the mind that had been his cradle since birth. Seesee was one of his family's dragons and had been a hatchling the year of his birth. Playmate, sister, ward and guide.

Sad thing you think of, Seesee said when he flung himself at her.

Yes. His throat was too tight for speech.

Why is it so sad to you?

That she could pose such a question about a blood sacrifice of someone she'd said she liked showed the gulf between human and dragon minds.

"You won't think it sad?"

No.

"I don't think I can do it. Give you Zlinda's blood."

Then don't.

"You don't need it to lay eggs?"

Again he saw, with insistence, the bleeding princess chained to the rock.

"But . . ." He shook his head. There was no point in arguing with a dragon. But in that vivid, awful image, a dragon claw was slitting open the victim.

"You could do it?" he asked, expecting a negative, even shock.

Yes.

Oh, for such a calm and distant mind.

Heart torn with grief, he said, "Then, Seesee, let it be so."

Chapter 8

I f the stream had been deeper, Rozlinda might have
thrown herself into it. She'd not swum since becoming
SVP, so she'd probably drown. As it was, she had to return to the man and his dragon and fly onward to Dorn.

She packed lingering items in her bag, only then remembering the bandage. When Ro had done such a
good job of tidying up she didn't want to leave mess, but
she didn't remember it by the stream. She looked at the
dragon.

Yum.

It made her smile a little, but she wondered. This
fondness for her blood was worrying, especially when
the dragon, too, must grieve the death of Cheelus. She
sensed, all the time, something unsaid.

At least her husband had thawed. He carried her
overstuffed bag to the dragon and wedged it in place.
When he gave her a hand into her seat, he might even
have tried to smile, and when he sat behind her, his arm
came around her strongly. She could imagine it was caring, except that she sensed the strain behind it.

With a roaring sound, the dragon lifted into flight,
throwing her back against him. Despite her will, parts
of her enjoyed it.

The tunic he now wore covered his arm down to his
elbow, but that still left his strong forearm to admire,
shimmering with pale hair and a narrow gold band.

Perhaps he didn't hate her after all. Perhaps the strain

was because he wanted to make love to her and couldn't yet, for whatever reason. She certainly knew how unreasonable rituals and traditions could be.

This morning's flight covered a long distance. The land beneath became rougher and the Shield closer, but that border of Dorn was still far away when they landed so Seesee could feed.

"What will she find here?" Rozlinda asked, looking at scrubby woodland.

"Deer, goat, wild pigs, even, if they venture out of the trees. Ready?"

Yesterday's walking had left some of her very unready, but she wouldn't complain. She shouldered her bag and said, "Of course." But she couldn't help adding, "Do you normally walk a lot?"

"If I want to get anywhere."

"What of the dragons?"

"They're not beasts of burden."

"What about horses, donkeys and such?"

"We have none."

"Why not?"

"Because the dragons would eat them."

"If you bred enough, the dragons could eat some and you'd still have some to ride."

"There is no 'some' with dragons and blood. They probably ate all the large animals in Dorn before my ancestors arrived. The settlers introduced draft and riding animals, and the dragons gobbled them up. People and dragons fought over it, but then the people discovered the advantages the dragons provided, so they tried your idea—they bred extra. The dragons ate as much as there was. More food meant more eggs, more dragons, more eating. A few animals could be preserved inside stone buildings, but apart from that . . ."

"They didn't eat the people?"

"No." But she heard a slight hesitation.

She said it for him. "Except Virgins of the Blood, of course."

"Except Virgins of the Blood. It's something to do

with the mind. A dragon can't eat unwilling victims. They seem able to make animals want to be eaten, but not people."

"But they ate the princesses. They could hardly have been happy about it."

"They could with enough hralla."

"I'm safe, then," she joked. "I need only stay away from soothing tea."

It fell flat. Rozlinda reminded herself not to attempt jokes until she understood the Dornae, if she ever did. With that in mind, she asked more questions and learned that the dragoners lived with the dragons on a rocky plateau called the dragonlands, while the other Dornae lived in the lower, fertile areas called, for some reason, the Dragons' Gift. The dragoner families each had some dragons as part of their family, but the dragons also formed a tribe of their own in some way. Doubtless it would make sense one day.

Dorn had no castles or grand homes, but Ro had a house as part of a group of houses belonging to his family. They ate little meat, but kept some poultry and small animals, which were not worth the dragons' effort to eat. There were fish from the highland lake and some from the sea, but the rough coast made fishing difficult.

The dragons mostly ate rock and earth, and the small plants and creatures that came along with them. They ate some fish from the lake, and even from the sea, now and then. It was only for egg-laying and long flight that they needed large amounts of blood.

Rozlinda listened and learned, but weariness caught up with her and she had to ask for a stop long before he was ready for one.

"I'm sorry," she said.

"I'm sorry not to have realized how hard this would be for you. We will simply take longer to reach Dorn."

Rozlinda was of two minds about that. Dorn still loomed in a foreboding way, but she longed for rest, for his proper house, a bath and a bed—with all that promised.

"If you can walk just a little farther, there's a small lake."

"Of course," she said, though she feared her walk had become a trudge.

She didn't know how he knew about the lake, but they crossed some rough land and clambered through trees to a tiny, pebbled bay on a narrow strip of water. She slumped down on a rock, resisting the urge to apologize again. She would get stronger. Clearly, she'd have to.

He climbed back into nearby woods and returned with a bowlful of berries. When she smiled as she thanked him, he smiled back. Things were definitely better. He looked up. "She comes."

Seesee swept down and plunged right into the lake, disappearing below the surface with something that sounded in the mind a lot like a child's *Wheeeeee!*

Rozlinda couldn't help laughing. "She likes water, I gather."

"Oh yes. We live around a lake and they spend a lot of time in it. There's sea nearby, as well, but it's rougher. Dragons are all for an easy life."

Rozlinda couldn't tell if Seesee swam or walked, but she came into the shallows and lay there, slurping in water. Then bubbles and steam erupted near her back end, and a whiff of sulfur drifted over.

"Fart," Ro said.

Rozlinda giggled, feeling more hopeful about everything. She stood up. "I'll just go into the woods."

But he rose. "No, I'll go and collect more berries. You'll be more comfortable here."

Rozlinda wasn't sure about relieving herself in view of the dragon, but Seesee seemed oblivious, so she went behind a rock. Afterward, she opened her bag, took out her soap and cloth, and went to the lake's edge to wash.

Ripples spoke of the dragon's lazy movements, but otherwise the world lay still around her. It was eerie to one who'd lived her life in a busy castle, but strangely beautiful. Was it like this on the edge of the lake in Dorn?

Bigger lake. Lovely lake. Home!

Home. Hers, too, and she wanted to fit in.

Rozlinda looked around and saw no sign of Ro, so she pulled out the strange clothes. She hid as much behind the rock as possible before untying the veil from around her waist and taking off her dress. The air was chilly, but that wasn't the only reason she shivered.

She braced to take off her shift, but paused. If she kept it on, it would veil her legs down to the calf. She quickly pulled the tunic on over it and fastened the loops to the neck. It would doubtless look ridiculous to a Dornaan, but it felt much better to her.

She sat to pull on the yellow hose, but they wouldn't fit over her full, lace-frilled drawers. She wasted time trying to think of a way around it, but then took off the drawers and hurried into the tiny substitutes. They were little better than bare skin, so she worked swiftly at pulling on the yellow legs and wriggling the top up to her waist, where she tied the strings.

She looked down at yellow legs, longing for a mirror. But perhaps not. How any woman could walk around uncovered to the thigh she couldn't imagine. She was pulling on the boots when waves splashed up onto the pebbles, almost reaching her.

She hastily moved farther up and saw that Seesee had shifted so that her snout was close to shore, and was using her long tongue to flick this stone and that into her mouth. She crunched with relish. Ro had said they ate rocks.

Tongue still gathering rocks, Seesee said. Rocks yummy.

She kept forgetting that the dragon could pick up her thoughts.

Nice clothes.

At least someone approved.

Or had it been yummy clothes, referring to the discarded dress and veil? She suspected it had.

"Sorry, Seesee. It's all supposed to go back home."

Everything should be as it should be.

It was peculiar to see the flick-crunch continue without pause as words formed in her head.

"Is everything as it should be?" Rozlinda asked, walking over to be closer, wondering if she could ask Seesee about Ro.

The long tongue slid sideways to flick her shift. Clothes funny.

"I feel half-naked. But then I suppose that makes no sense to you."

Flick, crunch. People funny.

"Funny ha-ha, or funny peculiar?"

What a stupid question to ask, but the more she conversed like this, the more natural it seemed. Seesee's "voice" was a deep rumble that should go with wise, aged eyes, but at the same time she often seemed innocently young.

Both. We like people. They do things.

"Do dragons not do things?"

Without people, not much.

"People do a lot of stupid things."

Funny, Seesee agreed.

Did Ro realize that dragons regarded people as amusement? He must. As Seesee was chatting, she'd try for more information. "How many dragons are there?"

Too few.

The same unhelpful answer.

"Too few for what?"

Rouar unhappy. Seesee's head swung around and her tongue flicked at the shift again, more strongly.

Rozlinda jumped back. "No, Seesee. You can't have it. I need it."

That tongue could stretch to extraordinary length. Seesee seemed to hook the shift and pull, dragging Zlinda to the water's edge. She was about to scream for help when the dragon spat it out, slimed all down one side.

"Oh, Seesee! Why did you do that?"

She couldn't stop it sounding like a complaint to a

young child. She crouched by the water's edge to try to wash it.

The water retreated as Seesee slurped.

"Give it back!"

She'd swear Seesee laughed.

The water level settled back, but Rozlinda gave up. She wasn't going to be able to get the viscous drool off without soaking herself.

When she felt a brush at the back of her thighs, she whirled. "You stop it! I don't know what it is with you and silk, but stop it. Right now." She was hand on hips, leaning forward, glaring at one huge red eye. Which blinked. Seesee resumed flicking stones into her mouth and crunching them.

Rozlinda wanted to rant on, but the dragon had stopped as requested.

Good rocks here.

All right. Rozlinda was definitely interested in the subject of dragon food. "But you like blood, too?"

Yes.

"Especially princess blood?"

Now.

Rozlinda didn't hear any threat, but she retreated. She liked Seesee, but she didn't fool herself that she understood her. Perhaps a princess would round out a meal of stones perfectly. She heard a noise behind and turned to see Ro returning. Thank heavens. He stopped and looked her over.

"You probably think I look ridiculous."

"No." He offered her more berries.

Rozlinda knew she shouldn't, but as she took some she said, "I hoped you'd be pleased."

"I am. It's the sensible thing to do."

Sensible. Admit it. She'd hoped he'd find her pretty in Dornaan dress. She'd hoped he'd forget she was part of the people who had killed his dragon aunt, or sister, or mother, or whatever Cheelus had been.

She pulled herself together. "I don't know what to do

with my gown and veil, with all of it. They should go back to the castle if the ritual is to be complete."

"All should be as it should be. Why not bundle the dress in the veil?"

Rozlinda made as small a bundle as she could, and tied it to her pack. It wasn't heavy, only bulky, but all the same, she resented that he wasn't offering to carry it.

Was she wise to try to be cheerful and adaptable? Perhaps she'd get better results by complaints and weeping fits, like Aurora and Izzy. It wasn't in her nature, however, so when Seesee came out of the water, she climbed back on, deliberately grateful not to be walking.

She had to admit that her new clothing was definitely better for dragon riding. She could sit astride and felt much more secure. Even so, she was glad Ro circled her waist again—more snugly, now the bulky veil was gone.

They took off, and she immediately felt a difference.

She'd never ridden anything astride before, and the undulations of the dragon's wings set up a rhythm between her thighs. Her mouth dried. Breathing normally became an effort, but she had to because his arm was around her and he might notice.

His arm. She wanted to stroke those fine, pale hairs.

Seesee flew on for longer than before. Had Ro decided to hurry to Dorn after all? Dorn, where they could complete this marriage. Oh yes, hurry, hurry to Dorn.

Her left hand rested now on the hard heat of his arm. Flexed there, reveling. His hand moved, fingers stroking just below her breast. Rozlinda tried to stay still. He might not know what he was doing, the sweet magic he was creating. If she moved, he might stop.

If he did know, did it mean they didn't have to wait until they reached Dorn? Oh, please . . .

The sun was sinking lower in the sky, bleaching blue but hinting at fiery red.

His thumb began to stroke the underside of her breast, protected now only by fine shift and light tunic. She leaned back into him, hoping he wouldn't notice. Wouldn't notice the flexing of her buttocks, either, or the depths of her breaths. His hand slid upward so his thumb could brush her astonishingly sensitive nipple.

Her breathing broke, her vision clouded and when she felt his lips at her neck, she stretched her head, welcoming him. It wasn't enough. She twisted to meet his lips.

Ah! Heady heat. Hunger.

The space was too tight for her to turn completely, but doing the husband-wife thing on a dragon no longer appalled her, not even when the dragon was probably *amused*.

Without a care for being high above the earth, she scrambled up and turned to sit facing Ro. She grabbed his head and kissed him hotly, deeply, thighs spread over his, swelling heat pressing into her throbbing ache, a strange vibration making her want to scream with pleasure.

She broke free to breathe, to grab his clothing. "Off. How?"

But he captured her hands. "No, no, we can't, we can't." He panted it like a man at the end of a desperate race, his eyes dark, sweat running. "Zlinda, we can't!"

Whether on command or on her own, Seesee plunged downward. Ro was thrown forward onto Rozlinda, so she claimed another kiss. She hardly noticed when Seesee landed, but then stillness surrounded them. Yet that vibration still ravished her, body and mind.

"What *is* that?" she whispered, head to head with Ro.

"Dragon." He said something in Dornaan, then shook his head, clearly struggling to make sense. "Dragon mating."

"That's what happens when they mate?"

Another head shake. "They don't. No sexes. Or both. That's what happens when we mate. When dragoners mate."

"Wow."

They were both sucking in deep, deep breaths, seemingly in synchrony. Perhaps she was running with sweat, too. She ached.

"Why can't we? Why?"

He took a deeper breath, let it out slowly and then helped her to stand. He took out his knife and cut off her shift at tunic hem.

"What?"

He ran off the dragon, carrying the bundle of her dress as well as the strip of shift. He tossed everything by the dragon's snout. "Are you insane?" he said.

Seesee merely blinked.

"Doesn't your survival matter to you? Doesn't Dorn's?"

Dorn survive without dragons.

"Tak durol."

Not true.

"Grashectalix!"

Happy.

"Fict!"

Rozlinda stumbled her way to Ro's side and grabbed his sleeve. "What's going on? Talk Saragondan!"

You and your Zlinda have babies. Dragons enjoy your babies. Happy. True.

Ro turned to Rozlinda, and she saw tears.

"What?" She brushed them away, but couldn't touch the anguish in his eyes. "Tell me."

He looked down at her hand, which he took in his. "This has all been a lie, Zlinda. I'm not taking you back to Dorn to be my wife. I'm taking you back to be the Sacrificial Virgin Princess in truth."

"You mean . . ."

"To feed your blood to Seesee so she can lay eggs. But I can't do it anymore." He turned back to the dragon. "Because she has been smearing you with dragon drool."

Rozlinda looked at the severed bottom of her shift—the part Seesee had deliberately sucked by the lake. "Why, Seesee?"

Like babies. Like Ro's babies. Like Zlinda's babies. Happy.

But it was all beginning to sink in, to become a block of ice in the heart. "So it was all to get the SVP back to Dorn for this sacrifice, and the passion was all drool. You really should send some of that in the tribute," she added bitterly. "It'd be a huge hit."

"Zlinda, don't." He reached, but halted himself before he touched. "Yes, that was the plan, but in hours it was dust in my hands. I admired your courage, your willingness to try to make something good out of your situation. Drool, queen drool, has sped everything to lightning speed, but my feelings are real."

"How can you tell?" she snapped, wrapping her arms around herself. "You'll still sacrifice me?"

"No."

"Not true."

"I can't do it."

"So what *are* you going to do?"

"Return you to your home."

"A discarded wife? No, thank you. You married me. You will take me with you."

"I can't do that!"

"Why not?"

"Because then someone else will kill you and I won't be able to stop it."

"But why? Seesee wouldn't eat my blood." She turned to the dragon. "Would you?"

Yes.

"Why?"

Have eggs.

Dazed, Rozlinda backed so she stood equidistant from both man and dragon head, even though confronting Seesee added nothing to understanding.

"You will explain everything to me. Everything."

Chapter 9

By the time Ro had finished, Rozlinda had been drawn back to his side, to hold his hand, to move into his arms. Entwined, they sat against Seesee's head, close to one big eye.

"So without my blood, there will be no eggs, and in time, no dragons." She knew the answer, but asked, "All my blood?"

Too much for life.

Was there sadness in the dragon's words, or was she adding that herself because she wanted the dragon to care? She settled into thought, but no amount of thought changed anything. She sighed. "I am the SVP. I will do my duty."

"No, you won't," Ro said.

"What is one life compared to a race? Two races, for you seem to think the Dornae will die out with the dragons."

"I was exaggerating. Our way of life will die out, but we'll adapt."

Dragoners go where dragons go.

Rozlinda swiveled to Seesee. "When the dragons die, the dragoners will die?"

"That's not true," Ro stated.

True.

It seemed to surprise him. "Why?"

Dragon things. You eat. You change. No more dragon things. You sicken. You die.

"That settles it, then," Rozlinda said.

"No it doesn't."

She looked at him. "Where does mother stone come from?"

"From Dorn. Why?"

"I know that. I mean exactly where. Is it from dragons?"

"Everything on Dorn is from dragons. Everything of importance."

"Then where does mother stone come from?"

He looked wary. "Dragon dung."

"Dung!"

"It's our fertilizer, but it also contains useful minerals. Because they eat rocks, we assume. Dragon-eye jewels and what you call mother stone, among other things."

"Hralla?" she asked. "Versuli?"

"Versuli's from drool. Hralla is a plant that only grows on the dragonlands."

Rozlinda surprised herself by laughing, hiding her face against her knees. "I'm imagining Aurora's face if she finds out mother stone comes from dung."

Laughter threatened to turn into tears, however, so she sobered and faced him. "It has to be, Ro. For the dragons, for your people, and for mine. Without mother stone, you see, every child of a woman of the Blood would die in the womb."

"Not in your lifetime. The stone won't run out for generations."

"How could I bear children, knowing daughters or granddaughters would face that? And dragons are special. They must not die out."

He covered his face with his hands.

She turned to the dragon. "There is no other way for you to have eggs, Seesee?"

Need princess blood. Lots. Rozlinda saw a young woman sprawled on Dragon's Rock, gushing blood in a way that had to be fatal. She knew Ro saw it, too. They sat there, a silent trio as the sun slid flaming behind hills, and evening softened colors with mist.

Desire stirred again, powerful enough to blank out even fear. Rozlinda reached to touch Ro, but then halted. No. But surely there was something they could do.

"Seesee, how much of a virgin do I have to be?"

No eggs.

"I don't have any eggs?" Rozlinda asked, bewildered.

No babies.

"I can't have had a baby? Well, then . . ."

Not start baby. Changes blood. But babies nice.

"You're not eating my babies." Rozlinda meant it as a dark joke, and she'd swear the dragon laughed.

Ro surged to his feet. "You're both monsters. She's bad enough, but *you!*"

"Which she, which you?" Rozlinda asked, looking up, surprised by how much she simply delighted in him.

"We're returning you to your castle."

Night coming.

"You can fly in the dark."

Need to eat.

The dragon heaved to her feet, waddled away and did her roaring leap into flight.

"How does she do that?"

"Internal gases. A giant fart."

Rozlinda burst into laughter.

Ro scowled. "She left to thwart me!"

"I can't imagine how you'll force her to take me back to the castle if she doesn't want to."

"We can walk."

"I'm a princess. It's beyond me."

"I'll carry you."

"Ro, I saw a vision of you, just before we realized a dragon had come."

"A vision?"

"You on the road. I don't think an SVP ever saw a vision before, so it means something. It means I'm different. I'd rather not be different in this way, but if I'm chosen to save the world, I must follow my Princess Way."

"Your Princess Way should have you back in your castle, doing whatever should come next."

"Marriage, but I'm married."

"There has to be a way out of that."

"If we both agree. I don't. If you take me back, I'll come after you. I'll walk."

"You're a princess. It's beyond you."

She rose and kissed him. "I'm a princess. Nothing is beyond me. I'll climb the Shield if I must. I will complete my journey."

He held her off with a bruising grip. "To death?"

"Everyone's journey is to death."

"I will die with you, then."

"That's not fair."

"It is *my* journey."

"Then love me. I don't want to end my journey without knowing love."

He tore free. "Don't! Don't you realize how much I want to take your virginity and make you safe?"

"But you heard Seesee. I only don't have to be *pregnant*."

"Same thing."

"Not if you'll give me some of the stones from your buckle."

He looked down at the tiny dragon eyes. "Why?"

"They prevent pregnancy."

"That's nonsense."

"Perhaps it only works on princesses of the blood, but it works. Three stones and I'm safe till my next flowers. Well?"

"It's nonsense."

"Trust me."

He looked from her to his buckle, then unfastened it. "You're sure?"

"Absolutely."

He pulled out his knife to prize stones free, nicking his hand because he was shaking. He stared at her as he sucked blood, and then he worked out more and poured them into her hand. Six of them.

"Better safe than sorry," she agreed, tossing them into her mouth and swallowing.

"How long till they work?"

"Almost immediately." She rubbed her hands, which longed to touch him, then held herself because she burned to be held. "Poor Aurora."

"Aurora, murderer of dragons?"

"I know, but we complained because she kept having babies when the mother stone was running out. But no dragon eyes came after her sacrifice. She had none to share with others, so she could hardly ask others to share with her. She has to have some sense of guilt."

"You have a forgiving nature."

"I must. You must. Everyone must." She looked at him soberly. "Your people are going to have to forgive mine for Cheelus. Mine must forgive yours for me. It will be hard. In fact, I need to write about this, about my willingness. Make sure I have time for that. Before."

He grasped her tense hands. "You are a remarkable woman, Rozlinda of Saragond."

She found a smile. "Seven years' training must be good for something. Love me, Ro."

"We're safe?"

"Yes. I promise."

He drew her into his arms and held her. It was tender for a moment, but another rhythm thrummed beneath, transmuting tenderness to hunger. And now the dragon was returning, beating wings, beating heart, beating need as great as theirs.

They kissed as Seesee circled and landed, her excitement wiping away any hope of control. They tore off clothes till skin slid against skin. Then they were on the dragon, beneath the wing, spiced with dragon smell, one with Seesee in mind and, it felt, in flesh as Ro thrust deep into Rozlinda again and again, and three minds spiraled in flight, then plunged deep into ferocious fire.

Gasping, running with sweat, Rozlinda heard a purred, *Good loving.*

"A dragon," she said, laughing, "is a queen of understatement." She inhaled perfume of man, woman and dragon, loving the hot weight of Ro still sprawled over her and the dragon heartbeat deep below. "Do all the Dornae do it this way?"

"Only dragoners." He moved off her, gathering her into his strong arms. "The dragons do the mind thing a bit with others if they're nearby, but this is special."

"Very. Very, very."

Sadness threatened, that this would all end tomorrow. She pushed it away and explored every inch of this wonderful man. She played with his long, lovely hair, with his wire-bound plaits and gold-bound arms. She straddled his dark, muscle-hard torso. So hot, hot, hot. She kissed, tongued and tasted while he did the same, the dragon *yum, yum, yumming* along with them.

Dragon madness plunged them together again, pounded them together again to explode into a million, brilliant stars.

"More," Rozlinda said when she had breath. "More!"

"For pity's sake."

She slid her hand over him and found him limp. "Poor dear. You need food. Seesee, did you bring food?"

Somewhere. The dragon sounded exhausted, too, but happily so.

Rozlinda giggled. She rose naked, stretching out to embrace the starry night, and then ran lightly down to earth. It was too dark to see bags or food.

"Can you breathe fire, Seesee?"

Only heat, and not even that right now.

Rozlinda giggled again as she groped around for Ro's pack. She dug into it, looking for his flame maker. He joined her and found it. Flame sprang up and they looked at each other, naked in its golden light. And smiled. And kissed.

He shut it off. "It won't last forever."

"We need a fire, then."

"Not much wood nearby as I remember. And no water."

"Improvident man."

"Are you willing to try a new dragoner experience?"

"Anything!"

She saw his smile as he lit the flame and used it to find the lump of meat Seesee had brought—and dropped. He wiped it on his tunic. Rozlinda remembered once being bothered by things like that.

She was chilly, however, so she climbed back onto Seesee and snuggled beneath the wing, waiting for whatever wonderful new experience her Dornaan husband would bring.

She would not be sad. How many people had a night like this? She was on a dragon, bathed in starlight, soon to make stupendous love again to the most wonderful man in the world. If this was all she ever had, it would be riches beyond dreams.

Eventually, he joined her with something on plates. Mushy lumps on plates.

She sat up. "Do I want to know?"

"Try it."

"I don't want to know, do I?"

He scooped some mush on his finger and held it out to her. "It's a prized delicacy."

She sniffed and caught the sweet spice of drool, but smelled blood underneath. "I knew I didn't want to know."

When he put it to her mouth, however, she sucked in a bit. And groaned. "Oh, my stars . . ."

He ate some himself, a noise deep in his throat. "Good, isn't it?"

Rozlinda grabbed her plate and scooped up more. The sweet, spicy taste burst intensely on her tongue. "I don't know why you'd ever eat anything else," she mumbled as she chewed and swallowed.

"Not healthy," he mumbled back, "only eating meat, even dragon chew."

That image made her hesitate for a moment, but it couldn't keep her from shoving more into her mouth, more and more, until it was gone.

Ro scooped up the last of his. "Remember that we only have small animals. Meat is a luxury. We eat chew only on very special occasions."

Rozlinda licked her plate to gather any remaining bits. "Then it's exactly right for now." She put aside the clean plate and licked her fingers as meticulously as a cat.

He captured her hand and began to clean it with his tongue.

"Not fair!" So she did the same to him.

They licked further and then shared a spicy kiss, rolling together into soaring, drool-fired, dragon-sung sex. Exhaustion overwhelmed them eventually, however, and they woke to the gray light and dewy damp of dawn. And to reality. They lay in each other's arms in silence. Seesee was silent, too. Rozlinda couldn't stop thinking, trying to find an escape.

"Isn't it a stupid system, to have only one fertile queen in a generation?"

"Yes, but it was their sacrifice long, long ago."

"Explain."

He stroked her hair, her shoulder. "Remember the animals, the food which led to too many dragons? It was a disaster for them as well as for people. They were eating too much dragon rock, and without that they can't make eggs. So they changed so they could have egg season only once every eight years, and the Dornae stopped keeping large animals. That worked for a long time, but the time came when they'd eaten the dragon rock down to the crater we now call the Dragon's Womb. That was when they began to fly over the Shield to seek the rock, which they found. But they also found unlimited blood, and the problem started all over again."

"Hence the Dragon Wars?" she guessed.

"Not immediately. The Dornae bribed the Saragondans with dragon eyes and hralla and sent a dragoner with each queen to control her appetite. Then Dorn ran out of the special blood, too."

"That's what happens when you eat all the carriers before they can have babies."

"Exactly. But the dragons sensed a new source—the royal family of Saragond."

"Why should that be? Your people and mine are completely different."

He pulled a face. "Actually, we're not. We're both descended from the rival twin princes, Lorien and Ulien."

"Because Lorien fled over the Shield. Our records say he and his followers perished."

"Whereas ours tell that he survived, and after some trials, prospered."

"How strange. But you are so different."

"Only the dragoners, and that's something to do with living with the dragons."

"Will I . . ." But she stopped her question. She wouldn't develop the same coloring, because she would soon die.

"So the dragons found the rock and the Virgin blood, and the Dornae controlled the feeding . . . . But we still have the Dragon Wars. The cause was supposed to be the way the dragons consumed good farm animals."

"It was. Despite all efforts, the dragon numbers were growing. And then there were the princesses. Your people weren't happy about that, either. So they decided to put a stop to it."

Terrible time. People not happy. Dragons not happy.

"It soon came to truce. To make sure there would never be war again, the dragons agreed that only one dragon in a generation would queen, so that few animals would be eaten and only a little princess blood would be required."

"One dragon flies to Saragond to eat," Rozlinda said, "then lays many eggs? How does she care for them all?"

A sense of humorous alarm came from Seesee.

"She doesn't. Her sisters each take one. Dragons complete the eggs in a pouch. This time . . . if we do this, Cheelus's sisters will raise the eggs."

They will be very happy.

"Because they never had eggs to raise," Rozlinda said, realizing. "Couldn't one of them have become queen instead of Seesee?"

"Apparently, to queen out of egg year, a dragon has

to have queened before, and Seesee is the youngest. Unfortunately, to do it, she needs a lot of Virgin blood."

The picture of the bleeding princess on the rock returned to Rozlinda's mind, and it wasn't Seesee's doing. "So be it, but"—she buried her face in Ro's chest—"with plenty of hralla, please."

Head close to hers, he said, "With all the hralla you want, brave beloved one."

"Am I? Beloved? Don't lie to me."

"Beautifully brave, endlessly beloved. I will join you in the next life. Believe that."

She moved back to look into his amber eyes. "I don't want that. Please live and enjoy dragon babies."

But she couldn't help thinking of their babies, which would never be born. Dark-skinned, pale-haired, beautiful babies.

She suddenly saw a vision that must be from Seesee. A plump, round egg being tucked into a pouch between the dragon's front legs. She understood then that the host dragon fertilized it in some way. Then she saw the hatchling, all goopy head and tail. Rozlinda tried not to think that it was an ugly little thing, but she knew Seesee would catch it. The hatchling turned green and gold, looking out huge-eyed from the pouch.

See?

Yes. You have lovely babies. It really will work? My blood?

The same vision as before. The bleeding princess on the rock, but now the dragon crunched into the blood-soaked rock.

So you still have a dragon rock in Dorn? Rozlinda said.

Ate all, long ago.

Rozlinda sat up. "Ro, where's the rock for the sacrifice?"

"It's called the Dragon's Womb. Don't talk about it."

He reached for her, but she grabbed his hand. "We have to. If I'm going to do this, it has to work."

"Seesee says it will."

"Didn't you hear her? She needs the green rock, and you said they ate that from the womb long ago."

He sat up, too. "She can talk to only one mind if she wants. You need more dragon rock, Seesee? More than you ate?"

For eggs, yes.

Exasperation rose from him like steam. "You could have mentioned it before."

Did. Made you unhappy.

He gripped his head. "The picture of the princess! Always on the rock. Always. We'll have to go back for more." He lowered his hands. "That's not all bad news."

More days and nights.

Better to go on to Dorn and make babies. Happy.

"No, Seesee," Rozlinda said. "That wouldn't make us happy at all."

Not true.

"It is true. People can be sad and happy at the same time. I'm sad to die, but I would be sadder to live and see the dragons die, see my family die. So in a way, dying makes me happy."

She wasn't sure it made sense to her, but the dragon didn't argue.

Need less blood for one egg.

"What?" Ro and Rozlinda said it together.

Dragoners want many eggs. Everything as it should be. But only one egg needed. In eight years, one queen. With rock and a little blood, make many eggs. Any dragon can raise the eggs. All as it should be again.

Rozlinda sensed the effort it was for Seesee to put together so much in people thought, and she thanked her. She looked at Ro and could see he was as afraid to hope as she was.

"Are you sure that will work, Seesee?" he asked.

No.

He dug his hands into his hair again.

Rozlinda tried. "Seesee, what exactly do we have to do to make sure that the dragons survive? No," she amended, trying to avoid ambiguity. "So they reproduce forever and ever."

"Dragons don't think like that," he said.

"We have to try. Seesee, it would make us very happy to have this clear."

She could feel the effort in the dragon's mind.

Need princess blood. Need rock. Make egg.

"We know that. But you said you couldn't be sure only one egg would work."

Never can be sure of what comes next.

"It's truth!" Rozlinda exclaimed. "She insists on absolute truth. There *is* no certainty of anything in life. So you could lay one egg without taking all my blood?"

Probably.

"Would that one egg survive?"

Probably.

"How much blood for two eggs, then, or three? We should be as safe as possible. How many eggs can you create without killing me?"

"Zlinda!" Ro protested.

Don't know.

Rozlinda ignored Ro. "Will you know when you are taking too much, when you are killing me?"

Probably.

She blew out a breath. "Right. We'll do that. It would be madness to risk all on one egg. I'll give you as much blood as you need to create at least three eggs—"

"Zlinda—"

"I *have* to do this," she told him. "It's my duty. My fate. I hope to live, but life would be meaningless if I failed. Seesee, you will take all the blood you need for at least three eggs. Promise me." She didn't know if she could command a dragon, but she tried.

Yes, noble princess.

It was an accolade, and Rozlinda savored it, along with hope. "Now we must return to Dragon's Rock—"

More nearer.

Carefully, Ro said, "There's dragon rock near here?"

Yes.

"Something else you could have mentioned."

No use. Need fresh blood on rock. Other rock close to princess.

He shook his head. "So if we get rock from there, go on to the womb, and give you some of Zlinda's blood on the rocks, you might be able to lay some eggs without killing her?"

"Why not just do the sacrifice there?" Rozlinda asked.

He pulled a face. "The Dornae are angry, Zlinda. They have burned for a war of revenge. They have been promised that their representatives will witness the sacrifice of the princess, and it needs to be so."

My dragon sisters need to see it, too. But they will be happy with one egg.

"Three eggs," Rozlinda said.

Much blood. You not happy. Ro not happy.

"I'll drink lots of hralla. I'll be happy. I promise. And Ro will, too, won't you?"

He glared at her, but said, "If it's the only way."

Good.

Rozlinda could wish the dragon didn't suddenly sound quite so carefree.

"You will take us to this rock?" Ro said, sounding as if he felt the same way.

Yummy rock. Go now?

His eyes met Rozlinda's, and they were both thinking the same thing. Dragon sense. But there was hope, so they quickly dressed and were on their way as the rising sun touched the nearby snows of the Shield with gold.

Chapter 10

They flew up to the rocky foothills, and there, sure enough, lay a greenish strip in a barren slope. Seesee landed and chomped.

Rozlinda laughed. "I think dragons like this rock for reasons other than eggs."

Seesee's response was definitely a *yum*. Then: *Rock precious. Only eat in egg year.*

"Remember, we're here to take some back," Ro said.

With a sigh, the dragon stopped eating and began to bite off small lumps and spit them out.

They needed bags, so Rozlinda unbundled the SVP clothing and they rolled rocks in the veil and pieces of skirt. When Seesee thought they had enough, she flew off to eat. When she returned, they loaded the rock and headed for the Shield.

The dragon soared high this time, far above land and into bitterly cold air, so Rozlinda shivered despite Seesee's heat and Ro's hot, encircling body. The sun was setting again as they swooped down, apparently gliding on the wind, into the land of Dorn.

Rozlinda heard a happy *Home, home, home!*

Though Rozlinda's heart hammered at the thought of what was to come, she marveled at the place laid out before her. The peninsula was mostly a rugged, russet, highland plateau, set with a turquoise lake like a long ring on a finger. All around the peninsula, sea crashed white on dark, forbidding rocks, but between the coast and the highland lay forests and fields like a lush, green skirt. The Dragons' Gift.

She seemed to understand things now as if sharing Seesee's mind. The dragon's dung, neatly shed off the highland, washed down to create the fertile land below. That explained the name, especially as the gift included dragon eyes, mother stone, and other useful minerals.

Then dragons rose up to welcome them, seeming small as birds down near the lake, but becoming huge as they swooped and circled nearby. Greetings and joy swamped Rozlinda's mind like hralla, for it was equally directed toward all three of them.

The croon of welcoming love she felt was only for her blood, alas, but she was here to give it. Then she hoped they wouldn't all insist on a share.

Silly. Only one dragon at a time.

Seesee with her honor guard of dragons circled the lake, which was edged by groups of houses surrounded by gardens. Pale-haired people spilled out, waving and ... singing. Yes, a harmonic chorus rose to greet them as they flew on toward a huge, dark crater beyond the head of the lake.

The womb, and some of the people running toward it, were ordinary-looking.

Ro had warned her. The representatives of all the people of Dorn had gathered for this—to see the princess die so the dragons would live. Some of their eagerness would be for vengeance. Would they let her live?

Seesee said, *You are safe from them,* and other dragons took up the promise.

Not safe from Seesee, but she'd accepted that.

Not happy.

Seesee sounded fretful, so Rozlinda tried to smother her fear.

"We should have started the hralla already," Ro said, and she knew he wasn't thinking happy thoughts, either. "It'll be there as soon as we land."

Despite every scrap of willpower, Rozlinda was shaking when Seesee settled in the dragon's womb, and cold despite Ro's arms tight around her.

He helped her to stand, then swept her into his arms to carry her down. To the watchers it might look like the act of a captor, but Rozlinda knew it was an act of love. She longed to be strong for him, but terror was sucking all the strength from her limbs. There were seats carved into the rock all around and people were filling them, lusting to see her die.

She didn't want to die!

A woman approached, a jug and goblet in her hands. A sorrowful woman.

"Thank you, Mother," Ro said, settling Rozlinda on the ground. He took the cup and put it into Rozlinda's trembling hands. She drank deeply—my, it was strong! Immediately, her shivering stopped.

So this plump woman with pale hair in a tidy bun was Ro's mother. "Hello," Rozlinda said, smiling, but hardly able to believe that women really did show their legs without a care.

The woman smiled back, but with tragic eyes.

"Don't worry. Everything's going to be all right," Rozlinda assured her, astonished by the brilliant colors of this world and the glory of dragons perching all around the rim of the womb like the spikes of her crown.

"It might be," she heard Ro say.

She offered him the goblet. "Have some."

He drained it, and from dragon minds came, Good. Happy.

She also sensed a croon over her lovely, egg-creating blood.

She smiled into Ro's still-troubled eyes. His mother had refilled the cup, so Rozlinda offered it again. "Have some more."

"I have to make sense. I love you," he said, then climbed back onto Seesee and addressed the people. Wonderful, beautiful Ro.

Without understanding the words, Rozlinda knew

he'd said something like, "I have returned with the princess."

A great roar went up—an ugly roar, abruptly stopped.

"That's better," Rozlinda said, drinking more of the limitless hralla. "Nasty people."

She felt a hand on her hair. Ro's mother's hand, warm and lovely. "The dragons corrected them. Now Ro's reminding everyone that dragons insist on happiness. That hatred and happiness can't exist together."

"They certainly can't." Rozlinda peered into the cup. Empty. Ro's mother filled it.

"Yummy hralla. Do you like hralla, Seesee?"

Like princess hralla.

Or was it *hralla princess?* Rozlinda giggled. "Hralla. Dragon gift. Dragon delights. Dragon sex is very good," she informed Ro's mother, and noticed alarm. "Don't worry. Dragon eyes, you know. Lovely dragon eyes. Lovely dragons with dragon eyes"—she giggled again—"and they all love me. I love them, too. Seesee, do they know I love them?"

You are loved, Rozlinda of Saragond, crooned the dragons. *You are a perfect princess.*

"Oh, good. I trained very hard, you know. Would be a shame to waste seven long years. I'm truly very, very happy to do this. I can't imagine anything I'd rather do. Anything at all."

Happy! It was a crescendo of dragons.

"Let's do it, then. Why are we waiting?"

Seesee coiled her neck and bit the bags off her back so they tumbled to the rocky ground. Her razor claws ripped the bundles open.

"Poor dress," Rozlinda said, not at all unhappily. It was about to happen. At last.

Seesee licked at the rock.

"Greedy, greedy," Rozlinda said, chuckling. "Ro's still talking."

Unhappy to release your blood. I do it?

It took a moment for Rozlinda's hralla-crazed mind to sort that out. "Can you?"

If it would make you happy.

"Oh yes." Rozlinda arranged herself on the rocks and smiled. "I can feel my beautiful blood wanting you, Seesee."

Yes.

She watched a claw etch down her thigh, slitting yellow cloth and skin beneath. Glistening red blood gushed. "Beautiful."

Beautiful.

Rozlinda quickly shifted so it would pulse directly onto the green rock. "Don't want to waste any. Oh, I forgot to write that explanation." It didn't seem to matter as it should, but she said, "You'd better try not to kill me."

Seesee chomped the blood-soaked rock. *Rouar unhappy if I kill you.*

"You're not to think like that. Eggs. There must be eggs."

Eggs. Seesee licked blood directly from the wound. Rozlinda giggled because it tickled.

"Zlinda!" She heard Ro's cry from a distance and tried to wave to him.

"It's all right. Absolutely perfect. I love you!"

Slit. The other thigh.

"Matching pair now." Rozlinda rolled on the rocks, loving the scent of her own blood on the spicy rock. "Why not do the back somewhere?"

It felt like the lightest stroking, but she knew her blood followed it, as it should. Dragon elixir. Virgin Princess blood. Seesee and all the dragons humming as she and Ro had hummed at lovely dragon chew, at lovely dragon sex.

She rolled again and saw green-dusted scarlet on her hands. Licked it. Delicious. Dragons sang in her mind. *Lovely princess. Perfect princess.*

She spread her arms. "Take more, more!"

Ro was still standing on top of Seesee, simply staring, death white.

"You should have had more hralla." She laughed at him as the dragon's tongue swept over her like a lover's touch.

Dragons. They were wonderful, wonderful creatures, and she was so happy to do this so they would never die out. "Make lots and lots and lots of eggs."

Thank you, they all sang in her mind as darkness fell sweetly upon her.

Her sense of smell awoke first. Strange aromas, but nicely dragonish. Then hearing. Distant noises of everyday things. Then sight, when Rozlinda raised her heavy lids.

Ro was looking down at her, and she smiled into his concerned eyes. She was inside somewhere. Cloth-hung walls. Deep reds and golds, like dragon eyes. Hralla still misted her mind, but she became aware of weakness and soreness. "I think I'm alive."

He stroked her face, his eyes loving. "I think so, too."

"It worked?"

"Probably, as a dragon would say." He lay beside her on the bed, resting his head against hers. "I died a thousand deaths."

She inhaled his delicious scent. "How perfect this is."

He laughed into her hair. "You're a mad woman, hralla or no hralla." He leaned up to study her. "How much do you hurt? Do you want more?"

She shifted her body, feeling only pulling stings. "Not too badly. Seesee will lay eggs?"

"The dragons say so. Not many, but more than one."

"Good." She snuggled, aware of lassitude, which probably meant considerable lack of blood. "Where am I?"

"In our home, of course."

"Our home." She moved to sit up to look around, but almost blacked out.

He gently settled her back. "You lost a lot of blood, and your wounds will take time to heal, even with drool."

"Drool?" she asked, but she smiled.

He smiled back. "Don't even think about it."

"I'm thinking about it. Doesn't a weakened SVP deserve some chew?"

He laughed and kissed her, deep and long. "All the chew she wants, beloved. And anything else Dorn can provide. You are our treasure, our precious gift. You will be a great lady in Dorn all your life."

She shook her head against his shoulder. "All I want is to be your wife and a bringer of peace. And mother of many pale-haired, dark-skinned dragoner babies, of course."

From nearby, softly, contentedly, came Seesee's voice. Lots of babies. Dragon babies. Rouar and Zlinda babies. Everybody happy, happy, happy.

The Dragon
and the
Dark Knight

❧

BY

MARY JO PUTNEY

Chapter 1

ENGLAND
IN THE DAYS OF KNIGHTS, LADIES AND DRAGONS

As a lad, Sir Kenrick of Rathbourne had thought that the life of a freelance knight would be a grand and glorious adventure. It wasn't.

The last tournament of the English season had just ended in a sea of mud from the relentless rain. Even Kenrick's tent was leaking as he sat wearily on a wooden stool so his squire, Giles, could take off his greaves. Every inch of his body ached, but at least he'd broken no bones.

He calculated his finances, wondering if the silver belt he'd won in the tournament would sell for enough to pay passage south for himself and his squire. "Should we cross to France and try our fortunes, Giles? It would be warmer there."

The blond youth looked doubtful. "Sunshine would be good, sire." He peeled off Kenrick's drenched and dripping surcoat. "But at this season, we might have to spend weeks in a Channel port, waiting for the weather to improve enough to sail across to France. By the time we reached a warm place, winter would be over."

Kenrick frowned, thinking of the weather and the difficulty of shipping horses across the Channel. "Very likely you're right. Wintering in England is more sensible." He raised his arms so his squire could lift the hauberk off over his head. "A pity the country is so peaceful. If there were a few little wars being fought, it would be easy to find a place for the winter."

"Especially for a knight so skilled as you, Sir Kenrick," Giles said loyally as he pulled off the hauberk with a ringing of metal links. The mail garment was splashed with mud up to the shoulders, and would require hours of cleaning.

Kenrick considered what castles might allow him and his squire to winter over. If the country was at war, he and his sword would be welcome anywhere, but in times of peace, a freelance knight, squire and horses were merely more mouths to feed during the hungry months. "I suppose we must go to Alveley. Since there's always a risk of Welsh raiders, the Lord of Alveley should be willing to have us."

Giles looked depressed. Alveley Castle was surely the most crowded and uncomfortable fortress in England. They'd spent the previous winter there, and had left eagerly at the first scent of spring.

As Kenrick stripped off the padded garment that protected his body from the hard links of the hauberk, he wondered what he could have done differently. Granted, as a bastard he had been fortunate to receive knightly training at all. That had come as a result of his boyhood strength and fighting ability. He had won his first tourney wearing borrowed armor.

Since then, he had become known as the Dark Knight, respected for his skills even though many sneered at the bar sinister that slashed across his scarlet shield and proclaimed his illegitimacy. Still, other bastards had established themselves comfortably. He had expected that by now he would have earned land and a wife.

Instead, though he did well enough in tourneys to support himself and his squire, he lived a hand-to-mouth existence with no place to call home. Once, a wealthy lord who admired his fighting skill had hinted that he would consider Kenrick a suitable match for his daughter. The fiefdom of a fine manor would have come with her. But the subject had been dropped, never to be raised again. Giles heard a rumor through the squires' grapevine that the lord's daughter had found Kenrick too dark, too frightening. Given the scar that slashed down his left cheek, he couldn't blame her for her reaction.

Whatever the reasons, he had never managed to impress a lord enough to be granted a fief of his own, and without land he couldn't take a wife. One night, deep in his cups, a baron had said that the trouble with Kenrick was that he was so by-the-saints independent. The term *stubborn* had been used also. The words had not been meant as a compliment.

After Kenrick dried himself with rough towels, he dressed for the feast that would be held to celebrate the end of the tournament. He hoped the great hall would be dark enough that the shabby condition of his best garments wouldn't be obvious.

Giles poured him a goblet of wine. "I was talking with some of the other squires," he said hesitantly. " 'Tis said that a mighty baron is looking for a champion who will be richly rewarded if he can successfully perform a dangerous task."

Even though this was surely no more than squire gossip, Kenrick couldn't help but be curious. "What kind of reward?"

"The fiefdom of a handsome manor by the sea." Giles poured a second goblet for himself. "In Cornwall."

"And what is the dangerous task?"

The squire said hesitantly, "To . . . to slay a dragon."

Kenrick almost choked on his wine. "Blessed Mother, that's a troubadour's tale! Do you know anyone who has actually seen a dragon? No, it's always a friend of the cousin of the baker's wife, who lives a hundred leagues away. There are no dragons."

"One of the squires I was talking with last night said he'd seen one," Giles retorted. "And . . . and I thought I saw one once when I was on the coast of Wales. I'm not sure since it was so far away. But it didn't fly like any bird I've ever seen."

"So you believe in dragons." Kenrick took a more cautious mouthful of wine. He hadn't known the boy was so credulous.

"I'm not sure," Giles said carefully. "But they might exist—there are so many stories over so many years. If the danger in Cornwall isn't a dragon, perhaps it is some other peril that you may conquer to win the fiefdom."

"Perhaps, if your tale is true. But if we were to investigate, we would need a name and location. Such tales are usually remarkably free of details. Who is the baron? Where is the estate?" Kenrick shook his head and finished his wine.

"Lord William of Penruth," Giles said promptly. "His castle is on the south coast of Cornwall."

Kenrick frowned and rested the goblet on his knees. "I've heard of Penruth. He's a rich and powerful man. Why would he need to lure a champion by such means? He must have a goodly number of knights and men-at-arms."

" 'Tis said that several of his own men died in the quest, and the rest refuse to try."

"They sound a poor lot," Kenrick said, but the detail made the story seem more believable. "So Penruth thinks a tournament champion would be better able to defeat the menace, whatever it is."

"Or he thinks it's easier to let freelance knights get killed," Giles said dryly.

"So cynical for one so young," Kenrick murmured. "Did your gossiping squires know if any tournament knights intend to accept the challenge?"

Giles frowned. " 'Tis said that several already have. None survived."

The squire listed several names. Two were men Kenrick had fought against in earlier tourneys. He hadn't seen either in a while, now that he thought about it. "If this is true, there may be real danger on the Cornish coast. Pirates or bandits, if not dragons."

He finished his wine in a gulp and held the goblet out for more. For the chance of a fiefdom, he would risk much. "Shall we venture forth to test our luck? At the least, it might be warmer that far south."

Giles' face glowed with excitement. "Yes, sire!"

As they swallowed the rest of their wine, Kenrick hoped they wouldn't regret this improbable quest.

Chapter 2

Kenrick pulled his horse to a halt as they reached the crest of a steep hill that overlooked Penruth Castle. The sprawling fortress stood on a hill surrounded by flat, grassy moorland. A river flowed across the moor and fed a moat that added to the castle's defenses. The cloudy sky and wisps of wintry mist that trailed around the stone walls gave the scene a strange, unearthly beauty.

"Cornwall is an uncanny land," Giles said as he halted beside Kenrick.

"Aye, but it is indeed warmer than the Midlands," Kenrick pointed out practically. "Now it's time to find out how true the squires' tale is."

"What if it is just a tale?" Giles said with a furrowed brow.

Kenrick shrugged and set his horse down the hill. "I've seen a part of Britain I hadn't seen before, so the trip is not useless even if there is no dragon and no reward."

In fact, he quite liked Cornwall, uncanny though it was. The land was far from Britain's best, with rocky hills and desolate moors, but there were also fertile valleys and coastal fishing villages, and the breeze had a balminess that pleased him. The thought of winning a fief here would be unbearably exciting if he allowed himself to dwell on it.

He concentrated on the steep path downward. He'd know soon enough.

* * *

"Sir Kenrick of Rathbourne," the man-at-arms announced to the lord of Penruth. "He craves an audience with you, my lord."

Kenrick and Giles had been admitted without problems, his knightly equipment a guarantee of his rank. Giles was left with the horses while the man-at-arms guided Kenrick to the baron's mews. As they walked across that bailey, Kenrick schooled his face to fierceness. More often he tried to look less alarming, but today he needed to look worthy of taking on a dragon.

When they entered the mews, and Kenrick was announced, William of Penruth turned to greet the visitor. He was a large, brawny man of middle years, his dark hair barely touched with silver. A magnificent falcon perched on his leather-clad arm.

He drawled, "You are here to slay the dragon, I presume?"

"Yes, and to win the fiefdom you have offered." Concealing his surprise, Kenrick held the older man's gaze steadily. This sober lord believed there really was a dragon? Perhaps this journey to Cornwall wasn't the frivolous quest he'd expected. "I would see the land first, to decide if it is worth the risk."

A gleam of interest showed in Penruth's eyes. "You're more practical than your predecessors. You may see the property if I decide your experience is sufficient. I will not allow you to challenge the dragon unless there is some hope you will succeed. The more knights who are lost, the harder it is to find new knights willing to try."

The implication that Kenrick was incompetent rankled, but he understood the baron's point. "I have made my living by my sword ever since I was knighted. Two years ago, I was champion in the individual competition at the great tourney of St. Aliquis." He pulled his sword partially from its sheath, revealing the superb workmanship and glittering blade. "I won this sword."

"Then you are a champion indeed, Sir Kenrick." The

baron fed a tidbit of raw meat to the falcon. Its curving beak slashed into the bloody flesh.

Actually, what Kenrick had been on that occasion was by-the-Virgin lucky. St. Aliquis had been swamped with rain. Knights and horses slipped around in the mud like drunken stoats. Kenrick's destrier, Thunder, was no beauty, but he was a stalwart steed in the mud. He had carried the day for Kenrick. Not that one should publicly give credit to a horse. He said tersely, "If you have further concerns about my skills, I shall be happy to engage with you or any of your knights so that you might judge for yourself."

"No need. You have convinced me of your prowess. Pray avail yourself of Penruth's hospitality. Tomorrow one of my men will take you to see the fief of Tregarth, which is on the way to Dragon Island, the beast's lair. There are a good manor and some decent fields, as well as a fishing village." The baron handed the falcon to his falconer. "Slay the dragon and Tregarth is yours, but the dragon's treasure is mine."

"There's a treasure?"

"So 'tis said. I've not seen it myself." Penruth fed another tidbit to his falcon. "But if a treasure exists, it is on my land and belongs to me."

"Of course." Kenrick was less interested in treasure than land. "A dragon, a treasure. The only thing missing is a maiden to be saved."

Penruth's brows arched. "Hadn't you heard? A maiden has been seen at Dragon Island, if the beast hasn't eaten her. Some poor mad village girl, I believe."

"Even village girls deserve to be saved from peril," Kenrick said, his voice edged. His boyhood rank hadn't been much above that of common villagers, and such folk had been his friends.

"By all means, save the maiden if you can," Penruth drawled. "But that will not win you Tregarth. Only slaying the dragon will do that."

"Have you seen the dragon with your own eyes, my lord?"

"I have. Do not underestimate the beast, Rathbourne, or your bones will join the others scattered on Dragon Island." The baron turned away, more interested in falcons than knights.

Kenrick left the mews. So there really was a dragon. This would be . . . interesting.

The next morning, a young knight named Sir Jesmond was assigned as their guide to Tregarth and Dragon Island. A couple of hours of riding brought them to the manor of Tregarth. The fief was Kenrick's dream. A spacious, well-fortified stone house was set among fertile fields and solid outbuildings. A hill curved partway around the house to shield it from the winds, and there was a view over the sea that caught Kenrick's imagination. He would risk much to win this place.

Sir Jesmond summoned the bailiff, Master Arnulph, who was not too busy at this season, and the man offered a tour of the property. The more Kenrick saw of Tregarth, the more he wanted it. As they looked out from a headland at the crashing surf far below, Kenrick asked the bailiff, "Have you seen the dragon?"

The bailiff hesitated. "Aye, I've see him flying. He gives me no trouble."

"He doesn't steal your livestock?" Kenrick asked, surprised.

"He has never harmed the manor or the village," Arnulph said firmly.

The bailiff didn't seem happy about Kenrick's mission. Did he not want Kenrick as a master, or was there another reason for his demeanor? "I'd heard that the dragon has destroyed villages and crops in this area," Kenrick remarked. "In fact, we rode through a burned village this morning."

"There's been no trouble here," Arnulph said again, his expression flat.

Wondering what the bailiff wasn't saying, Kenrick mounted his horse and they continued along the coast to the dragon's lair. The land grew ever more rocky and desolate. Finally, they crested a rugged hill and looked down on a bay that contained a massive stone outcropping that thrust high out of the sea. Though called an island, it was connected to the mainland by a natural causeway that would flood at high tide. The position was very strong for a castle, or for a dragon.

Sir Jesmond halted. "There's the cursed place." He glanced at the sky uneasily. "Dragon Island is larger than it looks, full of caves and little meadows. A perfect place for a monster's lair."

"Which is why the dragon has defeated all challengers." Kenrick studied the site with narrowed eyes. "How many knights have taken up your lord's challenge?"

"You will be the thirteenth," Sir Jesmond said flatly. "None have returned."

Kenrick felt a chill on the back of his neck. Telling himself not to be superstitious, he said, "Thirteenth and last, because I shall succeed." He collected his reins and started down the rough trail toward Dragon Island.

"You're going to try your chances today?" Sir Jesmond said with alarm.

"I only wish to scout the area so I will be prepared when I return in earnest."

Again the other knight glanced fearfully at the sky, as if he expected the dragon to appear at any moment. He gasped, his clenched hands startling his horse, when a winged creature appeared in the distance.

"It's an osprey," Giles said as he peered at the silhouette. "Not a dragon."

"Of course it's an osprey," Sir Jesmond said testily, as if he hadn't revealed himself in that moment of fear. "I shall leave you to your scouting. It's easy enough to return to Penruth. Just follow the coastline east."

"We'll have no trouble," Kenrick said, letting a touch of contempt show in his voice. The braver of Penruth's knights had already tried and failed, leaving only the cowards. "Come along, Giles."

The squire, to his credit, looked more excited than worried as they picked their way down the steep hill.

The path flattened onto a bluff that loomed over a rocky beach. By dismounting and peering over, Kenrick saw that the causeway to the island ran from the lower end of the beach. A narrow footpath zigzagged down the face of the bluff. "Giles, stay here with the horses. The tide is low, so I might try to cross the causeway to see what's on the other side."

Giles frowned. "Shouldn't you wear full armor when you do that, sire?"

Kenrick shook his head. "This is just a scouting expedition—I'm not out to stir trouble. Besides, full armor might be a bad idea against a dragon, since it limits agility. And carries heat."

Giles blanched at the thought of iron armor burned by dragon fire. "Perhaps you shouldn't wear the hauberk, either."

Kenrick shrugged. "Dragons have teeth and claws as well as flame. There are no rules for fighting dragons. I am just guessing what might serve me best." He slung his shield and sword over his back so his hands would be free. "But this is only a scouting expedition so that I can learn the ground."

"I shall wait here on the bluff."

"Pull farther back to the shelter of that old stone hut," Kenrick ordered. "This headland is too bare. You would be an easy target for a flying beast. If the worst happens, there's no point in both of us being baked for a dragon's breakfast."

Giles looked even more concerned. Likely he hadn't thought about the techniques of dragon fighting. Kenrick had thought of little else on the long ride south.

He tossed his reins to his squire. "I'll be back before the sun sets. If I don't return by then, ride back to Penruth and inform the baron that he must find a fourteenth knight. I name you heir to my horses and armor."

"Sire!" Giles exclaimed, horrified.

Kenrick chuckled. "Don't worry, lad, I don't intend to do anything to get myself killed. But it's good to make my wishes clear, just in case."

He turned and started down the footpath to the beach, feeling the thrumming excitement that came before combat. He was relaxed yet watchful, aware of everything happening around him.

He was ready for whatever might come.

Chapter 3

Dragon Island was peaceful in the pale afternoon sun. The steep footpath was bordered with tough little bushes that provided handholds as Kenrick scrambled down to the shingle beach. The only activity was the nesting of seabirds.

Halfway down the path, Kenrick halted to study the area more closely. The causeway was wide enough for only one man to pass. A horse could be brought along the beach, but it would have trouble crossing the causeway. A donkey would be better. The almost-island would make an impregnable site for a castle, though it would be damnably cold in winter.

He was about to resume his descent when he saw four shabby figures moving purposefully along the beach. These were no peasants or fishermen. They were armed with daggers and swords, and they wore boiled-leather cuirasses to protect themselves in a fight. Bandits. Perhaps a gang of thieves used the island for a hideout, and encouraged dragon rumors to keep people away? The crashing waves drowned out any conversation among them.

Since the bandits hadn't seen him, he crouched, partially concealed by a bush, until the four had crossed the causeway and were on the island. They moved warily, glancing upward often. Were they looking for a dragon, or watching for people on the island? He was glad that

Giles was too far from the bluff to be visible—the bandits might want to steal the horses.

With the men out of sight, Kenrick finished his descent and started over the slippery stones of the causeway. With so many tumbled boulders on the island, the bandits were unlikely to see him following. Since he couldn't see them, either, he carried his sword in his hand, all senses on alert.

He reached the end of the causeway and began climbing the steep hill. Several times, he passed blackened areas. It seemed unlikely that anyone would have built a cooking fire on this barren ground. Hard not to wonder if knights had been charred on these spots. There were no bones or other human remains. But there wouldn't be if the dragon had carried the cooked knight off for dinner. . . .

Chiding himself for too much imagination, Kenrick continued upward. Once he found a scorched, half-melted piece of chain mail about a foot square. The sight was chilling. Mail was not easily torn from a hauberk. Nor easily melted.

As he neared the top of the steep hill, concealing himself behind boulders whenever possible, he heard a rumble of rough male voices speaking in some dialect he couldn't understand. They sounded surprisingly close. He also heard the frightened baaing of sheep. Maybe the bandits were sheep thieves.

A woman screamed. He stopped in his tracks, shocked at the terror in her voice. Then he bolted up the rocky path, almost falling as pebbles shifted under his feet.

The path opened to a narrow meadow that was fenced in by rocks on three sides, with the other side open to the sea. Terrified sheep were fleeing along a narrow path that led from the far end of the meadow, their bleats fading as they vanished from sight. The screams came from a bright-haired young woman who was pinned to the ground by a bandit who ripped at her clothing with greedy hands.

Though the girl fought desperately, she was helpless against the man's strength. The other three bandits stood around the girl, cheering the would-be rapist and arguing who would get the next turn.

The girl's resistance ended when her assailant walloped the side of her head, knocking her unconscious. Pray God she was only unconscious.

Kenrick pulled the hood of his hauberk over his head, then armed himself with his sword in his right hand and his dagger in his left. Teeth bared and blades flashing, he charged into the narrow meadow.

The first man died howling as Kenrick's sword stabbed through his back. Hardened leather was not up to the slice of sharpened steel. As Kenrick yanked the blade free, the other two men who were on their feet spun about and reached for their weapons.

Kenrick used his dagger to deflect a sword thrust by the bandit on the left while he parried the man on the right with his own blade. These were not mere bandits, but trained soldiers. At a guess, mercenaries turned rogue. Though he'd taken one man down through surprise, he was now outnumbered three to one.

Too late for second thoughts. Even if he'd known how skilled they were, he could not have stood by and watched an innocent girl raped, perhaps murdered.

The fight was chaotic, a maelstrom of filthy men and deadly blades. The bandits landed punishing blows, but Kenrick's mail protected him from lethal injury. If he survived, he'd have bruises aplenty, and his left hand bled from a shallow gash.

His sword took a second man in the throat. Two down, two to go. The would-be rapist had risen, and he was the biggest bandit of all. He joined his companion in the fight, and the two of them began herding Kenrick back toward the cliff edge.

Not sure how close that lethal drop was, he lunged toward the man on his left, going in below the bandit's guard to deliver a deadly stab to the heart. Then he swung to face the last man, the rapist.

The brute had great skill, Kenrick grudgingly admitted, and he was quick on his feet. He also had the advantage of not having engaged four enemies at once, so he was fresh and full of strength. Step by step, he forced Kenrick back toward the cliff.

Barely holding exhaustion at bay, Kenrick fought on, looking for a weakness in the bandit's guard. He found it when the fellow slashed at his eyes. When Kenrick dodged, he slid on the damp grass and fell to one knee an arm's length from the cliff. The bandit moved in with a shout of triumph, his sword descending with killing force.

Kenrick spitted the bastard on his blade.

Gurgling blood, the bandit fell forward, then pitched sideways over the cliff. There were dull thumps as he struck rocky outcroppings on the way down. Finally, a distant splash. He would ravish no more maidens.

Dizzy and acutely aware of every blow he'd suffered, Kenrick staggered to his feet and crossed the meadow toward the unconscious girl. As he approached, her eyes opened and she pushed herself to a sitting position. Blessed be, she had survived the assault. Her plain, grass-stained gown was that of a village girl, but the wildly tangled red-gold hair that fell over her face would have won acclaim at the king's court.

As she flinched away from him, he said, "Demoiselle, you are safe now. Were you injured?"

She looked up, and he gasped as their gazes met. The girl was stunning, her features exquisite despite the bruises on her face. Her eyes were an amazing shade that shimmered between green and blue-gray, as mysterious as the sea.

And her figure—the ripping of her gown showed more than a gentleman should see. Kenrick knew he should look away, but couldn't.

The girl's gaze moved to the bodies of the bandits. "I . . . I am not seriously harmed, sir knight." She touched the bruise on her cheek, wincing. "I owe you great thanks." Her speech was surprisingly genteel, and she used proper English, not Cornish.

She was about to say more when a shadow fell across them both. That hard, menacing shape was no cloud. Kenrick jerked his head up and saw a great silvery dragon swooping down toward him, claws extended.

The girl screamed, "No!" and scrambled to her feet frantically.

Summoning the last shreds of his strength, Kenrick raised his bloody sword. He had never imagined how huge, how powerful, a dragon might be. The wings seemed to fill the sky. Despite their vastness, it was hard to imagine how they supported that massive, silver-scaled body. No wonder a dozen other knights had died here. No man could defeat such a creature.

Now he would be unlucky thirteen, but maybe the girl could be saved. "Get back!" he called to her. "I shall hold him off as long as I can!"

The dragon breathed out a stream of fire. Though it wasn't aimed directly at Kenrick, he was unable to control his instinctive jerk away from the blistering flames. With horror, he found himself teetering on the edge of the cliff. He scrambled to regain his balance, stabbing his sword into the turf to stabilize himself.

Then a blast of wind from the dragon's wings struck and knocked him from his feet. Slowly, inexorably, he tumbled over the cliff. For an instant he was falling free, too stunned for fear. *Better to die this way than be burned alive.*

He slammed into a stone ledge that broke bones before he ricocheted into space again. His last conscious thought was hope that the girl might survive.

Giles shivered through a long, cold night as hope faded. With the dawn, he grimly saddled up for the ride back to Penruth. He had seen the monstrous dragon swooping down on the island, fire flaming from its great jaws, and knew that there was no chance that his master could survive such an attack.

Sir Kenrick of Rathbourne, the most generous of masters, was dead.

Chapter 4

K enrick gradually became aware of his body again. A very painful, throbbing, beaten-up body. His ribs and left hand were bound, and his lower right leg was splinted. Had he been in a tourney where every horse in the field rode over him?

Piece by piece, he remembered the rocky islet, the bandits and the girl. Then the great dragon that had sent him to his doom.

Though he'd died unshriven, this place didn't seem hot enough for hell. But would he hurt so much in heaven? Purgatory, that would be it. Perhaps some of his sins had been canceled by his attempt to save the maiden, so he would suffer the torments of the damned for a limited time. Eons instead of eternity.

Dully he wondered if the damsel had survived. He hoped so. It would be good to know his death had accomplished some good. She had been a lovely creature. . . .

When he came awake again, his mind was much clearer. He opened his eyes and saw raw stone above. Yet his bed was comfortable and warm blankets covered him.

And the air smelled of flowers.

Ignoring the pain, he turned his head to study his surroundings. He seemed to be in a cave, a well-furnished one. Besides his bed, the rocky chamber contained a chest, a table, a bench and a wooden chair with arms. On the table was a rough pottery vase filled with fragrant golden blooms. Though Cornwall was warmer than the rest of England, flowers were still unexpected at this season.

His hauberk was draped from the back of the chair, his sheathed sword and dagger laid neatly underneath. He was grateful for that—armor and weapons were far too dear to replace.

Candles glowed in wall sconces, and there were even carpets on the floor, warming the cold stone. A piece of tapestry cloth covered the exit, and seabirds could be heard crying outside. He must still be on the island. But how had he avoided dying?

A shapely silhouette appeared against the light in the doorway. The maiden! He started to sit up, then fell back gasping on his pillows as agony lanced through his ribs.

"You are awake!" The maiden rushed to his side, then halted, her sea-change eyes wide and wary. The magnificent red-gold hair was plaited into a thick braid that fell past her waist. "You were so badly injured that I wasn't sure I could heal you."

Her exquisite, mobile face was enough to dissolve a man's wits even if he wasn't dizzy already. "I am Kenrick of Rathbourne," he managed to say. "I am sorry there is no one to introduce us."

Her eyes lit with laughter. "This is no royal court. I am Ariane. I am pleased to meet you, Sir Kenrick." She laid a cool hand on his forehead. "The fever is gone."

She pulled the blankets down to check his bandaged ribs. Her light touch sent a spark between them that startled her as much as him. He was embarrassingly aware of his nakedness below the blankets, and he tried not to think of who had undressed him.

She covered him again and stepped backward. "Would you like some broth?"

Kenrick considered the idea. Ordinarily broth was not very interesting, but it sounded right at the moment. "That would be very welcome, Mademoiselle Ariane."

"Ariane will do. We are not so formal here."

She turned to the table, where a tankard was steaming. He could smell the meaty scent of the broth, and wondered why he hadn't noticed it before. "I'm glad that you escaped the dragon, Ariane. I came here to slay it, but the bandits left me in no shape to attack the beast."

Now that he had seen the dragon, he doubted any knight could defeat it except through luck. Perhaps a large, heavily armed and armored group could manage it, but a single knight? No.

Ariane slammed the tankard back on the table and turned to glare at him, her braid swirling like a cat's tail. "I have had enough of idiot knights coming here and attempting to kill a dragon that has caused them no harm! Lord Magnus has been slashed with swords, shot with arrows, and stabbed with lances. If you hadn't been wounded by the bandits, you would have done the same. You should be ashamed of yourself, sir!"

He stared at her. "So you live here willingly and are not a prisoner?"

"Of course I'm not a prisoner! And I must tell you, sir, that I like Lord Magnus a good deal better than any knight I've ever met. That includes *you*."

"Magnus?" he said weakly. "That is the beast's name?"

"Yes. And he isn't a beast." She glared at him defiantly. "He's my grandfather."

Kenrick had struck his head much too hard. His wits were scrambled. Or Ariane's were. "He can't be your grandfather. He's a dragon. You're a human."

"You know *nothing!*" she hissed.

Yes, hissed, because as he watched, the lovely Ariane shimmered into a blaze of light. When the light cleared, the girl had been replaced by a dragon roughly the same size. Its shimmering scales were the same apricot shade as her hair.

"Christ have mercy," he whispered. "Have I gone mad?"

The dragon snorted and dropped on all fours, which brought the beast within touching distance of the bed. Its teeth were impressively long. And sharp. "Ariane?"

Warily he extended his hand, as if introducing himself to a strange dog.

She snapped her teeth at him. "Keep your handss to yoursself!" Eerily, her voice was Ariane's, despite the sibilance of her tone.

He withdrew his hand hastily. "I'm sorry, I meant no disrespect."

His temples pounded like drums. He closed his eyes, thinking that if he had lost his wits, madness was as real as the world he'd grown up in.

There was another possibility. He opened his eyes again. "Am I in Faerie?"

"Of coursse not." The dragon sat up on her haunches. Her eyes still echoed the sea. "I know of no other world but thiss one."

"Forgive my ignorance," he said humbly. "Will you tell me more about yourself and your grandfather and . . . and dragons in general?"

The dragon shimmered and was replaced by the human Ariane, looking exactly as she had before her transformation. Her brown kirtle and tan tunic weren't even wrinkled. "At least you are willing to admit your ignorance. So few men will."

He gave her a ghost of a smile. "Perhaps I should be offended on behalf of my sex, but I haven't the strength."

An answering glint of smile showed in her eyes. "You need that broth. Here, I'll help you sit up."

She slid an arm behind his back so she could prop him up with pillows. He caught his breath at her warm closeness. It was . . . distracting. Though she might not be a lady, she was most certainly a woman.

Despite her previous flare of temper, she moved him gently, keeping the pain to a minimum. When he was settled comfortably, she placed the tankard between his hands. He took a deep swallow of the warm, tasty broth and felt a little stronger.

He considered her garments. The fabric was plain but sturdy, a village girl's garb. He'd swear that the outfit was the same one she had worn when she was attacked, but the rips and grass stains had vanished as if they had never existed. "As a dragon, you were ... skyclad. What happens to your clothing when you are in dragon form?"

She lowered her gaze. "There's a trick to it. If one isn't careful, the clothing might not appear when one turns human again."

He tried not to think how she would look skyclad. "Can all dragons take human form?"

She nodded as she perched on the bench. "They sometimes find it convenient, though it becomes more difficult as they get larger and older. A dragon in his own form has great strength and magic, but human hands are useful."

"So you are a dragon." He studied her, seeing a mysterious, provocative quality he had never observed in another woman. "I hadn't known dragons were so beautiful."

She blushed. "I am only a quarter dragon. My mother was Lord Magnus's daughter. Her mother, Lord Magnus's mate, was human."

"Yet you have the dragon magic."

"Only a little. I cannot fly." For a moment, deep sadness showed in her eyes. Then she continued with determined cheer, "I will live the normal span of humankind rather than a long dragon life. But I have a bit of domestic magic, which is most useful when one lives in a cave."

"You have made this place very comfortable." He glanced around him, and was startled to realize that the light came not from candles in sconces, as he'd thought, but from globes of pure light set against the walls. "You created the lights?"

"Yes, light balls aren't smoky like candles, and they don't burn out." She sipped from her goblet.

He hadn't noticed the goblet earlier, either. He suspected she had made it appear. "Your grandfather killed the earlier knights in self-defense?"

"He didn't kill them," she said tartly. "As I said, he

causes no harm. Even with the knights who attacked when he was sleeping, Grandfather disarmed the brutes most carefully and carried them away to Southern France. None have returned here. I think they are too ashamed to admit their defeat."

"So no one has died at Dragon Island?"

"Only the bandits you killed, and they were no great loss. You would have died, too, if Grandfather hadn't caught you in midair. After I told him that you rescued me, he brought you here for healing rather than flying you to France. You might not have survived the journey in your condition." She frowned. "It isn't easy to catch a falling person. Lord Magnus pulled a muscle in one wing."

Kenrick wondered if his cracked ribs came from being held in those fierce dragon claws. "Then I am grateful to him. I thought I was doomed." He cocked his head curiously. "Why didn't you change to dragon form when you were attacked? With your teeth and claws, you might have been able to fight them off."

"They caught me by surprise and forced an iron torque around my neck. 'Tis not widely known, but iron makes it impossible to change to dragon form." Lines formed between her brows. "Somehow, they knew that."

"So they not only knew about dragons in general, but they knew that you had dragon blood and could be subdued with iron," he said slowly.

"Yes, and that's worrisome." She rose and took the empty tankard from his hands. "Sleep now, Sir Kenrick. You'll be stronger when you awake."

She was right—he was barely able to keep his eyes open. "How long have I been here?" he asked drowsily.

"Almost a week."

"A week!" He tried to struggle up in the bed. "My squire and Lord William will think I am dead!"

"Very likely." Ariane placed a hand in the middle of the chest and firmly pressed him back to the bed. "But there is naught to be done just now."

"Could you send a message?"

"We do not send messages to Penruth," she said dryly.

"No, I suppose not." Not when the baron was doing his best to have the dragon—Lord Magnus—killed.

He let himself slide into sleep. Perhaps this strange world would make more sense in the morning.

Chapter 5

A riane watched until the knight's breathing was slow and regular. Then she tucked the blankets around him, resisting the temptation to caress that dark hair or trace the pale scar that slashed down his face. She wondered how he had received that wound. Surely it must have come close to blinding or killing him.

She escaped outdoors, grateful for the brisk sea breeze that cooled her heated body. Blessed Mother, she had behaved like a silly girl with Sir Kenrick!

The reason why was obvious. Living out here with Lord Magnus, she had no opportunities to meet young men. She had seen the other knights only briefly, and they had all been angry and bad-tempered from being captured. One had even called her a dragon slut. She had been tempted to ask her grandfather to drop that one in the ocean, but she had controlled the impulse.

She followed a path through the rocky landscape till she reached her favorite thinking and dreaming spot. Wryly, she thought how her years on Dragon Island had made her agile as a mountain goat. It was unspeakably stupid of her to have been caught by those horrible bandits. She had been daydreaming, and almost paid a terrible price.

She reached her destination and sat down on a stone set against a boulder to form a seat. This little meadow faced south and caught the sun's warmth even in winter.

The bandits had taken her by surprise because she

had been thinking about her aloneness. Her grand-father was good company when his thoughts weren't elsewhere, and sometimes she visited the fishing village of Tregarth to buy supplies at the weekly market. The villagers knew she came from Dragon Island, and they looked out for her.

But most of her days were spent in solitude. As a mixed-blood dragon child, she would always be alone. Not dragon enough to fly, not human enough that any sane man would want to wed her. She could lie and pretend to be fully human. That would be easy, since few people believed in dragons. But every fiber of her being revolted at the thought of living a lie for the rest of her life. It wouldn't work, either. Someday she would lose her temper and turn into a dragon, and then where would she be?

Nor did she wish to marry a dragon even if there was one who wanted her. She was too human in her tastes to want the detached, intellectual life that was usual among dragonkind. It sometimes amazed her that her grandfather had ever managed to fall in love with her human grandmother.

Frowning, she drew up her knees and linked her arms around them. Sir Kenrick's arrival underlined her isolation. She hadn't expected him to be so ... reasonable. That he was brave was obvious—even a knight must think twice about attacking four armed men. That he was fit and muscular was expected, or he wouldn't have challenged a dragon. And it was honorable to protect a woman of no rank.

But honor and courage were expected of knights, and those traits were usually accompanied by pride and ar-rogance. Instead, Sir Kenrick had been good-natured. Even in the midst of his bafflement, he had struggled to understand rather than exploding into anger. It didn't hurt that he was amazingly handsome. No, not hand-some, even though his intense blue eyes had stunned her. He was too craggy, too fierce-looking, to be called handsome. Instead, he was compelling. A man who drew the eye and the spirit.

She grinned, thinking she would forever remember his shocked expression when she changed shape. The change had been a test, and he had passed. He had spoken to her when she was in dragon form, and not drawn back in revulsion when she had become human again.

A shadow fell across her. A moment later, Lord Magnus gracefully landed on the wide ledge a few feet away. Dragons were as fond of sunshine as humans. He stretched out his long body with a shimmer of bright scales, then settled on the hollowed stone and spread his wings to catch the warm sun. *What do you think of our knight?*

Because there were just the two of them, he used mind talk, and she replied the same way. *He might do, Grandfather. He is quite flexible of mind, for a knight.* She glanced away, hoping the canny old dragon couldn't read her feelings along with her thoughts. *He is Sir Kenrick of Rathbourne, and he seemed willing to believe you were not a monster who ate humans. I changed into dragon form, and while he was startled, he coped with the shock rather well.*

I hope so, for we need human help. Magnus used his back leg to absently scratch at a sore spot along his ribs. The eleventh knight had wounded Magnus with an arrow there, and it hadn't healed properly despite Ariane's best efforts.

He had other scars from the recent campaign to slay him. Though dragons were not easily killed, Ariane still worried when her grandfather was away for very long. If enough soldiers attacked all at once, they might manage to inflict mortal injuries. Weapons made of iron were the worst, for the wounds they made were slow to heal.

Something must be done, and perhaps Sir Kenrick was the man to do it.

The next time Kenrick woke, he felt almost himself, with only the normal number of aches and pains apart from his splinted right calf and ankle. He sat up and cautiously swung his legs from the bed. Though his right ankle hurt, he didn't have the feeling that attempting to walk would cause further damage. Ariane was a talented healer. After the injuries he'd suffered, he shouldn't feel this well this soon.

Garments were folded on the bench and a crutch leaned against it. Not his own clothing, which was designed to be worn with armor, but a long tunic and a hooded overtunic that were easy to don despite his splinted leg. There were also soft leather shoes that fit fairly well. The tunic was a little short, but it felt good to be clothed and upright again. The layered wool was welcome, since the cave had become rather chilly.

He lifted the crutch and tucked it under his right arm. The length wasn't bad, and using it reduced the strain on his splinted leg. He was experimenting with hobbling across the room when the entrance curtain was pushed aside and a huge dragon head thrust into the room. Kenrick almost leapt from his skin.

The dragon swung his head from side to side, as if sniffing the air. Then the enormous mouth opened and a narrow, fiercely hot flame blasted out.

The flame arrowed across the room and struck a large stone tucked into a corner. The dragon scorched the rock for the space of three dozen heartbeats. The temperature of the cave rose. Kenrick half expected the rock to start glowing, like coals in a blacksmith's forge.

The flame stopped as the dragon turned his head toward the other corner, which spared Kenrick from being set ablaze. Another stone was warmed by dragon fire. By the time the flame vanished, Kenrick had regained some of his composure. "So that is how the cave is heated? Thank you, Lord Magnus. It was cool in here."

The dragon turned his head toward Kenrick. He had the same sea-shimmer eyes as Ariane, and they were mesmerizing pools of deep, ancient wisdom. A man could lose himself in those eyes, forgetting to fight. . . .

Magnus rumbled a deep chuckle that rattled the furniture in the room. "Yess, this iss how the cavess are warmed. The sstoness hold the heat, gradually releasing it into the room." His voice had less hiss than Ariane's, but the sibilance was still unnerving.

Ariane squeezed her lithe body past her grandfather's head, which blocked much of the doorway. "Dragon fire builds up and must be discharged regularly, or it causes indigestion," she explained. "Heating hearth stones is a good use of the fire."

The need to expend the flame might explain the charred spots Kenrick had noted as he climbed the path to the island. "I have much to learn of dragonkind."

"There are few of uss left in your land," Magnus said. "Ssoon there will be none. But for now, we need your help, Ssir Kenrick."

"Me? What can I do that might aid such a powerful creature?" Since he was tiring, he sat down on the side of the bed.

Ariane perched on the bench. "William of Penruth is trying to destroy my grandfather," she said bluntly. "He is too much a coward to attack himself, so in the last year he has spread the story of a rampaging dragon. All lies, of course, but because of the reward he is offering, ambitious knights have been willing to try their arms against Lord Magnus. Penruth doesn't care how many knights are killed as long as there's a chance that eventually one will succeed."

"I saw burned villages on my ride down here." Kenrick kept his voice level and unaccusing. The last thing he wanted was to offend a dragon whose fangs were only a few feet away. "An alewife in one of the villages told me she had seen the dragon with her own eyes, his great wings flapping in the night like a demon."

"Villagess have been burned, but not by me," Magnus said flatly.

"Could a dragon from a more distant place be the raider?"

"It iss possible. A dragon will kill a human only in self-defense, and I can't imagine any of the English dragonss I know doing ssuch a thing." Lord Magnus looked a little embarrassed. "Though there have been occasional unfortunate incidentss."

Needing to understand, Kenrick asked, "You said that Lord William wishes to destroy Lord Magnus. Why would he want to do that if you are causing no harm?"

"Because he believes Grandfather has a great treasure," Ariane said, her voice edged. "Lord William is a greedy man. He would kill anyone if he might win gold."

"He did mention treasure when I talked to him," Kenrick said. "He was quite emphatic that any treasure found was his, though I thought little of his comment at the time. I thought that treasure was as much legend as dragons themselves."

"But dragonss are not legend. Now, ssurely, you are wondering if I have a treasure trove." Magnus's silvery eyes looked cynical.

"I am curious," Kenrick admitted. "But any treasure you might possess belongs to you, and Ariane is your heir. It has nothing to do with me."

Magnus's gaze was piercing. "You have an honorable heart, Ssir Kenrick. Ariane, show our guesst the treasure room."

"There is no need, Lord Magnus. Your treasure is none of my affair."

"Curiossity is a good trait, Ssir Kenrick. Once you ssee my treasure, you will underssstand more of the ssituation."

Ariane gave her grandfather a surprised glance when he suggested taking Kenrick to see the treasure, but she got to her feet obligingly. "Follow me, Sir Kenrick. Take care with your footing. The path is rough."

As Lord Magnus withdrew his head, Kenrick stood and adjusted the crutch under his arm. Though he was tired and his leg ached, he couldn't resist the mystery of the treasure. "I shall manage, Ariane."

Ariane pulled back the flap so he could hobble out of the chamber. A short passage led to another heavy flap, which explained why his bedroom hadn't been drafty.

As he pushed the second tapestry flap aside, he tried to remember any tales he'd heard of dragon treasure. He had a vague memory of a troubadour's song that described a fierce dragon lounging on a heap of glittering jewels, silver plate and golden coins. A maiden was tethered to his foreleg with a silver chain. Lying about on cold metal didn't sound like anything that would interest Lord Magnus, and Ariane certainly wasn't tethered against her will.

In the song, the knight slew the dragon and rescued the maiden. Obviously, the composer had never met a real dragon.

Nor a maiden like Ariane.

Chapter 6

Kenrick inhaled deeply when he got outside. The air was bitter cold, but intoxicatingly fresh. Magnus had disappeared. "Such a wild, beautiful place, Ariane. But lonely."

"I have my grandfather. There is no one I would rather have as a companion," she said, but her expression was wistful.

"Men and women are social creatures," he said as he followed her along a path that ran parallel to the sea. "Do you not wish for other women to share your days with? Or children, or . . ." He didn't quite dare say *a husband*.

"Enough, sir knight! My life is what it is," she said sharply as she paused to look back at him. "I am more fortunate than most. Is your life so perfect?"

He was silent for a dozen limping steps. "No. I am a wanderer who wants nothing more than land, a home, a family. I meet young boys who think that being a tournament knight is a glamorous adventure. They are wrong."

Ariane's gaze could be as piercing as her grandfather's. After a long moment, she nodded and turned back to the path. A short walk brought them to a narrow, barely visible cleft between two slabs of rock. She slipped inside. He followed her cautiously, careful of the uneven ground. He found himself in a passageway not much wider than his shoulders. If he were any taller, he would have to stoop.

The passage was illuminated by the globes of light

Ariane held in each hand. "Here." She handed him one of the globes.

He expected the ball to vanish, but the cool light continued to glow, creating a faint tingling on his palm. "This is a really useful piece of magic," he said admiringly.

"One of the best. Candles are messy." She started along the tunnel. It twisted and turned, taking them deep into the stony heart of the island.

As he ducked below a rocky arch, he asked, "A full-grown dragon couldn't possibly fit in this tunnel. Does Lord Magnus visit his treasure only in human form?"

"There is a large entrance that opens in the middle of a sheer cliff face. Lord Magnus can fly in that way. This cavern is his den when he's in dragon form."

Her voice changed in timbre as she stepped into a larger space. She raised the globe of light, at the same time making it brighter. "Behold the dragon's hoard!"

He stepped up beside her and surveyed the huge chamber. To the right was a vast area that contained what looked like the world's largest feather bed. It was covered with some tough fabric and was imprinted by the shape of a huge body. In the corner was a pile of nets, while a large tunnel curved out of sight at the far end of the chamber. He guessed that led to the cliff entrance.

The other end of the cave was furnished in human style, with wooden shelves and racks of cubbyholes. The shelves and cubbies held . . .

Kenrick gasped. "Blessed Mother and all the saints! I have never seen so many scrolls and bound volumes in my life!"

"A dragon's treasure is not cold metals and jewels, but the wisdom of the ages." Ariane moved to the opposite wall and touched one of the scrolls that rested in a cubbyhole. "This came from the great Library of Alexandria, which was destroyed a thousand years ago. Dragons saved as many of the precious scrolls as they could. More than anything, dragons love learning. They are great scholars, but not gifted with original thinking. This is why they enjoy humans."

Awed, Kenrick touched the illuminated page of a book that lay open on one of the tables. Having met Lord Magnus, he found this kind of treasure right and natural. Not baubles, but the wisdom of the ages. Lord William had been unable to imagine such treasure. "This illumination is exquisite."

"Thank you. It's the best work I've done, I think."

He looked up, startled. Ariane appeared shy but pleased by his words. "You are the scribe who copied and illuminated this? Saints above!"

Her gesture included the racks of scrolls. "Many of these are written in rare languages, a few forgotten by all but dragons. Lord Magnus reads the texts aloud, translating them as he goes, and I write down his words. I don't have time for full illuminations, but I make a pretty title page for each book completed."

"You are amazing," he breathed. "As learned as you are beautiful."

She cocked her head to one side. "You are not appalled at my learning?"

"I envy it." He paged through the book, which was written in Latin. "I read fairly well, but I'm not good at writing."

"Still, for a knight you are learned."

"I was schooled by the priest at the home where I fostered." He thought back to the years of his boyhood, and how enthralled he had been by the priest's knowledge. "I considered becoming a priest, but I didn't think I would like the confinement of the life." Besides, the church didn't accept bastards into the priesthood.

"It would have been a great waste if you had taken vows," she murmured.

The warm glow in her changeable eyes made his knees come near melting. There was timeless magic in this room, but the source was human, not dragon. More than anything on earth, he wanted to draw her into his arms, feel her warm body pressed against his. He settled for reaching out to touch her cheek. Her skin was delicate as silk against his rough fingertips. "I wish . . ."

"You wish what?" she breathed when he didn't continue.

Before he could come up with words to express the yearning she roused in him, she raised one hand and tilted her head. "Grandfather is coming."

Kenrick dropped his hand. He could hear nothing. "You have excellent hearing."

"I don't hear in the usual sense. Rather, I sense Lord Magnus's approach in my mind." She smiled a little apologetically. "I haven't much dragon magic, but I can talk mind to mind with the dragonfolk. I'm even better at it than Grandfather. When he wishes to communicate with another dragon, I send and receive the messages for him."

"Perhaps by the standards of dragons, you have little magic, but by human standards, you are a sorceress." He tossed his globe of light in the air and caught it again.

Her expression froze and she turned away. Lord Magnus's arrival gave her a good excuse. The dragon seemed to appear out of nowhere as he flew into the cavern from the tunnel. Once he was inside, he landed neatly in the open end of the cavern, then settled on the giant feather bed, looking as contented as a cat.

"What do you think of my treasure trove, Ssir Kenrick?" Lord Magnus said as he folded his wings against his body.

"It's wonderful!" Kenrick's gesture encompassed the room. "But not, I think, what Lord William hopes to find."

"He has been told what manner of treasure was kept here, yet still he threatens us," Ariane said harshly. "He judges everyone by his own greedy soul."

"Men blinded by the prospect of gold will believe what they want to believe." Kenrick caught the dragon's gaze. "You ask my help. What do you want me to do? I'm not sure that I have any abilities that would be of value."

Magnus breathed out a globe of light that floated to the roof of the cave and clung, illuminating the whole cavern. "You have lived in the world of lordss and kingss. You ssurely know great men. Do you think that an appeal to Penruth'ss overlord might help uss? If his overlord rebuked Penruth, the man might sstop ssending assassins."

Kenrick shook his head. "William of Penruth is sworn directly to the king. Edward will not intervene in a vassal's affairs as long as Penruth is maintaining order and sending taxes to the royal treasury."

Ariane sighed. "That's what I thought."

"But we had to assk," her grandfather said. He fixed his silvery eyes on Kenrick. "Wait here while I change."

He rose and vanished around the corner of the tunnel. There was a flash of light. A minute later an elderly man walked into the chamber, tall and dignified in dark velvet robes. He had silver hair and Lord Magnus's eyes.

Ariane said, "You forgot your shoes, Grandfather."

He looked at his bare feet in mild surprise. "I'm out of practice." After a small poof of light, his feet were covered with handsome leather boots.

"You should feel honored, Sir Kenrick," Ariane said as she seated herself on a bench. "Lord Magnus doesn't change to human form without good reason."

"It is easier to converse man to man than dragon to man," her grandfather said as he chose a seat.

Kenrick sat as well. It was indeed easier to converse with a man than a dragon, though he noted that Lord Magnus's teeth were in perfect condition, and rather pointed.

"Penruth is unlikely to drop his persecution of you," Kenrick said. "It costs him nothing to send knights errant. He will send them until one of them succeeds. Wouldn't it be easier for you to move away to a safer place?"

Magnus shook his head. "The age of dragons is almost over. There are few safe places left. I have been friends with the local villagers for many years. In particular, I have looked out for the fishing village of Tregarth, which is nearest. I have brought them food in times of famine, and kept trouble away. In return, they keep me informed of possible danger. In a new location, I will have no such support. Besides, Ariane has lived her whole life here. I will not take her away from her home."

"You know I will go anywhere with you." Ariane's face was pale.

"You are a good and loyal child," her grandfather said gently. "But you do not wish to move to a strange land."

"No," she admitted. "But even less do I wish to see you killed in front of me."

If a mob came and attacked Magnus, the violence would spill over onto Ariane. That knowledge made Kenrick's gut clench.

Magnus said, "Ariane, earlier I noticed what a fine dinner you are preparing for us. Perhaps it needs your attention now?"

She snorted. "You want to talk to our guest without my hearing."

Magnus smiled peacefully. "A man-to-man discussion is not out of place, child. We will join you soon."

She left the treasure room, her back stiff. Kenrick guessed that if she were a cat—or a dragon—her tail would be twitching.

And a very pretty little tail she had, too.

Chapter 7

Once Ariane was out of sight, Magnus remarked, "The child is right, of course. I do wish to speak to you out of her earshot."

"Why?" Kenrick asked.

"I want you to destroy Lord William," Magnus said bluntly. "I dislike violence, which is why I asked if the king might intervene to stop this persecution. But you confirm what I feared: that a diplomatic solution will not work. Force must be used. You are a skilled and honorable warrior. You have the strength to defeat him."

"I could probably defeat Lord William in single combat, but he would never accept a challenge from me. I am a mere knight errant, while he is a great lord. He would send his castle guard after me and I would be lucky to escape with my life." He frowned at Magnus. "There is obviously a feud between you and Penruth. I am not a political man, but I know that it would be folly to be caught between two angry lords."

"If you will not fight him for the sake of me and Ariane, will you do so on behalf of the people of Penruth?" Magnus said harshly. "I am convinced that Penruth is behind the attacks on his own villages. You fought the men who attacked Ariane. Did they seem like common thieves to you?"

"They had the training and weapons of mercenaries," Kenrick admitted. "But that doesn't mean they were in Penruth's pay."

"They knew enough about dragons to trap Ariane in human form with cold iron. Do you think any ordinary bandits would know so much about my kind?"

Magnus's words triggered the image of Ariane pinned down by that brute. The thought was even more disturbing now that Kenrick knew her. "You're saying that Penruth taught the mercenaries about dragons. That suggests he knew enough to hire a dragon, perhaps a foreign one unknown to you and Lady Ariane, to take part in the raids. Then he hired those villains to finish the job. Do you think they came here to kill you?"

"Perhaps. Four armed men would be more effective than a single knight." Magnus frowned. "But I think they wanted to hunt for treasure, and attacking Ariane was a convenient amusement along the way."

Kenrick's grip tightened on his crutch as if it were his sword. "They will harm no more women."

"No, thanks to your strong right arm. But what of Penruth's other mercenaries? I do not know how many villagers they have slaughtered, but even one is too many."

"You are making a terrible accusation. I have trouble believing that any lord would destroy the people he is pledged to protect." Kenrick shook his head. "It is against the natural order of things."

"So it is. Yet I believe Lord William cares nothing for the fate of his villagers if their deaths advance the cause of killing me." Magnus's gaze was piercing. "If I am right, can you, as a knight and a man of honor, stand by and do nothing?"

Kenrick thought of the burned village he had ridden through on his way to Dragon Island, and the new crosses in the cemetery beside the small church. "If you are right, I must act, even if it costs me my life. The code of chivalry demands no less."

Magnus exhaled roughly. "You are as honorable as I believed. If you do challenge and defeat Penruth, there will be a reward for you, beyond honor upheld."

Small profit in a reward if he were dead, but Kenrick said, "Time spent in your library would be a fine gift."

"You may have that, but I had in mind something of more worldly value." The dragon lord smiled, the sharp teeth visible. "You can win the heiress of Penruth. With William dead, the barony will need a strong arm to maintain order. Marry the heiress, and the whole of Penruth will be yours."

Kenrick's heart seemed to stop. To become a baron . . . "This heiress. She is of marriageable age and not betrothed?"

"Marriageable, not betrothed and the sole heir. Lord William is twice widowed. 'Tis said he is bargaining for a third wife, but he has no wife now."

Magnus was right. A knight who slew a murderous, dishonorable lord, then married the legitimate heiress, should have no trouble being confirmed in his rule. Kenrick could become a great and powerful man despite the bar sinister on his shield. His children would be lords and ladies. This was the dream of Kenrick's life, one that seemed so unlikely, he had ceased to dream.

Except—he thought of Ariane, and could not see beyond her to the heiress of Penruth. Would that unknown girl have Ariane's warmth, her beauty and intelligence?

Impossible. But Penruth's daughter would bring a dowry that would turn a homeless knight into one of the great lords of England.

Magnus rose and gestured for Kenrick to follow as he led his way across the cave and into the curved tunnel that led to the outside world. The dragon lord halted in the mouth of the cave, his gaze on the far horizon as the stiff wind tore at his robes and silver hair. "Ariane is in danger from Lord William because of her relationship to me. She has lost much in her life. I don't want her to have to choose between staying here and dying, or going to a strange place with no friends or family."

"As long as she has you, surely she will be happy."

Magnus turned to look at Kenrick, his eyes storm gray. "I will not always be here. There is a land to the west where only dragons live. No men, no swords, no seekers after treasure. Only dragons and books and leisurely discussions of the wisdom of the ages. More and more, it calls to me. Someday soon I will fly into the west, and I cannot take Ariane with me. I want her to be safe when I leave. That will not happen as long as Lord William is alive."

Kenrick's heart tightened at the thought of her alone and unprotected. "She has no one else who will take her in?"

Magnus shrugged. "The villagers in Tregarth know and like her. If the threat of Lord William is removed, they would take her in because of the aid I have given them over the years. There is a young man there, owner of a fishing boat, who might marry her if I provide enough dowry to overcome the fact of her tainted blood."

Kenrick frowned. "Tainted blood?"

"She is one-quarter dragon. That would not make her desirable in the eyes of the world," Magnus said dryly. "Nor will she lie about what she is."

"I had not thought of that." To Kenrick, her dragon nature was unique and fascinating. But not everyone would appreciate that. "This fisherman. He would treat her well?"

"I believe so, if Ariane would accept him. She has her pride." Magnus smiled fondly. "We dragons are an ancient race. We have much to be proud of."

It was unthinkable that Ariane become Lord William's victim. Barely more acceptable that she would become a fisherman's wife. But that fisherman had family and home and a means of making a living, which was more than Kenrick could offer.

First, Ariane must be made safe. "If you can provide me with proof that Penruth is behind the raids on his own people, I will challenge him. Whether he will accept my challenge, I cannot say. But I will proclaim his sins to the world and do whatever I can to subject him to the justice he deserves."

Magnus held his gaze, then nodded. "I can ask no more. Come, let us see what my granddaughter has cooked for our dinner."

* * *

The ducklings that had been slow roasting for hours were now crisp and succulent. Ariane turned the ducks on their spit, savoring the scent. She'd used torn bread and herbs to stuff the birds, and had roasted turnips and carrots as accompaniments. Plain food, but tasty. Absurd that she wanted to prove her cooking skills to Sir Kenrick, but there it was. She wanted him to think well of her.

Since she also wanted to show that they were not savages, even though they lived in caves, she set the table with the best plates and goblets. The heavy silver was fit to serve a king. Though dragons weren't obsessed with jewels and precious metals, they did like objects that sparkled.

She surveyed the great cave, which was warm and well lit on a cold, gray afternoon. This chamber with its hearth and comfortable furniture was the heart of the cave complex. Her own bedroom opened off it. The guest room where Sir Kenrick slept was adjacent but not connected. Often she cooked and ate alone, since her grandfather could not enter the room when he was in dragon form. It would be good to have company.

She heard the voices of the approaching men, so she poured wine and had it waiting when they entered the great room. Despite needing the crutch, Sir Kenrick kept up with her grandfather's long strides. He was almost fully recovered.

She took the goblets to the men, curtsying slightly. "Grandfather. Sir Kenrick."

The warm admiration in the knight's eyes made her drop her gaze, but her fingertips trembled when they touched his as he took the wine. His voice almost as deep as a dragon's, he said, "Thank you, Lady Ariane."

She glanced up quickly when he used the title. "Since your grandfather is a lord, surely you are a lady?" He raised the goblet to her in a salute. "I thank you for all you have done for me, my lady."

She liked his courtesy, even if it was incongruous in a

cave. Knowing how men's minds worked, she served the food quickly. Catching the attention of hungry men was an exercise in futility.

The laughter and conversation over the meal sounded almost normal, as if she and her grandfather were not of dragon blood. Even the stern, dark face of her knight lightened with laughter as Lord Magnus described the more amusing aspects of fishing for his meals.

She waited until the pears poached with honey and wine had been consumed before she said, "I assume your man-to-man discussion was about Lord William. Sir Kenrick, did my grandfather ask you to slay the baron?"

The knight choked on his last bite of pear, then shot her grandfather a guilty glance. "He did. How did you know?"

"Because Lord William is looming over all our destinies like a thundercloud. That must end." She caught Sir Kenrick's gaze. "When you fought the bandits, it became clear that they were not ordinary thieves but trained warriors, else you could have defeated them easily. Ever since then, I have been thinking about recent events, and I have realized that Penruth is behind all these evils. Not just urging knights to slay my grandfather, but also behind the dragon attacks which gave him the excuse to do so."

Lord Magnus chuckled ruefully. "I should have known I couldn't conceal the truth from you."

"Why would you want to? My life is also at stake here." She shivered. "There is danger all around us. I can feel it."

"Are you a seer?" Sir Kenrick asked with interest. "Is telling the future one of your dragon magics?"

"I cannot tell the future, but I can sense when there is trouble about."

"That is not a dragon magic, but a human one. Ariane's grandmother had the Sight." Lord Magnus finished his wine, his expression wistful. "She was an extraordinary woman. Ariane resembles her greatly."

Ariane remembered her grandmother a little, and it was true that the two of them had understood each other well. Ariane's mother had had a different nature. Less independent. Less clear-sighted. Ariane had paid the price for that.

Suppressing the memories, she said, "I think we must intervene during the next village raid. First, to stop the damage. Second, to reveal the truth to the people of Penruth. I don't think that the castle guard knows of Sir William's treachery. Most are honorable knights who would not accept such disgraceful behavior."

Kenrick frowned. "Do you have enough ability to see the future that you can predict the time and place of the next raid? Penruth is a vast, sprawling demesne. The raiders can easily strike and escape before we can reach them."

Ariane grinned. "The next attack will come tomorrow night."

Both men stared at her. "You are seer enough to see that?" Kenrick asked.

She shook her head. "The attacks have all come on the full moon. The next is tomorrow. I didn't realize until I thought back."

Her grandfather muttered an oath under his breath. "The full moon. The raids have been happening for a year now, and I never noticed. I am getting old indeed."

"Do dragons need the moonlight for night flying?" Kenrick asked.

"A good moon helps in navigation, especially when going to a strange place."

Ariane felt the familiar catch in her throat at the knowledge that she was unable to fly like her dragon kin. She was too human, too earthbound.

Kenrick said, "Do you have a way of learning the location of the next raid early enough for us to intervene?"

"I think so. I am good at touching the minds of dragonkind. Better, even, than Lord Magnus," she replied.

"Have you asked your English dragon friends who might be making these raids?"

"Yes, but no one had an answer except to suggest that it's a foreigner." She frowned. "I slept through the previous raids because they were not close, and I didn't know of them until later. Also, my ability is stronger when I am in dragon form. Now that I know a raid is likely tomorrow night, I will stay awake in that shape. I think that I will be able to detect any dragons that come near during that time."

Kenrick's eyes flashed. "Lord Magnus, forgive me if what I ask is a breach of decorum. If Lady Ariane can locate a dragon raid, would you be able to take me there so I could confront the dragon and the raiders?"

Lord Magnus nodded. "I have a leather harness that binds around my body so you can ride on my back securely."

"So that *we* can hold on securely," Ariane said. "I must come, too, to help you locate the dragon. If there is a dragon. If there are only human raiders, I will be unable to find them."

She was amused by the glance the men exchanged. Clearly, they would prefer to leave her here in safety, but they couldn't deny her value in locating the raid.

"Very well," her grandfather said. "Tomorrow we will attempt to prove our suspicions about Lord William."

"If you are right, it will be the first step in stopping his evil," Kenrick said softly.

His fierce, dark expression made Ariane glad that he was on their side.

Chapter 8

Full of good food and happy from the pleasant evening, Kenrick had settled in his bed when Ariane scratched at the tapestry door, then entered carrying a goblet. "You will need to be strong tomorrow night, so I've brought this posset, and I'll give you another healing treatment."

He caught his breath, mesmerized by the way the soft, magical light brought out the warmth of her red-gold hair and creamy skin. "I shan't need a posset. I'm tired enough to sleep till next Candlemas."

"This posset contains healing herbs, so you must drink it all," she said firmly.

He rose on one elbow, swallowing half the contents of the goblet at once. The hot drink had an astringent, not unpleasant, herbal taste. He drank again, more slowly. Safer to keep his attention on the posset than on his lovely companion. "This will help me fight raiders tomorrow?"

"This, and the healing treatment." She took the empty goblet from his hand. The brush of her fingers made part of him come awake with embarrassing thoroughness. "Lie back now, Sir Kenrick."

He obeyed, intensely aware of her presence. When she tugged at the blanket, he almost leapt from his skin. Before his imagination could run mad, he realized that she had exposed only his splinted lower right leg. Seeming unaware of his reaction to her, she laid her hands very gently over the throbbing pain of the damaged bone. She closed her eyes and her face smoothed out, becoming remote and a little stern.

Heat began flowing from her hands, heat so intense it almost burned. He had the strange feeling that the broken bones in his legs were being fused like metal fragments in a blacksmith's fire.

The energy radiating from her grew more and more powerful, then suddenly dissolved away. She removed her hands and opened her eyes, looking tired. "Sleep now, Sir Kenrick. Tomorrow you will be much stronger."

"What did you do?" he asked curiously. "I felt heat from your hands. Was it a kind of dragon magic?"

"I imagined the bone whole again and invoked healing power to speed that result. But that's not dragon magic, either. I was taught this by a healer woman in the village of Tregarth. She did say I was unusually gifted."

Ah, yes, Tregarth. "Your grandfather said you had a sweetheart in Tregarth."

"He must have meant Calum, who has been very kind." She had the expression of a woman who knew she was admired.

Well, Kenrick admired her, too. What man wouldn't? He would like to see that smile every day of his life.

But the days of his life might be very few. If he didn't get killed trying to stop the next raid on Penruth, Lord William's castle guard would probably finish the job when he challenged their lord. This was no time for a warrior to be thinking of soft smiles and softer flesh. . . .

As she rose to leave, he said impulsively, "Don't go yet. Stay and conjure yourself a glass of wine. There is so much I don't know about dragonkind." *And I don't want you to leave.*

"Very well." She sat down on the bench, her skirts falling gracefully around her ankles. A steaming goblet appeared in her hand. "I would offer you mulled wine, but best not to have it with that posset. What would you know?"

Where to start? "How does a creature as large as Lord Magnus stay aloft? It seems impossible."

She frowned. "It is hard to explain. There is a place that lies beside the world we know. When a dragon flies, much of his weight is held in that space. This is where we keep human garments when we change to dragon form. It is also where the additional bulk is held when a creature the size of my grandfather becomes a small human."

Intrigued, he asked, "What does this place look like?"

"I don't know. I can sense the space, but I can't see it. I am not dragon enough for that." A trace of bitterness sounded in her voice. "I cannot fly, I cannot breathe fire."

"Surely there are advantages to being mostly human. You said that humans are more imaginative than dragons, and that's a great gift," he said seriously. "Plus, dragons seem to be solitary, while humans can find joy in others of our kind. Friends and family are an even greater gift." He heard yearning in his voice and stopped, not wanting to further expose his weakness.

Her expression turned thoughtful. "True. I remember when I was a girl and my parents were alive and I had friends to play with." She sipped her mulled wine. "But such happiness is long gone. I have only my grandfather's company, and at heart he is a solitary creature. Most dragons are. Sometimes days pass and I don't see him because he is otherwise engaged."

Kenrick frowned, not sure what to say. While Magnus clearly loved Ariane, living on the island had to be lonely. She needed a real human family again. He wondered what had happened to her parents, but didn't want to ask about what was obviously a painful subject. "Your grandfather referred to a land in the west where only dragons live. Does that land exist in that other space you spoke of?"

Her brows rose. "He told you of this?"

"In passing," Kenrick replied. "It sounds as if there, dragons might be companions to each other. Not like here."

"Perhaps. I do not know what that land is like."

With her eyes downcast, she looked like a painting of the Madonna on a church wall. He ached to comfort her, and more, but this was not the time or place. "Will your dragon form continue to grow until you are the size of your grandfather?"

She shook her head. "Because I am only a quarter blood, I have reached my full dragon size. If I were ever to have children, they would be unable to change at all because they would have too little dragon in them."

"What lucky children they will be, to have a mother who is so beautiful, and who has the gift of healing." He yawned, no longer resisting sleep. As he drifted off, he thought he felt her hand on his hair. But maybe that was just a dream. . . .

Kenrick awoke the next morning able to walk normally, with no more than an ache where the bone had broken. Ariane was a masterful healer.

He spent the day cleaning his hauberk and weapons in anticipation of the raid that should come under the night's full moon. It was a quiet day, with all three of them keeping to themselves. Kenrick guessed they prepared for battle in their own ways.

After they dined and night had fallen, they gathered in the great library. Outside, moonlight shone on the sea, silver pure and cold as ice. Lord Magnus drowsed in the open area of the library, great eyes closed and his massive body crisscrossed by a heavy leather harness that included straps to secure riders.

Kenrick paced, following the tunnel out to look at the sea, then restlessly returning to the main chamber. Ariane was in dragon form to improve the odds of detecting the dragon raider. She was curled like a cat but with her eyes wide and her ears pricked with awareness. When the moon reached its apex, he asked, "Have you sensed anything yet?"

She flicked her tail with irritation. "No more than when you assked lasst."

"Sorry." Knowing she must be as restless as he, he paced away again. What if there was no raid tonight? Or what if Ariane was unable to sense the presence of a raider dragon? What if there was no other dragon, only Lord William's mercenaries? The terrified villagers might have only imagined a dragon attack.

If they were unable to locate a raid in progress, Kenrick didn't know how they might prove Lord William's treachery. Though his head had wanted proof before he supported Magnus's claims, in his heart he was already on the side of Ariane and her grandfather. But the world was a hard place, and evidence would be required if he was to charge a baron with the ruthless betrayal of his own dependents.

His gaze fell on the stacked nets in the corner of Magnus's den. "What are the nets used for?"

"For carrying objects. Cows, sacks of grain, scrolls." Magnus's heavy-lidded eyes opened a slit. "Some are larger, some are smaller, depending on the load. The fishermen of Tregarth make them for me in winter."

Kenrick frowned. "Perhaps we should bring some nets. They might be useful."

The dragon's eyes gleamed. "Indeed they might."

Kenrick lashed several of the nets to Magnus's leather harness. He was just finishing when Ariane reared up on her hind legs in excitement. "Another dragon iss flying into the ssky above Penruth!"

Kenrick spun around and Magnus snapped to full wakefulness. Her grandfather asked, "Do you recognize the dragon?"

"No. He is male and a sstranger." She concentrated. "Inland, to the north. On the far sside of Penruth. We musst hurry if we are to catch him!"

Earlier, they had rehearsed what they would do. Magnus bounded into the tunnel that led to the sea, followed by Ariane and Kenrick. At the mouth of the great cave, he straightened his legs and spread his wings.

Ariane scrambled onto her grandfather's back and settled between his shoulder blades. Kenrick buckled two pairs of straps across her, careful not to trap her wings. "Are you secure?"

"Yess." Her apricot scales shimmered. "Sstrap yourself on, Ssir Kenrick!"

He swung up behind her as if mounting a horse and buckled a strap across his lap. The nets were tied behind him. "We're ready, Lord Magnus."

"May the godss fly with uss," Magnus rumbled. He leapt into space. He had said he could easily carry two passengers, but when he launched himself outward he began dropping toward the sea. Kenrick's heart jumped into his throat as he tried to calculate the chances of them surviving a fall to the rocks.

Then the powerful wings caught the air and they soared upward, spinning through the moonlight as Magnus wheeled toward the land. He climbed higher and higher, until the hills below were only a dark blur decorated with occasional silvery clouds. Wind whipped around them, the winter cold biting to the marrow.

As Kenrick looked at the ground falling away, panic surged through him. He would face any man's sword, but soaring through the sky was terrifying. His fingers clenched the straps until his knuckles whitened.

"Issn't it magnificent?" Ariane threw her head back and spread her wings, giving a cry of exhilaration. Despite her dragon form, she was still Ariane to him. How could a mortal man ever understand a being of such complexity?

He could start by trying to understand her joy in flight. Fighting his fear, he looked around them and saw beauty in the clouds that shimmered below, in the contrast between the dark land and the ever-changing sea. And Ariane was beautiful, and Magnus, too. Fear faded, replaced by awe at his good fortune to share these days with creatures of such magnificence. He could not be a dragon, but willingly he would be their champion.

Chapter 9

They flew perhaps three-quarters of an hour, Magnus occasionally altering direction in response to mental commands from Ariane. In dragon form, her night vision was somewhat better than a human's, and she picked out the dark, clustered rectangles that indicated the widely scattered villages. Occasionally, a bright dot of fire could be seen. She wondered if any villagers would look up and see the dragon silhouetted against the moon-bright sky.

She arched and spread her wings again, feeling the blaze of the wind. The knowledge that she could not fly herself had less sting than in the past. Few people had the opportunity to ride a dragon through the sky like this. She was blessed to be part dragon, especially if the night ended in battle. At the same time, she was beginning to appreciate the advantages of being mostly human.

She twitched her tail as she settled again, and felt Kenrick's hand come to rest on the end. A frisson of pleasure buzzed through her. It wasn't lust, really. More a matter of reveling in the intimacy of touching.

She glanced over her shoulder and saw that Kenrick was scanning the horizon with interest. He'd been nervous earlier, she thought, but had adapted quickly. Seeing her glance, he smiled at her. Her claws involuntarily curled into her grandfather's scales. *Careful, child,* Magnus thought indulgently.

Wishing she could blush in this body, Ariane returned

to monitoring the progress of the other dragon. Speaking aloud so Kenrick could understand, she said, "I think the sstrange dragon musst be heading for the village of Tenholm. Nothing elsse iss near."

"Can you touch hiss mind?" Magnus asked.

"Yes, but he iss sso intent on looking for the village that he doessn't hear me," she said with frustration. "Also, hiss mind is different from that of the English dragonss I know. It iss like trying to understand a foreign language. I think he iss ssearching for landmarkss to locate hiss desstination. He hass been ssuccessful, and now he is desscending on the village."

"Then we musst catch hiss attention." Magnus pulled in his wings and stooped downward like a hurtling falcon. Kenrick's grip on Ariane's tail tightened, but he said nothing, even though a dragon's stoop must seem terrifying to a novice flyer.

The village came in sight, and Magnus leveled off into a glide. As they whizzed over the square tower of the church, Ariane saw the other dragon coming from the opposite direction. The beast was huge, noticeably larger than Magnus, and his scales were dark, almost black, the sign of a young dragon.

Ariane tried again to touch his mind, but the dark dragon was concentrating on his own business and not expecting to hear from another dragon. Her heart jumped when he opened his mouth into the fire-breathing position. *Lord Magnus!*

Her grandfather saw the danger as quickly as she did, and responded by blasting a narrow flame at the other beast. He didn't aim to strike but to signal their presence.

The black dragon's smooth flight jerked as he swung his head around to search for the source of flame. Ariane caught her breath. "He sseess uss! He should be able to hear me now."

"Tell him to follow us," Magnus rumbled.

Ariane obeyed, and managed to touch the black dragon's mind. He was startled, but willing to parley.

When they were south of the village, Magnus landed in a barren field. Kenrick unstrapped himself, then Ariane, and they slid to the ground. She took position beside him as the black dragon landed a dozen yards away. He kept his wings raised, which signified wariness.

"Sseldom do dragonss fight each other," Ariane said quietly to Kenrick. "But it iss not unknown."

Kenrick nodded and took a watchful stance, feet set apart and right hand resting on his sword. He was a splendid figure of a man. Ariane looked from him to the black dragon. The beast was impressive, but it was Kenrick who moved her.

Her grandfather called, "Greetingss, friend! I am Magnuss of Cornwall. How come you here, and why do you attack my villagess?"

"You are Lord Magnuss? I didn't know you sstill dwelled in the landss of men," the other dragon said respectfully, speaking with an accent Ariane didn't recognize.

The black dragon continued, "Why do you sspeak the language of men rather than the dragon tongue?"

"Because I am accompanied by a human friend, and courtessy demands that we sspeak in a language he can understand." Magnus waved a foreclaw at Kenrick and his granddaughter. "Allow me to introduce the famouss champion Ssir Kenrick of Rathbourne, and my granddaughter, Lady Ariane."

Kenrick gave a half bow, and Ariane inclined her head, dragon style.

" 'Tiss pleassed I am to meet you," the other dragon said politely, though he looked surprised to see a human. "I am Carthach of Donegal from acrosss the Irish Ssea. I did not know these villagess were under dragon protection."

"They are indeed," Magnus said sternly. "You have raided other villages in the area, I think?"

"Aye, every full moon for the last year." Carthach shrugged. "A sstrange businesss. The human lord of this demesne told me to fire the thatch of a different village on each vissit, and very particular he iss about which village iss burned. I cannot ssee the point of it, but who can underssstand human thinking, asssuming they are capable of true thought?" Remembering his audience, he glanced at Kenrick. "No offensse intended."

Looking amused, Kenrick said, "None taken, sir."

Ariane frowned. "Lord Carthach, why do you obey the bidding of a human? Particularly when the flight from western Ireland iss sso long and tiring."

"I do no man'ss bidding!" the Irish dragon retorted. "Thiss Lord William ssought me out and begged for my sservicess. I agreed because there hass been famine in the landss I protect, and I will not let my people sstarve. The human payss me in grain and livesstock." He shrugged his massive shoulders. "Perhapss he thinkss that burning down the cottagess will force the peasantss to build better next time. It makess no ssense to me, but I harm no one, and the human paid me well."

"So you set the fires, then fly away?" Kenrick asked.

"Aye. It doessn't take long to get little cottagess burning. I make sure the villagers ssee me before I leave. I can usually be home by dawn."

"Once a village is burning, armed mercenaries arrive and kill anyone who hasn't run away," Kenrick said harshly. "As news of the raids spreads, villagers have learned to flee as soon as the fires have been set, taking their aged and infirm family members with them. They see you and blame all the destruction on a dragon attack. No one who sees the murderers who come in your wake survives to bear witness. You may think that you hurt no one, Lord Carthach. But you bear responsibility in the deaths of many."

"Thiss iss outrageouss!" Carthach exclaimed, appalled. "To ruin the good name of all dragonss! How do the merceniess know where I will sstrike?"

"Lord William tells them. That's why he was so particular about which villages you burn. He is destroying his own land and people."

Carthach bellowed furiously in the dragon tongue,

then threw his head back and blasted fire into the sky. "How dare the human do ssuch a thing! We are forbidden to kill humanss except to defend oursselves, but I shall make an exception in this casse."

"No!" Lord Magnus boomed. "You know the law as well as I do. Only by our peace can we ssurvive in the landss of men until we are ready to fly into the wesst. If you break the law, you rissk harming all dragonkind. The lie that a dragon hass attacked humanss endangerss uss all. Your raidss have caussed a dozen knightss errant to come to my lair and try to kill me, and a dreadful nuissance it hass been."

Carthach's claws tightened, sinking into the earth. "Can I at least *frighten* him?"

"I undersstand the temptation," Magnus said, "but this iss a human problem, and besst ssolved by humanss." He inclined his head to Kenrick.

"Lord Carthach, will you ceasse burning villagess?" Ariane asked. "Surely there are other ssourcess of provissionss for your people."

Carthach sighed. "Yess, and all require more effort. But I can not ally mysself with a villain who betrayss his own people."

"An honorable decission," Magnus said gravely. Ariane sensed the younger dragon's pleasure in her grandfather's approval.

"The mercenaries must be near," Kenrick said. "They would have positioned themselves not far from the village and waited for the fires to start. We must stop them before they decide to move into the village and slaughter everyone, then set the cottages on fire themselves."

Ariane was chilled by the thought, but when she remembered the men who had attacked her on Dragon Island, she didn't doubt that the mercenaries were capable of such brutality. "We musst kill them all?"

"If necessary," Kenrick said coolly. "But perhaps they can be disarmed and captured. If that happens, could they be carried to a location far from here?"

The nets! No wonder he had suggested bringing them.

Magnus nodded his great head approvingly. "I can do that."

"Let me. I wish to make amendss for what I have unwittingly done." Carthach smiled, his pale fangs lethally long in the darkness. "There are placess in Ireland where the humans never sstop fighting. The mercenariess will be too busy trying to survive to ever come this way again."

Ariane thought that sounded like a fine idea. "To lure the mercenariess closse, we need dragon fire. Could you burn a tree or two, Grandfather?"

"Good thinking," Kenrick said approvingly. "Those two trees look more dead than alive and they aren't near anything else that might burn."

"It will be my pleassure," Carthach boomed. He turned and flamed the nearer tree, while Magnus did the same to the other.

Despite the dampness of winter, it wasn't hard to set the trees aflame. Ariane drew close enough to the fire to warm herself. She felt the cold more than a full-blood dragon, even when she was in dragon form herself.

Kenrick untied the nets from Lord Magnus's back and laid them out so they could be handled easily. Then he moved to stand beside her, not talking but pleasantly close. The fires were beginning to fade when he held up a hand, his face intent. "Men are coming this way, and from the sounds they're making, they may be Lord William's mercenaries." He pulled the hood of his hauberk up over his head. "I shall see if I can capture one for questioning before we engage the group."

"Yes!" Ariane reared up, clawing the air in anticipation.

He frowned at her. "I will go scout this band. Wait here."

"I will come with you," Ariane said, bounding to his side. "If needed, I can reach Lord Magnus and Lord Carthach by mind talk."

"That could be useful," Kenrick agreed. "Very well, come along, but be careful."

"Dragons are not easily destroyed," she said as they headed into a sunken lane. "Even a mixed-blood like me is tougher than most humans."

"That's true. But fighting begins in the mind, and if you are not used to fighting, you might hesitate at a critical moment." He took long strides, moving very quietly for a man wearing heavy chain mail.

Ariane hadn't thought of that. So he wasn't protecting her just because she was female, but because she was not a trained warrior. That made sense. He seemed to see her as she was, a woman, a dragon and an individual. Had any human ever done that? None that she could think of. Human men might desire her human body, but they had no use for her dragon side.

No other man had accepted her as a companion in battle.

Perhaps this one special man might even accept her tainted blood.

Chapter 10

They both fell silent as they neared the noisy group of mercenaries. Since the adversaries were advancing along the lane, Kenrick motioned for Ariane to scramble up the edges of the lane and through a gap in the hedgerow that topped the small ridge. She crouched on all fours while Kenrick knelt beside her.

No more than a minute passed before the mercenaries started to pass them. He counted ten. Enough to wreak havoc in a small village full of sleeping, unarmed people.

"Where's that God-cursed village?" one man growled.

"It has to be this way, Hob. I saw a blast of flame that could only be from a dragon," said an authoritative voice. Ariane guessed that it was the leader of the group.

"There should be more fire if the damned lizard did his job right, Drogo," the first one said. "Told you I don't like working with lizards."

Ariane's wings flared at the comment. Kenrick understood her fury at the idea of a magnificent dragon being called a lizard, but now was not the time for rage. He laid a calming hand on her back, between her shoulder blades. She folded her wings again, but the mercenaries had done themselves no favors by insulting dragonkind in front of her.

"He's done his job well on the other raids," Drogo said. "He should be gone before we reach Tenholm."

"He better be," Hob grumbled. "No telling how hungry he is."

After a pause, a third voice said uneasily, "Do you think Rafe and his lads were eaten when they went to Dragon Island?"

"Maybe," Drogo said brusquely. "I told them not to go there, but no, the bloody fools had to go treasure hunting. And now they're gone, and his lordship won't pay for replacements."

"No matter. Ten swords can handle a village full of stupid peasants," the third man said.

"Aye. We'll have good sport tonight." The leader peered into the darkness. "There, up ahead. I see the flames of the village burning."

The third voice said, "I thought the village was south of here."

"Then you're wrong," Drogo snapped. "Come on, we want to get there in time to see if there's anything worth stealing."

"Not bloody likely with these peasants," another man grumbled, but they all picked up their pace.

Mouth tight with anger, Kenrick waited until most of the group had passed before making his move. When the last man ambled by, some distance behind the others, Kenrick leapt through the gap in the hedge and brought him to the ground. He pinned the fellow down and clamped one hand over his mouth, using the other hand to hold his dagger at the mercenary's throat. The man stopped struggling while his companions continued walking, not noticing the drama behind them.

Kenrick waited until the others were well away, then dragged his captive back through the hedge and rolled him onto his back. Dagger still at the man's neck, he said, "I will take my hand away. If you shout, I'll cut your throat. Is that clear?"

The scruffy mercenary looked belligerent, so Ariane thrust her scaled muzzle into his face and growled. His eyes widened with terror and he became very still.

Satisfied, Kenrick uncovered the man's mouth. "Who has hired you to attack these villages?"

When the mercenary hesitated, Ariane growled again,

louder. The man said hastily, "The local lord did. Don't know why."

"Do you mean Lord William of Penruth?"

"Aye, he's the one."

Kenrick glanced up at Ariane. "It is as we thought. Lord William must be challenged. I suppose we should keep one of the mercenaries as evidence."

The man's eyes widened. "You're going to kill the lot of us? You want evidence, I'll talk, as long as you spare my life."

"We'll consider it." Kenrick frowned at his captive. "Ariane, in this other space, might you have some rope and a piece of fabric that can be used as a gag?"

Ariane nodded. "I can do that." She shimmered into a ball of light for a moment, then solidified again, rope and cloth in her mouth.

Kenrick took the rope and fabric, his eyes warm. "You are amazing," he murmured. "Can you ask Lord Magnus and Lord Carthach to draw back and ready the nets? They should be able to trap the mercenaries between them."

"They will enjoy that." She closed her eyes to send the message.

While she worked, he concentrated on tying and gagging his captive. He finished by lashing the man to the sturdy trunk of a nearby tree. Getting to his feet, he said, "The other mercenaries must be near the burning trees. Time for us to join them."

Her open-jawed grin would have terrified anyone who didn't know her. He grinned back. "You are the perfect partner for a night of mayhem."

She tossed her head, looking adorable as the light of the full moon shimmered jewel-like across her scales. "Thiss is far more exciting than copying manusscriptss!"

Side by side, they proceeded swiftly down the lane. Ariane was bounding on all fours, eager to take on the villains.

The sounds of dragon roars and humans alerted them to the fact that they were almost to the burning trees.

"Now!" Kenrick raced forward, his sword at the ready, with Ariane charging beside him.

They burst into the clearing and found the mercenaries huddled in terror between the two dragons. Magnus and Carthach were having a fine time shooting flames across the clearing to box in the villains. Kenrick grinned. "Let us administer justice, my lady dragon."

He stepped into the clearing and donned his fiercest face and voice. "Drop your swords, and you may live!"

After a stunned silence while the mercenaries gaped, the familiar voice of the leader shouted, "I'll not disarm myself so I can be eaten by these beasts!"

"You will not be eaten, only transported to a distant place where you will have a chance to survive," Kenrick snapped. "You will get no better offer. Now drop your swords, or be roasted alive!" Carthach shot a flame so close to the leader that Drogo scrambled backward, terrified, and threw down his sword.

Another man dropped his weapon, and then the others did, as well. Terror of the dragons was great enough that they were willing to grasp at what might be a hope of survival. Kenrick ordered them. "Back a dozen steps away from your weapons."

They obeyed, huddling into a tight knot. Kenrick glanced at Magnus. "Are you ready with the net?"

"Indeed we are, my boy," Magnus boomed. He clasped one end of the net in his foreclaws. Now that he looked closely, Kenrick saw that the net was stretched across the clearing behind the mercenaries, with Carthach at the opposite end.

"Now!" Magnus barked.

The two dragons swooped into the air while dragging the net forward to entangle the howling mercenaries into it. There was a wild scramble of limbs. Then the net full of men was raised high above the ground. Fifty feet above the clearing, Magnus transferred his end of the net to Carthach. Kenrick chuckled. "The men surely have daggers, but that far above the ground, they won't try to cut their way out of the net."

"Look!" Ariane exclaimed. "One of them escaped."

Sure enough, in the confusion and darkness, one of the men had managed to escape the net. Ariane and Kenrick raced after him, Ariane in the lead. As she closed in, she gave a marrow-chilling growl. The mercenary spun and yanked his dagger from a sheath. As he raised it to slash at her, Kenrick yelled, " 'Ware, Ariane!"

He pulled out his own dagger and hurled it with all his strength. It caught the mercenary full in the throat. The man choked, fell and died at Ariane's feet.

She jerked to a halt, staring down at the body. "Th-thank you."

"Mayhem isn't always amusing." He joined her, looking down into her face. "Are you all right?"

She nodded, a very human gesture. "I liked the chasse, but not the kill."

"The chase is more enjoyable," he agreed. "But sometimes the kill is necessary."

Above their heads, Lord Carthach called, "Now that all iss well, I shall take these villainss to the wesst of Ireland. Farewell, Lord Magnuss. I will return your netss ssoon." Carthach banked, his cargo net swaying beneath him, and headed west.

"Better him than me," Lord Magnus observed as he landed beside Kenrick and Ariane. "It hass been a long time ssince I had sso much energy. Ssir Kenrick, what are your planss now that Lord William's guilt has been proved beyond doubt?"

Kenrick shrugged. "I shall take my witness, the mercenary I caught earlier, and ride to Penruth Castle to challenge Lord William to a trial by combat. He will probably send his guard out to kill me. If I am lucky, some of them will hesitate to obey their murderous lord."

Ariane looked worried. "That sounds dangerous. What if you approach the castle at the head of a group of village folk demanding justice? Men armed with scythes and sickles and righteous anger."

"That would make it much harder for Penruth to ignore me. Can such a group be organized?" Kenrick said, surprised. "It is almost unheard of for laborers to stand against armed warriors."

"They will sstand if they are angry enough," Lord Magnus said. "We can sstart by waking the headman of Tenholm and turning over your captive, explaining what you have learned. They will hold the man prissoner, and sstart to sspread the word of Lord William'ss treachery. On our way home, we shall visit Master Arnulph, the bailiff of Tregarth Manor. He has influence and iss a friend."

Kenrick was still doubtful, but it was worth trying. He turned his captive, Hob, over to the headman of Tenholm and his strapping sons. Their rage at their betrayal by their lord was swiftly followed by a pledge of support. Kenrick made them swear not to kill Hob, because he was needed to bear witness to the lord's crimes.

When he returned from the village, Ariane had resumed her human form. She wore a simple gown and a beautiful fur-lined mantle to protect herself against the cold. Though her human and dragon forms were similar in height and weight, she looked smaller and more delicate now.

She was a demure lady, not the mischievous dragon who had fought at his side. The sleek scales of a dragon he could touch. With Ariane so cool and lovely, he kept his hands to himself, except when he helped her onto Lord Magnus's back.

The moon was setting as they took flight for Dragon Island. This time, the speed and height didn't worry Kenrick. Like Ariane, he threw back his head and laughed. The future was uncertain, but tonight, they soared.

Chapter 11

W hen Kenrick and his companions landed beside the bailiff's cottage at Tregarth Manor, Magnus wakened the bailiff by banging his foreclaws on the second-story shutters. The bailiff threw open the shutters and thrust his nightcapped head out the window. "What the devil? Ah, 'tis you, Lord Magnus. You have not called in some time. I have been worried with so much outcry against dragons."

"There iss a tale to tell about that, Masster Arnulph." Magnus gestured. "I think you have met Ssir Kenrick of Rathbourne?"

Arnulph peered downward and saw Kenrick and Ariane. "Didn't think I'd see you again, Sir Kenrick. I thought you'd vanish with all the other knights who set out to challenge Lord Magnus. Give me a moment to get dressed and I'll join you."

He was downstairs and outside in record time, with his solid, no-nonsense wife by his side, both of them wearing heavy cloaks. "So tell me this tale."

Kenrick described Lord William's treachery and their capture of the mercenaries. Arnulph and his wife were horrified by their lord's betrayal of his own people. When Kenrick finished, Lord Magnus said, "I told Ssir Kenrick that the common men of Penruth will stand at hiss back when he challengess Lord William. Did I sspeak true?"

The bailiff and his wife exchanged a glance. His wife gave a slight nod. "You did indeed, Lord Magnus," Arnulph replied. "Lord William has never been popular, and he has not treated the people of Penruth well. Word of this final betrayal will set tinder to flame, if there is someone to lead the challenge to his authority."

"I am willing," Kenrick said. "My great concern is how I might force Lord William to confront my challenge when he can so easily ignore me from within the safety of his castle walls."

"Three mornings from now, Lord William and his entourage will ride out from Penruth Castle to journey to the king's Christmas court," Arnulph said thoughtfully. "If you appear at the right time, when he is outside his walls, he will be unable to avoid you, and there will be many witnesses to your charges."

Kenrick rested his hand on the hilt of his sword. "I shall be there."

"If you are, you will find a goodly number of the common men of Penruth at your back," the bailiff said. "We shall spread the word."

Ariane suggested, "Let them wear their plainest garments, and perhaps hoods over their heads if they fear being identified."

Kenrick nodded approvingly, for common men would rightly fear challenging their lord no matter what the provocation. "Then we shall face Lord William, and may God choose the right!"

After their informal council discussed Kenrick's plan, Lord Magnus flew Ariane and Kenrick back to the island. "It hass been a good night'ss work, younglings," he said as they landed in the library. "Resst now, for the next dayss will be busy."

Ariane lit two globes of light, handing one to Kenrick before she led the way through the narrow tunnel that led outside and along the path to the main living quarters. With the villagers of Penruth behind Kenrick, the odds of success had improved. She hoped they had improved enough.

Kenrick escorted her through the kitchen and living

area. When they reached the tapestry flap that covered the door to her bedchamber, she hesitated, reluctant to end this exciting night. Never had she felt so alive.

Nor had she felt so lustful. She ached to reach out and touch Kenrick. Broad shouldered and irresistibly masculine, he fulfilled every romantic dream she'd ever had. And unless her intuition was sadly mistaken, he yearned for her also. But yearning wasn't enough. She must know something of his mind, as well. "Well done, Sir Kenrick. Not only will you do justice, but you may end up as the lord of Penruth yourself."

He frowned. "I'm told that Penruth has an heiress. If Lord William dies, she has the legal right to the demesne."

Wondering how much he knew about the heiress, she asked, "Are you thinking to marry her to solidify your claim to Penruth?"

His gaze shifted away. "What I am thinking . . . is how much I want you, Ariane. I am not a great lord with land or position to offer, but I do love you. If you will have me, I can surely find a position that will permit me to support you. Or I could live here, if that is your preference. Anywhere, as long as I'm with you."

She stared at him, not daring to believe. "How can you love me when I'm not even fully human? You've seen me in dragon form. Don't my lizard scales repulse you? Do you want dragon blood in your children?"

He turned and met her gaze, his eyes blazing. "Your dragon blood is part of what makes you rare and precious. You are charming and alarming in your dragon form, but certainly not a lizard. It is . . . is as if you're wearing a different gown, but your heart and soul are still Ariane." Tentatively, he reached out to take her hands. "You may be part dragon, but you're all woman. The most wonderful woman I've ever known."

She had seen desire in men's faces, but never had it been blended with such tenderness. Wordlessly, she stood on her toes and kissed him. He made a rough sound and his arms came hard around her, pulling them together while their kiss exploded like dragon fire. She clutched him, wanting this moment to last forever.

When kisses were no longer enough, she whispered, "Come inside with me, Kenrick."

He stepped back, his body tense. "Will Lord Magnus eat me if I take advantage of you?"

She laughed wryly. "He has been praying for a strong man to protect me so he can fly into the west with a clear conscience. He will be glad to give me into your keeping." She ran a hand down his chest, wanting to peel his hauberk away so she could feel his hard body against hers. "In three days you will be risking your life. Don't let us waste a moment of what time we have."

Still he hesitated. "I want you as my wife, not my leman, Ariane. I have little enough to give you but my name, and that is shadowed by the bar sinister. But it is all I have, and I wish the world to know that we are husband and wife."

"As if I cared for the bar sinister!" She clasped his hands hard. "Let us plight our troth together. I love you, Kenrick of Rathbourne, and I take you now for my husband in the sight of God. I swear I shall be faithful and true as long as we both shall live."

His smile was radiant. "In the sight of God, I take you for my wife, Ariane, to love and honor and protect. I swear I shall ever be faithful and true, dearest wife." He lifted her hands and kissed one, then the other. "And while we are now legally bound, I would marry you again in the church, after the danger is past."

Wishing she could be equally confident that their marriage would survive longer than three days, she tugged him around the tapestry panel that led to her chamber. "I will do so willingly, but now it is time to celebrate our marriage."

This time he came into her chamber gladly. She tossed the globes of light against the wall, dimming the glow so there was just enough illumination to sculpt the shape of his beautiful body. He asked, "Can your magic remove my hauberk?"

She shook her head regretfully. "Not when it's made

of iron. But I shall remove it quickly enough." The heavy metal garment weighed in her hands as she pulled it, jangling, over his head. She barely took time to drape it over the bench before she turned into his embrace.

They fell on each other with a hunger far deeper than mere desire. "Beloved," he murmured as he tugged at her tunic.

"This magic I can do." She gestured and her garments whirled across the room, coming to rest across his hauberk.

He laughed. "What a very useful skill. Can you do the same for my clothing?"

She gestured again, consigning his clothing to the bench, where his garments twined with hers. Her breath caught as he stood before her in all his male glory. Skyclad. Powerful. Burning with desire. She whispered, "Come to me, my dearest lord."

"You look so fragile, yet you are so strong." He rested his hands on her shoulders. "It is your differences that make you so special. I thank God that you can care for a man as ordinary as me."

Tears burned her eyes as she raised her face for his kiss. He asked worriedly, "Is something wrong, Ariane?"

She shook her head, her heavy length of her hair sliding over her bare shoulders. "You're not ordinary. Truly, I never thought to meet a man who would treasure my differences rather than condemn them."

"Then I am lucky indeed that the other men you've met were such fools." He scooped her up as if she were a featherweight and laid her down on her low bed.

They explored each other with wonder and passion, laughing together at the awkwardness of becoming lovers. She had not known desire could be so fierce, nor that fulfillment would transform every fiber of her being. After, as she lay contentedly in his arms, she thought that all the years of loneliness were redeemed by this one perfect night. "Fight well against Lord William," she murmured. "I don't want to lose you so soon after I have found you."

"No need to worry." He leaned forward and kissed her throat. "I have longed for a home, Ariane. And in you I have found one. I would die for you, but even more, I want to live for you."

As his mouth moved down her body, her hands clenched in his dark hair. In a fair fight, she didn't doubt that Kenrick would defeat Lord William. But from what she knew of Lord William, a fair fight was unlikely.

As she arched against her husband, she prayed to find a way to ensure that the battle would be just.

Kenrick had trouble keeping his eyes off his bride as they dressed the next morning. "You are as beautiful as the dawn."

She grinned at him as she combed her hair into an apricot-colored silken fall. "I might say the same of you, my lord."

He hadn't known that he was capable of blushing, but then, he'd never known a woman who looked at him with such an expression. "Will Lord Magnus be in the library? I must tell him of our marriage."

"We will tell him together. Truly, he won't eat you. He used to tell me that humans gave him indigestion." She stood and smoothed the wrinkles from her blue tunic. "When you go to Penruth, I will go with you."

"No." His objection was instinctive. "Lord William wants to kill you and your grandfather both. If I fail, you will be at risk if you are near."

"I shall stay within the circle of the forest where he won't see me, but I need to be there, Kenrick." Her eyes were as blue as the summer sea. "I have some magic, as you know. Perhaps I might prevent an injustice."

He frowned. He wanted to protect her from all danger, but he could do that better if he was alive, and perhaps she could help during the confrontation with Lord William. Reminding himself of her strength, he said, "Very well, but please, take care when near the castle." He offered his arm. "Now to announce our marriage to your grandfather."

Kenrick's concern about Magnus's reaction proved baseless. The dragon lord was curled up on his feather bed in the library, but his drowsy eyes opened as soon as Kenrick and Ariane entered the great chamber. "Sso, Kenrick, you decided you'd rather have Ariane than claim the heiress of Penruth by killing Lord William."

Once more, Kenrick felt like blushing. "How could I want an unknown heiress after I've met Ariane? I am deeply honored that she has accepted my pledge of marriage. Later we shall repeat our vows before a priest."

Magnus shrugged. "If you like, but the bonding hass already happened. A blaze of light ssurroundss the pair of you. I could not assk for a better husband for my girl."

"I will do my best to be worthy of your trust."

"Then don't let yourself be killed by Lord William. I hear he is considered a mighty knight." Magnus tapped his claws on the stone floor of the cavern. "It will not do for you to arrive at Penruth Castle on dragon back. You will need horsess."

Kenrick had been thinking about that, too. "It would be hard to issue a convincing challenge on foot. Do you know if Arnulph of Tregarth has suitable beasts?"

"Arrangementss shall be made." Magnus closed his eyes and lowered his great head onto his crossed forelegs.

His arm around Ariane's shoulders, Kenrick turned away, wondering what other preparations might be made. Now that he had someone to live for, he could afford no mistakes.

Chapter 12

On the second morning of her marriage, Ariane awoke with a luxurious stretch. She was discovering why marriage was so popular. Though it would be even nicer if her husband were still in her bed.

She closed her eyes and reached out mentally. Though she couldn't do true mind speech, as she did with dragons, she'd found that she could sense Kenrick's location and mood. At the moment he was outside the cave, concentrating fiercely.

Curious, she slid from the bed and dressed, donning a warm cloak over her tunic. Then she cut two chunks of bread and went in search of her husband. The morning was bright and bitterly cold, the sea smooth and icily silver.

She followed the sense of Kenrick's presence and found him in the small meadow where they'd first met. He was practicing with his sword, moving with incredible swiftness and agility despite the weight of sword and hauberk. He lunged, dodged, then spun about, as light on his feet as a dancer.

Seeing her, he lowered his sword and smiled, warmth lighting up his dark face even though he was panting like a bellows. "Good morning, my angel bride."

"Hardly an angel!" She tossed him a chunk of bread. "What are you doing?"

"It's been only days since I was seriously injured. Though you healed the injuries, my strength and stamina are much diminished." He tore off a mouthful of bread with his teeth. Despite the cold morning, sweat ran down his face. "I am trying to rebuild my strength as much as I can before I meet Lord William."

Her brows arched. "You don't expect God to deliver justice?"

"In my experience, God tends to favor the strongest right arm," he said wryly.

She was about to reply when her grandfather's thoughts touched hers. She frowned in concentration. "Lord Magnus says the horses have arrived. You'll find them at the top of the bluff."

Kenrick sheathed his sword. "I'll be interested to see what Magnus has found. Do you suppose he stole a couple of beasts from a field somewhere?"

Ariane laughed as they fell into step together. "Brute force is not his way. He probably asked someone who asked someone else. Even at the height of antidragon fears, he has had loyal friends all across Penruth."

Luckily, the tide was low, which made crossing from the island to the shore easy. She loved the way Kenrick took her hand to help her over rough spots. Not because she needed the help on a path she'd walked a thousand times before, but because his care made her feel protected as she hadn't since her father died so many years ago. Lord Magnus was certainly protective in his way, but this was different. She felt . . . cherished.

As always, the path up the bluff took all her breath. Even Kenrick was panting by the time they reached the top, but she was pleased to see that he showed no other sign of his recent injury. He had healed well. A pity she couldn't also mend his strength. He would need it.

At the top of the bluff, Kenrick scanned the area with narrowed eyes, then pointed. "Over there, by the old hut. Three horses are grazing."

He took Ariane's arm and they headed toward the hut. As they drew closer, he said with amazement, "That's Thunder, my destrier! They're my horses! How did Lord Magnus manage that?" His pace quickened.

A familiar blond youth emerged from the hut. "Sir Kenrick, it's true! You're alive!" He hurled himself at Kenrick. "I was sure you were dead!"

Kenrick hugged the boy, laughing with pleasure. "Alive and well, as you can see. Ariane, this is Giles, my squire. Giles, this is my lady wife, Ariane."

Giles blushed when he realized his effusions had been witnessed by a beautiful young woman. "I'm sorry, my lady. In my excitement I did not see you."

"No matter. I'm pleased to meet you, Giles," Ariane said warmly. "You have been staying at the castle?"

Giles nodded. "When Sir Kenrick didn't return from the island . . . well, I was sure he was dead. I took the horses and rode back to tell his lordship what had happened."

"He probably shrugged with irritation and continued about his business," Kenrick said as the destrier head-butted him. Thunder wasn't the handsomest of horses, but his heart and stamina were without equal. "I doubt he was much concerned about my fate."

"Er, no, sire, he wasn't. He muttered something about unlucky thirteen, then granted me permission to winter at the castle if I made myself useful." Giles made a face. "I hid your armor so none of the men-at-arms would be tempted to steal it. I've been working as a stable hand and sleeping in a drafty corner while wondering where to go come spring."

"How did you know to bring the horses here?" Kenrick asked, curious.

"Yesterday, an old man sought me out in the stables. He said you were alive and in need of your horses and arms, but I must tell no one. It seemed unbelievable, but—well, there was something powerful convincing about the old fellow, so I decided to take the chance he was telling the truth."

So Magnus had gone in person, and known exactly who to speak to. Typical of the dragon lord. "You brought my armor?"

"Aye, sire. It's in the hut. I smuggled everything out of

the castle in a hay wagon so no one would suspect, then hid it again. Today I took the horses out for exercise, and kept on riding after I retrieved your armor."

"You have done well, Giles! And just in time. Tomorrow I must challenge Lord William to judicial combat." Kenrick moved to the doorway of the hut and looked inside. Sure enough, everything was there, topped by his scarlet shield with its slashing black bar sinister.

"Sire?" Giles exclaimed, aghast. "Why would you do a daft thing like that?"

Kenrick turned from the hut to his squire. There was much to tell the boy about Lord William. And about dragons.

The bailiff's information had been confirmed by Giles: Lord William and his entourage would ride out this morning to attend the king's winter court. After a day of swift messages between Dragon Island, the manor of Tregarth, and the villages of Penruth, all was in readiness.

Penruth Castle stood on a hill surrounded by moorland, the river that created its moat rolling south toward the sea. To the west rose a hill crested with thick, dark woods. On this fateful morning, Kenrick sat astride his destrier in the woods, his wife and squire beside him. Standing behind and around them were more than a hundred hooded Penruth villagers. They carried scythes and rakes and hay hooks, and waited with eerie silence. The morning was heavily overcast, and the darkly garbed, hooded men were almost invisible in the shadows.

Ariane sat quietly on her palfrey, wrapped in her fur-lined mantle and wearing an abstracted expression. He knew she was worried, but there was nothing he could say that would relieve her fears. Earlier, she'd been in dragon form as if she intended to fight by his side, but as Magnus said, this battle must be between humans.

Giles was on Kenrick's other side. Tied to his saddle-tree was a rope that held Hob, the mercenary, on a long tether. Hob was willing to bear witness in return for his life, but Kenrick thought it best not to allow the rogue a chance for freedom.

Trumpets blared across the moor, and the outer gate of Penruth Castle was raised. Kenrick came to full alertness as a gaily colored procession rode out, banners flying. Dozens of farm folk had gathered outside the gates to watch the sight. Lord William's broad form was visible at the head of the column. He wore full armor and was followed by a dozen knights and a dozen more men-at-arms.

Kenrick waited until the procession was well outside the castle and the gate had been lowered. As he waited, some of the hooded men drifted from the woods to join the onlookers. "It is time," he said quietly as he gathered his reins.

"Go with God, my dearest husband." Ariane touched his gauntleted hand, her face pale but composed.

Kenrick inclined his head to her, then spurred his horse out of the woods and down the hill. Giles followed more slowly because he led Hob, who was on foot.

"Halt, William of Penruth!" Kenrick shouted as he thundered into the road in front of the baron. The procession ground to a halt, wagons creaking and riders milling in confusion.

Twenty paces from William, Kenrick reined in his mount and said in his most commanding voice, "Lord William of Penruth, you have hired mercenaries to slaughter your own people while laying blame on a dragon lord. I charge you with murder, treachery and betrayal of your sacred trust. For your crimes against God and man, I challenge you to judicial combat, here and now!"

There was an audible gasp from the listeners, and heads swung to look at their lord. William's eyes narrowed as he studied his accuser. "Kenrick of Rathbourne," he snarled. "I thought you were dead. Instead you've run mad. Out of my way, or I'll have my men kick you aside like a rabid dog."

"You will not brush me off so easily. I have proof of

my charges." Giles reached Kenrick's side, the tethered Hob panting beside him. Kenrick continued, "This man can testify that you hired him and his fellows to burn and kill your own people."

A ripple of unease ran through the entourage, and several of the men-at-arms frowned. All must know of the raids, but no sane person would suspect his own lord.

Hob raised his head and said brusquely, "Sir Kenrick speaks truth. I and thirteen other mercenaries were hired to attack local villages after they had been set aflame by a dragon. The dragon did not harm the villagers—that was our job. All of us, including the dragon, were hired by *him*." He raised his bound hands and pointed at William.

The baron's face turned a dark red. "Lies, all lies!"

"We think not!" All of the hooded men had joined the crowd, and now one stepped out and called, "The raids made no sense to us until we heard Hob's testimony. Then we knew we'd been betrayed by our own lord. Sir Kenrick has offered to stand as our champion that we might see justice done on behalf of our murdered kin!"

William looked shocked that a commoner was speaking so to him. He raised his arm and barked, "Ride the peasants down!"

There was an uncertain pause. At least a few members of his armed guard looked doubtful, as if unsure whether they should obey a lord who had acted so monstrously.

But others had no doubts. Knights were gathering reins and preparing to charge when a voice vaster than the ocean boomed, "Enough! No longer will you be able to hide behind the sswordss of your henchmen, William of Penruth." Lord Magnus dropped below the clouds as if conjured by magic. "The dragonss of Britain have come to ssee that justice is done!"

Another dragon appeared, then another and another, their great wings beating with awesome power. Kenrick recognized Carthach among the gathering throng. More than a dozen came, the wind from their wings hard against his face. When she was in dragon form earlier, Ariane must have summoned every dragon she knew to ensure that William would be unable to avoid this confrontation.

As the dragons wheeled above the moor, most of the drivers and servants in William's entourage ran screaming. The hooded men, better acquainted with Lord Magnus, stood their ground, though Kenrick could sense their uneasiness.

Lord William roared, "You are no knight, Kenrick, but a sorcerer who has bespelled dragons to obey his will. You'll not take my land from me with vile magic!"

Kenrick laughed. "No mere mortal can command a dragon. They are here to see that you cannot hide from your crimes. Prepare to fight, Lord William."

"Kill him!" William gestured wildly to his knights. "Kill the sorcerer, and the dragons will fly away!"

"Nay, murderer!" Magnus released a plume of fire between William and his knights. The other dragons wheeled into position and began breathing fire, creating a ring of flames around Kenrick and William. The men-at-arms were driven back until William and Kenrick were face-to-face in a large circle.

The dragons ceased their flaming and the fire died quickly on the damp turf. But they had done their job. No knight would dare come to the aid of his lord.

"You want to fight? Then die, damn you!" William yanked his visor down over his face and pulled out his sword as he spurred his horse forward.

Kenrick tugged his own visor down and wheeled Thunder to parry William's first blow. Though William was years older, he had power and cunning. The two knights hacked furiously at each other as they tested each other's strength and looked for weaknesses, letting the well-trained destriers keep them in position.

Kenrick's skill was greater, he thought, but as the savage struggle continued, he began to feel the weakness left by his recent injuries. His movements slowed and he was having less success with his thrusts and parries.

Seeing that he had the upper hand, Lord William managed to get around his opponent's shield to land a crushing blow on Kenrick's right arm. His hauberk saved the arm from being chopped off, but the force of the blow drove mail links into his muscles with shattering force. There would be massive bruises and maybe a broken bone. Arm numb, Kenrick swayed in his saddle, fighting the pain and fatigue as he tried to collect his remaining strength.

"Die now, you villain!" With a roar, William gripped his hilt with both hands and the heavy sword slashed downward in a killing blow that would finish the battle. Feebly, Kenrick managed to parry. Though it was a weak effort, his blade threw William off balance. With both hands gripping his weapon rather than reins or pommel, the baron lurched sideways. Unable to recover and weighted down by his armor, he fell awkwardly from his horse, snarling a vile curse.

A mounted man had a great advantage over one on foot, but honor required Kenrick to dismount so they could continue the battle on equal terms. Aching in every inch of his body, he slid from his horse.

The baron hadn't moved. Kenrick approached cautiously, sword at the ready. William was just the sort to pretend injury in order to lure his opponent close enough for an unexpected blow.

As Kenrick went down on one knee beside the baron, he saw that William's helmet was twisted at an unnatural angle. He pushed the visor up, revealing the other man's slack features. Gravely, he held the blade of his sword in front of his opponent's mouth. No trace of breath condensed on the bright metal.

Scarcely believing that the battle was over so abruptly, Kenrick rose wearily to his feet. "Lord William of Penruth is dead. He broke his neck when he fell."

There was a moment of absolute silence. Then Magnus's booming voice proclaimed, "God has chosen the right! The ussurper is dead, and Penruth can now be ruled by the true blood!" He caught Kenrick's gaze, and for a moment their minds touched. *Farewell, my champion. Live long and well with my dearest girl.*

Kenrick caught his breath at the suddenness of this farewell. *We will miss you, my lord. May you find what you are seeking when you reach your home in the west.*

Lord Magnus inclined his head. Then, with a whoosh of wings, he ascended into the clouds, followed by his dragon kin. Kenrick watched him go, tears stinging his eyes. The world would be a poorer place when dragons no longer chose to live among men.

Only moments had passed, and when Kenrick looked around at the remnants of William's entourage, he saw that the knights and men-at-arms were still stunned and uncertain. None seemed inclined to avenge their lord. He saw no young girls in the entourage, but perhaps Lord William had left his daughter in the castle.

The silence was broken by the thunder of hooves. He turned to see Ariane galloping down the hill. The hood of her mantle was thrown back and her red-gold hair streamed behind her like a banner of flame. She slowed down to ride through the crowd of hooded men, then halted her horse a dozen feet from Kenrick.

"You know me, people of Penruth!" she cried in a voice like ringing bells. As she spoke, the clouds broke and a shaft of sunshine broke through, lighting her with its golden warmth. "I am Ariane of Penruth, returned to claim my birthright!"

．

Chapter 13

Ariane's gaze swept the moor, touching every man and woman present. The great gate of the castle had opened, and servants were pouring out as they heard the news. These were her people, and many of them she recognized. Even more recognized her, she thought.

Arnulph, leader of the hooded men, pulled his scarf free to reveal his face as he dropped to one knee. "Hail, Lady Ariane!"

He had known she was alive, but many of the other people of Penruth had thought her dead. The villagers were the first to follow Arnulph's lead. As they knelt in obeisance, it was like a wind blowing over a wheat field.

"Hail to the Lady of Penruth!" Sir Alfred, one of the older knights who had served her parents, slid from his horse and bowed before her, tears running down his face. "Give thanks for God's miracle!"

The other knights followed Sir Alfred's lead. "All hail to our lady!"

Almost everyone in sight was now kneeling, except Hob. Released by Giles, he raced for the woods while attention was elsewhere.

Only Kenrick still stood, his expression stunned. She could feel his shock and confusion, and his painful wondering about why she had concealed the truth of her heritage. As he started to kneel, she extended her hand. "Never kneel to me, my dearest," she said softly.

He took her hand, and she held it as she dismounted.

Raising their joined hands above her head, she called out, "Kenrick of Rathbourne is my beloved husband and champion! Together we shall rule over Penruth with justice and compassion."

"Why didn't you tell me?" he said under his breath.

She glanced up pleadingly. "I'll explain as soon as I can. Please trust that my reasons were good."

She lowered their hands, her gaze steely as she studied the knights and men-at-arms. "Some of you I have known for many years, and I know you to be good men. Swear fealty to me and you may stay. But if any of you feel you cannot serve William's successor, or if you have committed crimes against the people of Penruth, go *now!*"

Her gaze came to rest on Sir Guiscard. As captain of William's guard, he had once tried to rape her. She'd used magic to escape. William had brushed off her accusation. Today, Guiscard paled under her hard gaze, and she knew that he would be gone before noontide. Several of the other guards looked equally uneasy. She guessed they also would leave before they could be accused of any crimes.

"Oh, my lady!" A middle-aged woman who had run down from the castle fell to Ariane's feet, her voice choked with tears. "I had thought you dead these many years!"

It was Margery, her old nurse. Ariane lifted the older woman to her feet and hugged her fiercely. "My grandfather saved me. It's so good to be home!"

Her hand locked in Kenrick's, she began walking up to the castle, receiving greetings from the people who had raised her. Old Roger, the stableman who had taught her to ride, said bluntly, " 'Tis good to have you home, my lady, and God be thanked that your new lord killed that devil William."

"One should not give thanks for death, Roger," she said, but her heart wasn't in the mild rebuke, since she felt exactly the same way.

Joyfully, she entered the gate into her castle. Kenrick

had said nothing during their walk, but she could feel his questions.

As they entered the inner bailey, she announced, "Today there will be a feast of rejoicing! Margery, tell the cooks to get busy. Now I must show my husband his new home." Breaking away from the crowd was a slow business, but eventually she managed to lead Kenrick up to the tower room that had been her mother's solar. The sky had cleared during their walk, and sunshine poured into the round room.

As soon as the door closed behind them, Kenrick dropped her hand, his face forbidding. "Why didn't you tell me Lord William was your father?"

"He was my stepfather." She stepped close and pulled Kenrick's scarlet surcoat over his head. "My mother, Lord Magnus's daughter, married Richard, the last true lord of Penruth. They were very happy together.

"After my father died, my mother felt overwhelmed by the responsibilities of the barony. In her worry and loneliness, she turned to William, who was captain of the castle guard. He wooed her with pretty words. She was fool enough to believe that he loved her, and that he would protect my rights as my father's heir."

Kenrick's face relaxed as she removed his helm and went to work on the breastplate. "You were able to sense his evil, I think?"

She nodded. "My mother refused to think ill of him, though I warned her. She learned after they wed that while he lusted after her position and beauty, he despised her dragon blood. He had an iron bracelet welded around her wrist so she could not change to dragon form. I think he was glad when she died in childbed, along with the babe, because that meant he could replace her with a wife of untainted blood. Of course, he had no real right to Penruth, but he was here, and strong. There was no one to take my side."

"So you ran away to your grandfather?"

She nodded again. "With my mother dead, I realized my life was worthless if I stayed at Penruth. In fact, as my mother lay cold on her deathbed, William hunted me through the castle. He wanted to kill me that night so he could claim that I had taken my own life in sorrow."

Ariane's hands stilled as she remembered the terror. She had been fourteen years old. "William trapped me in one of the towers. I used mind touch to call Lord Magnus. He flew to the tower and rescued me before William could break the door down. My stepfather announced that I'd thrown myself into the river from grief. I think he believed that I drowned myself rather than wait to be murdered."

"The campaign to kill Magnus began about a year ago," Kenrick observed. "Did it start because William learned you were alive?"

"I believe so. Several people in Tregarth knew who I was, so I suppose it was inevitable that word would get back to the castle eventually."

"And ever since, he has been trying to kill Lord Magnus, because then it would be easy to kill you." Kenrick drew her tenderly into his arms. "Thank God for your grandfather's strength and protection."

She clung as closely as she could, not caring about the hard armor he still wore. "Lord Magnus and I decided not to tell you I was the heiress, for fear that like William, you might want me for wealth and power while secretly despising my tainted dragon blood. My mother died of a broken heart, I think. I ... I had to know that you could accept me despite my dragon nature."

"Not despite. Because." He kissed the tip of her nose. "If God grants us children, I shall rejoice in the knowledge that your dragon blood will run in their veins. I love you, Ariane. For now and always." He kissed her again, claiming her mouth with a hunger that turned her to flame.

She returned the embrace with such enthusiasm that they bumped into the door with a clank. Half laughing and all frustrated, she said, "We have to get this armor off you so we can celebrate properly, Lord Penruth!"

He blinked. "I'm a lord now? I suppose I am." He

tugged at the fastening that held on his greaves. "I shall miss Lord Magnus, and I knew him only days. He ... was like the father I never had. Yet his departure will be much harder for you, for he was all the family you had."

"I will miss him dreadfully, but Penruth is my home," she said softly. "And you are my family."

He smiled, but his gaze was searching. "Lord Magnus was also your link to the dragon world. Will you grieve for the loss of your dragon life?"

"Some." She thought wistfully of her childhood dreams of being a true dragon, then let them go. With a smile of pure joy, she said, "But it's all right, my beloved, for I've found that in your arms, I can fly."

Anna
and the
King of Dragons

∞

BY

KAREN HARBAUGH

Chapter 1

1650, ISLAND OF KYUSHU, JAPAN

Anna Vanderzee gazed at the waterfall that fell from a small cliff into a large pond so deep she could not see the bottom. *Deep enough to drown in,* she thought. The Japanese villagers in the nearby town of Arita had warned her not to go too far up the stream, for there were bottomless pools where the water collected and one slip could cause a person to fall and drown. What was more, it was home to dragons; indeed, there was a dragon's cave not far from the village.

Nonsense, of course: Dragons were mythical things, her father had said, and did not exist. She put her hand to her cheek to wipe away a tear. Her very sensible father and mother would say such things no more, for they had died but a few days ago in a carriage accident. After surviving great difficulty at sea, it took a thing that could just as well have happened in Amsterdam to turn her life upside down. Stupid. It was so stupid, she thought angrily.

And now she was looking down at the pool from a great height, shivering, though the warm August sun beat upon her head. A mist wandered the surface of the green water, rising up only to disappear into the air. It looked cold, she thought, as befit the ice that had frozen her heart in grief.

The sun beat down harder, as if trying to warm the

chill inside. She had not enough money to go home to her own country, and even if she did, she did not know how she would make her way in the world. For all that she had learned of the healing arts from her father and mother, the Dutch would not care to have a woman physician in their midst. She would not be considered old enough to manage midwifery, though she had assisted in births and indeed many times doctored women who were birthing.

No one in Japan would welcome her services, either. She was a foreigner and her white skin, curly red-blond hair and blue eyes would no doubt frighten pregnant Nipponese women into hysterics, for her coloring was similar to their depiction of demons. All she had were her parents' few belongings at the inn at which they stayed, and her father's pistol in the bag at her feet. If there was some way of earning money, she could perhaps raise enough to pay for ship passage. . . .

But she did not know what kind of work she could respectably do. In Holland, the most populous part of the Netherlands, she could find a job as a chambermaid if she had to. But here . . . she was not sure she could even find brothel work, certainly not at the high-class ones where the women were treated with courtesy. She had seen how the low-class prostitutes were treated, and it was not with any kindness.

Anna gave a despairing laugh. She never thought she would come so low as to even think of such a thing. What else was there for her, then?

She looked down at the water again, and felt the mist that touched her face with curious warmth. The mist beaded on the tree leaves around her and the moist ground at her feet, the wet sparkling in the shifting light as a small breeze moved the branches. She sighed. One leap and she would drown, for she did not know how to swim well at all.

She closed her eyes. She could hear birds singing and the breeze flicking the leaves of nearby trees, and a warm draft of air caressed her face. It felt so much like the touch of her mother's hand that her heart constricted and she drew in a sobbing breath.

No, it would not be right to jump, even if she went on to work in the lowest of brothels. If she ended up working in one, surely there would be need for a midwife. Births, after all, were a consequence of such activity, and she would eventually be able to ply her medical trade amongst the poor and perhaps work up to a better station....

Or not. Anna winced, thinking of how strictly the classes were separated in this land. In her own land, one could rise from one class to another, be born of farmers and through hard work become a prosperous merchant. It was not so here in the land of Japan. Still, she would have a chance to practice her medical arts. There was that, at least.

The air was warm, but she shuddered nevertheless. One must be sensible, and she prided herself on her practicality. She would mourn her parents, but she would not insult their memory by committing suicide. They were in heaven, she was sure, and killing herself might land her in hell, and then she would not see them after she was dead, either. She sighed again. Drowning would mean she would not have to deal with her life as it was....

No. She would find work, even if it were in a brothel. But she could feel her soul shrivel at the thought. She was nineteen. In Amsterdam, she'd be ready to wed, even if she would not be old enough to work as a guild mistress at her craft. It did nothing to dispel her despair; it shamed her that she had come down so low. *Stop it!* she told herself. *This mooning about has no good purpose. Grieving over Mama and Papa is proper, but grieving over your future accomplishes nothing,* she told herself sternly. *There is nothing else you can do.*

Pressing her lips together firmly against further useless thoughts, Anna gazed down at the pool again. She was glad she took this long trip and found this lovely place. It had cleared her head, and she was ready to do what she must.

A sudden rustle in the bushes behind her made her turn swiftly on her heel. "Who is there—?"

Her foot slipped on the mud and she fell off the small cliff with a little shriek, down toward the pool.

The water hit her face and body, shocking her with its force, though it was unexpectedly warm. For one moment she struggled, swallowing water, then her despair came over her again. So it seemed she was going to drown after all. With luck, she would not go to hell, and would be able to see her parents again, for she had not meant to fall into the pool. She could feel her mind darken, and felt her sodden clothes drag her down, down, down. . . .

Something seized her waist, shaking her, and she gave up the water she had taken in, coughing violently, then gasped in air, not water. She was suspended above the pond in midair. Something still clutched her waist, and she looked down.

And nearly fainted. Huge claws curled around her, shiny with sword-sharp tips and glinting serpent scales. *No. Oh, no.* She closed her eyes again. Perhaps she *had* drowned, and now she was clasped in the devil's grip for her sins. That was it. She had not taken seriously the idea that suicide was a sin, for she was not a Catholic, and a lukewarm Lutheran for that matter, and a woman of science, like her father. But she could not deny that a scaly claw held her around her waist.

She gasped again, for something lifted her up, and something warm brushed her cheek. She clenched her teeth against her fear. If the devil held her, then it would do her no good to close her eyes and pretend he was not there. She would have to face her fate, whether it was eternal torment or burning in the pits of hell or whatever the punishment the devil sought to put on her. Cautiously, she opened her eyes.

She was thankful that she could not scream her fear— the sound had tangled up in her throat and could not get past her tongue. At least she could go to her torment with a semblance of dignity, even though the creature that gazed at her could probably feel her body shaking in its claws. Perhaps it would think she was shivering from cold rather than from fear.

She grimaced. Unlikely; the summer air was warm around her and the grip of the monster was also warm. There was little excuse for her to shake and shiver except with fear. She closed her eyes briefly once more, and took in a deep breath.

"Are you the devil?" she asked, proud that she had managed to speak clearly, without a tremble in her voice.

"Annata wa oni desu ka?" said the creature at the same time.

Dear heaven, the devil spoke Japanese! *Of course,* she thought bitterly. That would be her punishment. She was not even going to be in a hell that was populated by Dutch or even English-speaking demons; she would have to live eternally in one in which the denizens spoke only Japanese.

The creature turned her around, then upside down. Anna groaned. Oh, now she was to be upended so that her petticoats and legs would show—humiliation would also be part of the punishment for her sins. At least the creature's claws held her past her hips, and also held her skirts just a bit past her thighs so that nothing else showed.

"Hmm. *Kirei desu. Oni desu ka?*"

At least the creature's voice was pleasant—a deep musical baritone, and not at all grating, as she would have thought the devil's would be. However, that it thought her pretty was perhaps not promising. She felt the blood rush to her head, and hoped the creature would bring her right-side up again.

It did, and she sighed with relief, but flinched when it brought her up close to one of its large, round eyes.

"Hmm. *Oni . . . nai.*"

Oni. It meant "demon" in Japanese. She thought back to what it had said when she had asked if it were the devil; it had asked if she were a demon. It did not make sense. If she were in hell, surely the devil would know the difference between one of its own and a human soul.

She frowned. "No, I am not a demon," she said in Dutch, then switched to Japanese. *"Iie! Oni de wa arimasen."*

The creature seemed to start, and held her away from its face. She looked down at the ground—she was so far up!—and recognized the pool in which she had fallen. Then she looked at the creature before her.

She drew in another deep breath and let it out again. She remembered illuminated maps and pictures in books, and what the villagers said about the pond and stream.

A dragon had her in its grip. It looked *somewhat* like the mythical dragons on the corners of a sea captain's map, and the picture of one she'd seen in a book of saints. It was scaled, with claws and wings like those she'd read about in her homeland. But it was also different than the European pictures she'd seen; the eyes were not slitted like a cat's, but round and quite humanlike, and around the edges of the scaled jaws and along each side of its body were lengths of fine red fur.

She closed her eyes again, trying to think past the dizzying sight of the creature. Perhaps she was not dead and in hell after all. Her clothes still felt damp, and hell was supposed to be fiery hot. She glanced up at the sky—yes, the sun had moved across it quite a bit, and if this were the demonic regions, her clothes would have been dry from hellish heat by now.

"What are you going to do with me?" she said, then realized she had spoken English this time. *"Nan—"*

"Hoo-at aru you going-u to do wit me?" the dragon repeated, looking at her curiously, its head tilted to one side. *"Kore wa nan desu ka?"*

"Kore wa English hanashimasu."

The creature's eyes seemed to flare. "Ahhh. *Engurishu . . .*" It paused and seemed to frown. Anna closed her eyes and shivered. Was it angry? Would it eat her now?

"English," it said at last, enunciating slowly and carefully. A sigh came from the creature, and it sounded curiously happy. Anna cautiously opened her eyes.

She let out a breath and let herself relax, as much as one could when grasped by a large dragon. She pointed at herself.

"I am Anna Vanderzee," she said slowly and distinctly. *"Watakushi wa Anna Vanderzee."*

The dragon nodded and grinned, showing large, daggerlike teeth. She swallowed, trying not to flinch. *"Hai."* It paused, apparently in thought. *"Watakushi wa arimasu ka?"* it said at last, pointing at itself with its other claw.

"Dragon," she said. "You are a dragon."

"Duragon," it said. "Dragon. I am dragon." It pointed to itself again. *"Ryu."*

Anna bowed. *"Hai,* Ryu-sama," she said, using the superior honorific—"Dragon Lord," if *ryu* meant "dragon" and was not its proper name. "Very good," she said in Japanese, thinking praise for the dragon's efforts in speaking English would be wise, especially after discovering that she was not in hell.

A deep rumble came from the creature, and she hoped it was a chuckle. Certainly, it did not seem as if it would eat her or cause her harm; it had saved her from drowning in the pool, after all. But ... it would be best to know for sure. If she were to be eaten, she should ready herself now so that she would end up in heaven instead of hell.

"Are you going to eat me?" she said in Japanese, and was disgusted at herself, for her voice came out in a squeaky whisper. She cleared her throat. "Are you going to eat me?" she said, much louder.

The dragon jerked away from her, and a fiery light gleamed in its eyes. *"Iie!"* it said, and she could feel the heat of its breath against her cheek. "Did I not save you from the water?" it said in Japanese. "Besides, I wish to know more about you and your world. I do not eat sources of knowledge." It shuddered, as if the thought of losing such a source was horrifying. It shook its head and then gazed at her again. "You are a foreign woman, clearly. Are you a noblewoman?"

Anna shook her head. "My father and mother are gently born, but we are not aristocrats."

"Hmm." The dragon brought her closer, looking her up and down. "Do you read?"

"Yes, I cipher, as well, speak English, Dutch, French, Spanish and Latin, and know many things of . . ." She did not have the word for *science* in Japanese. "Of foreign medicine." She could not help feeling a sense of pride at her knowledge, for she had a gift for languages and learned them easily.

"Ahhh." The sound was contemplative, but she did not know whether the dragon was pleased by her answer.

"Have you books?"

"Yes, many."

"Ahh, soo desu ka?" This time the sound was definitely pleased.

She took in a deep breath—a pleased dragon was good, she thought. But would it let her go? "Will you let me go home?" she asked in Japanese.

Silence for a moment while the dragon considered her. "If I do, will you return?" it said. "With your books?"

A lump came into her throat; Anna almost wept with relief. "Yes," she said. "I'll bring my books, but not all at once, for they are heavy and I have no way of transporting them all by foot."

The dragon nodded. "Good. Promise, and I will let you go."

She drew in a deep breath. "I promise." *Anything to escape this creature,* she thought.

Slowly, gently, the dragon let her down, until her feet touched earth at last. "Good," it said. "Do as you promise, and all will go well with you."

She nodded. Her conscience pricked her; the dragon had let her go, though she had not been entirely sincere when she made her initial pledge, for she had made it out of fear. "I promise on my honor," she said again, this time meaning it. She gazed up at the creature towering above her, at how steam escaped from its nostrils, the sunlight shimmering on the iridescent scales of its head and golden on the rest of its long body, and how its tail curled around its legs like an oversized cat.

Anna drew in a deep breath, and then another and another. A dragon. Dear heaven. Her head suddenly swam, and she put her hand to her brow. She was talking with a dragon. She tried to draw in another, strangled breath, but could not. . . . And her sight darkened and she fainted.

When her eyes opened, the sun had only traveled a little bit farther across the sky—she'd been not more than half an hour unconscious, she thought. She rose, putting her hand against her dizzy head, and managed to gain her equilibrium at last.

A dragon. Surely it'd been a dream, she thought. Never mind that she was now at the foot of the pool instead of at the cliff way above it—perhaps she had somehow found her way down here and had fallen asleep.

Her clothes were still damp. She'd fallen into the water, that was it, and somehow managed to crawl out, she told herself. But the memory of swallowing water made her cough again, and she remembered the dragon. . . . And there was something in her hand—round things. She opened it—there were three gold coins, with a dragon curled around the hole in the middle.

Gold coins—money. She was surprised she hadn't dropped them. How had they gotten in her hand? She fingered the decorative figure of the dragon on the surface of one coin and remembered the dragon she had seen—thought she had seen—and what she had promised.

Well. Dragon or no dragon, she now had money, much more than enough to pay for her room at the inn as well as food. She could use some of the money to buy the delicate blue-and-white porcelain she'd seen in Imari and Arita, and sell it when she returned to Amsterdam. She could get a good price for it, she was sure. She would not have to find work in a brothel here in Japan, if she were careful of her money. Anna looked cautiously around her, peering into the trees and the bushes. She could see no creature other than a squirrel and a few birds that flitted between the branches.

Well, she thought. *Well. Dream or not, I have the means to live, and that is something at least.* She thought of the room she had at the inn and hope rose in her heart. Perhaps she could find work after all, and save enough for passage back home. The people in Imari and the surrounding area were fairly used to the way foreigners looked, so that they might not mind being doctored by one. A niggling doubt persisted, reminding her of her earlier despair.

She shook her head as she followed the stream's path to the village she had passed earlier this day. No, she was practical, and would not despair now that she had the money. She had more time now to try her hand at her art, and then she would see.

Anna's journey back to Imari was easier than going out, for she was able to take her time about it, given the amount of money she now had. The farmer had looked suspiciously at her when she stopped at the nearest farmhouse to buy food, and she could not blame him. She was sure she looked a bedraggled fright as well as a foreigner. But she did her best to smooth back her too-curly hair and straighten her very foreign Dutch bodice, petticoat and gown, and was glad when the farmer's manner changed when she extended her coin to him.

Indeed, he not only included a good meal made by his wife's hand, but a pony to take her the rest of the way to Imari, bowing profusely as he offered them. For a moment, the farmer looked troubled, for he had not the change to give her after they agreed on what he would provide for her. But the sheer fact of having money made Anna feel giddy, so she asked to stay the night, for a lunch to take with her the next day and for a bath, as well—private, thank goodness, for she felt she could not bathe in one of the public baths where both men and women bathed together. The Japanese had little shame over nakedness, she had found, and though she had become used to it a little, she could not bring herself to do the same. The farmer grinned and nodded and managed to find enough change, which he put in a drawstring bag for her.

Even so, she welcomed the farm wife's assistance with her clothes—which she suspected the woman did half out of courtesy, half out of curiosity. The farm wife bustled around the room, stoking the fire that heated the bath, laying out towels and soap. Anna pondered her for a moment—a plump, olive-skinned young woman whose hair was neatly contained in a pretty kerchief, and whose blue-and-white patterned kimono was tucked up to her sturdy knees for freer movement. Except for her clothes and high-cheekboned face and nub of a nose, she was like any farm wife one might meet in Holland or England. Anna smiled slightly. And no doubt one who gossiped with her friends whenever she visited the local village. If so, then perhaps she could tell her a little about dragons in the area.

"Sato-san," she said as the woman set a towel near the bath stool. "Do you know anything about a ..." Anna paused, trying to recall the word the dragon had used when it pointed to itself. "A *ryu?* It is very large and has a—"

The young farm wife's eyes widened and she sucked in a breath between her teeth. "*Ryu-kami-sama.* You have seen it?"

Kami-sama. It meant "spirit," or "god." Well, she did not believe it was a god, for as a Lutheran, she did not believe in such things, and if she had indeed encountered a dragon, it certainly had felt very solid and not like a ghost at all.

"Yes, I think I have."

Sato-san fell silent for a moment while she poured steaming water into a wooden bucket. She nodded slowly. "That is the way of the *kami-sama.* They are real—I have been tricked by the fox *kami-sama* myself—and there are times you wonder if they are only a dream.

But *Ryu-kami-sama* ... he is less likely to be mistaken for anything but what he is."

Sato-san lowered her eyes respectfully and bowed as she handed Anna a hot wet towel and some soap, and Anna, covering herself as best as she could with the towel, bowed in return.

She had to admit that she preferred the Japanese way of bathing. After washing and rinsing herself with the towel and bucket of water, she climbed over the edge of the barrel-like bath and sank into the very warm, almost hot water. She could feel her body relax, her muscles release.

Sato-san raised her eyes and gazed at Anna curiously. "Forgive me, but did Ryu-sama ask you anything?"

Anna was not sure how to answer her at first; she preferred to think the dragon a dream rather than real, for it upset her sense of the world even more than it had been, and that was bad enough. But this woman believed in it, and it would be disrespectful to pretend otherwise.

"It—he asked me a great many questions about myself and my language, and what I knew."

The farm wife looked thoughtful. *"Ah, soo desu ka?"* she murmured. "Did he seem pleased with your answers?"

"I believe so."

"Did he request anything of you?"

"Yes, that I return and bring my books with me."

"Ahh." Sato-san smiled slightly. "Then you did well and he is not offended." She gave Anna a sidelong look. "Did he give you anything?"

Anna hesitated again. "Three coins. One of them I gave to your husband."

"Oh!" Sato-san sat down suddenly on the bathing stool she had set out. "Oh, my." She stood again, and paced back and forth in an agitated manner. *"Doshimashoo? Doshimashoo ka?"*

Clearly, the farm wife was upset.

"I am sorry," Anna said, and tried to keep her voice calm, but she could not help feeling worried. "Did I do wrong?"

"*Iie, iie*— Oh, I do not think so. But the *kami-sama's* money is sometimes a trick, sometimes a reward." Sato-san's brow creased in clear worry. "My husband was pleased to be paid with a gold coin, but he will not be if the money disappears."

Anna frowned. "I doubt it will disappear. It felt very solid to me."

The farm wife shook her head. "A fox *kami-sama* once gave me a coin, but it disappeared when I came to the village shops! My husband scolded me, and the shop-keepers laughed. I felt much shame." Sato-san lowered her eyes again, her cheeks blushing.

Anna thought of the foxes in the nursery tales she'd heard as a child. She smiled comfortingly at Sato-san. "It was not your fault, I am sure," she said. "Foxes even in my country are deceivers. What can a mere human do against a . . . a *kami-sama?*"

Sato-san cast her a grateful look. "*So desu,*" she murmured. "You are very kind."

"Not at all." Anna replied politely. She grinned. "Besides, this time it is your husband that has accepted a *kami-sama's* money. If it disappears, then it is . . ." She tried to think of the word that would express just deserts, then nodded. "Karma for scolding you."

The farm wife's face brightened with mischief, then she put her hand to her lips to smother her laughter. "It is naughty to think so, but perhaps it will be as you say," she replied.

The farm wife chattered on, tidying up the bathhouse floor, and for a while, Anna rested in the fantasy that she lived such a life of comfort and friendliness, that she was not viewed with suspicion but with the kindness of this young farm wife.

She was glad to stay the night, for it was late by the time she finished her bath. As she settled into the soft futon mattress and pulled the cotton quilt over her, she thought over her promise to bring books to the dragon. The night was silent but for the whispered slide of the wood and paper *shoji* serving as dividers and doors be-

tween the rooms of the farmhouse, the soft padding of
the household's slippered feet on the woven rice stalk
mats, and the sleepy sound of crickets outside. She'd not
been inclined to return to the dragon's pool with her
books, but she remembered the farm wife's words, and
a shiver went up her spine. Perhaps it would not hurt to
do so. If the dragon did not appear, then she had lost
nothing but a day's journey, and she would still have
enough money to last her until she found a way to leave
for home or a way to earn money. If the dragon did appear again, then she would not incur its wrath, and she
had to admit that she would not want to anger such a
fierce creature.

Soon the house grew quieter, and the silence lulled her
eyes to close. Anna's thoughts flickered once more to the
dragon, and she remembered the farm wife's words about
the shape-changing *kami-sama*. She wondered for a moment if the dragon could also change his shape, but sleep
caught her at last before any answer came.

Anna woke with the first stirring of the farmhouse occupants, and she quickly rose and dressed herself as best
she could. She frowned at the wrinkles in her skirts as
she smoothed down the cloth to no avail, and then did
her best to fold up the quilt and put aside the futon. She
was sure it was not as neatly done as the farm wife would
like, but she was not used to such bedding; at the inn at
which she and her parents lived, they had bedding on a
framed bed, as they would in Amsterdam. She had nevertheless slept well on the futon, and felt well rested.

The farm wife came by not long afterward with a
breakfast of a boiled egg, rice and a savory soup made
of mashed and fermented soy beans—miso—of which
Anna had become fond. She made quick work of it, and
then requested the pony that the farmer agreed to sell
her for her journey back to Imari. Since he readily did
so, with many bows as he led her to the stable not far
from the house, Anna supposed that the gold coin the
dragon had given her was a good, solid, unmagical one.

Anna smiled and bowed from her seat on her pony and turned to leave, but a cry behind her made her turn around again.

"Chotto matte, kudasai!" Sato-san ran out of the house and stopped suddenly next to her husband. She poked him sharply with her elbow. "What are you thinking, husband? Our most honorable guest must not travel alone! There have been rumors of bandits about. She must have a stout guard at least."

The farmer hesitated, frowning at his wife in annoyance, but bowed toward Anna. "The Nakagawa clan have fierce warriors, and bandits would not dare come to our province."

His wife gave him another nudge with her elbow. "Huh!" she said. "Even so, we should not be so dishonorable as to let our guest travel without escort. What would the village headman say? Especially since you know you can buy another pony—no, two!—with what she gave us!"

The farmer's wife shot Anna a meaningful look, and Anna thought of the dragon. Was Sato-san concerned about real bandits or the dragon? Or both?

The farmer looked guilty, and bowed with regret. "My apologies . . . I have been remiss. The Nakagawa clan has had their own problems to attend to lately; I thought their guards might not be available. It would be best if I took you to our village headman, and he will know what to do."

She glanced again at the farm wife and then bit her lip and looked away for a moment to suppress sudden laughter. Sato-san had made a ferocious face and clawing motions with her hands, then quickly put her hands behind her and an innocent look on her face when her husband glanced at her.

Anna shook her head and smiled. "You are very kind, but I shall be well and encounter no harm," she said. Clearly, the farm wife feared the dragon might come upon her again and thought its mood might be unpredictable. Besides, Anna doubted any human could fight it—a samurai might try, but she couldn't afford such protection if she were to save her coins for passage to the Netherlands. She had been given three coins and had spent one already. Besides, the dragon had displayed only curiosity about her, and she felt it was probably benign.

She bowed from her seat on the pony. "I thank you for your hospitality; I have had a very pleasant stay here, and I shall tell others of your generosity."

The Satos bowed low, but looked troubled. "I was thoughtless," the farmer said, bowing again. "My wife is right; you must be escorted. Please let me make amends, and take you to our village headman, so that he may find a guard for you."

She smiled at them and bowed. "You are very kind. But I did not encounter any trouble on my way here, and I think it is unlikely that I will encounter any on my way back. And if I do, then I have my knife and my father's pistol to help me." She patted the bag she carried at her side.

The Satos continued to look doubtful. Taking advantage of their indecision, Anna smiled and bowed to them once again, took a deep breath, nudged the pony with her heels, and went on her way. A glance back at them showed the farmer running off down another road, with his wife making shooing motions with her hands. Anna hoped they would not bother going to the village; she had always traveled freely in her own land, with a maid or with her parents, and even on her own if the shop she wished to go to was but a street away. A light, warm breeze scurried around her, tugging at her skirts as if it were trying to hurry her down the road. She smiled at her imagination and pressed her heels to her pony's side, urging it on.

Chapter 2

Lightness had settled in Anna's heart as she traveled, despite her misfortunes and the way her beliefs seemed to have upended themselves. She shook her head as her pony ambled down the sunlight-speckled road. She never thought she would meet a real dragon, for she had thought they were merely myths.

Thinking of the dragon made her look about her at the woods on either side of the road. The *clop-clop* of her pony's hooves echoed under the trees, and Anna remembered the Satos' talk of bandits. She began to feel uneasy, as if someone were watching her, and took out her father's wheel-lock pistol. She carefully primed it and hoped it would go off properly. There were times it did not, but it had a sturdy stock, and she could easily hold it by the barrel and hit someone with it if she had to.

She rode up a hill, and when she crested it, she could see the harbor below, with tiny Japanese fishing boats mixed with Dutch sailing ships, looking like so many toys sitting on the deep blue of the water. Her heart twisted within her at the sight. Would she ever see Holland again? *Perhaps,* said a soft voice within. *Perhaps.*

She smiled wryly at herself. Only perhaps? Surely she could do better than that. If the dragon was real, she could sell him more books, raise the money needed for a fare back to her homeland, and if she did well, acquire a dowry if she wished.

Yet the notion settled oddly in her heart as she descended the hill, and she knew a small reluctance. She pondered it and thought of the dragon again. That was it—she was a scholar as her parents had been, and who could claim to have seen and spoken to a dragon? It would be too bad if she did not come to know it better—if it were not merely a dream, of course—and note down her observations. Perhaps she could present her notes to the university when she returned to Holland. . . .

She shook her head. If they would even acknowledge such a thing as truth from a woman. Regardless, she would note her observations, and perhaps they would be of use someday.

Something roused her attention, and she looked about her. The woods by the sides of the road were too silent; no birds sang in the canopy of trees arching above her, and the *clip-clop* of her pony's hooves sounded too loud in the space around her.

"Hello?" she called out in Japanese. She held her pistol tight in her hand.

A small rustle sounded, and two men emerged from behind two trees on either side of the road. They wore rough kimonos tucked up to reveal dirty sandaled feet, and their eyes were shadowed by the bandannas tied over their foreheads.

Anna swallowed. They approached with a menacing swagger and long knives in their hands. She suppressed the fright and the shiver that went up her spine, and tried to turn the pony back up the road. Her pony halted and snorted with suspicion instead, and she groaned with frustration. Digging her heels in its sides and shaking the reins did nothing to make it move.

"A foreign woman!" cried one of the bandits. "She will have money on her, I am sure."

Anna swallowed and kicked the pony again. It did nothing but snort and rear a little, almost unseating her. "I have nothing of worth," she said in Japanese. "Let me be."

"Oh, ho!" said the other bandit. "She speaks our language." He nudged the other man with his elbow. "If she has not much money, as she says, let's sell her to the whoremaster."

Fear choked her. They were not dragons as Sato-san feared, but worse. *Stupid!* She should have hired someone to accompany her, for even though a stout peasant might not be proof against a dragon, he might have been of some help against bandits.

She held up her pistol. "Stop! If you try to harm me, I will shoot you."

The men paused, then laughed, coming closer. "You have but one weapon, and there are two of us. We will take our chances."

She swallowed and eyed the distance between the men and herself. She could shoot one of them, but she'd have to prime and reload the pistol before she could shoot the other, and he'd be upon her before she could finish. But she was quick, and could jump from the pony and run to gain herself time and distance. How far, for how long, she was not sure, but she had not much choice, since the pony refused to move and just cropped grass. The men continued to advance.

She aimed at one of the men and pulled the pistol's trigger. At the loud explosion, she jumped from the pony, still clutching the pistol as her feet hit the ground. Ignoring a loud rip as her dress caught on the saddle, she ran just as the two bandits charged at her.

Running up the road she had just traveled, she was glad she had eaten and rested well at Sato-san's farmhouse. But the bandits must also have been well fed and rested; a glance behind her showed them gaining on her, and she was not sure whether she would find help before the bandits caught up. She noted with satisfaction that her aim had been true; blood ran between one man's fingers as he clutched his shoulder and ran after her.

She glanced to her left and right—woods, and it might be possible to escape the men there. The *slap-slap* of their sandals against the ground grew louder. Her breath came harder; she did not know how much longer she could run.

A flash of light caught her attention—the sun glinted on water some distance away—a stream or a pool. The image of the dragon came to her mind, and she veered toward the water.

Foolishness! she thought. It was not her dragon's pond, only a stream that fed into a small pool, and shallow at that. But at least she could go across it, and perhaps if she were lucky, she'd not slip and the men would fall behind.

They did not. As she ran she looked for some kind of weapon besides her pistol. She was tiring quickly, and if she had to stop, at least she could fight. The stream had large rocks lining each bank. *Good,* she thought. Rocks might cause some damage to these bandits, if she threw them hard enough.

She stooped to gather some as she crossed the stream—shallow, but filled with treacherously slick stones and moss. She was almost across now, but the bandits' splashing behind her sounded too close. She turned and with as much strength as she could muster, threw the pistol and the rocks she had at them.

"Ai!" The pistol's stock hit one man neatly on the forehead.

"Bakayaro! Idiot! Don't get in my way—ow!" A rock hit the other near his eye.

Anna grinned fiercely and turned to run again, but pain lanced through her instep, and she gasped, falling, her hands crashing through the ferns that hid the rock on which she'd twisted her foot. A triumphant laugh sounded behind her, and hands grasped her skirts. *Please,* she thought, closing her eyes tightly. *Someone help me.*

A loud, terrified cry sounded from one of the bandits. A harsh *swish* sliced the air behind her, and another cry was cut off midscream. Then silence.

She waited, closing her eyes even tighter. There was only the sound of her own shaking breath hissing from between her clenched teeth as she huddled amongst the ferns. Anna pushed herself up, looking cautiously around, then moaned when she caught sight of what had become of the bandits.

She'd seen enough death, illnesses and surgeries when she'd worked at her father's side not to feel ill, but such an execution . . . her stomach clenched and she felt queasy. Anna looked away and tried to get her bearings.

She almost missed seeing him, for a soft mist had risen from the forest floor, dappling the light and shadow that played amongst the slender birch branches and green leaves fluttering upon them. His form almost blended with the arching trees, and his black, white, and forest green kimono seemed to shift beneath the beams of light filtering through the branches.

Only the red that gleamed on the edge of his sword stood out stark in his surroundings.

"You killed them!" she cried, shuddering.

The samurai raised his brows in clear puzzlement.

"You killed them," Anna repeated, this time in Japanese.

The puzzled expression did not disappear. *"Hai,"* the samurai said. "I think that is obvious." His expression changed to one of surprise. "Did you not want me to stop them?"

"Yes—no—that is, surely you could have done it without killing them." Anna rose to her feet and brushed off as much dirt from her dress as she could, while averting her eyes from the erstwhile bandits.

"I recognized them: They are known criminals and would have done worse to you," he said. He stepped out of the trees' shadows, and in one smooth motion, wiped the blood from his blade and returned it to its scabbard.

She looked up at him then and could not help staring for a long moment before remembering her manners and bowing low. He was taller than most Japanese men, and his face was lean rather than broad. His well-sculpted cheekbones looked as severe as his high-arched nose, his straight dark eyebrows that swept upward to his temples, and pulled-back hair, black as a crow's wing, looked equally as severe. She had imagined him a part of the forest when she'd first spied him, and the impression did not dissipate, for his movements were lithe and sinuous. His appearance reminded her of the descriptions of the elfinkind in her mother's English nursery tales: otherworldly and dangerous.

She glanced at him again and bowed in acknowledgment. "You are right, but I am sure I would have outrun them." She glanced at the sun—she would need to hurry now, for the sun was at its zenith, and if she wished to reach Imari before it became dark, she should leave now. She turned away from him.

"Oh, ouch! Oh, dear—" She gasped and bit her lip as pain shot through her foot.

"If you had not hurt your foot," the samurai concluded for her. Anna felt a spurt of annoyance at the amusement in his voice, and the blush that rose in her cheeks.

But he was not looking at her in return, for he had gone to the edge of the stream and was washing his hands, presumably of the blood from the bandits, she thought, shuddering. He stood and shook the water from his hands. "You are far from Nagasaki. I am surprised you were not accosted before."

"My parents were given permission by your emperor to travel as far as Saga and Imari."

The samurai raised his brows, but bowed in acknowledgment. "You have been much honored," he said. "Only a few foreigners have been allowed such a privilege. To what town were you traveling? Arita? Imari?"

"Imari," she replied. "But if I must, Arita, if I cannot get to Imari before sunset."

He nodded at her foot. "You will have to stop at Arita—and at whatever village you may encounter on the way. You will not be able to travel far on that foot."

She lifted her chin but bit back a groan when her foot began to pound. It was a sprain, at the very least, and she would have to bind it soon to keep it from swelling more than it had already, and to keep it stable. "I have a pony," she said, but even she could tell her voice did not sound confident.

"You will still not reach Imari by sunset," he said. He looked at her for a long moment and then sighed. "I will take you to your pony, and then accompany you to the next village or farmhouse." He shook his head. "You should have agreed to let Sato-san's village headman find a guard for you. If you had, I would not have had to stay at a distance from you."

"You followed me!" Mixed embarrassment and relief momentarily scattered her thoughts, and then with a deep breath, she said, "I did not ask for, nor can I afford, a guard."

The samurai raised his brows. "Was that why you refused an escort? *Honto,* had you offered payment to anyone assigned to guard you, it would have been declined as an insult, for it is the ruling *daimyo*'s duty to ensure travelers are guarded on their travels." He looked at her curiously. "Were your parents not guarded when they traveled?"

Anna bit her lower lip before replying—she felt such a fool! "They were occasionally, but they never told me anything about the details. I assumed they paid for the service." She lifted her chin again. "I believed I could manage quite well by myself, and so I did—"

The samurai gave a disbelieving snort. "As I witnessed only moments ago."

"I would have, if . . . if . . ." She shrugged. "I see no profit standing and talking to you when I could be on my way to Imari."

"Arita," he said. "You will not make it to Imari before dark." His voice became sympathetic. "It is brave of you to continue with an injured foot but, *honto ni,* it is not practical." He stepped toward her and held out his hand.

I do not want anyone's help, a stubborn, frightened part of her insisted. But her step backward only made her stumble and cry out in pain.

His hand shot out and grasped her arm before she could fall, and pulled her upright. She stared at him again, for his face changed from grim solemnity to mischievousness, so that he seemed more elfin than ever.

"Are all foreigners so stubborn and clumsy?" he said, grinning.

She pulled away. "I am not clumsy," she said haughtily.

"Stubborn, though?" He still smiled, and she could not resist smiling in return.

"We Dutch are known to be so, and I have heard the English are, as well. Since I am both Dutch and English, I suppose I have twice the stubbornness of anyone else."

He laughed and bowed. "I see. But I hope you are not so stubborn as to refuse assistance?"

Anna paused and gazed at him again. He seemed genial enough, but she caught sight of the bandits again and shuddered. He was pleasant enough now, but he had spared not one thought of the two bodies not far from them while they had conversed.

Neither have you, an accusing voice said in her mind. She pressed her lips together. Well, she was thinking of them now.

She pointed to the bandits' bodies. "Should you not do something about the—them first?"

The samurai's brows rose. "I have already done something about them. They are now dead, as they deserve."

Such arrogance! But then the lords of the land—the *daimyos*—and the samurai who served them had absolute say over every aspect of their people's lives. She should expect no other attitude from them. Anna almost stamped her foot, but the pulsing pain in it gave her pause. But the bodies—it was not right to treat them as if they were nothing. She crossed her arms and then frowned. "You cannot just leave them there!"

He crossed his arms, as well, and she could not help thinking he did so to look more imposing than he already was. "There is no reason for me to do anything about them, and to try would be impractical." He jerked his head toward her foot. "What would be more useful would be to take you back to your pony and then to the nearest farmhouse or inn to tend to your foot." He looked her up and down. "And your clothes and hair. They are quite torn and dirty."

Her hand flew to her hair, and she could not help trying to dust off her skirt in a self-conscious way. But she collected herself and put her hands behind her back in defiance.

Which quickly wilted. Her practical self made her sigh and nod, albeit reluctantly. "I suppose you are right. It is not as if either of us could bury them or carry them away anywhere." She eyed the samurai sternly. "But you *will* send someone to take the bodies away?"

"Of course," he said. "I cannot have them fouling the place, so close to the stream where our people drink."

Well, he had a sense of responsibility for the people under his *daimyo*'s rule, at least, she thought. "Very well, let us go," she said. "The sooner we leave, the sooner I can splint my foot to keep it from swelling."

But a step forward made her realize her foot was more badly injured than she had supposed, for she was only able to hobble a few inches at a time. The samurai shook his head, looked about for a moment, and then pointed to a fallen log. "Sit. As you said, it should be bound up."

Anna had thought the same thing earlier, so she hobbled to the log and sat, even though her first—admittedly impractical—impulse was to refuse.

The samurai knelt, and she gasped when he took out a long, sharp knife from its scabbard tucked in the sash around his waist. She gave another gasp as he cut a long strip of cloth from her skirt, and stared at him in outrage.

"How dare you!" she said. "You have ruined my dress!"

He took her foot in his hand, and she sucked in a pained breath. "Your dress is ruined already," he said.

"And taking a strip of cloth from *my* clothes would paint a disreputable picture of me, and reduce the trust in my clan. Any villager would assume the bandits had succeeded in attacking me, as well. Now tell me how to care for your foot. I will do so, and then we will be on our way."

Anna said nothing for a moment, then sighed, showing him how her foot was to be wrapped so as to keep it immobile. His hands were warm and soothing, she thought, and very deft for one who was clearly a warrior instead of a healer.

"Would it be so bad for you to be the least bit untidy?" she could not help saying. Even after his fight with the bandits, he still looked quite tidy.

He cast her a pitying look as he let down her foot again. "I do not expect a foreigner to understand." But he smiled suddenly, and the laughter in his eyes stopped her from blurting angry words. "No one will know anything about bandits when we enter the their village. All they will see is a young woman whose clothes are torn and a mess, and a man whose clothes are also in disarray. *Honto,* they will not be thinking of bandits at all, but of something very different."

Anna blushed and looked away. "I understand," she said. She picked up her now sodden shoe and tried to put it on, but it would not fit over the bandages on her foot. She bit her lip against the pain, then she heard a sigh from the samurai.

"You won't be able to walk at all to the pony," he said, and she shrieked as he scooped her up in his arms, as easily as if she were a leaf instead of a sturdily built Dutchwoman.

"What are you doing? This is hardly proper! We have not even been introduced!" Irritation flared; her words were ineffectual against his strength, especially since he simply walked back to the stream, navigated it easily, and continued up the other side toward the road. He even managed, she noted, to pick up her pistol and return it to her on the way.

"You are right," he said. "We have not been properly introduced. I am Nakagawa Toshiro, of the Nakagawa clan."

She let out an aggravated breath at the amusement in his voice, and at how her face flamed hot again. But there was no place to hide her blushes except against the fine silk of Master Nakagawa's kimono, and she could not deny the truth of what people would think if both of them were dirtied. At the very least, she wished to maintain some of her dignity.

"I am ... pleased to meet you, Nakagawa-sama," she said with as much control over her temper as possible. "My name is Anna Vanderzee, daughter of Hendrick Vanderzee, professor and doctor of medicine." She could not help feeling pride and a little sadness when she said her father's name.

"Your father is a *sensei*," Nakagawa-sama said. "That is an honorable profession."

"Was," she replied. "He and my mother died some days ago."

"You have no other family?"

"No. I do not," she said, pressing down her sorrow. For a moment she thought his arms tightened around her, but then the trees thinned out in front of them, and with a few steps, they were on the road to Imari again.

The pony was still there, cropping grass as if nothing had happened. Anna gave it a disgusted look and then sighed as Nakagawa-sama lifted her onto its back. She gave him a smile and bowed as best she could from her seat.

"Thank you for giving me aid against the bandits, Nakagawa-sama, and for carrying me to my pony. I am conscious of the debt I owe you." She hesitated, for she was aware that now she was under obligation to repay the samurai for saving her life, and the Japanese were strict about honor and repayment. Yet she did not know this man, and a statement of willingness to repay this debt of honor could put her in more trouble than she was in already. She gazed at him, at how he stood at respectful attention as if she were a general and he a mere soldier.

Nakagawa-sama bowed. "It was nothing," he said formally—a ritual reply, she knew, and not a dismissal of her obligation.

"You saved my life and my virtue," she said. "I would be honored to repay you." She looked away, biting her lip. Her words were a farewell, but were also an acknowledgment of debt to which he needed to reply. A quick glance at him revealed an assessing expression, and she felt a tension between them. He could, if he wished, ask anything, from lifelong fealty to the use of her body, and according to the rules of their country, she would be obliged to obey, especially since she had no family in this country to share the obligation or pay the debt.

Unless I find a way to leave this country before he claims the repayment, she thought. Her conscience pricked her; even if this had happened in her own country, she'd be indebted to him.

He is not your countryman; he is a foreigner, not at all like you. Do you truly owe him anything at all? She bit her lip. It was an argument she had heard from other Europeans, and they had acted on it, particularly the Spaniards. She frowned. She would not act like a Spaniard, especially since they had tried to occupy her own country.

The silence stretched thin between them, then the samurai bowed. "I will accompany you to Arita, and then to Imari."

Anna sucked in a dismayed breath. "You put me under more obligation to you," she said. She needed no more ties to this land; she wished to leave as soon as she could.

Nakagawa-sama gave her a sidelong look she could not interpret. *"Hai,"* he agreed. "But my saving of you would be for nothing if you were attacked again along the road, and it is still my duty." He took the pony's reins in his hand, and the contrary animal moved forward obediently—now that there was no threat of bandits, Anna thought bitterly.

She had to admit that traveling with Nakagawa-sama—Sir Toshiro, as such a knight would be known in her own land—was easier than traveling alone. Their appearance in the first village through which they passed gathered a small crowd and pointing children who laughed at her untidiness. But a cool glance from Nakagawa-sama scattered the children, and the gossiping groups of men and women were silenced and melted away.

When they stopped at an inn, the innkeeper gave her a knowing look, even though it disappeared under Nakagawa-sama's glare. Her blushes returned at the speculative glance the innkeeper's wife gave her when the samurai ordered a meal in private quarters, and a kimono to replace her dress.

"No, you cannot—it is not right that you buy me clothing—I will not be further obligated to you," she whispered fiercely once the *shoji* closed after the innkeeper had left a tray of food for them in the room.

His gaze was coolly unconcerned. "You at least owe me obedience in this, Vanderzee-san," he said. "If I wish to feed and clothe you, what concern is that to you?"

"They will think me your . . . your mistress," she hissed. "It is not right."

"What peasants think does not matter," he replied, as he picked up his chopsticks and lifted some noodles from a delicate porcelain bowl. "But if it bothers you, it's better they think that than something worse." He waved a hand in dismissal. "Which they will if you continue to look as you do now."

Anna opened her mouth to protest, but a knock on the *shoji* sounded, and at Nakagawa-sama's acknowledgement, the door opened. The innkeeper's wife entered the room with a neatly folded stack of cloth, which she laid near them, respectfully backed her way out of the room, then slid closed the *shoji* once again.

Nakagawa-sama poked at the cloth with the clean end of the chopsticks. "Adequate, I suppose," he said. A half-suppressed sound of dismay came from behind the *shoji*, and he gave Anna an amused look. "Too bad it is not better. You are a foreigner, but while I am your guard, you are an honored guest of the Nakagawa clan, and daughter of a renowned *sensei,* who was given permission from the emperor in Osaka to travel our lands."

Anna bit her lip and looked away to keep from laughing, as a hastily whispered discussion from behind the *shoji* ensued. It was only a few moments before the innkeeper himself knocked on the sliding door and bowed until his nose nearly met his knees.

"Forgive me, Nakagawa-sama! My silly wife brought the wrong clothes—" An indignant gasp from what must have been his wife sounded behind the screen. "Please accept these instead, too poor for your use, but it is the best we have in our miserable inn." With another bow that put knees and nose to the floor, the innkeeper extended the clothing toward them, and at Nakagawa-sama's nod, Anna moved forward and accepted them.

"You are very kind, innkeeper-san," she said. "I am sure these clothes are excellent, and perfect for me."

The innkeeper bowed to her, and lower to Nakagawa-sama, keeping an anxious eye on both of them.

"You have served as expected," Nakagawa-sama said with a nod, "but you must do better next time." The innkeeper's shoulders relaxed in relief at this formal acceptance. Bowing again, he exited the room, closing the *shoji* firmly, although Anna smiled slightly to note that his footsteps did not go far.

This time Nakagawa-sama moved forward and lifted the cloth with his hand, turning over one piece after another.

"Much better," he said, and smiled at Anna.

"I would have been satisfied by the first set of clothes," she said. "Beggars cannot be choosers, after all."

He looked at her curiously. "You are not a beggar. You are a *sensei*'s daughter, an honored caste."

Anna could not help the sadness in her chuckle. "I am indeed a professor's daughter, but have few funds. I have nothing but my parents' belongings and my own, and so must find work, or else I might indeed become a beggar. With luck, I will save enough funds for passage on a ship, and to buy some goods at Imari, and so set myself up well once I return home."

"Hmph," he said, looking at her contemplatively. "Even so, the first set of clothes was not satisfactory for anyone under the Nakagawa clan's protection." He nodded at the clothes next to their serving trays. "These are better." He glanced at the shoji and smiled slyly. "They are of good quality, in fact."

A relieved sigh sounded from the other side of the wood-and-paper wall, and the *pad-pad* of footsteps told Anna that the innkeeper was on his way to serve his other guests at last.

"That poor man was shaking in his sandals at the thought that you were displeased," Anna said, when she was sure there was no one by.

"As he should have been," the samurai said. "You are to be treated as an honored guest. Anyone who thinks otherwise will know my displeasure." Anna felt sure a Nakagawa's displeasure was more than a simple rebuke. He nodded at the bowls in front of her. "Eat. You need strength to heal as well as travel."

The scents of the food registered on her senses at last, and she realized how weary she truly was, for the food had not pierced her awareness until he spoke of it. The dishes before her in the tray were set precisely so that they looked fit for a still life that even Rubens or Vermeer might wish to paint. A stirred cooked egg lay atop some noodles in a savory broth, and in a separate bowl was some steaming rice. A black-and-red lacquered plate held a mackerel broiled in soy sauce on a fan of green onion. She hesitated ruining the precise picture before her, but the scents came to her nose, and her mouth watered. With a deep sigh, she plunged her chopsticks into the mackerel and popped a piece into her mouth. She managed not to moan at the salty taste, but could not help closing her eyes. It'd been a long time since her meal at the farmer's house.

When she opened her eyes again, Nakagawa-sama was staring at her, a bemused look on his face.

"What is it?" she said, lifting a hand to her chin and wondering if she had spilled any sauce.

"I ..." The samurai paused and then took in a deep breath. "You use the *ohashi* very well," he said at last.

She was almost sure he was going to say something else, but had changed his mind at the last moment. She shrugged. It did not matter. "I learned some years ago, since it seemed useful to do so." She dipped her chopsticks into her bowl. "See? I can even pick up a single grain of rice with them."

"So you can," he said, and once again she heard the amusement in his voice.

He seemed perceptive; though he continued conversing easily and smoothly, he did not ask why she had been traveling alone past Arita. Anyone else would have been curious, she thought, as they finished their meal, bowed to each other, and went their different ways to bathe and then rest for the night. But no doubt her reluctance showed when Nakagawa-sama skirted close to the subject, and so he diverted their conversation to an area less hurtful: her father's work in this land, and the knowledge she herself had of medicine and science.

She appreciated his care in not prying; she felt chagrined at her foolish despair, even though it was understandable. Her heart ached painfully for the loss of her parents, and she was unsure of her future. But she had her life, her knowledge, and her good health, and that was a beginning.

She was being sensible *now,* she thought as she snuggled down under the quilt. She had a task, though a strange one of conveying books to a dragon, and Nakagawa-sama would accompany her to the inn her parents had once occupied. A companion on her journey would be comforting. The samurai had been fierce and alarming, but he would protect her from further assault, and could possibly while away the time in conversation. Her thoughts turned to the dragon; it had also seemed fierce and alarming, but it had done nothing but turn her upside down and request books of her, and had even given her money.

She sighed. It was a strange country, this Japan. She was not sure she liked it as much now that her parents were gone. But as her eyes closed in sleep, a thread of excitement wove its way into her dreams, telling her that perhaps adventure was not to be scorned, even by a practical Dutchwoman.

Chapter 3

A nna didn't mind the trip to Imari the next morning; it was because of Lord Nakagawa's company,
she knew. As she rode the pony, she smoothed the fine
kimono that she wore, clothes befitting one of the es-
teemed scholar class. They felt odd; she was used to
the boned corset she'd worn ever since a child. Instead,
the wide sash—the *obi*—around her middle served to
hold her upright, though it was not as stiff as the corset.
She could breathe and move freely about in it, and she
thought she could become accustomed to it easily. The
blue cloth was very fine, with an intricate flowered pink-
and-green pattern woven into it, and the pink obi con-
trasted beautifully with it. She had not seen the like even
in Amsterdam; she now wore it because of Nakagawa-
sama's generosity. A breeze unloosed her hair from
the bun in which a maid had put it, and Anna frowned.
Nothing could be done about her curly hair that refused
to stay put in the smooth, neat Japanese style.

She glanced at him as he walked by her side. He was
very curious about her country and all that she had seen
of the world as she traveled with her parents to Japan.
He nodded thoughtfully at what she relayed to him
about her homeland, and marveled at what she could
tell him about other countries, as well, although he was
skeptical sometimes.

"A creature whose nose is like an arm, and which
can pick up rocks and even food with it?" He shook his

head. "Surely you are mistaken—unless you are try-ing to make a fool of me." His brows lowered and he frowned in a threatening manner, but she could see the glint of amusement in his eyes.

"No, it is as I say," Anna said, laughing. "They are com-mon in the land of India, and I know I was not mistaken, for I walked all around it, to see if its owner had some-how cleverly attached a false nose over its natural one. But it was very much part of the animal, for I touched it to be sure."

"How I wish I could see such things for myself!" Nakagawa-sama said. He sighed and shook his head.

"Perhaps you can travel to distant lands yourself someday."

He said nothing, and a glance at him revealed a grim look. "It is forbidden." His voice held a note of finality.

She wondered if she had offended him somehow, for he seemed to withdraw into himself. But after a mo-ment, he pointed out a bird she hadn't seen before, and told her of its habits and of local folk tales. Clearly, he did not wish to talk of traveling outside his country. She sighed. Their emperor—or, she suspected, their military ruler, the shogun—disliked foreign influence and did not want samurai leaving for other lands. To disobey meant severe punishment, even death.

The other animals he pointed out, as they passed below green-leaved trees arching above the road, were like those in her land, but colored differently in some ways. Even the fox that looked at them curiously from the side of the road seemed a brighter red than those in her own country. For a moment, the samurai stopped and gazed back at the fox, and she wondered if he would take it for its fur, as many of her own countrymen would. But he merely gave her a quick smile before he turned his attention to the fox and bowed slightly in its direc-tion. The fox gazed back for a moment, and then with a small yip, ran into the forest.

"A friend of yours?" Anna asked, jesting.

Nakagawa-sama smiled. "Yes, of course." But the

smile did not quite reach his eyes, and his bow had been stiff, as if he had given the fox some warning.

Anna nodded but glanced at his now solemn face as they continued down the road. She was not sure the samurai was joking; she remembered Sato-san speaking of the fox kami-sama. She had almost dismissed Sato-san's story, but did not because of her own experience with the dragon. One could not, after all, dismiss a very large dragon. But a fox . . . well, it was a brightly colored one, and she had seen foxes before.

She shook her head and shivered, looking about her at the birch branches above and the mossy rocks to either side of the road, at the occasional veils of mist that arose from the ferns and brush. It seemed as if the curtain between the real world and one beyond the senses was very thin here, and would part if she would put out her hand in the right direction.

Even her noble escort, Nakagawa Toshiro, had appeared silently out of the mist and without warning. A fanciful part of her wondered if he, too, would disappear as easily as he had appeared. She hoped not—not because she fancied him, of course, but because he was necessary to her safety. She glanced at him again. No, he would not leave her until he saw her safely in Imari. She felt sure of that.

And then the road opened into a field bright with sunshine, and the otherworldly feeling dispelled. Field-workers bent over green rice paddies, their kimonos tucked up in their sashes, and when they caught sight of Nakagawa-sama, they stopped their work and bowed. It was an ordinary picture no different from her own land, where peasants would bow to a passing liege lord.

Anna shook her head at herself. One dragon did not mean the rest of the world had become supernatural. Indeed, it was simply a different sort of animal, native to Japan, in the way elephants were native to India, except dragons apparently could learn human things.

And from whom did the dragon learn? Anna shrugged and ignored this annoying thought. The day was too beautiful and her companion too pleasant for such distractions.

When they came to Imari at last, her innkeeper gazed at her in a worried way, and bowed very low to Nakagawa-sama.

She bowed, and could not help the anxiety showing in her voice when she asked, "I know I have been gone for longer than a day. . . . But I hope you have kept my possessions about?"

The innkeeper bowed in return, lower than necessary, and gave a nervous glance at the samurai, who watched him expressionlessly.

"I . . . my great apologies, Vanderzee-san. This is but a poor inn, and we do not always have room, and I was not certain, when you did not return immediately—"

Anna's heart sank. She'd been such a fool! She had no reason to think that the innkeeper would keep her room available for her; she had indeed not intended to return. "I see," she said. "And my belongings?"

The innkeeper bowed low, and another glance at Nakagawa-sama's face made him look even more uncertain. "I had them put away . . . I cannot remember. . . ."

"You *will* remember, innkeeper." The samurai's voice was harsh. "Vanderzee-san is under my protection. You will have her belongings brought to her immediately. She will look them over to ensure all that she owns is present. If they are not, then I will not be . . . pleased."

The innkeeper paled and bowed low, over and over again. "Of course, Nakagawa-sama! No doubt my servants have misplaced them; I never doubted that Vanderzee-san would return. But servants! One can never get good help these days!" The innkeeper bowed again, backing away as he did so, then ran, calling for his servants and scolding each as he found them.

Anna looked at the samurai. "He could not know I would return," she said.

"Did you leave a note saying you would not?"

"No . . ."

"Then he had no right assuming you would not return,

and removing your belongings—if he has not already sold them—was all greediness on his part. He is fortunate you did not accuse him of theft." Anna gazed at him and thought his serene expression no doubt belied his intent if the innkeeper did not return all her goods. Nakagawa-sama would certainly mete out swift punishment if any of her belongings were lost or damaged.

In the hour in which the innkeeper and his servants gathered together her family's belongings, she once again sat with Nakagawa-sama, partaking of tea. He said very little as he sipped his tea, his body tense as he sat on the floor pillow. He had escorted her to Imari, as he had promised, she thought, and now they would part. She wondered if she might see him again. He had been an interesting companion in their journey here, and she had to admit she felt safer while he was at her side.

He stayed only few minutes after the innkeeper had returned and shown her to another room in which he had set out all her family's belongings. She was vastly relieved to find that her father's books had not been discarded; they were valuable in and of themselves, and even more so since she had promised to bring them to the dragon.

She sighed and turned to Nakagawa-sama, giving a respectful bow. "I thank you, sir, for saving my life, and ensuring my well-being. I understand I owe you much, and though I wish to return to my own country—" She bit her lip, knowing how problematic that would be, but continued nevertheless. "I will do what I can to repay you."

The samurai gazed at her for a moment, then sighed. "It was nothing, and my duty to maintain the law as a samurai bound to my lord and the Nakagawa clan." She almost thought he was about to say something else, but he nodded at her foot. "I hope your foot heals well." He hesitated. "If . . . if you find you are in need, send a message to the Nakagawa clan, asking for me, and I will do what I can to aid you."

She shook her head. "You are too kind, and I am under

much obligation to you already. If there is anything I can do for you or your clan, I will use what knowledge and skill I have to help." She smiled. "My expertise is mostly in midwifery, but I have other areas of medical knowledge. But perhaps I may be of service to your wife—"

He bowed, stiffly this time, and his face looked a little grim. "I am to be wed next week, if all goes well. If you continue to live in our country, perhaps I will call upon you for your services someday."

Anna dismissed the sinking feeling at finding that he was to be married. It was no concern of hers, except where it might give an opportunity to repay him. She bowed and smiled. "Many blessings and congratulations on your upcoming marriage, Nakagawa-sama. If your future wife, or any lady of your clan, will need a midwife, I would be pleased to be of assistance."

"I will let you know." With a last bow, he left the room silently, and the room was empty except for her and her belongings. She stared at the doorway where he had been and shook her head. Nakagawa-sama had not seemed happy when he mentioned his upcoming wedding, and had amended his words with *if all goes well.* She wondered how it might not; he was a handsome man of an aristocratic and clearly wealthy family. He was also an amusing companion, as she had experienced. She could not imagine any young Japanese lady refusing to be married to him. Or perhaps he was to be married to someone he disliked. But then why would he have said "if all goes well"?

She shrugged. It mattered not. As with all aristocrats even in her own country, the bride and groom had little say over who they might marry, for these were political alliances and not made for love. She was lucky that she was only of the gentry, instead of an aristocrat. She could have a say in who she married, when it came time for her parents to choose a prospective groom. . . .

But her parents were not alive to do this, and she was far from anyone who might act as a parent and introduce her to an eligible gentleman of her own country.

The thought tore at her, and her heart constricted with pain; with the death of her parents, even that option was closed to her.

She hugged herself, looking at her father's trunk, at various crates and boxes that held his clothes, her mother's and her own clothes. The daylight was dimming now, and she could see the flicker of the inn servants' lamps as they passed by to light the torches outside the inn and the lamps within each room. She gazed down at the kimono that Nakagawa-sama had procured for her. She could wear her own Dutch clothes now, and now that her mother . . . Anna swallowed desolate tears, determined not to give in to more weeping. Her mother's clothes were hers now, and with some alteration, she could wear them. She was handy with a needle, and it was fortunate she was similar in form to her mother, so very little sewing would be needed.

She opened the trunk that held her and her mother's clothes, and began to lift them out. The scent of lavender wafted up, and she could not help pressing her face into the bodice of her mother's fine wool dress. It also smelled of the particular rose scent her mother often wore.

Tears rose past Anna's resolution to be done with grieving, and she could not help the huge sobs that wracked her body. The comfort of her mother was available no longer, and neither was her father's warm guidance.

The sorrow she'd held at bay while her parents' bodies were buried, while she stayed at the Satos' farmhouse, and while she traveled with Nakagawa-sama now tore at her, made worse because she was alone and would have no comfort now from anyone.

After a while she grew aware of the silence around her and blushed. She'd been noisy in her grief, and it was clear the servants and those around her had left to give her privacy. . . . Or to get away from the noise.

Anna wiped her eyes with the back of her hands and brushed at the tearstains on her mother's dress. She would probably weep again over her loss, but for now she needed to find work to support herself. She had one gold coin left, aside from the one she was reserving for passage home, enough to maintain herself for a while. In that time, she could sell to the dragon what books of her father's that the creature deemed valuable, and save more, especially if she made good investments.

She closed the trunk, not wishing to change into her Dutch clothes just yet. *I will save them for my journey to Amsterdam,* she thought. She did not know how long it would take to save enough money for a ship's passage, and it would not do to have worn or torn clothes. She could hardly appear in a kimono in Amsterdam, after all! And it would profit her more to remain in a kimono while she tried to find work, for acceptance of the Japanese's ways would make them regard her kindly. She looked around the room. The work of putting everything in its place would soothe her, she knew.

By the time she was done, she had all her belongings in order, and the books she would bring to the dragon set aside. She gazed at the books with mixed regret and anticipation. Such books were costly, but she could not think of that now. Instead, she thought of the dragon— seeming more illusionary now that she was so far from it—and shook her head in wonder. Four years ago, she had thought coming to Japan an adventure; she never knew it would turn her whole world on its head.

Nakagawa Toshiro, of the noble Nakagawa clan, moved from the hall next to Vanderzee-san's room. He'd heard her grief, and was sure it was over the loss of her parents. Disturbed to find he had turned back to comfort her, he stopped himself. Instead, he glared at an approaching servant, who scuttled away in alarm, and the lack of other servants near the young woman's room told him that the servant had correctly assumed he had wanted no one to impose on her privacy.

For all that she was a foreigner, she was a sensible,

even strong young woman; she had ceased her weeping after a few minutes, and he could hear her move trunks and boxes within her room. She had been brave when confronting and fighting the bandits in the woods, as well.

Nakagawa-sama moved silently away from the room, and out into the busy street. He frowned as he made his way back to the road to Arita. He should not have let himself become involved with such a woman. But he could not help feeling curious about her. He had seen foreigners from time to time, but most of them had dark hair, similar to his own. She, however, not only had hair that curled like the dancing waves of water in a rocky stream, but it was the color of gold with a cast of red, very much like the coins he had in his coffers. He wondered if it would feel soft, or if it would feel as stiff as gold threads. He shook his head at himself. Curiosity was a part of his nature: He could not help wondering about the strange and the different, and what wonders occurred beyond his native seas.

He sighed. He would see her again; he often had business in Imari, and she had things to sell, which meant she would need to travel. For now, however, he would go home, for the marriage his uncle had arranged for him would occur in a few days.

He could not help feeling resentful at the thought. The girl chosen for him was a silly thing who was accomplished in all the suitable wifely skills, but if she had more than half a brain, he was not aware of it. However, she was of a good family, and he could not be too particular. This was the second marriage his uncle had arranged for him; with luck, this bride would be too stupid to do anything but acquiesce to it.

Nakagawa-sama frowned, then shrugged. What was it Vanderzee-san had said? That beggars could not be choosers? He was hardly a beggar, but in the matter of marriage, he felt almost as if he had not much more choice than one.

The sun was half below the horizon by the time he

reached the edge of town, and soon the woods surrounded him. He sighed, for he felt more comfortable in the woods than in the city, and looking about him for the path that would lead him home, stepped from the road, and faded into the trees.

Chapter 4

Much to her relief, Anna found that her foot was not broken but sprained. Still, it was frustrating: If she wished to heal properly, she would have to stay off it and elevate it as much as possible. However, two weeks had passed and much money was spent in that time, and her injured foot made the search for work difficult. Few thought a limping woman—especially a foreign one—would be an effective doctor.

She fingered the two coins she had transferred to one of her necklaces. She had planned to sell her pony so as to raise additional money for her passage. While her foot was still healing, however, the pony was of great help in traveling about the town, and would hasten her journey back to the dragon. For now, it made sense to keep it. She frowned in frustration. What was she to do?

Letting out a sigh, she turned to the collection of books she had shelved in a cabinet at the corner of her room. She'd avoided returning to the dragon for as long as she thought she could.

She thought of her last trip to and from the pool not far from Arita, and she shivered. Though she did not want to encroach on the samurai's generous offer of help, she knew she would be safer having an escort, considering what she had experienced. She sighed. She certainly could not afford another assault, sprain or worse.

Anna brought out a piece of rice paper, ink and a brush. She had learned a few characters of their language, enough to spell out their words in syllables, and hoped that her rendition would be legible. She had made herself learn the characters, even though she hoped to leave this country soon; she did not want to spend more money having someone else scribe her words. Besides, she thought, it might come in handy someday, should she want to return to Japan.

The idea had crept into her in the last few weeks, yet another option for her life. She was not sure her reputation would survive a trip back to her own country to the point where she could marry respectably and practice her trained profession, regardless of how well she guarded her virtue. Like it or not, she had to face that fact. But if she were well chaperoned, she could possibly act as interpreter to merchant shipmen and earn her keep that way. And ships were ever in need of those who understood the healing arts.

However, a handsome fortune could overcome a lack of perceived virtue. If the dragon gave her even one gold coin for the books she would bring, she could use the money to buy Japanese wares, and then sell them in Amsterdam. There were porcelain and fine silks to be bought here, which would fetch more than three times the money she spent. If she could find passage for herself and her goods, she could amass a tidy fortune and live well on it. These thoughts heartened Anna as she quickly wrote out a request for escort, waited for the ink to dry and then folded it.

A maid came at her call and bowed as she accepted the folded note. The girl's eyes widened when Anna gave her instructions on where it was to go, and bowed again, lower, when Anna gave her some copper coins from her purse. She smiled wryly as she watched the maid hurry away. It was obvious that the Nakagawa clan had influence even in the city.

She furrowed her brow, thinking of it. The *daimyos* and samurai had the strict obedience of the people wherever they went, but she could see that Nakagawa-sama had a slightly different effect. He seemed always of good nature those times she had glimpsed him walking or riding through the streets of Imari, but people seemed to keep a farther distance from him than they did the other samurai. It was not that he was cruel or unkind at all. Indeed, she had seen him snatch a small peasant child from beneath the wheels of an oncoming cart, and soothe the child's weeping until he returned her to her mother's and father's arms. She knew not all aristocrats would care about the life of a lowly peasant. And yet the parents had taken the child from him with fear in their eyes, and had trembled as they fell to their knees in a bow, begging forgiveness for the child's unruly behavior and their own thoughtlessness. Clearly, they thought they would be punished.

But he had merely told them to be more careful, and gave them a few copper coins before turning away. Anna had seen the encounter while standing at a potter's stall in the market, and had seen a look of . . . well, the closest she could think it might be was loss on his face. As if he had wished the peasants had not been so afraid of him. Anna had stepped forward to greet him, but he had already turned away and disappeared like mist into the busy crowd. She wondered why he would care about the attitude of a peasant, when no other samurai would.

She shook her head at the memory and went to the cabinet that held her father's books and began to select what subjects she thought the dragon might be interested in, and bound them with twine. Pain tugged at her heart when she pulled the books down from the shelves; selling these books felt like parting with dear friends. It would not hurt to look them over again, just a little. . . .

A light tapping made her start, and hastily she put aside the book she was reading. She slid open the *shoji* door.

"Oh!" She could not help staring at Nakagawa-sama, for it was he and not his servant.

His brows rose. "Did you not expect to see me?"

"I . . . I did send a note," she said. "But I expected a servant for escort."

The samurai waved a dismissing hand. "I was in town,

and am returning to my family's house today, so it is nothing for me to escort you." He looked her up and down, and a hint of a smile tugged at one corner of his lips. "I see you have bought another kimono."

Anna felt a mix of gladness and frustration; confusion followed on their heels. She had no reason to be glad at his presence, for a servant would have done just as well, and her reaction annoyed her. More reasonable was her frustration: She would have to be rid of him before she went to the dragon. The samurai would no doubt feel obliged to challenge the dragon, even fight it, as he had with the bandits. Who would not think such a dragon would be a danger to her? She could not afford obstacles to her trade with it; it was the only way she could quickly raise the money for passage back to her country.

And then he had noticed that she had bought another kimono. It was of pink silk and had flowers embroidered at the hem and edges of the sleeves—not of the finest, but it suited her station in life as a scholar's daughter. It had pleased her that he had noticed, but it shouldn't have; he was married by now, and it was wrong to encourage his attentions. The difference in their stations must discourage anything more than a friendship.

Yet she had no choice but to travel with him and accept his escort. To refuse, especially after she had accepted it but weeks ago, would be an insult, and her parents had emphasized the importance of adhering to the strict decorum of the Japanese. She would figure out what to do when the time came. She bowed. "I am pleased to see you again, Nakagawa-sama. Please wait while I gather up my belongings."

He nodded and stood at attention by the doorway. "I will need to know your destination, Vanderzee-san."

She noticed how he stumbled a little on her name; he had said it carefully and slowly the last time he had traveled with her. She smiled at him as she chose two more books to take with her to the dragon. "You may call me Anna, Nakagawa-sama. It is my given name, but in my country a woman may allow a man to use her given name if he is respectful about it."

He bowed. "I am honored, Anna-san."

"It is easier to say, is it not?" She grinned.

"Indeed." An amused look appeared in his eyes. "But I still need to know your destination—for your own safety. I will send a courier ahead to notify the prefecture guards along the way that we will be traveling on their route, especially if I determine there is a shorter route than is usually used."

She suspected he knew she was trying to avoid telling him her final destination. "I will be going not far from the village where you left to follow me. It is near the Satos' farm." She hoped this was all the information he required.

He raised his eyebrows, obviously wishing to know more.

"There is a . . . scholar who lives in the woods nearby. He wishes to buy my father's books so that he can study them." She blushed at her near lie, and hoped he thought she was embarrassed to admit she had to sell her belongings to survive.

He bowed in acknowledgment. "As you wish," he said. She sighed in relief at his apparent acceptance of her explanation, and hurried to gather the books and her belongings.

The ride to the village near the Satos' farm did not last long at all compared with her journey many weeks ago. Nakagawa-sama knew a shorter road than she had traveled before, and this time neither a recalcitrant pony nor bandits hampered her. Instead, she and the samurai conversed as if the span of time since they last met had not gone by at all, and talked of more important things than identifying animals in the woods.

The news of the Tokugawa Ieyasu Shogun's actions was always of import; the English Anjin-sama still held a high position with the military ruler, and for now the English and the Dutch were allowed to trade and move about fairly freely, even though the Portuguese still tried to conspire against them. Her parents had not told her of this land's politics, and she had not been that interested, for she had been not more than fifteen years of age when they had arrived in Japan. Instead, she'd been interested in the colorful silk clothes, the different plants and animals, and, of course, she had focused on her studies. They had emphasized the importance of learning the strict and intricate protocols as well as the language. It had not been difficult to learn; she had an ability to pick up languages quickly, and her rote memorization was excellent.

She did know enough to avoid the Portuguese, however. They saw Protestants as heretics, and would be glad to see her gone, along with other Dutch and the English. She frowned. Truth to tell, her own people could be ruthless, as she had seen on her voyage to this land.

"Is there something the matter?"

She blinked at the samurai and then realized she had grown silent. "My pardon, sir. I was thinking of our different peoples, and thinking of our . . . natures, I suppose. When I return to my country, I will need a chaperone on my voyage." She scowled. "I am of marriageable age, you see. Young women are allowed to travel short distances alone in my country, or with a maid for longer ones, but traveling across oceans, without family . . . it would call my virtue in question, even if my fellow shipmates were all gentlemen—which sailors usually are not." She looked away for a moment. "I would again be in danger. But if I had a stout chaperone or guard of some sort, and if I could gather enough goods to trade once I returned, I could still find myself a husband, or establish myself in a respectable trade."

"Is this your wish?" They passed from under the trees into a clearing, where the sun felt very warm, and Nakagawa-sama brought out a fan, which he waved lazily in the air in front of him as he rode.

Anna hesitated, and also took out her own fan—a lovely confection of delicately carved sandalwood sticks and painted silk that she bought as soon as she saw it—

and waved it in front of her face, partly to conceal her own surprise at her hesitation. She thought of the bustling streets of Amsterdam, and the fields of grain and grass, and then her mind turned to the equally bustling streets of Imari. The two seemed to blur in her mind, and suddenly she felt unsure.

"Yes, of course," she said at last, in spite of her uncertainty. "Who would not want to be with their own people?"

Nakagawa-sama said nothing, but closed his fan with an irritated snap, and rode ahead for a little while. Had she said something wrong? She gazed at him sitting in his saddle; for a moment his shoulders sank before he sat straight as a board once again. It was not long, however, before he seemed to regain his good humor, and rode by her side again, engaging in trivial chitchat about the emperor's court. Anna strove to be attentive, for as he talked, an air of loneliness seemed to cover him, and it pained her that he who had been kind to her should feel so.

Even so, she could not help mulling over the two cultures. In some ways, she would have more freedom in her country; she could find work and perhaps marry. Here, work was difficult to find, and she was certain no Japanese would wish to marry her. *Your countrymen are here, as well, and you are the only Dutch woman, for that matter. Anyone would think of you as a wife.*

Yet she had not seen them as potential husbands. The thought shocked her. Why hadn't she? She looked at Nakagawa-sama, at his clean-shaven face, well-styled hair, and his neat clothing.

As they rode, it became clear to her: Her countrymen who lived and traded here were . . . uncouth compared to Nakagawa-sama. She thought of her last three weeks in Imari, and remembered she had avoided the Dutchmen and Englishmen who appeared there. She had even come close to one Dutchman—a tall man with hair as blond as her own—and had moved swiftly away. He hadn't noticed her, for she had worn her kimono and a broad, conical hat to shade her from the sun. He probably thought she was yet another gently born Japanese woman, for her hair and face had been totally hidden from him.

The faint, clean scent of sandalwood wafted in the air; it came from the samurai who rode next to her. She took in a quick, despairing breath. It was the Dutchman's smell that had made her walk quickly away—it had repulsed her. He was no doubt new to the country; he had not adopted the Japanese custom of bathing daily, as she had, and his clothes had been rimed with salty sweat and dirt. Remembering it made her feel momentarily ill. But she and her parents had not bathed as the Japanese did before they came to this land. It had not seemed unpleasant then. She'd become used to the customs of this land.

"Is there something the matter?"

Anna blinked, and discovered that her pony had stopped while she was lost in thought. She shook her head and put a smile on her face. "No, no, it was nothing. An unpleasant thought—of little worth, so I shall not bother you with it."

He bowed slightly in acknowledgment, though she could tell he was still curious.

She smiled. "I was thinking of the long journey ahead of me—on the ship, when I return to my country." She sighed. "It will not be pleasant."

"How so?"

Her smile became rueful. "There are storms, and months where you do not see land or are not able to leave the boat. And ..." She paused only a heartbeat before she said, "One must learn to defend oneself from pirates." The memory of the dirty conditions upon a sailing ship struck her suddenly, but she put it aside. She did not want to think about that right now.

"Tell me what it is like," Nakagawa-sama said.

"Often boring," she said. "But I will tell you of pirates, and how we defended ourselves, for that is far less dull."

Barbary pirates had assailed their ship, and these

were the most vicious around. She told him how the crew had blessed themselves for bringing a large store of ammunition and weapons, and how they had used cannon and musket to keep all but one pirate from invading the depths of the ship. Even she had been given a pistol and dagger, and had been taught how to use them. She'd kept both the dagger and pistol, for her parents had learned how truly dangerous far lands and seas could be.

"And the one pirate? What happened to him?" Nakagawa-sama's voice sounded just a little breathless, and she smiled to think she told the story well.

"My mother shot him," she said. "He had managed to sneak down into the cabins, and when he came into our room, she had her pistol ready for him."

"Ahhh." The samurai let out a satisfied sigh. "Your mother was a brave woman. I can see you inherited her courage."

A blush of pleasure warmed her face, but she shook her head. "You are too kind. Now that I look upon my actions in your land, I have been more ignorant and foolish than brave."

"*Honto,*" he said, and the mischievousness in his grin took the sting away from his agreement. "But foolish or not, it is better to be brave than a coward, and if ignorant, one can always learn."

She could not deny his words, so she thanked him again, and then looked up as the trees parted to reveal the Sato farm in the distance and the small road that led to their house.

They rode quickly past the farm, though Anna wished she could stop to chat with the Satos. Perhaps she could visit them for a bit on the way back. The thought lifted her heart. She liked the Satos, and the farm wife in particular. She realized that she did not know the woman's given name; she would remedy it when she passed this way again. It would be good to have a friend here.

If you were going to stay. The thought came unbidden to her, and it surprised her. She had, for a short while, forgotten that she meant to return to her own country. She had thought instead of cultivating friends.

She glanced at the samurai who continued silently at her side, and the idea of friendship fluttered up to her attention again. He would be a good friend, she thought. He was amusing, intelligent, and did not seem to think less of her for being a foreigner. But no, she could not think of that; she was to leave soon. Besides, to form a friendship with a married man—he must be so by this time—was not appropriate. She frowned slightly. If he were so recently married, why was he here, escorting her? She glanced at him, at the good humor in his face, and did not want to disturb the moment between them. She would ask him later, she thought.

Her thoughts disturbed her to the point where she almost missed the path off the side of the road that would lead her to the dragon's pond. Shaking her head, she stopped her pony.

"I must part from you here, Nakagawa-sama," she said. "The . . . scholar is very solitary, a hermit, in fact, and would be disturbed by more than my presence." She slipped off her pony and unlaced the packages of books she had tied on her saddle.

The samurai descended from his horse. "It is my duty to accompany you, for these woods—as you know!—are not safe. How far into the woods is this hermit?" His manner became cool and professional; Anna imagined this was his usual manner when he was formally guarding.

"It is but a few moments away," she said. "It is not necessary for you to accompany me."

"A few moments can bring great harm," he said sternly. "Remember how close the bandits were to hurting you. Indeed, you *were* hurt."

Her foot twinged at the memory. "I remember," she said. "But I also respect the . . . hermit's wishes for privacy." She looked away and down the path that led to the dragon's pond, vexed at her own lie. But it was necessary. She did not want a confrontation between the dragon and Nakagawa-sama.

Yet it *was* a dragon. For all that it had not harmed her, and, in fact, saved her from drowning, she did not know what such creatures would do if vexed or displeased. She suspected that since the dragon had long, sharp claws and large, sharp teeth, it could be quite terrible if it were angry.

She looked at the samurai, whose face and stance did not look as if he would back down. She sighed. Truly, she would not mind his protection should the dragon turn vicious.

She sighed again, this time in resignation. "Very well. It is not precisely a scholar or a hermit. But I was not injured when I first met . . . it. In fact, it saved my life." She smiled. "As you did. You may watch if you feel it is your duty. I beg you, however, that you keep yourself well hidden and make no noise. I do not know how the creature will react if it knows I have company."

"The creature," the samurai repeated, but bowed in assent. "Very well." He unsheathed his sword. "I will be silent and keep hidden, since you ask." She swallowed nervously, seeing the weapon, but turned and walked resolutely down the path.

He was true to his word. Anna looked behind her to see if Nakagawa-sama followed her, for she did not hear his footsteps and his clothes did not disturb the bushes nor the ferns on either side of him. One more glance behind her as she approached the cliff above the dragon's pond froze her in her steps, for the samurai had disappeared, with only one fern leaf moving to show that he had been there at all. She let out a sigh. Of course. He'd promised he would hide himself.

She reached the small cliff at last, and careful to stay far enough away from the edge so that she would not slip and fall into the pond, she looked about for the dragon.

The grove was empty. The stream fell from the cliff she stood on to the pond below, burbling happily. The leaves of the trees stirred around her, but it was not from great wings that whooshed from above, but from a simple summer breeze. She frowned. Had she imagined it after all? Her frown became an embarrassed wince. She supposed it would not hurt to call for it, she thought, even if she felt silly doing so.

"Ryu-sama!" she called. "Honorable dragon! I am here with my books, as I promised."

A strong wind caught her, blowing awry her hair, and she stepped back from its force so she would not fall. She looked up, pushing stray strands of hair from her face, and managed to choke down a shriek. She had not imagined it after all.

Sunlight glinted off golden scales and sleek, strong wings. The dragon let out a breath—warm as it touched her cheek—and the fine wisps of fur around its chin and down its body fluttered in the wind as it circled down to the pond.

Anna cast a hasty and warning glance behind her as the dragon floated down to the ground. She did not want Nakagawa-sama to appear and challenge the dragon, no matter how surprising its presence. Nothing moved from the trees or the bushes behind her—good. It seemed he trusted her to handle this herself, and her heart warmed at his confidence in her.

"I have brought the books I promised you," Anna said, when the dragon was finished settling itself on the ground.

It looked up at her and inclined its head. "Bring them down," it said.

Anna looked over the cliff. It seemed higher up than she remembered, and there were not the footholds she thought had been there.

"It will take me a while," she said. "The way down is difficult, and I do not want to damage the books."

"You are right," the dragon replied. "I will carry you down." And his claw came up and clasped her around her waist.

Anna clenched her teeth together, although she could not help her voice squeaking when she said, "Thank you, honored dragon, for saving me the time and the untidiness that climbing down would have cost me." She hoped Nakagawa-sama heard her, so that he would not dash out to fight the dragon. A relieved breath escaped her when he did not, although a breeze suddenly scurried through the ferns a little to the right of the path to the waterfall cliff. She remembered stories of the stealth of the samurai; no doubt he hid his movements with the movement of the wind through the forest.

"Show me the books," the dragon said.

Anna quickly untied the packages she had brought and laid them down on the wrappings, so that the moist ground would not damage the books. "Here is a dictionary that translates Japanese words to English and Dutch, and back again," she said. "There is also a book of mathematics, and one that has pictures of foreign animals." She touched the books tenderly; the last was one her mother had illustrated, and had hoped to publish when they returned to Amsterdam. Anna had hoped to keep it so as to publish it for her. . . . But it was one of the few books she was convinced a dragon might like.

"Ahhh." The dragon's sigh definitely sounded happy. It reached down a huge claw, and with surprising delicacy opened the cover of her mother's book and looked at the first page, then turned each page slowly. It looked over each picture, and its breath came out in puffs that sounded very much like a chuckle. "Very good," it said after a few moments. "It shows animals I have only glimpsed, and some I may never see."

Anna gazed at the dragon's huge wings, now folded behind it. "But . . . can you not fly and see them for yourself?"

The dragon looked at her, its head coming down to peer at her with one eye. She swallowed and managed to stand where she was. "It is difficult," it said. It moved away again to gaze at the book. It clicked its claws together, steepling the tips contemplatively. "I lose one claw for each ten—what is the word in your language?" She picked up the dictionary and held it aloft. Quickly it leafed through the pages. "Yes, ten leagues I travel from the shores of my native land. As a result, I have difficulty acquiring those things far away from my home."

So it would not follow her should she decide to leave Japan, she thought with relief. *When* she left Japan, she corrected herself. Pity stirred in her heart. The dragon sounded wistful, as if it dearly wished for adventure, and the knowledge that the world could bring it. It must be difficult to be crippled when so desperately searching for knowledge.

"I have traveled far," Anna said. "Across half the world. I could tell you a bit, if you wish." She cursed herself as soon as the words left her lips. Nakagawa-sama was waiting in the woods, and she did not want to take advantage of his patience. "But only for a few minutes; I must begin to travel soon, or else I will not arrive home before dark."

The dragon bowed its head, and she told it some tales she had told Nakagawa-sama when they traveled to Imari. It nodded when she was finished, and thanked her politely.

"Please bind up the books so that I may carry them," it said. "It would not do to leave them here where it is damp." She did so, and the dragon dropped a gold coin next to her. Her heart lifted when she picked it up. It was a great deal of money, and more than what she had expected, for the dragon had already given her three gold coins in advance.

"Many thanks for your generosity," she said, and bowed deeply. "I would be glad to be of service again."

The dragon looked at her curiously as it took up the books by the strings with which she'd bound them. "Would you? Are you not frightened of me?"

Anna looked at it, at how it loomed over her. It was very large, and, yes, frightening. But ... she was not frightened of it as much as she was when she first met it.

She shook her head. "A little at first," she said. "But I do not think you mean me harm."

The dragon showed its teeth in a grin. "Your trust honors me, and I hope we might be friends. I promise, I shall never harm or allow harm to come to you as long as you are in Japan."

Anna returned the bow. "Your friendship honors me." She *was* honored, she realized. It was a great, powerful creature, and she knew no one who could claim to be friends with a dragon. It let out a long sigh, and she gazed at the creature curiously. If it had been human, she would have thought it sounded forlorn.

"Is there something the matter, Ryu-sama?" she asked.

It shook its head slowly. "No . . . or rather, I wish others were as brave as you."

It *had* been a forlorn sound. "Surely you have friends, other dragons—?" she asked. It fluttered its wings, a frustrated movement, she thought.

"There are other dragons, but we are few in number, and rarely meet." It held up a five-clawed forefoot. "Our movements are restricted, and I do not relish losing claws; if you ever see a dragon with fewer than five claws, it is because he is far from home. Fewer claws make it difficult to hold things, turn the pages of foreign books or unroll scrolls. And those who are not dragons—except for humans—do not understand the need for books or learning."

"So . . . there is no one to converse with about the books," Anna said slowly.

"Hai," said the dragon.

As she watched as the creature touched the books she had put before it with a reverent claw, her fear of it drifted away. How could she fear a creature of such reason and intelligence, and who cared for books and learning as deeply as she did? She understood exactly how it was not to have anyone with whom to discuss new ideas, or marvel over something just read or newly discovered. She was in the same position herself. Her heart melted, and she stepped forward and patted the dragon's claw in a comforting manner. "I understand," she said. "It becomes lonely without a companion who does not understand one's thoughts or interests."

The dragon drew back a little as if startled at her sympathy. "Are you, then, lonely?"

She winced; she had revealed more of her feelings than she had wished. But she nodded nevertheless. "I am a Dutchwoman in a foreign land, where even my countrymen would find my interests ... not the usual feminine interests."

Again a discontent arose within her. The truth was, even if by chance she stayed here in Japan, she could conceivably find someone with whom to talk—Nakagawa-sama, for example. Her mind leapt to the conversation she'd had with the samurai: Even as the dragon was prohibited from leaving its home because of the loss of its claws, so was the samurai because of the restrictions of Japan's ruler. The dragon had even fewer options, for who would wish to talk to such a ferocious-looking thing? Or even think to do so? It must have hundreds of tales to tell of its life and habits, and yet no one would know of them because of the natural fear of such a creature.

But home. What about going home? The thought arose as she found herself slipping toward the edge of staying here in this country. She could not, of course. She had already purchased goods to sell in the Netherlands, and she did not want to lose her investment. It was best if she left soon. She put aside her newborn regret and wistfulness, and draped practicality over her emotions again.

She looked up at the cliff from which she had come down. It would take a bit of time to climb it, and she did not wish to dirty her kimono. She gazed at the dragon again uncertainly, then banished her nervousness. It would take care to put her safely up on the cliff, she was certain.

Anna bowed to the dragon. "I need to return to the inn at Imari. May I impose on you to please set me up on the cliff again? I don't wish to look untidy on my return home."

The dragon grinned again. "Of course," it said, and she held her breath as it picked her up and set her safely up above the waterfall. This time, she felt only a little nervous, and she was glad that she showed none of it.

"Thank you," she said. "If you wish for any more books while I am still in Japan, please let me know...." Her brow wrinkled. How would the dragon let her know? Its appearance in Imari would cause a great deal of disturbance. "Is there a way you might send a message to me?"

The dragon looked at her for a moment. "There is." Two claws came up and clipped at one of the tufts of red fur on the side of its jaw. A few strands floated down, and the dragon caught it deftly with the tip of one claw. It extended the wisps of fur to her. "Take these," the dragon said. "If you wish to call upon me, hold them in your hand and ask for me, and then I will either send a messenger or I will come myself."

The fur was as soft as silk, she thought, as she took it and tucked it into one sleeve of her kimono. "Thank you, Ryu-kami-sama. I will keep it safe, I promise you."

The dragon bowed in return, but the movement was hesitant. "Must you leave?" it asked. "I have enjoyed your stories, and then there are the books—perhaps, before you leave Japan, we could discuss them.... If you will not be leaving immediately?"

Again Anna felt pulled between practicality and sympathy. She would indeed like to converse longer with the dragon, but she had to leave to prepare for her journey to the Netherlands. In addition, Nakagawa-sama was waiting above in the woods beyond the cliff's edge. She could not keep him waiting forever.

"Please forgive me, Ryu-sama," she said formally. "But I have a companion who is waiting for me most patiently so that we can travel back to Imari. I would not like to return his generous protection with ungrateful delay."

The dragon let out a hot puff of breath, which if it had come from a human would have sounded like definite frustration. But it bowed again. "Very well," it said. "I will be contented with what books you may wish to send me—or bring to me." The last few words held a note of wistfulness, which tore a small hole in Anna's heart.

"I will try my best," she said. The words almost stuck in her throat. Truly, the dragon was a gentle-minded creature, and she hated to hurt it in any way.

"Thank you," the dragon said, and then with a rush of wings, flew up and away from sight.

Anna gazed at the creature until it was not much more than the size of her little finger, and then turned away. She sighed, and the thought came to her that perhaps she was being a fool; a dragon was a marvelous thing, and to refuse to learn of it was not at all scholarly. But irritation at herself arose again. She had determined her course, and she would travel it. To do otherwise was impractical.

She had one more gold coin. It would be enough to buy some wares—silk, certainly, and then some of the delicate porcelain from Arita and Imari, as well as some fine cedarwood boxes in which to put these purchases. It'd be enough to go back to Amsterdam, especially if she agreed to give a percentage of her profits to whatever sea merchant gave her passage. She'd have to find a companion, and it would mean she would have to find one amongst the very poor, for few else would leave this land.

She walked along the path a few steps, and then jumped, startled, for Nakagawa-sama suddenly appeared beside her. "I wish you would give me notice when you appear," she said, irritated. "You startled me, popping up like that."

"I did not pop," Nakagawa-sama said. "Samurai do not pop. It would be undignified."

She frowned. "Very well, you did not pop. But you did startle me."

He gave an acknowledging nod, but grinned. "My apologies. It is my training to walk silently." He gazed at her for a long moment. "So, it was not a hermit, but a dragon."

Anna sighed. "I did not want to deceive you," she said. "I was not sure what you would do if you were confronted by a dragon, and I was not sure what the dragon would do if it saw you, especially since I did not tell it you'd be here."

"You were not afraid of it?"

She smiled a little. "I was, but it did not harm me the first time I met it, and only asked for books. It is an intelligent creature, and was gentle when it picked me up. So I believed it would not harm me."

"Most women would be frightened into screaming if they saw a dragon." His voice was admiring, and she blushed.

"It would have done no good to scream and act in a silly way. I might even have annoyed it, and then it might have eaten me out of annoyance." She chuckled. "I am not certain I would have blamed it if it had. People who scream when no harm is offered them would annoy me, too."

The samurai burst out laughing. "Indeed," he said.

"Besides," she said. "It offered me friendship."

His brows rose. "You would be friends with a dragon?"

"Why not?" she said. The thought settled into her, oddly comfortable, after she said it—why not indeed? "It is very large and fierce-looking, and I imagine it would be a good friend, especially if I ever found myself in trouble."

"You are fortunate; it is a golden dragon, and so a king among them." The samurai bowed slightly. "You are very brave indeed, Anna-san."

She shook her head and denied it in the formal Japanese manner, but warmth flowed into her heart at his words. She smiled at him as he lifted her onto her pony, and for a moment she was conscious of the warmth of his gaze and the strength of his hand on her waist as he looked up at her.

He is no doubt married, she reminded herself. She turned away resolutely, then thanked him as she took up the reins.

She reminded herself again when they arrived in Imari,

late in the afternoon. As Nakagawa-sama escorted her
to the inn's entrance, she smiled at him. "Thank you for
your escort," she said. "And for your understanding." She
hesitated as she gazed at him, wondering if he wished
for refreshment, and wondering if her offer was wholly
unselfish. But the words rushed out of her: "Would you
care for some tea?" she said.

Nakagawa-sama bowed slightly. "No, but I thank you.
I need to return to my family."

His wife, Anna thought. "Very well." She made herself smile. "Give my good wishes to your wife," she said.
*There, I have said it, and know that anything more than
a cordial acquaintance is impossible. . . . And that is a
sneaky way of finding out if he is indeed married, isn't it?*
she told herself.

His brows rose. "I am not, unfortunately, married."

"Oh!" Anna blushed, more from guilt at her con-
versational manipulation than at her faux pas. But
she did so much want to know. "I—I am sorry! I
thought you had mentioned— Please pardon my error,
Nakagawa-sama."

"I did mention it," the samurai said. "But the arrangement did not go as planned."

She blushed even more and looked away, confused
about how to respond. "I hope . . . the bride and her family will reconsider such an honorable offer," she said.

"I do not," he said, and there was a hint of laughter
in his voice.

She looked at him, startled, and then pressed her
hands to her cheeks, for they flamed hotter than ever.
He looked at her with kindness and warmth, and his
hand for one moment had extended out to her before
dropping properly by his side.

It was impossible, Anna thought. There could be no
alliance between them, no proper one, except friendship. They came from different lands and people, and
even if that were not an obstacle, certainly their stations
in life were. Pain twisted in her heart, and she realized
she wished they could be in a closer relationship.

"You have been very kind," Anna said, and could not help the trembling in her voice. She cleared her throat and squared her shoulders. "I . . . the dragon has been generous, also, and I now have enough to pay for passage to my own land. If . . . if I could ask you one more thing: to escort me to a Dutch ship in two weeks." It would take that long, she thought, to select her wares, pack them, and find a merchant ship to transport her.

Silence stretched between them, and when she dared look at him, he had returned to his professional formal stance again. "Of course," he said, his voice neutral. "But . . . did I not recall that you promised the dragon more books?"

Anna gnawed at her lip in indecision. "It is true." She sighed, remembering the strands of fur the dragon had given her. "I will not go against my word. I will see what books might please it, and see that they are transported to his lair."

The samurai bowed in acknowledgment. "Very well. A good evening to you, Anna-san." He mounted his horse once again.

Anna watched him guide the horse through the busy street, then turned back to the inn and to her room. There she took out the gold coin she'd been given, and then the strands of dragon fur. Carefully, she tucked the coin into her purse, and then considered the red strands in her hands.

They were as soft as feathers and fine as silk. It was a wonder that the dragon did not have matted fur because of its fineness, she thought. She twined them around her fingers and then began to braid them. She would make a bracelet of it, and put it around her wrist. That way, she'd not lose them, and would have them handy should she ever need the dragon's help.

She smiled to herself. It would be a memento, she thought, for she doubted she'd need the dragon's services. Even if she did need help, she might still have to defend herself, anyway, for there was a limit to how far the dragon could travel.

It came to her that it would be nice to have something of Nakagawa-sama to remember, but she shook her head at herself. There was no chance of such a thing, and to wish otherwise was useless. She would be gone from Japan in a few weeks, and that was that.

Chapter 5

Two weeks later, Anna faced the Dutch ship *De Voortman* with unease. It was a worthy enough ship, and its crew had a good reputation as hardy men and good in a storm or a fight. But the captain had seemed too eager to have her aboard as a passenger, and it was her experience—or at least, it had been that of her parents—that women were not welcome aboard ship, especially on a long journey. But the *De Voortman*'s captain had been the only one who hadn't leered at her or rejected her outright.

She glanced at Nakagawa-sama, who stood in formal guard stance at her side. She'd sent a message asking for escort to the docks of Nagasaki, and again he arrived, instead of someone else. The laborers she had hired were now carrying her goods of silk and fine Arita porcelain to the docks and then aboard the ship. She had also remembered to purchase a box of sandalwood and painted silk fans. Surely the fans' delicate and refined beauty would attract and sell well to the noblewomen of her own country. The samurai had looked over these purchases and nodded. "I will escort you myself; these are valuable, and it would be a pity if bandits attacked you on the way to Nagasaki." He then ordered the cargo to be loaded on a Japanese barque, rowed around the coast to Nagasaki harbor, and then unloaded onto the city docks, accompanied by a contingent of lesser samurai under Nakagawa's command.

She had hired a beggar girl—Miyoko—to accompany her on her long journey. The girl was perhaps in her teens, and had a scar across one cheek that made her unmarriageable, and she had fallen to begging. Anna had taken her away to the inn, given her a bath, and bought her a few good cotton kimonos to wear. The girl had been so grateful that she had scarcely stopped bowing since her bath. Miyoko-san also stood at Anna's side—away from Nakagawa-sama, for she was very frightened of such a high-caste samurai, but tried to show courage for her fate by staring at the sailing ship with determination.

The wind shifted and brought the sour smells of the docks to Anna, and she could not help wrinkling her nose. She took out her fan and waved it before her face, but it did little good. She glanced at the samurai beside her and caught a fleeting expression of disgust on his face before it became smooth and polite.

He looked at her, and for a moment Anna thought indecision showed in his eyes before he said, "Are you certain you wish to leave . . . Japan?"

As she looked at him, she knew she did not. Indeed, she wished to stay, to see him every day, now that she knew that this was the last she'd see of him. But it was too late: The porters had already loaded her cargo onto the ship. She needed only to board it, and then she would be gone. She turned to her maid and gestured toward the ship. "Go, Miyoko, and prepare my room. I will follow shortly." The girl bowed, and with a deep, resolute breath, walked up the gangplank.

Anna lowered her eyes, then gazed at the ship before her, feeling that she might weep if she looked at the samurai. "Truthfully, I am not certain, Nakagawa-sama," she blurted. Taking a deep breath—how stupid she'd been to blurt out her thoughts like that—she looked at him firmly. "That is, it is a long journey and dangerous. But it will be more difficult for me to live here than it would be in Holland. I cannot find respectable work here. I can live in the inn for only so long before I will have to find somewhere else to live, and I do not want to live as a beggar or a ... a prostitute. So I fear I have no other choice."

"You might stay with me," Nakagawa-sama said.

She gasped and looked at him, her heart pounding hard. He did not look at her, but pink colored his cheeks as he stared straight ahead at the ship before them.

Silence fell as Anna tried to gather her scattered thoughts. Finally, she swallowed and said, "You do me great honor, Nakagawa-sama; I am surprised and overwhelmed by your generosity. But would not your family question your friendship with me? If you gave me work to do, would they not suspect that you intend something else?"

A frustrated expression crossed his face. "It is not only friendship I offer, and not work," he said in a rush, stumbling over his words. He pressed his lips together and frowned, clearly frustrated at himself. "That is, I would offer you security, you would be well cared for...."

Anna bit her lip, then let out a sigh. "I am sorry, Nakagawa-sama. No matter how illustrious the man who offered, it would dishonor my family if I became a man's concubine, whether he was a man of my own country or one of Japan."

"Not a concubine," he said.

She stared at him. "Not a concubine, more than a friend, and not work? Are you asking me ..." *Surely not,* she thought. *Surely not.*

"To be my wife," he said stiffly, not looking at her.

She closed her eyes. *Oh, if only it were as simple as that,* she thought. She stared at the *De Voortman* rising and falling in the water before her. She was already materially invested in the journey, and could establish herself well in Holland. Here in Japan, she was an outsider. What Nakagawa-sama proposed ... her heart twisted in pain. She would like to be his wife, for she loved him. He would care for her, and he listened to her with respect; rare in her land and in his own. She wasn't sure she would find such a man in either country.

"Why?" was all she could ask.

He looked at her then and said simply, "Because I've come to love you."

She put her hand to her lips, pressing down confused words. It was not customary for a man such as he to say this; it was a concession to her own customs. Finally, the beating of her heart slowed, and she drew in a deep breath.

"I am very honored, Nakagawa-sama, and I wish it could be so. But both of us know such an alliance is unequal at best. You are a samurai and son of the noble Nakagawa clan, and can only marry a woman of your own class. I may be of good family, but I am a foreigner and not of the nobility, even in my own land. Your family would object, and rightly so. I do not wish to cause trouble for your family."

She pressed her lips together to keep down her sorrow. It would be best if she left now, before her heart broke from thinking too much. She turned to him and gazed at him for a long moment. Quickly, she tiptoed and kissed his cheek, then ran to the ship and up the gangplank.

She let herself look at him once she was on the deck. He stood there, a surprised look on his face, his hand on his cheek where she had kissed him. With a last wave, she turned away.

There. That is the end, and I shall never see him again. The words brought a lump to her throat, but she had done enough weeping for the past month. She needed to see to her maid and to her belongings below in the cabin.

Again the sense of unease came over her as she walked to the door that led down to the room the captain had assigned her. The sailors working the ropes and the decks looked at her, and then their gazes slipped away as she nodded to them. She caught sight of the captain issuing orders to the men. When he turned and bowed to her, she made a short wobbling curtsy, clumsy because of the sudden dip of the ship as it moved away from the dock, and because she had almost bowed in the

Japanese way before she remembered that she was traveling to Holland, now dressed as a Dutchwoman, and must act like one.

As she descended from the deck to her cabin below, she almost gagged. Pitch and tar assailed her nose, and the smell of once-rotted goods, and underneath, the smell of chamber pots not yet emptied. Dismay came over her; she had forgotten the conditions on board ship—oh, not the dangers of the sea, for those stood out in her mind in her travels with her parents. But the smells and the dirt—she hoped she and especially Miyoko would not become ill from it. For all that the girl had been a beggar, the Japanese were not brought up in such dirt, and might be more susceptible to it than a European might.

Anna swallowed bile as more stench came to her nose. She was not sure she could stand it herself, and was almost wishing herself back on the shores of Nagasaki, by Nakagawa-sama's side.

Stop! She said to herself as a well of sadness within her threatened to overflow. *You are returning to Holland, and there is no turning back.* She succeeded in stemming the tears she felt; she'd stopped them so often lately that she was sure she was an expert at it now, she thought bitterly.

She came to the door of the cabin to which the captain had given her the direction, and hesitated. It was strangely quiet within; she expected there would be some bustling sounds inside, since she had directed Miyoko to tidy the room for her. She put her hand on the door and pushed it open. . . .

To find Miyoko on the cot, mouth muffled and hands tied. Shock froze Anna for a moment before she rushed forward. "Dear heaven!" she cried. Dread rose as she pulled at the knots around Miyoko's wrists.

The ship rose steeply and fell, almost unbalancing Anna, but it was nothing compared to the fear that threatened to freeze her limbs. Remembering the dagger tucked in the sash around her waist, she let out an impatient breath at herself and cut the ropes. "What happened?" she asked the girl.

"I ... the captain ... I thought ... he tied me and then ..."

Anna closed her eyes, feeling ill. "Did he touch you aside from tying you up?" she asked.

Miyoko shook her head. "No, because I bit him, and then he tied me up and said he would have use for me. . . ." She gave Anna a frightened, trapped look. "And for you."

Anna mentally cursed herself. She should have looked more extensively for a ship and not settled for one whose captain seemed genial enough. But there had been so few, and this was the only one that had agreed to take her as a passenger. She searched the room for her pistol—there, it was still in her trunk, under her petticoats, and she quickly primed the weapon. She smiled grimly. No doubt the captain did not think a woman would have a pistol, much less know how to use one.

She looked at Miyoko and thought it would be well if she, too, had a way to defend herself. She took the girl's hand and put the haft of the dagger in it.

"Do you know how to use this?" Anna said. The girl nodded slowly. "And I don't mean to kill yourself; I mean using it on anyone who tries to harm you. You will not commit *seppuku*, do you understand? This is to be used to defend yourself."

Miyoko grinned. "Yes, Vanderzee-san, I will use it to defend myself."

Anna let out a sigh of relief. "Very good. Now walk behind me, and beware!"

She moved cautiously to the door of the cabin, and carefully looked around the threshold. A shadow shifted to her right, and she swung around to level her pistol at it, but a hard hand caught her arm and she dropped the pistol as she was shoved against the wall. She leaned her face away as the fetid breath washed over her. It was the captain, of course.

Anger and fear made her struggle, but a slap dizzied

her, and she half sank to her knees. "Did you truly think I'd agree to have a woman aboard without more than you offered me in goods?" the captain said. He pressed himself against her, and she gagged with disgust.

"I thought you might be an honorable man, sir, and keep your word." *Miyoko,* she thought, *where are you?*

Her pistol lay on the floor, not far from where they stood. If the captain could be distracted, she might be able to struggle away and get it. With luck, the gunpowder hadn't dislodged when she dropped it. The captain's face came closer, and she turned her face away again.

Suddenly, he jerked and let out a cry, falling limp to the floor. Miyoko stared at her, and then at the captain; the dagger Anna had given her was stained with blood, and the maid's eyes were wide with fear. She looked at Anna. "Vanderzee-san, this is a bad ship with a bad captain. We cannot stay here."

"You are right," Anna said. "And I am sorry to have brought us here." She looked at the captain—blood oozed from his back, and though he still breathed, she did not know if he would live or die. Regardless, there were still the sailors and the ship's first mate to contend with. Anna closed her eyes in guilt and shame. She had assumed that because she traveled safely with her parents, she could do the same on her own, and her grief for her parents had had urged her on to return to her family's homeland. But she had made a stupid and dangerous mistake.

She and Miyoko had to escape the ship; surely the threat of the crew was worse than drowning in the open sea. She turned to Miyoko. "Help me take the captain into our cabin," she said. "I do not know if he will live or die, but regardless, it will keep questions at bay until we can find a way to escape this ship." She paused. "Can you swim?"

Miyoko nodded. "*Hai,* and very well, too."

"Good. Come with me."

They dragged the captain into the cabin, and Miyoko thoughtfully cleaned up the blood that had dripped onto the floor. No one would slip on it or discover it and so alert the crew to what she and Anna had done.

Anna picked up her pistol and tucked it in the sash around her bodice, then brought out a shawl to cover her shoulders and also conceal the weapon. Miyoko cleaned off the dagger and tucked it in her obi, well hidden by her kimono sleeve. They made sure that the door to their cabin was locked from the outside, and hoped that the captain was disabled enough that he would not make a disturbance.

Something soft rubbed against Anna's wrist—it was the bracelet she had made with the dragon's fur. *Will it work?* she thought hopefully. Would the dragon hear her now that they were already under way? She wound the dragon-fur bracelet around her fingers and held it tight as she and Miyoko climbed up to the deck. *Please let this work,* she thought. *Please.*

A brisk wind and bright sun momentarily blinded her as she came up out of the darkness of belowdecks, but she quickly recovered and looked around. The sailors were still occupied adjusting the sails, but it seemed they were well under way now and their activity had slowed. She looked down at Miyoko and nodded. "Come up, it's all right . . . so far."

Once Miyoko found her feet on the deck, they walked swiftly aft, Anna with her shawl crossed tightly around her shoulders so that she could hold on to the pistol tucked into her sash.

There Anna leaned against the railing and stared at the horizon. She could still see the thin faint line of islands that marked the port of Nagasaki. Her heart sank. How would he hear her above the whistling wind and the distance between the ship and the shores of Japan?

She took a deep breath. "Nakagawa-sama—" She stopped, shaking her head. Stupid! She was to call the dragon, not the samurai. She'd become used to thinking of Nakagawa-sama as her guard, and so his was the first name to come to her lips.

She shook her head and tried again. "Dragon-kami-sama!" she said. "Honorable dragon! Help me and my maid, Miyoko. Take us from this ship where our lives are threatened. The captain of this ship has tried to harm us, and we need protection."

The wind continued to whistle past her ears, tangling her hair and whipping her skirts about her ankles. She strained to discern any change in the horizon, any movement that would indicate a dragon's flight.

There was nothing but the wind and the waves. She could not expect the dragon to appear immediately, she told herself. It would take some time to hear and to fly to the ship.

She glanced at Miyoko, who held her hand to her brow as she peered out at the sea. The maid's shoulders slumped.

"I do not think it is much use to appeal to the kami-sama," Miyoko said. "They are fickle, and do not always do as they are asked."

Anna cast a glance behind her. The sailors continued their work, only glancing at them occasionally.

"What shall we do?" the maid asked.

Anna gazed at the sea behind the ship, dark between the froth stirred up by the ship's wake. She had heard one could float if one did not struggle in the water. She hoped she would not panic once she reached the water, and had enough sense to do what she had to do to survive.

Anna gave Miyoko a reassuring smile. "I am sure the dragon-kami-sama will come, but it will take a while, for we have traveled far already from Japan."

Miyoko looked dubious. "And if it does not?" she asked.

Anna swallowed before she said lightly, "Then we shall have to jump and swim the best we can to land." And she would do her best to survive, for she realized her survival meant Miyoko's, as well. If Anna died and Miyoko managed to reach land alive, then Miyoko would be bound by the custom of her country to commit *seppuku* for failing to keep Anna alive—even if there was no way she could do so.

Miyoko nodded. "I can swim well, so I shall not fail you," she said, nodding her head with determination.

"Good," Anna said, and thought it best not to let her know that she herself could not swim well at all.

A few more moments passed as they gazed out at sea, and still nothing appeared on the horizon but a thin line of clouds. Anna glanced behind her. Still the seamen worked, and it seemed no one thought the absence of the captain remarkable . . . yet. Her hands dripped sweat, even though the wind had picked up and pierced through her shawl. She glanced at Miyoko, who hugged herself and shivered.

The captain's body would be discovered soon, Anna thought, and she strained to see Japan. The now distant land was becoming a thin line rather than an undulating form on the horizon. The air continued to cool and the clouds above thickened and rolled toward them. The ship pitched suddenly, and Anna and Miyoko grasped the railing that separated them from the sea below. She noticed the crew's worried glances at the sky. *A storm,* Anna thought with dread. *If the dragon does not appear, then it will not matter whether the ship's crew discovered the captain; if the storm is strong enough, the ship could founder and sink.*

Lightning flashed and thunder boomed but a heartbeat afterward. A shout sounded against the scurrying wind, and Anna looked toward it.

The first mate was at the belowdecks door, pointing downward and shouting at the men. Her heart pounded hard as anxiety filled her throat.

They'd found the captain.

Anna turned aft, quickly checking her pistol. It was still primed. She glanced at Miyoko, who had moved her hand to the dagger tucked in her obi. Clearly, the maid was ready to defend herself and Anna. Anna took in a deep breath. She had but one shot, for it would take more than a minute to reload and prime the pistol after firing, so she had to do her best to hold off the crew until the dragon came.

The ship began to pitch and roll wildly now; the wind swirled around them furiously, and rain hit the deck with an angry rush. The first mate strode forward, his men behind him.

"You and your Nipponese girl here tried to steal from our captain," he said.

"You are wrong," Anna said, pushing back wet, straggling strands of hair from her face. "It was the captain who tried to thieve from me, and when we resisted, he gave us violence."

The first mate sneered at her. "My own eyes have seen the captain dead as a herring." Anna's stomach twisted with nausea. There was no real concern in his eyes; clearly the man cared not for his captain or for the truth. He took a step closer.

Please hurry, dragon, Anna pleaded mentally as she pulled out her pistol. "I'll be pleased if you'll keep your distance," she said.

The first mate laughed nastily. "Do you think I'm afraid of that?"

Anna stared at him, anger steadying her hand. "You should be," she said. "I've used it before."

Her answer made him pause, and he held up both his hands. "Well, little miss, you don't want to be holding a dangerous thing like that, do you? Give it up, and we'll deal well with each other."

His answer only made her anger flare more. "But I *like* dangerous things like this," she said. "Especially when I might have a chance at causing such scoundrels as you and your captain some damage." If she could keep him talking, it might buy her time, she thought. . . . If the dragon came at all.

"You wouldn't want to do that, would you?" the first mate said, his voice clearly wheedling. He eyed the pistol with deep unease, which made Anna smile.

"Yes, I would," she said, and was surprised to feel fiercely cheerful at the thought. "A great deal. I would like to see your bloody carcass shot through and your soul in hell, in fact." The first mate looked more uncomfortable than ever, and Anna could not help feeling glad. She felt a nudge to her side.

"Should we not jump and swim?" Miyoko asked.

Anna barely kept herself from shuddering. "Not yet," she said. "I'm trying to keep them at bay until the dragon-kami-sama comes."

"Forgive me, but I doubt it will work for long," Miyoko said. "There are many of them, and only two of us." The ship heaved again as if to emphasize the maid's words.

"You have but one pistol and one shot, miss," the first mate said. "You can shoot, but the rest of us will certainly capture you then."

Too true, Anna thought, biting back a grimace. She put a smile on her face instead. "But which one wishes to be the one who dies?"

The men behind the first mate looked uneasy, and some stepped back a bit.

The wind and rain blew against Anna so hard, it seemed needles pricked her face. Lightning flashed again and thunder sounded with it, almost as one. She jumped and nearly lost hold of her pistol. The first mate leapt for her, and fear made her hand tighten on the trigger.

A loud report sounded, and the first mate screamed. But as Anna backed away, she could see she had hit his shoulder, not his chest. He might live from such a wound.

And she could not prime it now, not before the rest of the men came for her. She grasped the pistol by the barrel, glad that the stock was heavy and had a metal ball at the end. At the very least, she could cause some damage with it if she hit someone.

"It is too late to jump, I think," Miyoko said. "It has become too stormy."

"Then we shall fight," Anna said. Her maid nodded and brought out her dagger.

The ship heaved again, but the first mate looked about him before gazing at her again, sneering. "Witch! I'll have you, girl, now that you've spent your ammunition, and make sure you're burned at the stake at the next port." He turned, shouting to the sailors behind him. "Get the sails in order. Jan, Dirk, Jean—I think we can handle these females now."

Witch. Anna shuddered. First used and then burned. She glanced at the sea beside her; the storm had turned it dark and swirling. Surely she and Miyoko would be sucked into its depths.

A hand reached out for her, and she struck at the first mate with her pistol. A hoarse cry beside her proved that Miyoko had made her dagger known. She swung with her pistol, but she knew she could not keep it up for long. Her dress dragged her down with its rain-wet weight and hampered her movements. A glance to her side showed that even Miyoko faltered for a moment before slashing out with her dagger.

A sudden glancing blow caught her jaw and she staggered, her pistol clattering to the deck. Rough hands caught her, and though she could hear Miyoko still fighting, she knew the girl would be caught, as well. She closed her eyes, clasping the dragon's fur bracelet once again.

"Nakagawa-sama! Dragon-kami-sama! Mother! Father!" she cried, desperation making her call out the names that had meant the most to her in the last few years; the words were pleading, her last hope.

A roar sounded, half-obscured by the wind and rain, and then once again, louder. The sailors' cries mingled with the shriek of the wind and boom of thunder. She opened her eyes.

The dragon arose from the waves of the sea as if it were a part of it, curling up around and over the side of the ship until it flowed onto the deck toward Anna, Miyoko and the men who still held them. A sharp prickle pressed against her throat.

"Tell your creature to leave, or I'll slit your throat." The first mate's voice shook with fear, but he held firm.

"I cannot," she said. "I have no control over it except to call it."

"Liar," the man said. He pressed his knife a little closer to her neck.

"Dragon-kami-sama! I ask you not to attack, for this man would do harm to my maid and myself."

The dragon paused its advance toward them. "This man deserves to die—as do those who helped him."

Anna swallowed. "Yes, of course, but you see he would kill me before you got to him."

The dragon bowed its head a little. "Very well, what would you have me do?"

Anna looked at it, thinking swiftly; it seemed very obedient for a dragon, and a king of dragons at that—she remembered Nakagawa-sama had said it was a king. And did not Sato-sama say the *kami-sama* changed shape, as well?

The first mate gave her a kick. "Tell it to go away."

"What difference does it make?" she said to him. "You will have me killed, anyway."

"Sooner or later: It's your choice," the man said.

She gazed up at the dragon. "I wish," she said carefully, "that such a frightful dragon as yourself would disappear."

The dragon bowed again. "Very well," it said. And suddenly it was not there.

But Nakagawa-sama was, samurai sword in hand.

Faintness threatened to overcome Anna, but she managed to retain enough wit to elbow the first mate in the gut and knock his knife hand away—his injured side, thank God.

She twisted away, and was glad to see her maid had had the same presence of mind, even though the poor girl must have been not only exhausted but frightened at the sight of the dragon.

The first mate scrabbled at his side for his own sword, but Nakagawa-sama struck, then struck again as the men who had seized the two women ran forward. The samurai swirled, a dance of steel and death as more men attacked him. Anyone would have thought it impossible for one to defeat so many, but the samurai did, with a seemingly lazy elegance.

Anna averted her eyes, going to her shivering maid and holding her around her shoulders. Sharp cries came to her ears, and then silence, only the wind and the shushing of the waves sounding in her ears. She looked up. The clouds had faded to a light gray, and she could see once again the summer sky behind them. What men were left stood back, wary and fearful.

"Bring this ship about," she heard Nakagawa-sama say in Dutch. She swiveled around, staring at him. "And bring it back to Nagasaki. Or you will know my displeasure, and I will do with you as I have done with these ... vermin."

"But the winds, they're in the wrong direction—" the helmsman protested, but was cut off by the samurai's stare.

"I will arrange it to be otherwise," he said, and lifted his hand to the sky. The wind stilled, then began to turn. The sailor backed away and turned to the helm again.

Nakagawa-sama turned to Anna, and she stepped back, almost stumbling over Miyoko, for the maid was crouched in a deep bow, her palms and knees on the deck. "Get up!" she whispered loudly to the girl. "It is only Nakagawa-sama."

Miyoko shook her head. "No, it is the dragon-kami-sama, perhaps even the king of dragons. I dare not."

Anna glanced at Nakagawa-sama, who had a decidedly amused look on his face. "The deck is very dirty, Miyoko-san," she said gently. Surely that would make any cleanliness-conscious Japanese recoil upright.

Miyoko jerked as if to rise, but remained on her knees. "I am very sorry," she said. "But I dare not."

Anna looked at the samurai—dragon—whatever he was. A feeling of misuse arose in her, and irritation threatened to burst into heated words. She pressed her lips together. No, she would not talk to him; she would maintain a dignified silence until they arrived in Nagasaki.

A large grin suddenly appeared on his face, and she could stand it no longer.

"You speak Dutch!" she exclaimed indignantly.

"Dragons learn quickly," Nakagawa-sama said.

She let out a frustrated breath. It was *not* what she wanted to say. "That is, you are a dragon, and a ... a ... well, you are not what you seemed," she said, crossing her arms. She looked down at the maid at her side, still bowed. "And *do* tell my maid she can rise. She is doing no good like that."

Nakagawa-sama's grin grew wider. "Rise, Miyoko-san," he said. The maid glanced cautiously at him and rose, and crept just slightly behind Anna. "You have done well in protecting your mistress," he continued.

Miyoko bowed, blushing. "It ... it is nothing—my duty—I would give my life—" she replied, stumbling over her words.

"You will be well rewarded," he said, and the maid looked almost to faint at the promise of such good fortune. He turned to Anna and held out his hand. "I will take you and your maid back to my home. It is of no use for you to stay here, as I am sure these men will do as I requested." He gazed at them, and a visible shudder came over the men who met his gaze.

But Anna stepped back. "But you are not what you seemed—you deceived me."

A sad look passed over his face. "I did not wish to; I had little choice. Come, let us not talk of it here, but later, when we are on land."

Anna hesitated, but Miyoko spoke up. "Vanderzee-san, I am afraid of the dragon-kami-sama, but I think it would be better to do as he—it—he says. Also, I think a dragon will smell better than this ship does."

Anna hesitated, suspended between irritation at Nakagawa-sama and amusement at Miyoko's words. But she nodded at last. "Very well," she said.

A rush of wind blew against her face, making her blink. The dragon was before her again, and she held her breath as it—he—caught her by her waist. A small squeak sounded from her maid, and she saw Miyoko had also been caught up in the dragon's claws, and that she had her eyes tightly closed.

Her stomach seemed to lodge in her throat when the dragon made a sudden leap into the air, but she swallowed and forced herself to keep her eyes open. She was being held under the dragon, and below her was the sea, sparkling with the setting sun and reflecting the deep blue of the now clear sky. The dragon rose quickly, and soon the ship seemed as small as an acorn floating on water. She held out her arms, feeling the wind whip the hair from her face and her skirts flapping behind her. Except for the warmth of the dragon's claws around her waist, she could imagine herself flying by her own power. *This must be what eagles feel like,* she thought.

Nakagawa-sama's claws. She frowned. No, the dragon's. She let out an impatient breath. She would not think of that now. The pleasure of flight was too new and wonderful for her to keep hold of her temper.

Too soon the land grew larger beneath them, and even sooner they passed over the hills that separated Nagasaki from the rest of Kyushu island. The trees below grew larger and they landed, and the dragon set Anna and Miyoko gently on the ground.

Anna could not help stumbling a little, but when she held her hand out to gain her balance, Nakagawa-sama caught it. For one moment, she looked at him, startled. Her face grew warm and she looked away.

And found herself gazing at a large house, surrounded by a serene garden of rocks and evergreen bushes, with spears of iris leaves guarding a bubbling spring.

"I . . . I thought you lived in the woods, in a cave . . ." she said, then shook her head. "I do not know what to think."

The samurai gazed at her for a moment, then transferred his attention to her maid. "Miyoko-san, go into the house and inform the servants within that I wish

them to give you clothes, food and a bath, and to prepare the same for your mistress."

The maid's face brightened and she bowed, over and
over again. "*Hai,* thank you, thank you! You are too
kind, Nakagawa-sama! Too kind!" She backed away, almost stumbling, then turned and ran into the house.

Anna looked at him, shaking her head. "You will not
gain my favor so easily," she said, but pressed her lips
together to suppress an involuntary smile. "I do not like
to be deceived, after all."

He nodded. "Yes, I remember you said you were
stubborn."

"I did not—" Anna exclaimed, then remembered that
she had indeed said so some weeks ago. "Very well! I
did say it, so you are well warned. There are many things
I will need explained before I—" She stopped, biting
back the next words, for they made her feel uncertain
and a little afraid, and she wished an explanation from
Nakagawa-sama first.

The samurai lifted his brows. "Before you—?"

She shook her head and put on her most stubborn
look.

He sighed. "Very well." He walked slowly to where spring
water flowed, and sat on a rock near it, trailing his fingers
in the water. She noticed one finger seemed deformed and
cut off at the knuckle, but as the water flowed over it, it
slowly became whole again. She swallowed, remembering
what the dragon had said about the limits to how far it
could travel, then also remembered that samurai who
lost their hands or fingers were not considered as worthy as those who were whole.

"I am half-dragon, half-human," he said. He did not
look at her, but at the water that he continued to stir
with his fingers. "You are an educated woman—I assume
you know that the *kami-sama* can change into whatever
shape they wish?"

Anna nodded.

"My mother is the favored youngest daughter of Lord

Nakagawa, the *daimyo* of the clan, almost as fierce a warrior as a man, and met a dragon-kami-sama while she pursued bandits. She did not know he was one such, proceeded to marry him and conceive a child." He smiled slightly. "It is said that when my father found I was a boy, his delight was such that he lost control of his human form and became the dragon he was. Let us say that my mother was not pleased to be deceived."

"Understandable," Anna said tartly.

The samurai's smile turned wry. "They argued and he left, never to be seen again. Perhaps he departed to his home amongst the *kami-sama*, for in all my travels, I have not seen him."

He glanced at her, an uncertain look, then continued. "Given my history, there were few women willing to . . . agree to an alliance with me. A difficulty, since I am the last male Nakagawa in my clan. And unlike my father, I preferred they know my other shape before any alliance was made."

Anna frowned. "Except for me."

A frustrated expression came over his face. "You do not know what it is like. I am only half-dragon, and so maintaining my human shape is not difficult for me, and indeed I prefer it, for I can read and study much better as a human than as a dragon. But that did not matter to any of the young women whose families agreed to an arrangement of marriage. Before I could explain what I was, my habits or my preferences, they screamed, fainted and acted in ways that strained my patience past endurance. When they insisted on being released from the engagement, I was only too happy to do so." He glanced at her again. "You were the first who did not."

A warm feeling flowed over her heart, but she shook her head. "You are wrong. I did faint, after you . . . you flew off."

He grinned. "I know, and I am sorry, for you were very brave, even to the point of conversing with me. I admit I must have tested your courage, for I have never seen a woman of your country before, and thought perhaps you might have been an *oni,* because of the color of your hair. You were in more danger than you knew; dragons are the enemy of the demonkind."

A shiver went up her spine. "Why did you decide I was not?"

He smiled slightly. "You spoke to me, and your voice was soft and sweet, without the growl of an *oni.* What was more, you brought me books, as you promised. *Oni* do not honor promises." His voice warmed with gratitude as he spoke of books, and her resistance to him melted; it was a rare man who cared for them as she did. "I was intrigued," he said. "And you knew stories of places I wished I could visit. I grew to care for you more than I could admit at first."

Anna smiled a little, blushing. But she shook her head. "And yet you did not tell me that you were a dragon before you asked me to marry you."

He sighed. "It was not what I wished, but you were leaving, and I did not know my own heart until we stood at the dock." His frown turned into a mischievous grin. "And it would have caused a terrible disturbance if I had changed into a dragon in front of everyone. Definitely not the proper way to propose marriage to a woman."

A spurt of laughter escaped Anna's lips, but she shook her head. "Even so, I cannot think your family would agree to a marriage with a foreign woman, however desperate they would be for an heir. Even if I were not foreign, certainly I am not of noble birth."

"Honto," he said, but his grin remained. "So I applied to have you adopted into the Nakagawa clan, and my family was agreeable. Now you are Nakagawa Anna Vanderzee, a lady of the *daimyo*'s family, and eligible to marry any samurai." He hesitated and his expression sobered. "If you wish."

Anna stared at him, speechless, suspended between impossible hope and uncertainty. She knew now that she did not want to return to the Netherlands, even if she could somehow magically do so; she had become too used to this land, the culture and refinement. She would ever be a foreigner, walking between the two worlds of her own heritage and her adopted country. But she would live like that in her own country, for her experiences in foreign lands and her lack of family would set her apart from her countrymen, as well.

Then there was Nakagawa-sama. She gazed at him, at how he looked at her earnestly and with a little despair. Despair, she realized, because he, too, was different from his own countrymen, and also walked between two worlds: that of mortals and that of the *kami-sama*. Her heart went out to him, and she went to sit by his side, dipping her hand in the water and taking his hand in hers. In this, they were alike.

"You arranged for my adoption into your clan, even as I was on the ship?"

"In case you decided to return," he said, and shook his head. "Yes, my family thought I was mad to do so. But I understand that the heart often overrules reason."

"And no doubt being half-dragon can also overrule one's family," Anna said tartly.

He laughed. "Perhaps so. I have always found them agreeable to my suggestions." He cocked his head, looking at her. "As I suspect you probably will not, as my wife."

"As I probably will not—as your wife," she agreed. "I am stubborn, as you know." He looked a question at her even as his expression brightened. "Yes," she said. "I will marry you." She put her hand to his cheek. "Agreeing to marry a dragon is most unreasonable, and I assure you it simply is not done in my country. And I find my reason most definitely overruled."

A deep sigh came from him, and he drew her close, tentatively, and put his lips to hers. They were soft and gentle, and then as she let out a breath, insistent.

He parted from her then and took her hand. "Thank you," he said, then stood up. "Come and meet my family."

Anna stood, as well, and a feeling of trepidation came

over her. But she need not have feared, for they went forward into the house to curious faces and welcoming smiles.

She need not have fretted over her reception, she thought wryly, as one day turned to the next in the Nakagawa household. Nakagawa-sama's—Toshiro's—family's greetings and reception were tinged with relief. At last their only son would be married, and she knew his having been refused more than a few times had been an embarrassment. Perhaps marrying a foreigner was not what they had hoped for, but she would show them they had acquired more than a simple woman who would bear children.

However, it was soon clear that Toshiro had told them of her knowledge, and as she went through the next few weeks preparing for the marriage ceremony, members of the family and clan came to her for help when they were ill or had some wound to heal. She settled into the clan's daily life easily, and found that she had a place and a function beyond that of wife.

And she made friends—the Satos, whom she visited—and the Nakagawa women. They delighted in hearing her tales of foreign lands and of the land of her birthplace, as they prepared her for her wedding.

The day came when she was in front of the Shinto priest, and she said her own vows according to her beliefs, bowing stiffly at the end of it, for her kimono was very elaborate and many-layered. She was aware of a frisson of fear, for there was the marriage bed ahead of her, and ... well, he was a dragon, or part dragon. But her husband's mother had survived such an alliance, and so perhaps there was nothing, after all, to fear.

Anna was left quite alone in her own chamber that evening, after great merry-making and dancing, with even the villagers celebrating and feasting, and when her husband—what an unfamiliar thing to think!—came to her room and moved close to her under the silken quilt, she opened her eyes to see that he was no different from any man she had seen, except his chest was smooth of any hair and firm with well-toned muscles. And as he kissed her and touched her body, it was as any man might, she supposed—but then any supposition and thought fled as she gave into sensation and the lovely, sinuous flow of his body moving over hers. She let his long black hair trickle through her fingers like cool water, and then she could do nothing but hold on to him, for heat made her body shake, and she did not stop until his movements within her ceased with his long, soft sigh.

Anna also sighed when Toshiro rolled over and pulled her close, and she laid her cheek against his chest. She closed her eyes and felt her body relax against him—so comfortable and oddly familiar, as if she had come home after a long journey.

Home. She sighed and snuggled closer to her husband. *This* was home, she thought, as she felt his hand move over her hair and then her body again, as she whispered, "I love you," into his ear.

They loved long into the night, and then in the morning to the singing of larks, and when the dawn broke, Anna could see the wonder and the gratitude in her husband's eyes.

"I have heard that a man is emptied when he beds a woman," he said as he caressed her face. "But I feel as if I have been filled instead."

"Yes," she said. She could hear the rustling of servants outside their shoji door, and knew there would be more feasting and celebration as soon as they rose and dressed themselves. But Anna did not want to rise yet. She kissed Toshiro and drew him to her. "Thank you," she said. "For bringing me home."

And knew, as he made love to her again, that it was true.

Dragon Feathers

⧷

BY

BARBARA SAMUEL

Chapter 1

A brisk autumn breeze swept rust-colored leaves into eddies as Penny Freeman made her way up a narrow Santa Fe lane. Low clouds hung over the tops of the trees, holding close the fresh gin and cinnamon scents of juniper and rattling scrub oak. Penny puffed as she climbed the steep hill, her lungs unused to the high altitude, but despite the labor and the gloominess of the day, the young widow felt something moving in her veins that almost felt like a hint of happiness.

It had been a long time. The past year had been an endless, blurry year of widowhood that had seemed, at times, as though it would ruin her completely.

A fresh start in a new place, with new goals, was exactly what she needed. The Realtor had not held much hope that she'd be able to find a house in her price range, but on the phone today, Sally had sounded very cheerful.

"I just had a call this morning about it—it's been empty for a year, but the caretaker wasn't ready to let it go till now," the Realtor said in her drawling South African accent.

At first, Penny had found it surprising that her real estate agent was an immigrant from such a faraway place, but Santa Fe was filled with people who'd come here from somewhere else.

As Penny herself had. She had not yet met a single person who was actually a native of Santa Fe. "Is there a reason it's so inexpensive?"

"I haven't seen it, but the neighborhood is good. An old woman lived there, and the place needs work, but it's in your price range."

Which said it all. Penny was eager to get settled. She'd already been in town for more than three weeks—never dreaming that it would take so long to find a place to live. Classes started next week, and she wanted to have her living arrangements worked out by then.

Class. Her heart, already pumping hard as she climbed the hill, took another leap. She'd been accepted as a student by famed weaver and *curandera* Señora Maria Libélula. The weaver accepted only a handful of students every few years, and Penny was both nervous and excited that she'd been among the anointed.

Sally's directions had led Penny to this steep lane, almost invisible from the main street, and too narrow for cars. A small settlement of ancient adobe houses, with gardens hidden behind their walls, stretched along the lane here and there. Most of them had obviously been remodeled and well tended by the wealthy occupants who'd had their house numbers inlaid in expensive hand-fired tiles on the thick adobe walls. Most of them, she noticed, were accessed by a private drive that looped up the steep hill from the main drag. Very wealthy folk, these.

She puffed to the top of the hill and discovered that the lane ended there, in front of the house. No signs marked it for sale, but the gate hung a little awkwardly, and upon examination, she saw it had lost a hinge. Pausing to catch her breath, Penny had to admit to mingled dismay and relief.

Speaking of old! The small adobe house tucked beneath the sheltering arms of a tall, stately cottonwood tree appeared to be one of the oldest she'd seen. Corners were all very round, not quite even, the porch with its vigas, the enormous logs used to brace the ceiling, very dark with age and weather. The windows were painted the traditional turquoise to keep out bad spirits, and a low wall encircled the yard. Such as it was. The ground was mostly bare dirt, though a climbing rose, withered in the November air, clung to a trellis. Perhaps there were other plants, as well, hidden beneath the unwatered soil.

Penny leaned on the gate to catch her breath, admiring the line of dark blue mountains she could see beneath the arms of the tree. The deep porch, furnished with chairs and table made quaintly of twigs, faced west so one could view the sunsets over the mountains. Spectacular!

She turned in an admiring circle to evaluate the view in the other direction. Mountains, the brilliant sky, a frame of tree branches—

She frowned.

The views were much too nice for the sum they were asking. Millionaires had obviously purchased the houses she'd passed on the way here. What was wrong with this place that it had stayed empty for a year, in one of the most exclusive, inflated real estate markets in the country?

Letting herself in through the gate, she climbed the steps to the porch and pressed her face to the window to look inside. Light fell in squares, like yellow cake, on a tiled floor. Time-darkened vigas showed between whitewashed stretches of plaster overhead, and in one shadowy corner, Penny could make out a kiva-shaped fireplace. A kindling of desire moved through her—it was beautiful!

What could be so wrong with it? Probably nothing structural, since the millionaires would do exactly what they'd done elsewhere along the street: gut the internal workings to start fresh within the shell of an old house.

But there had to be something wrong for the price to be so affordable. Would it be something she could live with? It wasn't as if she could afford to be particular in this market, but she did have some resources, thanks to the life insurance settlement and her late husband Alex's strong sense of savings. Her quilts brought in a small income, but she'd come to Santa Fe to study weaving, and she wanted to devote herself to that while she was here.

Rounding the house, she saw again the neglect of the yard and the withered window boxes. A scent of cotton candy hung in the air, mingling with the butterscotch scent of a long-needled ponderosa pine protecting the kitchen door. As she came around the house, the silky gray promise of rain edged the horizon, and the view was so vast, so beautiful that she almost just left without bothering. *Something* had to be wrong.

Sally arrived, out of breath and cheerful. "Good morning, Penny," she sang. "Let's take a look, shall we?" Pulling out a set of keys, she unlocked the door and led the way inside. "As you see, it's quite small."

Penny nodded. Living room, bedroom through a pair of French doors, back through the living room to the kitchen and the bathroom that had obviously been carved out of the kitchen area at some later date. A small windowed room jutted off the back—perfect for her looms and threads.

"What's wrong with it?" Penny asked.

"It's tiny," Sally said, but something funny crossed her face. "And neglected, obviously."

"I can see that. But I'm sure most of the houses along this lane were this small at some point, and this has the nicest view of all. Is it plumbing? Foundation? What?"

"No!" Sally said. "The inspections have all been done, and I've got the paperwork in my car for you."

"Is it haunted?" Penny asked, and she wasn't joking.

Sally looked at the ceilings, the walls. "It's old enough, all right. But I haven't seen anything about that." Her nose wrinkled. "But . . . it does have an odd *smell*, doesn't it?"

Penny breathed deeply. "A little." A minute ago, outside, she'd been thinking it smelled like cotton candy. Inside, it made her think more of brown sugar and butter, a mixture her mother had used to cook ham for breakfast. "I guess it could get a little cloying, but you'd just open the windows or something."

Sally gave her another odd look.

"What?" Penny asked.

Sally shook her head. "The smell is quite odd."

Again Penny breathed in. "It smells like sugar."

"Let's look around outside, shall we?"

They headed out to the porch, which Penny now saw looped around to the west. At the turn, a flash of color caught her eye and she knelt to pick up a feather. It was like a peacock feather, the same length, with the eye at the top, but instead of blue, the feather was shades of pink. It was in perfect condition. "Look at this!"

Sally turned around. "Pretty," she said dismissively, heading without mercy to the end of her errand.

Penny twirled the feather in her fingertips, admiring the dye job. Extraordinary! At each point of the eye where the feather should have been green or turquoise or sapphire, it was shades of cotton candy and strawberry and crimson. The scent of sugar came off it a little more strongly, and Penny held it to her nose, calling out, "I think it must have been the old woman's perfume," she said.

"What?"

"The scent in the air," Penny said. "This looks like it might have come from an old-fashioned boa or something."

"Right." Sally held a palm to her eyes as she examined the roofline. "Everything appears to be in order, girl. Don't know what to tell you about why it's so cheap, but you might want to jump on this one. The land itself is worth a fortune."

Penny looked at the house, back over her shoulder at the view. She twirled the feather in her hand. There was a sense of welcome and happiness in her as she stood there—and for the second time in six months, she did something wildly impulsive. "I'll buy it," she said. "But I have to move in within the week."

"Do you want to think on it overnight?"

"No," Penny said definitely. "No, I want this house."

"All right, then. I'm sure we can work something out." Sally shivered in a sudden gust of wind. "Come back down to my office."

                        *   *   *

Eight days later, Penny stood outside the whitewashed
adobe wall that surrounded the hacienda where Señora
Libélula held her classes, and took a long slow breath.
The morning was bright and crisp over hills pincushioned
with sage, the sky an improbable color of blue that people back home in Missouri had likely never seen. Penny
never had, until she and Alex had come here on their
honeymoon just four short years ago. Something about
this vivid sky, the smoky scent of leaves in the air, made
her remember that stretch of weeks with a pang. How
happy they had been, how full of hope and anticipation!

    Firmly, she put the memories aside and focused on
today. Which was a very good day, too, for Penny was
beginning a year of study with the famed Señora Maria
Libélula, one of the most brilliant and temperamental
weavers in the world, descended from a line that stretched
back seven centuries to the Maya and to Spain.

    Unlike many artists, Señora Libélula was also a re-
vered teacher of her arts, but she accepted only seven students at a time, and only at her whim. It was notoriously
difficult to be accepted, and there was, as far as anyone
could see, no particular set of standards that made her
more likely to accept one over another—there was an
entire Yahoo! group on the Internet devoted to trying to
decipher it. Thus far, there was nothing identifiable.

    Her students were of all ages, from all walks of life,
from all over the world. Most were textile artists of one
sort or another, but not all. One of her best-known students had been a painter before she came to Señora
Libélula.

    Penny came from a long line of champion quilters,
and had started making quilts of her own when she was
barely old enough to hold a needle. By the time she was
in her early teens, she regularly swept the top prizes at
local fairs and craft shows and was invited to exhibit her
work at a textile arts show in Chicago. Until her husband's death last year in a car accident, she'd been quite
happy with her choice of career.

But when Alex was killed, it was as if something in her died with him, even as something else was being born. Her fingers burned not to cut the fabric of others, but to make fabric of her own. She wanted to dye it, spin it, weave it herself. Her friend Juney, a weaver from way back, had suggested that Penny apply to Señora Libélula's class, and to her amazement, she had been accepted within days.

Fated, Juney said, obviously trying not to mind. She'd applied three times.

Now Penny was here, acceptance letter and introductory materials in hand, a bag of supplies hanging heavy over her shoulder. She wore jeans and a soft, long-sleeved T-shirt, and a jacket she'd surely shed by noon, even if they worked outside.

The gates burst open suddenly, and a woman came swirling out. "Welcome!" she cried.

Penny blinked. The woman had masses of black, shiny hair and dancing dark eyes, and she wore a fringed velvet shawl in a paisley swirl over her turquoise dress. Her hands, white and long, seemed younger than they should have—and yet, what age should she be? It seemed the señora had been weaving a very long time, but this woman appeared to be only forty or so. Impossible, but that was how she looked.

"Hello," Penny said shyly.

"You must be Penny Freeman," she said. "That milk-fed skin, those rosy cheeks. You have to be the farm girl."

Penny frowned, pulling herself up to her full height. "Not really. I mean, I'm Penny, and I'm from Missouri, but a farm girl? No."

The woman's eyes tilted upward with her slightly ironic smile. "Ah."

"Anyway," Penny said, extending her hand, "I am very happy to meet you."

"I am Señora Maria Libélula." She clasped Penny's hand between both of hers. "And I am very happy to meet you at last."

"Are the other students here?"

"We are still waiting for one more, but yes, the others have arrived." Señora Libélula did not drop her hand, but kept hold of it firmly. "You bought the house on the hill, yes?"

"Yes. How did you know?"

The woman's smile was as mysterious and pleased as a cat's. "I hear of most things—but in this case, the house once belonged to an old, old friend of mine. How do you like it?"

"It's wonderful!" Penny said. "I've only been there a few days, but I feel very much at home. It needs some work, but I'm sure I can find someone to help me."

"What sort of things need doing?"

"Oh, just little things," Penny said. "A cabinet door that's off its hinges, and some loose tiles here and there; a window that doesn't lock properly." She shrugged. "I had an old house in Missouri—they all have their troubles."

"Ah. Well, perhaps I know someone who will help you."

"I'd be delighted."

"Now come. Let's meet the others."

Penny allowed herself to be led through the gates, looking around eagerly. Flowers in clay pots and mosaic pots and tall urns lined the base of the wall, still blooming in the heat stored by the adobe itself. Penny turned around to admire a copper-colored vessel planted with what she thought might be—

Orchids? How could orchids be growing outside in Santa Fe in November? Everything about that was just wrong. Maybe they were fake—but why, then, was the young man, too neatly dressed to be a gardener, pouring water into the pot?

She peered over her shoulder—first at the flowers, but then at the man, who wore his hair long in traditional Native American fashion, so the color of the sleek black showed in glossy sheaths, a color also illuminated by his red shirt, so finely woven it seemed to shimmer over his strong shoulders, his lean waist. *Not like silk,* Penny thought, *but—*

"This way, my sweet," Señora Libélula said, and tugged Penny down a hallway lined with windows, then into a large, open room where a cluster of other students sat around a big butcher-block table.

The room was vast. It was well lit by skylights, and had a row of windows looking north to a courtyard where a white goat placidly grazed. White walls lined with open-box shelving held a dizzying array of goods. One long row held yarns and threads in a dazzlement of colors—Penny wanted to rush over and plunge her hands into the turquoises and burnt umbers and the endless host of subtly varied whites—beige, eggshell, brilliant white. All of them. Her fingers tingled in anticipation.

"Everyone, this is Penny," Señora Libélula said.

The others greeted her as if they were in a twelve-step meeting: "Hi, Penny."

"Have a seat," Señora Libélula said. "We're only waiting for one more."

"Here I am," came a breathy voice from the doorway. "Andy Alistair."

Penny turned to see a tiny, fifty-something woman with a cloud of salt-and-pepper hair. Behind her was the young man from the garden. His face was almost adamantly Mayan, she thought, the angles and planes exaggerated, as if it were carved out of some exotically beautiful wood. Their eyes met, and in that fleeting instant, she felt an arc of attraction, a spark of heat that blazed in his black eyes only for the length of time it took to feel the sensation rush down the river of her spine to her hips.

Then, as if a wall slammed down between them, he was expressionless, cool. Penny hurried over to take her place at the table. She was, by at least a decade, the youngest person in the room. The next-closest person was a man in his forties with the grizzled beard of a mountain man. The oldest was a woman who looked to be in her late sixties, with the leathery wrinkles of someone who'd spent a lot of time in the sun.

The young man stayed at the doorway in that elusively intriguing red shirt, his arms crossed, his mouth in a firm line. Even though she had angled her body away, she could feel the lure of him, silent and beautiful and intriguing. Was he Señora Libélula's lover? Son? Friend? Penny was sure the fabric must have been created by the famed weaver herself. It was like something from a fairy tale.

She found herself sneaking another glance at his face—and was startled to slam into his gaze, fixed on her, not with that aloof hostility she'd picked up a few moments before, but with curiosity, measurement, as if he wondered just as much about her as she wondered about him.

"Everybody," Señora Libélula said, "I will introduce you to one another in a moment, but before I send him away to do some work for me, I would like you to greet Joaquin. He is the one who knows everything about this hacienda, so if there is some trouble or you have some wish, let him know. I believe all of you, except our lovely Penny, are staying here for the duration of our studies together."

Startled, Penny looked up. She had not known that staying at the hacienda was an option. Were they paying for the privilege? She'd won a full scholarship. Perhaps that was why she had not been told.

Nonetheless, it made her feel left out. A brush of heat moved along her chin.

It helped only slightly when Señora Libélula smiled, as if including Penny in some inside joke. "Say hello to Joaquin."

Penny looked at him, not realizing until she started that she was out of synch with the others when she said, "Hello, Joaquin."

His black irises were deep as a cave. "Hello."

Her classmates chuckled. Joaquin did not smile, only lifted one hand, almost in ironic dismissal, and stepped out of the room.

"All right, everyone," Señora Libélula said. "Let's introduce ourselves, shall we?"

Chapter 2

On the first Saturday morning after classes began, Penny slept late. When she opened her eyes and saw the hands of the clock pointed to nine o'clock, she couldn't believe it. Nine o'clock! She ordinarily woke up at five, a habit born in her Midwestern childhood and not easily shed.

Sleeping at all had become something of a luxury since Alex was killed. She'd had so much trouble at first that even her mother, so antidrug as to be cartoonish about it, had nagged her into getting a prescription sleep aid. Penny, desperate after three months of very short stints of sleep, had used them briefly, but found they made life even more difficult to manage.

In this house, the first night, she'd fallen asleep deeply at ten p.m. and slept through until seven without stirring at all. Her bed seemed triply comfortable, the pillows exactly right, the comforter thick and cozy.

It was crazy, but she felt cradled in this house. As if she were crawling into the lap of a great mother, who stroked her hair and sang her soft lullabies. Maybe, she thought fancifully, the old woman who had been Señora Libélula's friend was now a benevolent and protective ghost.

After a little more than a week, the shadows that had marred her face for a year were beginning to disappear, and her skin began to look again as if she were her true age of not quite thirty instead of the fifty she'd looked for a while there.

This bright November morning, she'd slept till nine a.m., and she supposed she'd earned it. The past week had been a whirl of activity. She had moved her meager belongings to the house, hiring a trio of burly laborers and a burro-drawn wagon to cart her things up the narrow lane. It had delighted her on some weird level, this quaintness. She didn't own much, so it wasn't as problematic as it might have been.

Bringing groceries up the hill in the wintertime might prove to be daunting. Unlike some of the other houses along the route, a back road to the house was not a possibility—her backyard dropped off in a steep cliff, and the lane was too narrow for cars. In some places, that would prove daunting, but Santa Fe's central area was small and easily walkable—a boon to Penny's thinking. She loved walking.

It was almost eerie how well her things fit here—as if they were destined. The couch and love seat that had seemed strange and impractical in the bungalow in Kirksville fit perfectly in the living room here, the deep red and copper fabric glowing against the Saltillo tiles and sand-colored walls. The wood matched the vigas and the wood around the windows. Even her cat, Puff, a massive male snowpoint Siamese, fit in these rooms with his nearly black points and splashes of white and his sapphire eyes. He sat just now on the wide windowsill, his long black tail twitching, and dozed in the sunlight.

As she lazily ate her breakfast, content with only herself for company and the sound of the house itself around her, she realized with a shock that she was happy.

Happy! Imagine that.

Almost immediately, she felt guilty about it, as if she were letting Alex down. He'd been her soul mate—how could she ever really be happy again?

But the sensation was undeniable, and not even guilt did much to dilute it. She hummed under her breath and she made a list of the things she needed to do. There was homework from Señora Libélula—figuring out how to set up her own house loom, which Señora had loaned her since she wasn't staying at the hacienda. There were many floor looms there and she could use them whenever she wished, but the señora wanted her to have something at home, as well. She sipped her coffee and peered at the wooden slats, the screws and washers. Hmmm.

A knock sounded at the front door. Puff woke up with a trill and rolling eyes, then leapt off the windowsill and trotted toward the front door to see who it was. He meowed, the sound an almost pained yowl.

Penny chuckled as she followed behind him. "I hope no one ever tells you that you're not a dog," she said, and swung open the door curiously.

"Oh!" Her hand flew to her throat, where a pulse had started to pound, for it was Señora's right-hand man, Joaquin, who stood there. Puff looked out, too, putting his paws on the screen door and sniffing the air. His long black tail was in alert position.

"Um," Penny said. "Hi."

"Hello." Joaquin's hands were tucked loosely in the front pockets of his jeans and he wore a plain, washed-soft chambray shirt. "Señora said you might have work for me to do?"

The cat trilled a greeting, lifted one white-smudged black paw to bat at the screen. *Hello!*

Joaquin bent and scratched his finger against the screen. "You're a beauty."

"Don't encourage him," she said, shaking her head.

He grinned, scratching a nail along the screen. Puff batted it with a muscular paw.

"I do have some little things that need doing," Penny said, and pushed open the door, glad that she'd washed her face and traded her pajamas for jeans and a sweater. "Would you like a cup of coffee? I just finished breakfast."

"That would be great." He came inside and frankly looked around. "Are these quilts your work?"

Penny nodded, looking at them through his eyes, abstracts and fairy tales, in very strong colors that had not always been appreciated in Kirksville. "I was thinking this morning that it's almost as if I made them to go on these walls."

He looked at her. "Maybe you did."

"I guess." Shrugging, she led the way into the kitchen, took a moon-and-stars mug from the cupboard and poured coffee. All the while, she was acutely conscious of her body, of the movement of her thighs and feet, of her hair falling down her back and in need of cutting, her ragged nails as she handed him the steaming mug. "Do you need anything in it?"

"No. This is fine." He looked around him, then directly at Penny. "This is nice, but why didn't you stay at the hacienda with the others? It's not like a dorm— everyone has a bedroom, and there's a special courtyard for students only."

Penny shrugged. "Until I got to the school, I didn't know that it was an option."

"Oh." He seemed startled. "So you just bought this house for a year? Will you flip it?"

"Flip?"

"Fix it up and sell it for a big profit when you leave."

"No, that's not in the plans. I mean, I don't really know what I'm doing. Maybe I'll stay longer. Santa Fe might suit me."

"No family?"

Penny took a breath against the razor edge of the words: "I'm a widow."

"I'm sorry." The words were sincere, his black eyes direct. "And your parents, sisters, brothers?"

"I don't have any siblings, and my parents were well into middle age when I surprised them. They've passed away now."

He nodded, that full mouth in an expression of consideration. It was impossible to figure out how old he was. At the hacienda, she'd been thinking he was a little older than she—midthirties, perhaps—but up close, she saw that he might be younger, maybe only in his early twenties. His skin was fine and smooth, marred by not a single sun line or laugh line or other flaw.

Too bad. She looked away. The first man she'd even noticed at all since Alex died, and he was too young. She took a breath, met his eyes with false cheer. "So, are you related to Señora Libélula?"

"She's my mother."

"Oh!" Penny laughed, oddly relieved. And then she felt silly, as if her attraction was too obvious. She looked away.

And suddenly, beneath her feet, Penny felt—or heard, she was never quite sure which it was—a fine, warm sound. She went still, cocked her head. "Do you hear that, or is it my imagination?"

"What do you hear?"

"It's a very soft vibration. I keep thinking it must be like the Taos hum or something. Some people hear it, some people don't."

"I hear something, but I'm not sure what it is."

"My Realtor thought I was imagining things."

Between them, Puff burst into a loud, insistent purr and rubbed against Joaquin's shin. They both laughed. "I think," Penny said, "you can say you've made a friend."

He bent and picked up the cat, an armful. "I like cats. They're smart and independent."

Penny admired the length of his fingers stroking through Puff's silky fur, the long, lazy movements. She felt suddenly flushed and looked away. "Well, I suppose I should show you all the jobs that need doing."

He met her eyes, his so very, very dark that it was impossible to read anything into them. But his lips quirked the smallest bit. *Lovely lips,* she thought with yearning. "Let's do it."

It was too soon for romance, Penny told herself. And maybe he was a little too young. And it might not be a great idea to involve herself with Señora's son. There were a lot of reasons not to think of Joaquin in that way.

Somehow, she was doing it anyway.

When Joaquin was busy fixing a hole in the wall surrounding her yard, Penny took out the pieces of the loom Señora Libélula had sent home with her yesterday. Penny had worked a little with looms, and the pieces came with instructions, but after thirty minutes, she was flummoxed. With a sigh, she put down the screwdriver and went to seek out Joaquin.

She found him working on the wall, a bucket next to him. As she watched, he dipped his hands into the bucket, brought out a reddish muck and smeared it over the wall, patting it into place as if he were sculpting. "Is that adobe?"

He straightened, his wrist cocked. "It is. My grandmother taught me to make it."

Her fingers itched. "Can I try it?"

"Go ahead." He gestured toward the bucket. "It's easy. Just stick your hand in the mud, get a good handful"—as he spoke, he demonstrated the process—"and smear it on."

Penny yanked the sleeves of her sweater high on her arms and dipped a hand into the thick, cool mud. It had an oddly pleasing heft. With a cupped hand, she scooped out a handful and slapped it on the wall. It landed with a sloppy smacking sound, and Penny laughed. "It sounds like meat hitting a counter."

"A little."

"Like this?" Penny asked, patting the adobe into place, smearing it a little to make a texture.

"Doing good." He picked up another handful of mud himself. "This was the job of women, remudding the house every spring."

"Really." She watched his hand, dark and sinewy, smooth over the wall, his index finger making a pattern as he moved. "What did the men do?"

"They went to the fields, out with the sheep. Women took care of the house and everything in it. Men took care of the livestock—except some chickens or something, maybe—and the fields. The men brought home the mutton, the women cooked it."

Penny smiled at the play on words.

He dipped again and gestured for her to do the same

thing. "You work that way, I'll go the other. Each person has a style, a signature."

"Wouldn't that mean two styles meeting would also be style?"

"Yes." He smiled, very, very faintly, and flickered a glance toward her. Again she felt the frisson of his presence, a sense of power and strength that seemed to come from some inner core.

"Did you grow up around here, Joaquin?"

"My family has been in Santa Fe for nearly five hundred years," he said.

"Wow. So you're a native." She plucked a glob of mud from between her fingers. "Not very many of you."

"More than you think."

"Five hundred years is a very long time."

"It's a very old place." He patted the cool mud down in a lumpy spot, and she found her gaze on his wrists. "How about you? Where are you from?"

"A small town in Missouri. Not for five hundred years, though. My father was a professor, and my mother came to the school there from another little Missouri town, and that's where I grew up."

"What's it like? Missouri? I've never really traveled much." He slapped and smoothed the adobe, his hair shining like a wing in the sun, his body lithe, his hands graceful. Penny felt a whisper of something over her breasts, her belly, her thighs.

Stop it.

"It's green," she said. "Humid. In the springtime, day-lilies bloom insanely. I made a quilt of a scene of daylilies once."

"Sounds pretty."

"Why haven't you traveled?"

He glanced toward the sky, maybe back toward the hacienda. "I have obligations here."

"Obligations?"

"Yes," he said, and smiled gently, but did not elaborate.

Penny measured him for a moment, wondering what

duty kept a young man tethered to a place. "Do you mind?"

"No," he said, and there was strength in the word. He reeled back on his heels and surveyed the work, slapped a final pat of mud on the wall. "I think we're finished here. What's next on your list?"

"My loom," she said, remembering. "I can't seem to fit it together."

"Let's take a look." They went back inside, the cat trailing behind, and there were the pieces of the loom, scattered over her table. Penny pointed him toward the bathroom so he could wash his hands, and she hurried over to the kitchen sink to wash hers, wondering if she had anything to feed him if she invited him to stay for dinner.

Puff skittered around the kitchen, diving and dancing with some toy he'd found. Penny glanced over her shoulder and saw that he had her pink peacock feather, diving for it with both paws, then tossing it up in the air.

"Hey, that's mine, you bratty cat!" She swooped down and took it away from him with a little huff. "There are a million feathers out there. Go find a different one."

He glared at her and slunk away. Penny took the feather into her bedroom to put it back on the dresser where she kept it—and discovered it wasn't the same feather. The first one she'd found was still stuck in the blue vase in front of a small mirror where the beauty could be magnified.

This one had stronger scent, too. She held it to her nose, breathing in the somehow soothing, rich aroma of hot sugar.

She went back to the kitchen. "Sorry, Puff," she said, bringing the feather with her. "You found this one fair and square." He'd leapt up into the living room window and he studiously ignored her, his tail switching back and forth across the wall. Penny chuckled. "Come on, I'm sorry." She tickled his ears with the long feather. He twitched them but didn't turn around.

Cats.

"Where did you get that?" Joaquin boomed out from behind her.

She spun around, feeling guilty for no reason she could name. "The cat had it," she said, and scowled. "I thought he'd stolen it off my dresser"—she waved toward her bedroom—"but he found it outside and brought it in, I guess."

He stared at the feather as if it were something she'd stolen. Mulishly, she met his gaze, refusing to be intimidated.

After a moment, he said gruffly, "Let's fix your loom, and then I will have to be going."

Stung, Penny nodded. Her little romantic vision of a supper shared, and perhaps—

Oh, don't be stupid, she told herself, heat in her face as she stomped into the kitchen. Men like this always had a cadre of women. And it wasn't as if Penny was a great beauty, after all. Or Hispanic or Indian. She'd already learned that it was considered slumming for members of the older cultures to mix and marry the newer arrivals— that is, the Anglos.

"In here," she said, and tossed her hair out of her eyes. Better not to want what you couldn't have. Life should have taught her that much already.

He didn't speak as he put the loom together. Penny tried several lines of conversation, but they all failed. It wasn't until he was on his way out, moving through the living room, that he spoke again. He paused in front of a large quilt. "Are those daylilies?"

Penny crossed her arms. "Yes." The quilt was one of the fairy tale series. It showed a princess with long, dark hair sitting in a field of orange daylilies, thousands and thousands of them. She'd worked hard to capture their shape and the gradations of color, and the quilt had taken four Best in Shows.

"You're very talented."

"Thanks," Penny said.

At the door, he paused and took a breath. "Look, I'm sorry I sounded angry. There's a lot going on here, and I like you and don't want you to be hurt."

A pinch moved in her lungs. "What do you mean?"

He shook his head. "There are things I'm not at liberty to say, but just be careful, all right?"

"In my house?"

"You're safe here. Very safe," he said with a faint smile. "And I don't mean to be mysterious—it's just that there are things I cannot discuss."

Penny blinked. "Okay."

For one more moment, their eyes were in communication—worry, reassurance—and, Penny was pleased to note, interest both coming and going. "Will it be all right if I come back later to check your furnace for you? My mother was insistent that should be done this evening."

"Of course."

"I'll see you," he said, and disappeared into the night.

Beneath her feet was the soft, warm hum.

Chapter 3

Penny walked down the hill to the plaza, hoping to get supper at a little café she liked. She had forgotten that the tourist trade would be in full swing on the weekends, no matter what the time of year. The hostess warned her that it might be a substantial wait for a table.

Penny hesitated. It wasn't the waiting she hated. It was watching everyone around her. All the couples. The usual husbands and wives, boyfriends and girlfriends, but also sisters and friends and knots of relatives. It sometimes seemed that Penny was the only person who had no one left.

And it wasn't that she didn't like her own company. In fact, she'd always been a little too solitary, a little more of a hermit than she should have been. She knew she was eccentric and shy, and her head was filled with things other people seemed to find a teeny bit odd: myths and fairy tales and archetypes, and how to express everything in color. In high school, she'd dated very little, finding boys to mostly be very shallow and too needy.

And that was what had made finding her husband so miraculous. They'd clicked from the first moment of their meeting, at a poorly attended string quartet performance her sophomore year of college. They'd been inseparable ever after. Alex had been as distracted and geeky in his way as Penny was in hers—a classical bass player and computer gamer who also loved long hours in his own mind. The two discovered they could happily occupy the same space without speaking for an entire afternoon—Penny clipping and stitching and arranging her fabrics, Alex playing games and creating maps and practicing his bass. They'd been wildly, peacefully happy.

The worst part of being a widow was the sense that no one would ever understand her again. And yet she had to live, didn't she? Sooner or later, she'd have to get used to doing things alone.

"I'll wait," she told the hostess.

It was not easy to wait in her solitariness. Candles flickered, laughter swirled, flames snapped in the kiva fireplace. When a table did become available, she did her best to enjoy the meal, but finally admitted to herself that she was wretchedly lonely. More than a little depressed, she walked back up the hill in the cold, moonless night.

As she walked up the hill, she mulled the strangeness of everything. The fact that no one had told her everyone stayed at the hacienda. Her house coming suddenly available just as she needed a place. Joaquin's reaction to the feather. His hint that there were forces at work that she didn't know about. Was the feather some sacred thing, a symbol used in some exotic Mayan or Spanish festival? Was the house a place of—*spirits* or power or something?

She trudged up the hill, crisp wind swirling up beneath her jacket. A sound of wind rustled the trees, moving as if from a great distance down the valley. She hunched her shoulders, bracing for it to slam into her as she neared her home.

Instead, it seemed the air went completely still. The leaves did not move. A vivid wash of that fantastic, sugary baking smell filled the air. She paused to inhale it, a scent of carmelizing apples and brown sugar, butter and maybe hint of something else. It was very strong.

As she stood there, she caught sight of the lights of Santa Fe sparkling below, a magical sight, the lights scattered over the hills and bluffs and mesas like spilled rhinestones. She found herself smiling, as if the scent in the air had soothed her.

The air seemed to grow even more still. Penny felt a ripple of anticipation on her spine, the kind of whispering movement over the hairs in her body that came from lightning, but when she scanned the sky, there was no sign of a storm, only the bright, clear stars overhead.

She had a sense of being watched, but in a benevolent way, and then there was an odd, sweeping sound, a whoop, and a blast of strong, scented wind flung her hair into disarray. She pulled the mess out of her eyes and looked around, but there was no one there.

Then it seemed, faintly, as if she heard the flap of wings, impossibly large. She turned in a circle, slowly looking for the source, but she saw nothing.

Nothing at all.

Determined not to sulk, Penny decided to go down to the square in the morning, where an art show and farmer's market were in progress. She put on a warm sweater and boots, and tied her hair into a braid. As she headed out to the gate, however, she halted. There, as if fallen from the sky, were three pink feathers in a little heap. They looked old, worn, the fringes grimy and some bits torn.

But even more intriguing was a soft fluff of other feathers, the length and shape unlike any feather she knew of. Squatting to pick them up, she could smell that bakery scent again, very strong. Apple fritters, maybe. The short, wide feathers were the size of her palm, almost square, with a graceful arch at the tip.

And they were unmistakably pink, a pale, soft pink like baby booties, but slightly shimmery, with a hint of crimson at the very, very edge. She ruffled them against her palm, picked one up by the stem and twirled it around—how could you dye feathers so exactly this way? She held one up to the sunlight. Was it painted? She couldn't tell.

Dyeing was actually on the agenda for this afternoon. The students had all been sent home with a skein of freshly spun nubby wool, to dye with whatever dyestuffs they wished, drawn from a huge array of natural materials Señora Libélula had collected over the years.

Penny gathered the feathers from the ground and walked around the perimeter of the yard to see if she could find any more. There was only one—stuck in the joint of a tree. High enough she had to stand on her tiptoes to tug it down.

Perplexed but charmed by the beauty, she tied some of them together and attached them to her purse. Perhaps she would wander over the hacienda after a while, ask Señora Libélula how such a dyeing was accomplished. Perhaps that would be her task this afternoon, to reproduce with dye this very intriguing color. Cochineal, perhaps? Cochineal were the silvery skeletal shells of tiny, tiny beetles that lived inside cacti. They had to be collected by hand and were much prized for the lovely color they gave to natural fabrics, pink to magenta.

Yes, perhaps that would work. How to make the edges take the color more darkly?

It was a lovely artistic puzzle, and Penny hummed to herself as she walked down the hill to the fair.

Going to the market was the right idea, Penny thought two hours later. She ate an Indian taco from a vendor, fry bread piled high with beans and cheese and crisp lettuce and tomato, and admired the wares of the artists— painters and Native American potters and silversmiths from the nearby Pueblo nations, photographers and fabric stylists and craft folk. The autumn air was crystal clear, the sunshine as bright and clean as first dawn. She couldn't get over the weather in the Southwest; by now in Missouri they'd have out their heavy coats and gloves and hats. Here she was, wandering around in a light jacket and jeans, the sun so warm on her head that it almost made her sleepy.

Flute and guitar music played somewhere in the

square, and Penny ambled toward it. A small band of dark, tiny musicians played wooden pan flutes and stringed instruments for a gathered crowd. She joined the onlookers, happily swinging her head in time to the music.

A hand grabbed her arm just above the elbow, jerking her out of the drifting reverie. "Where did you get those feathers?" a man demanded in her ear.

She yanked out of his grip. "Let go of me!"

He stepped back a pace, but his stance was fierce. A tall, pockmarked Native American with flat black eyes stared at her harshly, his mouth turned down at the corners. "Where did you get them?" he asked again, pointing to the feathers she'd tied to her purse.

She fingered them, wondering suddenly if they were from some sacred bird she'd never heard of, the pink eagle or something. It was illegal to own the feathers of sacred birds unless you were Indian—she did know a little bit of local culture. "I—they . . . um . . . I found them," she said.

The man narrowed his eyes and spat. Raising an angry finger and pointing, he uttered something that sounded like a curse. Penny shrank away, both from his tone and stance and from the attention he attracted. Another man, smaller but as dark and fierce, hurried over. In some language Penny didn't recognize, he soothed the first man and hurried him away.

A pair of pale, stout tourists stared at her curiously, as if she were part of the local scenery. She ducked away, turning to the vendor on her left, who sold bear-claw necklaces. "Do you know what he said?"

The woman shook her head slowly. "It wasn't Indian."

"Or Spanish," said her rotund husband.

A tall man with a wonderful, thick, Old World mustache stepped forward. He was dressed in Santa Fe casual—jeans and an elegant shirt and very expensive, well-worn boots. "It was a form of Mayan. He said you have the feathers of the dragon god."

Penny touched the feathers protectively. "They're dyed peacock!"

He nodded. Extending one dark, long-fingered hand, he said, "I am Paul Rodriguez. I teach New World mythology at the college."

She accepted the hand, shook it crisply. "Penny Freeman."

"May I?" he asked, pointing to the feathers.

For some reason, the request made her feel slightly uncomfortable, but Penny lifted her purse from her shoulder and held tight to the strap while he put on a pair of reading glasses and examined them.

"Extraordinary," he commented, and let them go. He lifted his fingers to his nose. "Odd odor to them. Is that the dye, do you suppose?"

"I think they came from a feather boa from the old woman who used to live in my house." She smelled the feathers, inhaling the scent with the same cooling pleasure she always felt. "I think it was her perfume."

He looked at her sharply. "Odd perfume."

Penny lifted a shoulder.

He tucked his hands behind his back, urbane and elegant. "Do you know the tale of the dragon god?"

"No."

"If you would be so kind as to join me for a cup of coffee, I'd be happy to share it with you."

Penny glanced over her shoulder, fearful that she'd meet the angry Mayan-speaking Indian. "All right."

Chapter 4

At The Plaza café, an old Route 66–era landmark, Penny and Paul settled in over heavy ceramic cups of coffee.

"The dragon-god cult takes several forms," he began, "as with so many other myths. They all have their roots in the dragon god of ancient Mexico, Quetzalcoatl. He's a feathered serpent, a god of war and soldiers."

"Okay, I've heard of him," Penny said.

"The intriguing thing is, on the New Mexico plateau, the legend met the legend of La Llorona and morphed into a goddess whom women worship. She is said to grant the prayers of women, particularly those who grieve or have lost children. *Curanderas*—healers—made petition to her for healing powers, and there are said to be secret festivals celebrating her."

"I'm not very familiar with the legends around here," Penny confessed. "What is La Llorona?"

"The weeping woman. Depending on which version of the story you hear, she was either a poor, beleaguered servant girl who was jilted by her married lover, or a creature of vicious vengeance who drowned her children to get back at a man who scorned her." He was quite handsome, if a little too old for her. "A *curandera* is like a witch."

"Isn't she more of a healer?" Penny asked, frowning slightly. "I know that term. My teacher is a *curandera* and—"

His body went still. "Who is your teacher?"

"Señora Libélula."

He stared at her for a long moment. "Is that so?"

A chill ran down her spine, but she could not have said why. His expression was implacable. "Do you know her?"

"We are acquainted." He sipped his coffee, outwardly calm, but Penny felt a sense of waiting agitation in him. "You must be a very talented artist, then. Señora Libélula only accepts the best."

She inclined her head. "Perhaps. I'm honored to be her student. She's a very good teacher."

"I'm sure." He smiled very slightly. "There is a legend around here that the dragon goddess is not a myth at all, but real. She is our Loch Ness monster."

"A dragon," Penny repeated with skepticism.

He smiled. "Many have reported seeing her fly. She's said to be enormous and benevolent, and very, very ancient."

"So what do I have to do with any of it?"

"I would have said nothing, but our friend in the marketplace seemed to think those feathers belong to the god, and he was not happy. If I were you, I would be very careful."

Penny had the sudden sense that he was trying to frighten her—as if there were a big sign that said, CUE SCARY MUSIC. "I don't know anything about any of this," she said.

"One can be injured by ignorance," he said. "And it's wise to remember that religion is not reasonable."

She narrowed her eyes, unable to shake the feeling that he was deliberately trying to frighten her. She lifted a shoulder, made a joke. "I have an attack cat, so I'm safe."

He grinned. "I am fond of cats myself," he said, seeming to accept her change of subject. "What do you have?

When they finished their coffee, Paul insisted on walking her home. To be honest, she didn't mind the company.

The weather had gone blustery again, and it seemed there was something in the air. A little company up the hill wasn't so terrible, especially company as intelligent and handsome as Paul Rodriguez.

As the house came into sight, however, she saw Joaquin standing on the porch, his face severe and shadowed. His arms were crossed over his chest, and for the first time, she noticed how powerfully muscular his shoulders and biceps were. A swift vision of him without his shirt blistered over her imagination, an impression of toffee-smooth flesh and that thick black hair lying on his shoulders, and a naked belly—

She blinked, embarrassed at the detail and suddenness of the vision. "Um. Thank you for walking me home," she said, turning to shake Paul's hand.

He eyed Joaquin, then turned to accept her handshake. "Is he your boyfriend?"

"No," she answered, and didn't add any detail, though he clearly would have enjoyed it. "Thank you again."

He held her hand a little longer than necessary. Penny allowed it, but she felt her attention drawn away into Joaquin's realm, a physical capturing that was as powerful as if each and every cell in her body had a transmitter programmed to the Joaquin station. Her body buzzed, tickled, fizzed. She tried to slip out of Paul's grasp. "I have to go."

"Have dinner with me this week," he said. He wrinkled his nose, covered his face suddenly. "What *is* that smell?"

She inhaled, catching a faint whiff of the sugary scent. "You don't like it?"

"No!" His face wrinkled and he back away. "You can't mean that you do?"

She lifted a shoulder. "It smells like sugar to me."

He kept his hand over his nose. "Not to me." He shook his head, backed away. "I must go. Will I see you soon?"

"We'll see. So long."

"Take care, Penny," he called.

She waved a hand, hurrying toward the porch and the

watchful Joaquin. "Hello!" she said breathlessly, only then remembering that he'd been angry with her the last time he was here. She halted, the pleasure spinning out of her. "Are you still mad at me for whatever it was?"

He took a step down toward her, his ink black eyes alive and kind. "No." A swath of his heavy hair fell forward, sliding like silk over that shoulder she had imagined naked. It gave her a jolt.

The scent of sugar increased, as if they were right over a hot pot of bubbling molasses and butter, and it made Penny feel dizzy and off center. Her breasts were heavy, hot, and the palms of her hands tingled, and with a vividness that shocked her, she wanted to taste Joaquin's tongue, to see if that was where the scent came from.

And for one second, he seemed, too, as if he were buzzing, alight. His cheekbones flushed a dark caramel and his lips parted, and he stared at her mouth as if he would climb in.

A crack came from somewhere, breaking the spell, and both of them took a step backward. "What was that?" Penny said.

He seemed to know she meant both the noise and the odd spell that had fallen over them. "I don't know." Taking a breath, he wiped his face and seemed to remember she had come up the lane with someone else. "Who was that?"

"Uh." Penny looked over her shoulder. "I met him at the market." She told him the story of the scary man and Paul's rescue and the story of the dragon god.

His jaw went tight. "You should be careful. Don't show the feathers around anymore," he said. "Be careful of the professor, too. I don't trust him."

"What's going on?"

"Probably nothing much." He cocked his head and smiled. "Come on, I have some things to show you."

In the middle of the living room was a collection of items. "I was cleaning up in the basement," he said. "These were all down there."

The scent was very strong now, heady and dizzying, and Penny knelt to touch a wooden frieze. It was elaborately carved and inlaid with what seemed to be pink granite, showing a creature somewhere between a dragon and a snake and a bird. Penny brushed her fingers over it. "This is beautiful!"

"I'm pretty sure it's supposed to be Quetzalcoatl," Joaquin said.

Penny's head jerked up, and something like fear rushed into her mouth. "That's who the professor was talking about."

He shrugged lightly. "Well, as legends go, it's pretty pervasive around here. I think the artist who used to live in the house must have carved it. It's probably worth a lot of money if you want to find a buyer."

"Oh, no! I would never want to sell it." She pointed to the east, a space that seemed to just be waiting for it. "I'll hang it there."

She brought her attention back to the other things: a bucket with artists' brushes and small tools, probably for the carving; a box of what seemed to be old clothes, none worth much by the look of them; odds and ends of small paintings; a small, egglike sculpture made of rose quartz; and a plain white box with a lid, the kind sold in office supply stores for files. "What's this?"

He smiled slightly. "Open it."

Penny tugged off the lid, and an explosion of scent filled the room. Inside the box were hundreds of pink feathers, maybe thousands. She laughed and plunged her hands into the treasure, bending her head to inhale the scent deeply. "What *is* that smell?"

Joaquin was still, standing by the threshold into the kitchen. "I don't know," he said.

"Come put your hands in these feathers. They feel wonderful."

He didn't move, his black eyes fixed on her face.

Penny smiled slightly. "Come on. You'll like it." She raised a hand, extending it toward him.

As if he were a puppet, he collected up his limbs and made his way over, his knees collapsing beside the box.

Fiercely, he plunged his hands into the feathers, up to the elbows. Penny followed suit, letting the downy softness swirl over her wrists and the delicate flesh on her inner arm. She laughed low in her throat. Her hands brushed Joaquin's, buried the feathers, and she pressed her palms into his playfully. He laughed, too, and there was suddenly a brightness in the world, a connection.

He raised his head at the same minute she did. Their eyes met over the box, and the world both narrowed and swelled at the very same instant, as if there were only this, only Joaquin's eyes and Joaquin's hands. The place where they touched seemed very hot. She found her gaze straying to his lips, full and ever so slightly chapped, and wondered if he would kiss her. The pad of his index finger pressed into hers, and then abruptly he stood up. Feathers, freed by the gesture, floated in the air. One clung to his jean-covered thigh. A few wisps stuck to his wing-black hair, and Penny smiled gently, standing to brush them away.

"I have to go," he said.

"Right this second? Would you like some tea or something for all your trouble?"

"No," he said gruffly, his head bent. "Thank you."

"Well, at least let me"—she stepped forward and held out a hand to pluck the feather fronds from his hair—"get these out of your hair."

He raised a hand and caught her arm around the wrist, fiercely. His eyes burned black as oil bubbling in an iron cauldron, and despite herself, Penny felt her breath catch, both in desire and fear. He was powerfully strong, and his body was so close she could feel his heat radiating out from his belly and legs. The sheen of his hair, falling in that satiny curtain, gave her a vision of it falling on her bare neck, chest, breasts. As if the vision caught him, too, he swayed slightly forward, his lips only millimeters away. Her breasts brushed his chest. One of his feet settled between both of hers, as if to use a knee to ease her legs apart for—

"There is much you do not yet understand," he said roughly.

"Tell me!"

He shook his head, his eyes so close she could see each individual eyelash, and the truth that there was nothing but unbroken blackness in his irises. The breath of his mouth touched her upper lip, moist and hot, and she shivered in yearning. "I cannot."

He released her so suddenly that Penny stumbled backward. And he bolted without even looking at her. Bewildered, Penny sat back on her heels and looked at her cat, sitting on the windowsill. "What was that all about?"

The cat blinked lazily. *Who knows?* he seemed to say. *Who knows?*

Bemused, Penny plunged her hands back into the feathers, small and large, peacock style and not. A dragon god? Could such a thing exist?

How ridiculous! Taking feathers from the box, wondering where the old woman had acquired them, she began to arrange them on the floor in random patterns. They were beautiful and she could use them.

But they were *not* dragon feathers. Not.

Chapter 5

There had been so many odd happenings the day before that on Monday, Penny went in early to school so she could speak with Señora alone. She found her in the garden just outside the studio, her long black hair caught loosely in a barrette at her neck, humming breathily as she hung tied bunches of yarrow upside down. Silver bracelets shone on her dark wrists. Her hands, long and finely boned, were as beautiful and strong as one would expect from an artist.

"Señora," Penny said, "I'm sorry to bother you so early, but I wanted to talk to you before class, if I might."

"Of course, Penny!" She did not wear jeans or even trousers as modern women did, but always long, light skirts that swirled around her legs and slim ankles. It gave her a slightly Old World appearance. "What's on your mind?"

Pulling out the feathers, Penny said, "Do you know what kind of feathers these are?"

Señora smiled her elusive little smile, like a cat turning up the edges of her mouth, and took them from Penny's hands. "They look like dyed peacock to me. Did you use cochineal?"

Penny shook her head. "I found them like this." She paused. "You don't recognize some sacred bird or something?"

She shook her head, lifted the feathers to her nose. "Hmmm."

"What does it smell like to you?"

"Morning, and grass. Let's take them to the others and see if anyone else knows, hmm?"

The other students were still eating breakfast in a hushed, well-lit room. Glass pitchers of orange juice and milk, and carafes of coffee littered the table. The students read the newspaper, chatted quietly.

With a stab of yearning, Penny wondered again why she had not been told of this arrangement. She would have enjoyed being with the other students, made part of the group. All her life she'd been an outsider.

And yet, even as she thought it, she realized she didn't want to leave her cozy little home on the top of the lane, or her cat, or the pleasant silence or humming warmth late at night. It was almost as if Santa Fe had called her and then offered her a home, a nest for her to nourish her gifts. The others did not seem as inclined to stay here.

With a shock, Penny realized she fully intended to remain.

"Buenos días," Señora said.

"Good morning, Penny," said Alina, the wild-haired woman. "Would you like some coffee?"

"Sure," she said, settling in the chair Alina patted for her.

Señora raised the feathers, thrust them toward the table. "What do you each smell on these feathers?"

Obligingly, they passed the feathers around, hand to hand. Most smelled nothing at all, but they landed last in the hands of the older man, who said gruffly, "Goat shit."

The others laughed. Señora said, "To me they smell of fresh dew, like morning." She smiled benevolently at Penny. "What do you smell?"

"Brown sugar, bubbling. Butter and caramel. Sweet things." She took the feathers and inhaled deeply, close. "It's wonderful."

The old man tried again, coughed. "Nope. Goats. I know that smell."

Señora gave Penny her feathers. "Perception is everything," she said. "Remember that." For a moment, it seemed the famed weaver was speaking only to Penny. Her eyes were kind but somehow urgent.

Then she turned to the group. "I hope you've all brought me your dyeing samples. It's time for class to begin." With a swirl of hair and skirts, she spun around. "Come along."

It was only later that Penny realized that Señora had not asked anyone if they knew what the feathers were, only what they smelled like.

She barely glimpsed Joaquin through the day—he was always working, digging, trimming, watering. He had a green thumb of mythic proportions, judging by the gardens around the hacienda, and he never seemed to tire. Penny admired his energy and eye for beauty and arrangement. A stand of begonias with polka-dot leaves, for example, straight and clean next to a thriving stand of fluffy dahlias in a sunny spot.

Señora seemed driven, moving the students from task to task all day. As Penny walked toward home in the soft dusk of a Southwestern November, her brain felt overstuffed, vaguely achy with information overload. Dyestuffs were the subjects today, the lessons they worked with. Indigo and madder and saffron; larkspur and mesquite and the shimmery bodies of cochineal. She was nearly drunk with the saturation of color, swaying to a wave of blue, then a swell of pink and another of vivid yellow. Flowers and branches, powders and sticks—all with their own particular gift to the artist.

It seemed, twice, as she walked through the quiet, suppertime streets, that she felt someone watching her. Once, she was sure she heard footsteps and turned around with a frown, but there was no one there. Only the empty lane, lamplight spilling from a window to the sidewalk. Chiles perfumed the air.

Overtired, she told herself, and kept walking. *Overstimulated.* Paranoid after the odd encounters yesterday.

The feathers were safely tucked away in her bag, out of sight. She'd get home and have a nice sandwich and some hot chocolate, and curl up and read for the rest of the evening.

The sense of being followed walked down her neck again suddenly. Determined to stop indulging her imagination, she refused to turn around, but she did find her ears straining backward for the slightest crunch of gravel beneath a heel. Nothing. Only that eerie sense of being stalked.

There was a sudden whir, like wings, and startled, Penny whirled. She saw a bird taking flight from a nearby bush, its wings black against the graying sky. It let go a squawking protest, and seemed to alert others in its clan as it flew. They burst into the air as if terrified. She shivered, watching them, but there was still no one behind her.

The trees rustled and a shadow detached itself from the long shadows by the walk. Penny's heart clutched as she peered through the gloaming to make out what it was.

A big black cat, muscular with yellow eyes, leapt from the top of a fence post. He sauntered by lazily, his tail in the air, as if his work was done for the day. "You half scared me to death, you silly cat."

He blinked up at her but kept walking lazily, headed up the hill toward her street. Oddly comforted, she followed him. He walked all the way to her front gate, as if a soldier taking the maiden to her door, then looked back over his shoulder. "I'm fine," she said. "Thank you."

The cat leapt up on the fence and dived over, his body gleaming and sleek, and disappeared.

"Now I'm talking to strange cats," she said, and shook her head. Santa Fe was getting to her. Or maybe, she thought, yawning mightily as she let herself into the house, she was just working really hard. Her own cat greeted her, and Penny dropped her bag on the table and kicked off her boots. "I'm so tired!" she said, and the cat circled the spot on the floor where she'd laid out the feathers yesterday, sniffing curiously at the perimeter.

"What do *you* smell?" she asked, stroking his long back. "Sugar? Goat shit?"

He purred as if it were catnip, and rubbed his face on it. Penny chuckled and stretched out on the couch. "I just need a little nap," she said. The cat jumped up with her, purring on her belly. In the air, she heard the soft sound that so often came at night, rising as if from the very walls of the house. As she drifted off, she thought whimsically that it sounded almost like a purr. She imagined a cat like the Cheshire Cat in *Alice's Adventures in Wonderland,* but as big as a house, purring away.

She fell asleep, and her vision of a cat morphed in the dream world into a huge female bird god, covered with small pink feathers on its chest, and wide pink wings and a throaty purr—

A noise, sharp but unknown, jolted her out of the dream, and in the darkness, she felt something brushing over her face. The sugar scent was very strong, still somehow alluring and beautiful. A powerful wind brushed over her body and she leapt to her feet.

And she must have sleepwalked, because she wasn't on the couch any longer but on the front porch, and the noise she'd heard was a flurry of shouts and screams. She saw Joaquin, his back to her, warning off a trio of three men. One was the mean-looking, pockmarked man who confronted her at the plaza, and he was carrying something she couldn't make out.

The air filled with an odd sound, and Penny looked around, trying to figure out what it was. And then—impossible!—it was as if the creature from her dream had come to life, rising into the sky on enormous wings, the slow, powerful flaps creating a tempest of wind. It rose behind the men, who did not appear to see it.

Penny gaped, a shiver rushing over her arms, her spine. What could it be?

A *dragon?*

There was no such thing as a dragon. She had to be dreaming. It was dark. There was no moon. How could she see the creature so clearly?

The pockmarked man cried out a warning, again in his odd language—pointing back to her on the porch. Joaquin turned and cried out, "Penny, go back inside!"

"What's going on?"

"Just go. I'll tell you later."

The men backed away, and Joaquin moved with them, headed down the hill, rifle in his hands.

"Joaquin!" she cried.

"Not now, Penny! You're safe now. Go to bed."

She raised her eyes to the sky, unsettled and more than a little frightened. There was nothing there. Puff sat on the porch, unconcernedly licking a paw and using it to clean his face. The prosaic, relaxed aspect of the cat made Penny realize how ridiculous she was being. The men, okay—that was something to be afraid of. She wondered what they wanted, why they'd been outside her house.

And why Joaquin had been here, too. She stood there in the night, next to her cat, and listened to the stillness. In the distance, the town of Santa Fe winked and sparkled in undulating waves over the hills, a peaceful, placid scene.

She looked to the top of the trees, but of course they were perfectly still, not moving in the wake of a wind created by enormous wings. Of course not. "That was some dream," she said to Puff. He licked his whiskers.

Riled up and restless, she knew she'd never go to sleep right this minute, so she built a fire in the kiva fireplace in her living room, then went to the kitchen to make a cup of chamomile tea. The clear hay smell of it rose as she waited for it to brew, her hip propped up against the counter.

A gentle knock on the front door startled her, but she had a feeling she knew who it was. She peeped through a small window in the door, and opened it to Joaquin. "I just wanted to make sure you're okay," he said.

Penny shyly tucked a lock of hair behind her ear. "I'm fine. Are you?"

He nodded, but his brow was troubled.

"Come in and have some chamomile tea," Penny said, pulling the door open.

For a moment, he hesitated, then came through the door gingerly. "That would be nice."

She pointed to the couch. "I'll bring the tea." When she returned with a tray, he was scratching Puff's big head, and the monstrous cat was slumped against his leg, purring loudly. Penny chuckled. "He is your pal."

"I like him, too." Joaquin gave her a crooked grin. "He's a manly cat. A monster-truck-driving cat."

Penny sat down next to him on the couch. "A monster, anyway." She poured a cup of tea and dropped some honey into it, and passed it over. "Did you have cats as a child?"

"My mother loves animals. We've had everything—and cats aren't as hard on a garden as dogs, right?"

Penny nodded. "We always had dogs, never a cat. My mother didn't like them." With a little pinch, she thought of her mother's patrician bearing, her thin nose and blue eyes. "She fell in love with Puff, though. She spoiled him terribly." With a sense of surprise, she brushed away a tear. "I must miss her."

"I can see that. How long has it been?"

"My father died suddenly of a heart attack, and although my mother wasn't quite seventy, she just didn't thrive without him. She got sick and died within a year."

"It's sad," he said. His eyes were warm, patient. Penny didn't think she'd ever met a man who listened so well. "But also a tribute to their love for each other, isn't it?"

"I guess so," Penny said. "I think, in some ways, the fact that they were soul mates made it difficult when my own husband died when I was only twenty-eight."

"And you're thirty now?" He grinned impishly.

"Not quite. How did you know that?"

He wiggled his eyebrows. "I wanted to make sure I wasn't too old for you."

"Too old! How about too young?"

His face was enigmantic. "I'm older than you are."

Penny peered at him. "I want to know your face cream, then. You don't look it."

He took a sip of his tea, put it aside. "It's all part of the same thing, Penny. There is still a lot I can't tell you, but I want you to know I'm watching over you, that you're safe."

"Thank you." She scowled. "What were those men looking for?"

"It's a cult, or rather an old, old covenant. Some think it goes back to Spain. They think you might have some answers they want."

"Do I?"

His black gaze was steady. "In time, you will."

Penny made a split-second decision to trust him. He'd given her no reason to distrust him so far. "Shall we talk about ordinary things, then, señor?"

He laughed, and she liked the sound. "That would be great. What ordinary thing would you like to talk about?"

"Tell me about the most spectacular accident you had as a child and all the gruesome injuries." She sipped her tea. "Or tell me about the first time you fell in love. Or—how about this: What's your favorite movie of all time?"

"Oh, that's easy," he said, *"Last of the Mohicans."*

"No way. Mine, too!"

His grin lifted on one side. "Obviously, we're soul mates."

Penny grinned. "Obviously."

He stayed for an hour, and they only talked. And talked and talked. They shared a taste for historical movies and books, for comedy on television, for walking over driving. He loved showers. She loved baths. She liked the smell of clothes that had been hung out to dry in the sun, and he said it was his favorite smell.

And when he left, he only pressed a chaste kiss to the middle of her brow and melted into the night. It was comforting to know he likely still lurked, that all would be well as long as Joaquin, dutiful and kind and a good listener, was in her corner.

Chapter 6

After class the next evening, all Penny really wanted was a nice glass of crisp, cool wine, a bowl of soup and a pool of relaxation. Oh, and a very hot shower to ease the sore muscles in her shoulders. Señora Libélula seemed never to tire, but Penny wasn't alone in her weariness tonight. The whole class had been grumbling about it. She was looking forward to a restful supper.

But as she made her way through the grocery store, basket tucked into her elbow, she found herself looking over her shoulder, feeling that prickly, insistent sense of someone watching her. Testing the plumpness of a crimson pile of tomatoes, and again in the pasta aisle, she cautiously looked around, thinking of the men in front of her house last night, the oddity of Joaquin being there in the middle of the night, a rifle in his hands. She needed to think about that—but in truth, she was too tired to do it tonight.

And she was obviously just being paranoid. Her scans of the aisles showed only the ordinary evening customers. A good night's sleep would probably do wonders for her state of mind. She paid for her purchases and carried a string bag of chicken, onions, and pasta into the sharpening evening air.

A man stepped out of a plain black car in front of her, slamming the door smartly behind him. He gave her a polite nod. "Good evening."

She acknowledged the nod and detoured around him.

"You don't remember me?" he called after her. "Paul Rodriguez?"

She turned. Tucked the bag tighter to her body. His face came into focus. The thick mustache, the elegant bearing—it was the professor from the college. "Oh. Yes."

"I'm sorry to bother you, but I've been thinking about this ... er ... situation." He lifted a shoulder and a brow simultaneously. "I haven't been entirely honest."

"Is that so?" A part of her was poised to dash away if the situation required it. The other part was curious. Thinking of all the oddities from the past week, she cast an eye around the area for lurking henchmen or weird mythological creatures. The back of her neck was tight. "What did you hold back?"

"I was hoping you might have a cup of coffee with me, let me explain."

She shook her head. "I have a lot of homework." She made a move to go around, to head toward the hill. Darkness was thickening in the east, falling like a net curtain from the horizon to the mountains, closing the city in. "I need to get home."

"Please," he said. Quietly. "There is much you should know. One drink?" He pointed to a café behind her, well lit and modern. "It is important."

Penny considered. What could it hurt? "All right."

"Thank you." He came toward her, gesturing ahead of himself with an Old World courtliness she found very appealing. He held the door to the café open, and she swirled in ahead of him, only then—suddenly—realizing that she'd been wearing skirts almost constantly since arriving here.

Hmm.

They settled and ordered coffee once again, and Penny folded her hands. "Tell me."

"There is more to the dragon legend than I spoke of."

Penny sipped coffee, raised her eyebrows. Waited.

"*Curanderas* say the feathers shed by the dragon are very powerful for healing, and they make pilgrimages to a shrine to petition to find them. It's said that the feathers grant longevity and can cure any number of diseases."

Penny wanted to chuckle, but his dark eyes appeared to be perfectly serious. "And you think those feathers I found are dragon feathers? Don't dragons have scales?"

"Well, I don't know. I've never seen a dragon. Have you?"

"Not that I know of."

"Just so." He shook a packet of sugar, neatly tore the edge away. "The legend is that the dragon chooses her protectors, a man and a woman who keep her safe from the world of human beings."

A faint, silvery ripple moved on Penny's spine. As if he noticed, Paul leaned forward. "She is also said to have a very powerful scent—some find it repulsive, some compelling."

Penny blinked, thinking of the reactions of her classmates. Señora smelled grass and morning. The man in her weaving class had been repulsed. *It smells like goat shit.*

She almost shuddered, but it seemed important to appear to be unmoved.

She'd never asked Joaquin what he smelled, but it appeared that he found it appealing, too, since he'd plunged his hands into the box with her.

To distract herself, perhaps lighten the mood, she joked, "I'll be sure and find a big sword to protect myself. Who is it I'll need to find? St. George, right?"

"I don't know." He looked at her very intently.

"Surely you don't believe in a dragon!" she cried. "You're a man of science!"

"Exactly. I am a man of higher knowledge. If the evidence points to a dragon, then I must postulate that there is a dragon." His eyes glittered. "And imagine what a coup for a scientist to discover such a thing, no?"

"I suppose so."

"Will you help me find out if it's true, Penny?"

"Don't be ridiculous." She shook her head. "I'm done."

"Wait!" Urgently, he grabbed her wrist, and there was force and fury in his grip. "Just listen one more minute."

"Let go of me," she said, her voice low and dangerous.

He did. "Believe or don't believe," he said. "But know that there are those who do. They will not hesitate to kill you if they think they can have access to those feathers."

She thought of the incident last night and lowered her eyes quickly.

"So there has been trouble already, hmmm?" he said.

She met his eyes and lied. "Nothing more than what you saw at the square." Sliding sideways, she picked up her string bag. "Leave me alone, Professor. If I want to talk to you, I'll come find *you*."

He stood, giving her a slight bow of the head. "Very well. If you need me, I will be at your service."

"I'm sure I'll be fine."

As she walked up the hill in the dark, however, she felt uneasy. A wind tossed the upper reaches of the trees, and she kept scanning the sky for some giant birdlike creature. A shadow moved along the street, and she nearly leapt out of her skin until she realized it was a passing car headlight making the outline of a shrub look like a man rushing toward her.

A dragon.

How could there possibly be a dragon in the modern world? Not that Penny believed there had ever been any to start with. And yet—

Every culture had tales of them. The legends circled the globe, from the evil dragons of medieval lore to the red dragons parading down the street on Chinese New Year to—now—the feathered serpent of the Mayas.

What if one had survived, and it was indeed the creature leaving behind those beautiful feathers? Something like excitement leapt in her belly.

What if?

All day, she'd been hoping to see Joaquin and ask him what had been going on last night. He had never appeared, and when Penny asked Señora, she said she hadn't seen him. Perhaps, she thought, turning on to the lane that led to her house on the hill, he'd be waiting at home.

If there was a dragon, what did those men want of her? The professor was easy—he wanted fame and attention. The others—she wasn't sure. The Indian had seemed very angry both times she'd seen him.

Whatever. She sighed with the difficulty of trying to sort it all out. Her head ached as she trudged the last stretch of the hill to her house. A nice bowl of soup, some wine and good night's sleep. That was what she needed.

A lamp, burning in friendly welcome, lit the living room window, and Penny called out happily, "Hello?"

But only Puff came running to fling himself into the sybaritic rope trick of cat and ankles. "You'll do," she said, and laughed, rubbing his head for a minute. "Okay, come on. Let's get supper." She shed her coat and carried her bag into the kitchen.

There on the table was a fan, exquisitely made. *For you,* said a note in a beautiful hand. *Joaquin.*

It was woven of the pink feathers, and laced with beautiful beadwork. She waved it in the air and the extraordinary scent wafted out, along with a hint of man and cinnamon, and she thought of his hands doing this small, precise work with a sense of dizziness. A vision of his long, dark fingers came to her mind, fingers lacing feathers, lacing through her hair, down her back; his mouth pressing lightly to that very sweet place at the base of her nape—

Stop it!

With a little shake, she put the fan away where Puff wouldn't bother it, and focused on fixing some supper.

Somewhere in the middle of the night, Penny awakened abruptly, her heart pounding. At first, she only lay there, blinking, trying to pinpoint what had awakened her, and it was hard to even remember where she was. The room was lit from the wrong side, the bed was so soft—

Oh. Yes. Santa Fe.

In a rush, the rest came back: *dragon, feathers, men, danger!*

She sat up in her nightgown and listened carefully. There was a rumbling sound, and that rustling sound of wings. Tossing the covers away, she snatched her robe from the chair and rushed out to the back porch, which was where the sound seemed to be coming from.

And there, unmistakable now, was an enormous bird with long, elegant wings and a tail like a phoenix, held aloft in a graceful pose. It seemed to hang there for a long moment, as if allowing Penny time to absorb the astonishing sight of it, as big as a flying elephant.

Penny could only gape, her hands clutched to the front of her robe. It seemed to glow softly in the darkness, opalescent, fantastic, a creature born of a dream.

And suddenly, Penny remembered dreams she'd had as a child, of a being made of downy feathers, cradling her when she was sad or afraid. It seemed it might have been *this* creature. How was that possible?

After a long, long time, the creature made a quiet noise, a trilling softness like an eagle, flapped the muscular wings, and disappeared. A feather, perfect and whole, floated down and landed at Penny's feet. She knelt to pick it up, and a fresh, hot scent of buttery brown sugar came off it. With a soft laugh, she inhaled it, thinking of what the professor had said: *"The feathers are said to have a strong odor. . . ."*

Emotion crowded into her throat. Tears of wonder and honor pricked her eyes. A dragon! It was *real!*

A shadow peeled away from the dark wall, and Joaquin said, "It's me. Don't be afraid."

"I wasn't," she said, and extended the feather toward him. "Did you see it, too?"

He nodded.

"What do you smell on these feathers?"

His sleek black hair fell forward as he bent in to inhale the scent. "It smells very clean, like soap or shampoo. Like you." He lifted a hand and brushed away a lock of her hair.

Penny went still, aware of her slight dishabille, and looked up into his face. He smoothed her cheek with the tips of his fingers, then took her hand. "She has shown herself, chosen you, so now I can show you," he said. "Come."

Chapter 7

He led her back into the house and through a door in the kitchen to the dark, cold cellar. Penny had come down here only twice, the first to see what was there, the second to stow some boxes. Unlike many cellars, it wasn't spidery or particularly off-putting; it was just cold and unappealing. No reason to linger.

Joaquin flipped on the light and moved behind the furnace, down a short, black hallway that seemed to end in nothingness until he pressed through a narrow place. "This is the only bad part," he said apologetically. "Hold your breath for a minute and push through. It's not far."

Penny sucked in her breath and let him tug her through the earthen passage, feeling it press into her breasts and tummy and bottom. It might have panicked her but for his hand clasping hers firmly.

She stumbled a little when they half fell into the area beyond, then gasped in wonder, for it was a very large room, a natural cave lit by torches hung on the wall. The rocky floor was covered by rugs woven of some shimmery fiber Penny had never seen, and there was an air of absolute serenity. It was plain the dragon must sleep here. Tufts and piles of feathers were scattered about, and a pile of the fantastically beautiful rugs were coiled into a nest to one side. The scent of sugar and butter was rich as a morning of baking.

Penny's heart squeezed and she looked up at Joaquin in question. "The dragon?"

He nodded. "This way." Letting go of her hand, he headed through an archway. A series of rooms opened, one upon the other, natural cave space, smoothed by years of water that no longer flowed. Finally, they had to squeeze through another narrow passageway to enter the final room, where a spring burbled from the wall and tumbled down the smooth red wall to a pool carved by eons of water pouring into it. An altar of some sort was set to one side, and obviously it was visited by healers of many traditions—there were candles of many varieties and offerings of corn and beadwork, scarves and bread.

She moved to the altar, feeling again the sense of sacred quiet, of a reverent, powerful holiness. Her throat was tight with it. Once, long ago, she'd made a trek to an ancient church on a hill in France, and this felt like that—a place of women. Not a cathedral sense of grandness, but a place of the Mother. "How do people get here?"

Lifting an arm, Joaquin pointed to a narrow fissure in the rock. "Through there."

"They can just walk in?"

He shook his head. "It is a very steep climb to the opening, and the place is hidden behind the waterfall, and then up through a narrow passageway. It isn't easy." He raised a brow. "And Señora Libélula's compound guards the path."

"She knows?"

He nodded, crossing his burly arms.

Penny looked around. "But how can the—creature—get in and out? That's too small."

"There is an opening high on the cliff for her. Sometimes rock climbers try to get in, but the smell sends them back." Joaquin walked to a spot before the altar and pointed upward. "She can only leave at night, obviously, but she longs for the feeling of air on her wings."

Penny followed and looked up. A slice of night sky showed through an opening. "She?"

The sound of great wings came to them, and Penny

raised her head, a primitive sense of terror and honor
and excitement burning in her throat. She found herself
shrinking back toward Joaquin, who put his hand on her
shoulder. "Do not be afraid."

A scented wind heralded the dragon's arrival, and a
flap of wings—and then, suddenly, she sailed downward
toward them, as graceful and weightless as a scarf, despite her great size. Her fine, long wings looked both
sturdy and graceful; her chest bowed outward, and her
face, despite the fierce ridges on the sides, was somehow
kindly.

She was larger than an elephant and the pointed tail
seemed muscular, a rudder she coiled around herself
as she settled on the cave floor. Her great clawed feet
crossed and she lowered her head, as if knowing how
frightening her size could be.

Transfixed, Penny gaped, gathering wondrous details.
And entirely pink! "I would have imagined a dragon to
be like a snake," she said quietly. "But she's like a bird."

"A bit," Joaquin said, and squeezed her shoulders.
"You may approach. She likes to be petted on her
chest."

Penny bit her lip, then took a step and another toward
the dragon. Her wings and tail were covered with the
large peacock feathers, astonishing in such huge numbers. There was greater variation in the smaller feathers
on her chest—some were pale violet, and pink, and a
few crimson. Her wings folded softly over her back.

Her great eyes were a clear amber, with the long
pupil of a reptile or a cat, and she blinked as Penny
crept closer, feathery brushes of eyelashes making her
seem very much a girl. She bowed her head, and Penny
reached out a hand, fingers trembling, to brush it across
the broad nose.

Penny caught her breath in wonder. The dragon
lifted her head, and Penny moved closer to stroke the
long, feathered throat and the beautiful chest with their
shorter, multicolored feathers. A low, familiar vibration
suddenly commenced, and Penny looked at Joaquin.

She pressed her hand gently to the spot on the dragon's throat where the sound came from, and she cried, "She's purring!"

He smiled.

After a time, the dragon floated over the wall and into her lair, and the two humans followed, for where the dragon went, there was warmth. The creature curled up in her nest of rugs and tucked her nose beneath a wing, and the humans settled at her back. She purred softly, the sound rumbling through the cave ceiling, Penny knew, to the floors of the house above. "I always wondered what that sound was."

Absently, Joaquin smoothed the feathers along her rump, as if she were a dog, his long brown hands graceful and strong. Penny wanted to touch them again, feel him, but she looked away. Leaning on the warm body of the dragon, she said, "Now, tell me about all of this."

"The professor told you most of it. She is an ancient creature who is beloved by healers because of the properties of her feathers." He smiled. "She has been waiting a long time for you," he said. "The former caretaker has been gone for three years."

"So, am I the caretaker, then?"

"Not until you choose. It's up to you."

"How was I chosen?"

He shook his head. "We don't know that part. The old caretaker was here for as long as my mother can remember, and they were friends, but the old woman had come to Santa Fe with the Mabel Dodge Luhan crowd—almost a hundred years ago."

"Wow."

"We know some things," he said. "If you choose this path, you will live a long time. The dragon's companion and defender is always a woman, a young woman who will not age as others do. And she is allowed to choose a consort, who will also age very slowly."

A ripple of heat went through Penny. "A consort?"

His black eyes seemed made of pools of ink, hot and unreadable. "A man to be your companion."

Penny bent her head. "I see."

"There is a price you will pay for the long life," he said, touching one finger to her chin and tilting her head up. When she met his gaze, he said, "You will not have children if you go this route."

"Why?"

"It appears to be practical. A mother should not outlive a child."

Penny caught her breath. Nodded. "I see."

"There is a story that one of the early protectors was torn between the needs of her child and the needs of the dragon. The rule was made then."

Penny frowned. "So will I be sterilized if I choose this path?"

Gently he said, "It more seems that the dragon chooses those who are"—he scrambled for a kind word—"unable to have children."

Penny thought of the years she'd tried with Alex, and smiled sadly. "In this case, that's probably true."

Joaquin touched her face. "I am not able, either," he said. "A great sadness to me."

"I'm sorry."

He nodded. "The other condition is that you will not be able to leave Santa Fe. She will need you here."

"And what would my tasks be?"

"Only to be here. To come show her love and make sure she is all right, that if she is unwell, she has food and water, that none get in to hurt her." His mouth tightened. "There is more danger now than there has been. Satellite pictures, curiosity seekers; men like Professor Rodriguez, who want to make a name for themselves." He lifted his eyebrows. "Even airplanes make her life more difficult."

Penny laughed. "I can just imagine what a pilot would think of her!"

His eyes crinkled upward. It made him look a cousin

to the dragon—slightly exotic, otherworldly. "Right. So one of the biggest things you do is deflect interest, keep her safely hidden from the curious world."

"Are there any other dragons in the world? Is she the only one?" It seemed to her that it would be unbearably lonely.

"We think there are. Sometimes, she flies away and doesn't come back for a week or two. We think she is going to Mexico to mate, but thus far, she has not had any offspring, at least not in the time we have been keeping records."

"What happened last night, Joaquin?"

He shook his head, his lips tightening. "They're Indians from Mexico. They want to prove she exists for political reasons."

Penny frowned. "Political reasons?"

"Her feathers genuinely are healing. The *curanderas*—the traditional Spanish and Indian healers—know the ways to use them, and it is believed that money can be made for indigenous people by publicizing the methods."

"But," Penny protested, "she needs her feathers for herself!" She leaned into the dragon protectively, feeling the pulse of warmth and heat beneath her cheek. The dragon lifted her head slightly, and then, reassured, fell back to her doze.

"Exactly," Joaquin said. "She must be protected."

Sleepily—it was the middle of the night, after all—Penny yawned. She could easily fall asleep right here, next to the dragon. "What about you?" she said.

"What about me?" Was it her imagination, or was he moving closer?

"How did you come to this?"

"My mother, as a *curandera*, made offerings often when I was a child." He was definitely closer, rising on his knees to reach for Penny. "I grew up walking to the shrine with her, and one day, the dragon showed herself to me. My mother wept in happiness. Not many men are so honored."

He was right over her now. Penny looked at his beautiful mouth, the full lips, the white edge of a tooth just within. "Does she have a name, the dragon?"

His gaze lowered to her mouth, and he said with measured cadence, "We all call her something different."

"You? What do you call her?"

His chest touched Penny's. "Rosa."

"Oh!"

His hand slid through her hair, palm cupping her ear. "Are you going to kiss me, Joaquin?"

"If you don't mind."

"I don't mind," she whispered, and he edged over her, putting their bodies lightly in contact and tumbling her backward into a downy pile of cashmere-soft feathered blankets, and covering her mouth with his own.

Sparks of pleasure arced through her, and she made a soft, surprised sound. He, too, seemed startled, and raised his head for a moment, until Penny reached for him, pulled him down to her again, and their mouths opened, hotter than they should have been, and his body seemed to radiate something she'd never experienced, a silvery sparking that made her skin feel as if it glowed and pulsed itself. Her breasts felt sparked, and her thighs and the spot low between their bellies, where their root chakras glowed, seemed to get very, very hot.

Penny opened to his kiss, inviting his tongue into her, a silky thickness, a skilled dance. He suckled her lower lip slowly, then released it, moved his fingers lightly on her right breast, flicking a light touch over the nipple. His hips nestled closer, and she felt his erection, thick and hot, pressing into the heat of her own sex. Next to them, the dragon purred softly, a sound as rich as any music.

Joaquin abruptly lifted his head. He sucked in a breath, as if he'd been underwater, and touched her cheek. "I did not mean to—" He looked at her mouth, touched her lower lip with the pad of his index finger. "I have been wanting to kiss you like that since I first saw you, standing in my mother's garden."

"Me, too." Penny swallowed. "I need to think about all of this," she whispered. "Take it in, understand what it means."

"Of course." He straightened, and the dragon made a soft noise, settling more deeply into sleep with a hollow snore.

Penny laughed—it was a very doglike sound. With a sharp sense of fondness, she put her cheek to the beast's long spine and sighed. She was like a combination of the best qualities of dogs and cats. And birds, too, she supposed—those silky feathers. As if the creature—Rosa—heard her thoughts, she roused a little, opening one amber eye, and her tongue slid between great jaws to slip along Penny's arm, a loving lap. Her tongue was slightly rough, her saliva almost burning hot, and it smelled fantastic.

"Tomorrow," Joaquin said, "look at that place."

"I will." She smoothed the skirts of her robe, realizing she still wore her nightclothes. Her feet were in slippers. By the time they made their way back to the basement stairs and into the kitchen, dawn stained the far east horizon.

Joaquin paused at the door and touched one finger to her cheek. "Think carefully. You seem a woman who should have a child." He pressed a kiss to her forehead and melted into the evening like a ghost.

P enny did not go back to her bed. Instead she took a shower to wash the sleepiness and strong scent of the dragon off her skin. As she toweled away the water, sunlight angled through the bathroom window, illuminating her body for her. She stopped for a moment and looked at her breasts, her belly, the dark triangle of hair, her thighs.

A body that would bear a child?

In truth, she had made peace with it, though she had once wanted one with Alex. Her art had always been her child—the fabric and the quilts, the piecing together something beautiful out of scraps. She did not mind children, but it was not a hardship to imagine never actually having one of her own.

So that part was not difficult. She had other concerns, and as she dressed, she tried to organize her chaotic thoughts so she could speak with Señora Libélula before the other students arrived.

Joaquin's mother. Who knew Penny had been drawn to Santa Fe by the dragon, and knew the house should be hers.

Penny found Señora in her garden, singing to the orchids blooming against the wall—the exotic flowers evidence of the powerful healing qualities the señora boasted as *curandera*. Healer, weaver, witch—surrounded by magic. Even in the bright sunlight, there was no age on her face, no lines or wrinkles. Her black hair lay thick and glossy on her shoulders, as long as a girl's.

"Good morning, Penny," she said, turning with her watering can in hand. "I expected you. Come." She waved toward a small café table nestled in a sunny corner of the patio. It was set with plates and silver and a basket of oranges. "Let's have our breakfast and you can ask me the questions I know must be burning in you."

Penny trailed the slender form of her mentor to the table and accepted a cup of steaming hot coffee, poured into a delicate pink cup painted with a stylized dragon. She laughed softly. "Aha."

Señora smiled. "We have our little jokes here and there." She served pastries and butter, passed a pot of jam toward Penny. "Isn't she beautiful?"

Penny blinked away an emotional tear. "Yes. The most beautiful thing I have ever seen."

"Me, too." She cut into a Danish, took a bite and put down her fork. "Once upon a time, I was groomed to be her caretaker, you know." She shook back her beautiful hair. "Hazel O'Neal, the old woman who lived in the house on the hill, found me when I was seven. She was already very old then, and she knew she would have to move on in time."

"How did she choose you?" Penny asked.

"She saw a weaving I had made of a small pink dragon, and invited me to come to visit her. We made the trek up the back of the bluff to the shrine, and when I fell in love with those feathers and that scent, she knew I was her successor."

"The scent is a sign?"

"Yes. If it's sugary or sweet, like morning, you have the capacity to be her priestess."

"So . . . what happened?" Penny asked. "Why did you not become the successor?"

She smiled softly. "I was a heedless young woman. I fell in love, and I nearly let that love lead me to betray Rosa." Her mouth sobered. "Instead, I only betrayed myself. I bore my lover a child, and he left me for another town, another girl. Hazel was very angry with me, because of course she had to begin again to find some-one to follow in her footsteps."

"Why couldn't you do it if you had a child?"

Señora's grand dark eyes softened. "The protector and her consort are granted extended lives. Not a child."

"Ah." Penny nodded.

"Too painful for a mother to bury her child, live long after he is old and dies." She shuddered delicately. "So . . . when I made my error and Joaquin was born, Hazel and I conceived the idea of the school to draw a pool of possible successors. I had nearly despaired when you applied."

Penny frowned. "How did you know I would be right?"

"The smell of your sample work, your quilt. That is why we require the submission of actual fabric. I took it to Rosa, and she chose you."

"Just like that?"

"There were other things. The body of knowledge is old and sometimes hard to interpret, but there are sym-bols Hazel trained me to look for—the daylilies in your work, the loneliness you expressed—but it's the mark of the pink dragon we find."

"I don't remember a pink dragon in my work."

Señora smiled. "Don't you?" She took a picture from a stack on the table and held it up for Penny to see. "Now do you see it?"

Penny laughed and brought her hands to her mouth. The quilt was a mosaic in shades of pink and crimson and candy floss, and when viewed at a distance, the pat-tern of dragon feathers was obvious. "How funny!"

Penny sat quietly and let it all wash over her. "Will I be able to continue my studies with you? Can I still learn to weave and make my fabrics?"

"Oh yes!" Señora Libélula bent over the table and put her long hands around her student's. "You are a very promising weaver and a fine artist. You must continue that work. It's one of the elements we must have. With-out the art—"

"A woman must have either art or a child."

"Yes."

"And I may also choose my consort?"

"Of course. Or do not choose." She dipped her head, a gesture of advice. "I would choose one, so you will have a companion with whom you can grow old. Very, very old."

"How old?"

"I don't know. Hazel remembered the American Revolution. She pretended to have arrived with the artists' colonies, but she came as an indentured servant to a Spanish colonial family."

Penny's heart felt pinched. "So long!"

"Yes." With her fingertips, she nudged a dish of cheeses toward Penny. "Do not decide this morning, *m'ija*. A day or two will not make any difference."

It seemed wiser to plunge into her studies after so many revelations, and as she walked home again through the crisp dark, Penny was delighted to realize she'd hardly thought of the situation all day. Not Joaquin, not the dragon, not the decision she had to make. Art could do that—distract a mind and heart from almost anything.

Working her fingers, tired from the new action of learning to spin, an exacting and difficult process, she thought of what to do. The night rustled around her, making her jumpy again, as she had been the night before. Once, a man with his head down, like a drunk, bumped into her, but he muttered in slurry Spanish and listed onward.

Normal life. But it didn't keep her from feeling jumpy as she turned onto her dark lane. It felt as if someone watched her, and she paused, turning around to see if she could pick out the professor's car. She didn't see it. Or any other pedestrians. Her imagination was boiling over.

Raising her eyes toward the darkening sky, a part of her sang with wonder of the idea of seeing the dragon again, all affection and evocative scents.

Another part of her thought—*two hundred years!*

Three hundred! It was so long. It stretched ahead, hollow and unimaginable. But she would be doing it to protect Rosa. To be sure no one tried to come to her and take all her feathers for any scheme or even a good cause. The idea made her stomach hurt. It made her feel fierce and protective.

And she would not have to be alone. She could choose a companion.

As if he were drawn by her struggle, Joaquin waited for her at her house. He sat on the porch with a candle burning, and said, "Sit down. I have cooked for you. Would you like wine?"

"Cooked?" She echoed. "You can cook?"

His very white smile flashed. "Yes. I am a very good cook, and I thought you might be very tired after such a big night."

On the porch glowed a portable clay fireplace, shaped like a cone. Penny sat down and stretched her stiff fingers toward the flames. The smoke gave off a scent of mesquite.

"Here you are," Joaquin said, returned with two glasses filled with white wine. He dashed back into the house and returned with plates piled high with a fluffy mass of rice, and chicken cooked with saffron and a chunk of fresh, grainy bread.

"Wow. You weren't kidding!" She grinned. "A man who cooks is a treasure to behold."

He winked. "I'll be right back. I'm going to get the butter. Anything else?"

Penny shook her head, a pleasant tingling just below her ribs. It was a warm surprise to discover she could find herself falling in love again. She thought of his lips, of the sparking electricity that had flowed between them last night. He was intelligent, smart, sexy—

Falling in love?

She touched the recognition with an inner probe, trying to get the sense of it. Love?

A rustling in the leaves made her turn around, happily expecting the dragon to be rising from her secret entrance. Instead, the one time she should have been paranoid, she wasn't. She saw a figure rushing toward her, and managed to half stand before someone else tackled her and threw a blanket over her head, effectively stifling her scream.

Thrashing, slamming back and forth, Penny fought with whatever she had, but although her captor nearly dropped her once, he grabbed her again, and in seconds she was loaded into a car and it was driving away.

Penny's captors seemed to drive a very long time. When at last they got to wherever they were going, she was overheated and choking in the blanket, and feeling desperately afraid. A man roughly pulled the blanket off her head, berating the other man in a language she recognized—and her heart sank. It was the language the pockmarked Indian had spoken at the square.

When she could catch her breath, she looked around the area, but it was too dark to make out much more than the reality that she was out in the country somewhere, no longer in town. The desert hush lay in the air, broken only by the hooting of an owl, high in some unseen tree.

The man who took her arm now, not unkindly, was tiny and brown, his hair a dusty black cap. He said something to her, and from the rise at the end, she thought it was a question, but she just shook her head. Her stomach growled.

It was no surprise to find the pockmarked man seated within the house. He gazed at her with flat eyes and gestured for her to sit down on a couch shoved beneath the window. There were two other men in the room, both looking nearly as dangerous as their henchmen, all of them with the high, tilted cheekbones and pecan-colored skin. Not brothers, but definitely from the same village. The one with the scars looked at her and said something in his language. A man sitting on the edge of the desk translated, "He say the dragon is causing you too much trouble. You should go home."

She nearly agreed with him, then remembered that her goal was to convince people that Rosa did not exist. "I have no idea what you're talking about. I came here to go to school with Señora Libélula."

Scar Man flipped a photo at her, and Penny picked it up. It showed a night sky and two dragons flying in the light of a full moon. Two? She looked at him, frowning, not pretending quite so much now to be ignorant. She waited for the translation of a long speech.

"He say you lie. These two live in Oaxaca, but she comes to Santa Fe to roost. She will have baby, and it brings a lot of money."

Penny shook her head. "I don't know what you're talking about."

Desk Sitter slammed his fist on the desk. "He'll kill you, lady. You better tell him how to get to that big bird."

Penny just looked at them. Shrugged.

In that moment, she knew she wasn't going to leave the dragon, that the creature, so rare and fine and valuable, deserved a protector.

Silence fell on the room. Penny wondered if they would kill her.

In the distance came the sound of wind, gathering as wind did in these bluffs, rolling itself into a force that swirled into a giant power and slammed into whatever objects were in the way.

Outside, someone screamed, and the men inside leapt to their feet. Volleys of conversation sailed back and forth, and one of the men grabbed her. "Come on."

She stumbled a little, and the man holding on to her arm jerked her hard. They went outside, into the light of a moon rising in the east. The wind had flown over the house and settled, for now the night was absolutely still. In the driveway, the white-garbed man who'd taken her inside was now crumpled in a heap.

Or was he?

Penny looked closer and saw that he appeared to be kneeling. Which could mean only one thing. She smiled softly. "I think we have a dragon," she said quietly, and stepped out into the open.

A single, high-throated cry rang out, terrifying and gentle at once, and Penny turned to see Rosa perched on the rooftop, her wings outstretched and flapping in a slow, graceful way. Beside her was Joaquin, heavily armed with a very serious-looking rifle.

The scar-faced man swore. He looked to his henchmen, but they shrugged: *I'm not gonna do it.*

He made a threatening move toward Penny, and the dragon . . . roared. Not like a lion, exactly, but close. Not exactly the growl of a savage dog, but close. It was low and vibrant and quite simply the roar of a dragon. Gracefully, she flapped her long, leathery, feathery wings and lifted her enormousness from the roof of the cabin. The wind swept Joaquin's hair around his severe face and shoulders, and Penny felt her heart squeeze—yes, she was falling in love.

Had fallen.

Rosa swept her graceful body into flight and hung, her wings flapping easily, above the humans below for a moment. Her great amber eyes seemed to glow. Her tail, so long and muscular, suddenly looked quite dangerous.

The men scattered, screaming. Only the pockmarked man stayed where he was, transfixed, his face paling. He crossed himself and fell to his knees, muttering what seemed to be a prayer.

Gently, gently, the dragon settled beside Penny, bending her splendiferous, feathery soft muzzle to her shoulder. "Thank you," Penny whispered. The dragon purred.

Joaquin said, "Climb onto her neck."

Penny did. She settled into a little crook just above the joint between wing and neck, a perfect seat with a sturdy fluff to cling to, but it was nonetheless terrifying when the dragon flapped that muscular wing and lifted off. She paused to let Joaquin climb on, and Penny clasped his hand.

He grinned, his eyes alight with wonder. "Are you ready? You've never done anything like this before."

"Ready."

"Hold on!"

And Rosa lifted into the dark Southwestern night, high above the little roads with tiny cars traveling though vast loneliness, and above the bluffs, and suddenly, there was Santa Fe, spread like a magical vision below them. Penny shivered in delight and wonder—the brown sugar and butter scent enveloping her, the smooth muscular wings arching through the night. Joaquin held her hand, his thigh close to hers, and as she looked at him, it seemed both impossible and fated that she should be here. With him. With Rosa, impossibly flying on the back of a dragon who would grant her a very long life.

Suddenly—guiltily—she thought of Alex. He had not crossed her mind in days and days. It almost felt as if he belonged to another life.

And then she thought of his office, cluttered and covered with a thousand fantasy creatures, but mainly dragons. How he would have loved this!

She had not died. For Alex, she would live and love and protect a dragon he would have adored.

It did not take long to return to the hill, and Penny found it thrilling to dive into the hidden entrance, ducking at Joaquin's urging, to the lair of the dragon. She set down gently in the hidden back room, and waddled, as if weary, back to her nest of feathery blankets.

"Where did the blankets come from?" Penny asked.

"My mother wove them." He smiled. "I have found something out. Very important." He took her hand and circled around to the other side of the blankets. Two eggs, red laced with pearlescent pink, sat side by side in the nest. Rosa nosed them protectively and settled with a sigh over them.

"Babies!" Penny cried. "That's what those men said. That there are babies, and they would be valuable."

Joaquin nodded soberly, the gun still in his hand. "She

is in more danger now than ever. I don't think her enemies will abate—they will only be more insistent."

She was stuck on the dragon babies. "The babies will be so cute! Imagine."

He smiled gently. "Yes." Taking her hand, he said, "She needs you, Penny. You see that she is rare and magical. I will help you in whatever ways I can—but she has chosen you for a reason."

"I have decided," she said quietly. "I had decided before, but now I am quite, quite sure. I will serve the dragon, and stay in Santa Fe."

He squeezed her hand, lifted it to his mouth and kissed it, then kissed her wrist. "Thank you. Thank you."

She took a breath. "I also wish to choose a consort."

His eyes fixed on her face. Still and waiting. It was hard to keep herself from swaying to kiss him. "Have you?"

"Yes. But no one has told me how to do it, how to make it official or whatever. I assume that once it's done, it can't be undone?"

"That's true." He took a breath. "You just choose him."

Penny put her hands on his face, bent her head to his. "I choose you, then. Will you be my consort, and live with me five hundred years?"

He kissed her back, and as before, the meeting of lips was hot and full of hard sparks that moved in her belly and breast and thighs.

Then he took her hands in his own. "The first day I saw you at my mother's house, with your beautiful eyes and swaying hair, I thought, *I would like to kiss that woman.*" He bent and kissed her.

"The second time I saw you, in the classroom, I thought, *I would like to hear her speak.* And your voice sounded like morning.

"Then I saw you at the house, and you were so kind and intelligent, and I knew that Rosa had chosen you for her own reasons, but also, I think, for me. She chose me. She chose you." He bent in and kissed her, his lips as rich as life itself.

The dragon, settling over her eggs, began to purr. Her eyes half closed, and Penny laughed. "And we choose each other."

He raised his head. "Yes."

And then there was no need for talk, only hands and lips and kisses, and when they lay, tangled and sated, Joaquin leaned close and whispered, "I love you."

Penny brushed her hand through his hair. "I love you, too." And the future, long and sweet, filled with dragons and dragon babies, Joaquin and her art, reeled out before her. She snuggled close and laughed.

Dear Reader,

I hope you have enjoyed this unique anthology.

Mary Jo Putney and I have stories in another innovative science fiction/fantasy romance collection from NAL. *Irresistible Forces* contains stories by three romance authors and three science fiction authors, making for a very special creation. Two of the stories were nominated for the Sapphire Award for best Science Fiction Romance of the year, short form—Lois McMaster Bujold's "Winterfair Gifts" and my "The Trouble with Heroes." Against such competition, I am very proud to have won.

Mary Jo's story is "The Alchemical Marriage," a sixteenth-century story from her popular Guardian series. Two mages must join together to protect England from the Spanish Armada. My story is far-future science fiction, and takes place on an apparently idyllic settlement planet that has one small problem—some kind of alien life force that rises unpredictably to consume humans to dust. When my hero has to sacrifice all to destroy the enemy, only Jenny Hart can bring healing to a survivor of the Blighter War.

Irresistible Forces, (NAL, 2004; ISBN: 0-451-21724-1) edited by Catherine Asaro, contains stories by Catherine Asaro, Jo Beverley, Lois McMaster Bujold, Mary Jo Putney, Jennifer Roberson, and Deb Stover. It can be ordered at any bookstore or online.

—Jo

About the Authors

Jo Beverley is widely regarded as one of the most talented romance writers today. She is a five-time winner of Romance Writers of America's cherished RITA Award and one of only a handful of members of the RWA Hall of Fame. She has also twice received the *Romantic Times* Career Achievement Award. Born in England, she has two grown sons and lives with her husband in Victoria, British Columbia, just a ferry ride away from Seattle. You can visit her Web site at www.jobev.com.

Mary Jo Putney graduated from Syracuse University with degrees in eighteenth-century literature and industrial design. A *New York Times* bestselling author, she has won numerous awards for her writing, including two Romance Writers of America RITA Awards, four consecutive Golden Leaf awards for Best Historical Romance, and the *Romantic Times* Career Achievement Award for Historical Romance. She was the keynote speaker at the 2000 National Romance Writers of America Conference. Ms. Putney lives in Baltimore, Maryland. Visit her Web site at www.maryjoputney.com.

Karen Harbaugh is an award–winning author and RITA finalist who has published eleven fantasy/romance novels and three novellas, with more forthcoming. She graduated from the University of Washington with a BA in English, and has also had various other occupations such as quality assurance analyst, technical writer, legal word processor, and whatever other job might add to her store of miscellaneous knowledge and get her out of the house from time to time. She is happily married to a software engineer and has a college-aged son. When she is not writing stories, she does volunteer work, knits, cooks, spins yarn, gardens, watches reruns of *Buffy the Vampire Slayer*, and occasionally finds time to annoy her cat, Newman. Visit her Web site at www.sff.net/people/KarenH.

A passionate hiker and traveler, **Barbara Samuel** likes nothing better than setting off at dawn for a trip—anywhere! Her favorite places so far include the Tasman Sea off the coast of New Zealand, the pungent streets of New York City, and the top of her beloved Pikes Peak. Between books, she's currently planning trips to India and China, and a long rest in the damp and misty United Kingdom. Barbara has won five RITA Awards from the Romance Writers of America. You can explore her columns on rambling around France and Scotland, working the Pikes Peak Marathon at 12,000 feet, and many topics about the writing life at www.barbarasamuel.com. She loves to hear from readers at awriterafoot@gmail.com.

New York Times Bestselling Author
Jo Beverley

Lovers and Ladies

For the first time in a single volume:
two long unavailable yet beloved
romance classics from Jo Beverley!

The Fortune Hunter
A stunning beauty rejects the charming suitor who isn't
wealthy enough to save her impoverished family.
But she can't so easily dismiss the memory of their
sweet shared kiss.

Deirdre and Don Juan
The dashing Earl of Everdon is most eager to marry
someone—anyone—who will bear him an heir.
But when he meets a quiet, well-bred lady who fits
the bill, he must resort to an amorous dance of
deception to gain her acceptance to his proposal.

JO BEVERLEY

A LADY'S SECRET

When Robin Fitzvitry, the fun-loving Earl of Huntersdown, encounters a cursing nun in a French inn, he can't resist the mystery. He offers to help Sister Immaculata reach England, expecting amusement on the tedious journey home from Versailles.

Petre d'Avernio is not exactly a nun, though she has spent years in an Italian convent with her mother, whose death has left her in danger. She must find the only person who might protect her—her true father, an English lord who does not know she exists. The gorgeous earl Robin Fitzvitry will be a dangerous ally, but she's glimpsed her pursuers and must race to the coast. She will resist him, use him, and eventually escape him with her virtue and secrets intact—she hopes.

JO BEVERLEY

LADY BEWARE

For generations, the Cave family has been marked by scandal, madness, and violence. But after earning a reputation for bravery in the army, Horatio Cave, the new Viscount Darien, has come home to charm London society and restore the family name. He means to start with the lovely Lady Thea Debenham.

The magnetism between them is immediate, but can Thea trust the dark, sexy "Vile Viscount"? And will Thea's brother Dare—the most dashing member of the Company of Rogues—believe that Horatio does not deserve the cursed Cave reputation?

Available wherever books are sold or at penguin.com